Other Voice

"A powerful picture of a refugee's struggle." — *Kirkus Reviews*

"It is a well-told story of what happened to central Europe and Europeans in the middle part of last century. I found it well written and very engaging." —Mark Evans, *Historical Novel Society*

"This is a heartbreaking story about war, racism, and man's inhumanity to man, a story that describes the reality of post WWII Czechoslovakia in lyrical and compelling prose. Readers will love the way the conflict is developed, especially the internal conflict taking place within the protagonist. The story is beautifully told, and it has psychological depth. Joe Vitovec articulates brilliantly on the themes of love, patriotism, war, and friendship." — *Readers Favorite*

I liked the author's voice and tone in sharing the research as well; it remained engaging, never lapsing into an information dump. Author uses good instinct for depth of detail. Sensory detail such as "thuds" that have sound and feeling of impact stand out throughout the book. With crescendos and whines of engines, author builds an incredibly experiential book that can be felt as much as seen. Very well done. Character building is a forte of the author, as is crafting settings and movement. I appreciated each instance of author demonstrating the value of place, allowing the reader to immerse in the scene and be affected by all that surrounds them. Very well done. —Nicole Howard, *Readers Digest*

Vitovec delivers a riveting story in beautiful and poignant prose, reminding us that the impact of war can be total, even for those who never set foot on the battlefield. A book for political leaders, teachers, students, and anyone with a desire to not repeat the past. It's a book that serves to remind us of what we have and what can be taken from us at a moment's notice. — *Chanticleer Reviews*

FULL CIRCLE
A Refugee's Tale

By

Joe Vitovec

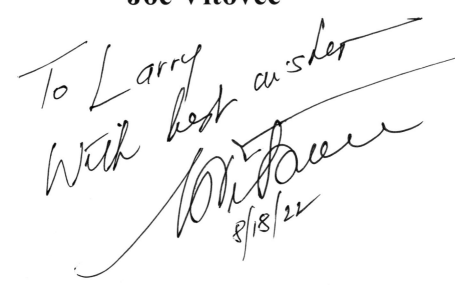

To Larry
With best wishes

8/18/22

FULL CIRCLE: A Refugee's Tale
Copyright © 2015 by Joseph A. Vitovec
GENRE: HISTORICAL FICTION
All rights reserved

Cover design by Joseph Vitovec
Original watercolor art © by Joseph Vitovec
All rights reserved
Print ISBN: 9 780692 594315
Electronic ISBN: 9 781370 953400
ASIN: B-016HIOVXU

First Published in 2015

"The pattern of our lives is essentially circular.
We must be open to all points of the compass."

Anne Morrow Lindbergh

"Freedom is a product of awareness: awareness of choice of the
possibilities, of alternatives. Seizing freedom is a matter of
courage, of willingness to face alternatives and, on occasion, to
pay the price of being different."

Raymond W. Mach
Early Czech Texas immigrant

Part 1.

AMERIKA

CHAPTER 1

When the boys first heard the sound, it was just a murmur. It came to them on the wind, at first only as a distant purr and then as a staccato of harsh clatters of metallic pings and grinding squeals punctured with booming thuds.

"Hey, you hear what I hear?" Rolling over on his stomach, Jan nudged Jakub sprawled next to him, strangely self-absorbed.

Jakub's mouth gaped open. The straw he'd been chewing on fell out of his mouth.

The growl became more distinct, growing louder until it burst into a crescendo of low clanking rumble overlaid with the high-pitched whine of powerful, revving engines and booming explosions of open exhausts.

Sprawled atop a moss and lichen-covered ledge that jutted out like a massive jaw from the grizzled face of ancient granite, the two boys gazed intently into the valley spread below them – a giant earthen bowl, with forested flanks dropping steeply toward a quicksilver sliver of a river and a checkerboard of maturing fields. Čekaná, their town. Two hundred or so dwellings and fifteen hundred souls. A cornucopia, out of which spilled all the good things one could wish, or at least all the good things that mattered and made life whole. Jan caressed it with his eyes, and frowned. The pastoral vision was fouled. A thick mustard-colored cloud rose and drifted above the huddle of pastel-colored stucco houses that blocked his view of the stretch of the main road leading out of town. The sound grated on his nerves. Squinting into a waning sun hanging low in the opalescent sky, he rubbed his eyes with the back of his hand and grimaced. "What *is* that?"

"Can't see anything yet." Jakub ran his finger through the unruly strands of his curly black hair, tucked them under his cap, and pulled the brim down to his eyebrows.

The air trembled. One by one, birds stopped singing. The chirping of crickets faded away. Even the goats, absorbed in their foraging among the bushes, raised their heads and cast wary looks in the direction of the noise.

The cloud advanced slowly toward the outskirts of town. Finally an angular shape emerged into plain sight...then another...and another...

"Jesus! Tanks!" Jan shrieked. "Those are tanks!"

Both boys stared into the valley, slack-jawed.

"And trucks too—" Jakub squinted. "Can't see with all that dust."

"Never seen one up close. Sure wish we could be—" Unable to hide the welling flood of resentment and envy, Jan glowered at the goats. "Bet all the guys are there, watching it all, and here we are. Wonder where they're going."

"My dad said there was some trouble up near the border." Jakub sighed. "With the Germans. The rabbi told him."

"Yeah, that must be it. I heard something too...at home...but I didn't know what they were talking about."

Resembling a string of animated toys, still trailing clouds of dust and fumes, the convoy lumbered westward deeper into the undulating chain of mountains, deceptively low but densely forested and in places impenetrable—the border of the Republic.

As Jan's excitement waned, a strange feeling in the pit of his stomach took over—a gut-wrenching, nauseating sense of anticipation. For days now, trains full of soldiers rumbled through the town's railroad station at odd times without stopping, their whistles blowing, smoke trailing in great horizontal smudges as they sped westward, leaving behind the lung-searing smell of burnt cinders and steam-laced wisps of smoke. At first, their passing barely drew any curiosity from the town folk, but now, their shrill whistles made everybody jumpy.

Things were not right, of that he was sure. It was written in the faces of his mother and father and some of their friends—in their worried looks and terse comments as they hunched over the latest newspapers, usually followed by animated discussions. Words such as "Anschluss" and "Hitler" and "Austria" filled their hushed conversations, along with talk about riots in some of the border towns. They railed about someone named Konrad Henlein, whom they called Hitler's agent provocateur and whose name his father always prefaced with an obscenity, and of the Germans demanding something called autonomy in the Šumava region they now called *Sudetenland*.

The boys hiked down a series of switchbacks with the goats trailing close behind, and stopped when they reached a grassy knoll with a stony bench under a stand of birches—their favorite stopping place.

Jan threw himself on the weathered, lichen-covered slab and fixed his gaze on the canopy of birches swaying gently in the breeze, revealing and concealing a mottled patch of the sky, with the sun just kissing the tips of their rustling crowns in a kaleidoscopic display of color. The cool air felt liquid. The nagging feeling vanished. He stretched and gave Jakub a friendly shove. "You coming tomorrow, right? Same time?"

Jakub shrugged and pursed his lips, and shifted his gaze to the toes of his bare feet.

"Hey, you coming, right?" Jan looked at him squarely. "Something wrong?"

Jakub tugged at his shirt and brushed some invisible dirt off his shorts. Finally he shook his head. "Can't tell you."

"What do you mean, you *can't* tell me? I *always* tell you everything. You know I do."

"Dad said, not to tell anybody. Made me promise. Said he'd take the strap to me if I say anything."

"But I am your friend. Friends don't keep secrets. You know, I won't tell. He'll never know. C'mon."

Jakub finally looked up. "I really shouldn't, but will you promise not to tell anybody if I do? I mean, not even your folks?"

"Sure. So what's so special you can't tell me? C'mon—"

Jakub's lips twisted into a sheepish grin. "Gotta have my picture taken." He rolled his eyes until they resembled a pair of milky marbles.

"You? A picture?" Jan's chortle died in his throat under Jakub's reproachful look.

"It's not funny. I knew I shouldn't have told you." Jakub tugged nervously at his suspenders. "I shouldn't have—"

" Aw, c'mon. I don't understand. What's so secret about a picture? We take pictures all the time."

Jakub squirmed. "Not that kind of a picture."

"Then what? Tell me."

Jakub shrugged. "Dunno. Some special pictures. We're all going. Need the pictures for some papers. Dad says we're going to Switzerland to stay with my uncle for a while, but nobody's supposed to know."

"Swit-zer-land? Jesus!" Switzerland was as remote as the moon, but Jan envied Jakub the unexpected adventure. "When?"

"Soon as we get the papers. From Austria somewhere. Some kind of permit or something."

Jan frowned. "You never *said* you had an uncle in Swit-zer-land!"

Jakub shrugged. "I didn't know."

Jan looked at him skeptically.

"Really! I didn't know, I swear. Dad just told me yesterday."

"So how long you gonna be gone?"

"Don't know. Promise you won't tell?"

"Told you I wouldn't. We can shake on it, if you want."

They spat into the palms of their hands, and shook them in a solemn oath to seal their pact.

* * *

"Jakub go with you again today?" Mother looked up sternly from her work.

Jan avoided her gaze and fidgeted.

"How come you're palling with him all of a sudden?"

He felt her flinty grey eyes boring through him and cringed. "I like him."

"But how come *him*?"

"You wouldn't let me play with Zdeněk, and he sits next to me in school. He's smart. I really like him." He looked up at her sheepishly.

Mother rolled her eyes, the way he saw the statue of Holy Mary in the church with her eyes perpetually gazing heavenward, and sighed loudly.

Slouched stone-faced next to the radio, beads of sweat glistening on his furrowed brow and prematurely balding head, Jan's father Tomáš barely acknowledged him as he entered. Burning perilously close to his fingers, a forgotten cigarette spilled its ashes on the unfinished coat in his lap. The announcer's grave and sometimes breaking voice filled the room:

"... our fatherland... too. Adolph Hitler promised them help, and his troops are now massing at our borders. His Majesty King George's envoy, Lord Runciman, whom we believed to be our friend, has left Prague after he sided with Hitler against Czech interests, hoping to gain time for England. This act, combined with the increased tension and riots in the Šumava region, leaves our republic in an extremely difficult position. Therefore, President Beneš has declared a state of general mobilization for all males between the ages of twenty and forty effective immediately. Further instructions will be posted in all towns and villages as soon as they are printed. Pravda Vítězí! Truth always wins!"

Choked with emotion, the announcer's last words vanished in the muted strains of the national anthem.

"Dad? Mom? What's going on?" Jan searched their faces.

Lena, his mother, gave him a blank stare, covered her face with her apron, and burst in tears. Huddled around a large worktable, six young girls – four seasoned seamstresses and two apprentices – stared into their laps.

6

"Those whores!" Father's jaws worked as though chewing on the words. The bulging veins on his temples throbbed in rhythm with his heart. "Those fuckin' whores!"

Mother shot a dark look in his direction and snarled, "Watch your language. The boy's home."

"Aw, the boy's old enough." Father dismissed her with a toss of his head.

She began to wail. "You never listen to me. He never listens to me!" she cried out to the girls.

"Sorry, boy," Father finally acknowledged him, "but there's been trouble up along the border. Riots. Damn Germans! Even in Vimperk...and that's what, ten kilometers? Practically next door."

"We saw a convoy. Tanks," Jan blurted.

Father nodded gravely toward Mother and the girls. "I told you. I knew it. I knew there was going to be trouble, ever since Hitler took Austria. And now even that whore Runciman sides with them." He wiped his brow with a handkerchief, laid down the coat he was stitching, and patted Jan on the head as he strode methodically past him to an old armoire. After some rummaging, he pulled out his old crumpled sergeant's uniform. It had been years since he had worn it. He laid it out on the cutting table, lit a cigarette, and without a word, proceeded to slice carefully through the seams.

Mother let out a shriek. "JesusMary, Tomáš, what are you doing!"

"Didn't you just hear? There's mobilization!" he shot back, not breaking his rhythm.

"You fool, didn't you hear? They only want forty-year-olds. You're almost fifty; you're too old. You don't have to go!

Oh my God, my God, what's he doing?" Pleading, she turned to the girls, but they averted their gazes, stone-faced and mum.

"I have to," Father protested.

"You...fool...you...damned fool..." Gasping for air between sobs, her face twisted in anger.

"I have to go. I'm going. This is just the beginning, can't you see? In the end, everybody'll have to go. Everybody!"

"Oh my God, he's serious...he really wants to go!" she wailed, looking desperately for support from the young women who remained silent, eyes downcast, embarrassed. "You can't just walk out on me! You have a business to run! What am I supposed to do here by myself? Oh, my God...Holy Mary...please, help me—"

"I said, I have to go!"

"You always were pigheaded and foolish. Doing stupid things. Promising to change, but never did, like all the other Neumans. You're all the same! What I ever saw in you I'll never know! All you give me is grief. You'll never change! You'll never change. You'll never change..." Her last words dissolved into a series of sobs.

Continuing methodically to rip the seams, puffing deeply on his cigarette, Father ignored her.

"And the boy—what about the boy? What about him? He needs you! He needs you home and not gallivanting with your pals, playing soldiers, risking your life and ours...everything we worked for, everything we saved—"

"For chrissake, stop it! Dammit! I have to go, can't you see? All this will be nothing if the Germans get it, nothing! Don't you understand? Nothing! I've got to go...we *all* have to go!"

"Oh my God, oh my...God, oh...my...God..." Whimpering softly now, tears tracing glistening rivulets down her cheeks, Mother pulled Jan close to her and buried his head in her bosom until he gasped. Her fingers, hard and calloused from years of stitching, dug into his back. "My boy, my dearest boy, oh my God...go talk to that fool of your father and beg him to stop. Beg him not to go. Beg him not to leave us." She moaned and stopped to catch her breath.

Listening to her wheezing, feeling the jerky heaving of her bosom and the hard ribs of her corset against his skin, dismayed and embarrassed, Jan looked at her through tears. He had seen his parents argue before, but not like this. He had never been called upon to take sides, never been drawn in. What to do?

"Speak to him!" she ordered, eyes red-rimmed from crying. "Speak to that drudge of a father. Speak to him."

He'd never seen his mother this way. Ordinarily unassertive, fortyish, but old for her age (he also thought her dour, until he realized that she was merely tired, having to get up before dawn to milk the goats, then fix the daily meals, maintain the house and garden, shop, and help with sewing until late at night, using a pair of scratched ill-fitting glasses no longer fit to correct her declining vision), short and stocky, her two long black braids streaked with grey, normally twisted in a bun at the back of her head but now unraveled down to her waist, she towered over him as she clutched him to her bosom. He felt trapped.

"Speak to him!" She gave him a hard shove.

His insides twisted in a knot. "Dad?" he croaked, feeling his mother's eyes burning through him like a pair of coals. "Dad? Please?"

Fuming, Father shot an angry look at her. "I'm sorry, Son, but when your country calls you, you go. You must always go when your country needs you. You must always defend your country."

Mother let out a howl. Her fist flew to her mouth and her plump body shook hysterically as she glared at her husband.

Huddled on a stool in a corner out of everyone's way and silent until now, Jan's grandmother stirred. A tiny shriveled figure hidden in untold layers of skirts and a perpetual sweater, with a face wrinkled over wrinkles, she gazed at him compassionately through half-closed sunken eyes. "There's going to be a war and your father wants to be in it," she said with a heavy sigh. She fished out a crumpled handkerchief and blew her nose. "They just announced it over the radio. I don't know what to tell you, boy. I've seen it all before. My poor Jeník, your namesake... your uncle...wouldn't listen, either, and the war took him in Serbia. My poor boy." She stared vacantly into space and her pale eyes grew shiny with tears. She reached for Jan and pulled him over to her bosom. "I don't see that you can do anything about it, boy, you know how stubborn *he* can be." She nodded weakly in Father's direction. "Your poor, poor mother."

Not accustomed to seeing his mother in such distress – she tended to be stoic and tight-lipped when angry, even when crying – Jan found himself flooded with emotion but empty of words. "Mamie, please don't cry, everything will be all right," was all he could muster, hugging her tentatively, feeling utterly weak and useless. Something was happening. He knew nothing about war except what he saw in the cigarette-smoke-laced cinema newsreels – surreal herky-jerky black and white snippets of distant places like Spain and China and Ethiopia overlaid by the excited voice of the narrator—enough to stir in him a sense of adventure but insufficient to understand the full meaning of what they really purported to show. All he vaguely sensed was that his – their – life was about to change.

"Dad?" he whimpered.

"Yes, Son?"

"Is it true? Is there going to be a war?"

Father's jaw worked as though he wanted to answer, but no words came out. Finally he looked up at him through misty eyes. He had never seen his father cry. Slowly, deliberately, and without a word, the crusty old man put away the uniform and uncharacteristically, silently but passionately hugged him. The strength of his embrace took Jan's breath away. Immobilized in the clutch of his father's sturdy arms, Jan became aware of his sinewy body underneath the thin worn shirt, the oddly sour smell of tobacco and sweat, the sandpaper coarseness of his stubble. It was the first and only time in his memory he had experienced the strength of his father's embrace.

Years later, when he understood these things, Jan Neuman would see these hazy late-summer days of 1938 as the days his childhood ended forever. He would polish the memories of these days and burnish them with reverie until they glimmered with the unnatural shine of regret, never permitting them to acquire the usual patina of distance and time. He would nurture them in the crowded niches of his mind, and dream of things that might have been but never were.

CHAPTER 2

The air vibrated with the staccato rolls of drumming and Jan sat up with a start. His mother was already up. "Mo-om? What's going on?" He rubbed his eyes.

"What's that crazy man Paleček doing, making such a racket so early in the morning?" Grumbling under her breath, she slipped hastily into a robe. "Oh! JesusMary! The mobilization!" She turned ashen, crossed herself three times, and flung open the window to hear what she feared the most.

Fully awake now, Jan squeezed in beside her. Standing there ramrod-straight, looking pompous, hands a blur of motion, old man Paleček cut an imposing figure. A slight, wizened, thoroughly disagreeable man with an enormous drooping mustache under a hawkish nose, he would put on a frayed blue uniform trimmed in red and gold whenever the occasion demanded, strap on an old snare drum and, after delivering a few snare rolls at strategic street corners around town, ceremoniously, in a croaky singsong monotone, pass on important proclamations and edicts to all within earshot.

The Palečeks lived in the poorhouse right next to the old synagogue on the other side of the river. In addition to being a town crier, the elder Paleček earned a living grave digging and doing odd jobs for whoever was willing to pay.

Jan avoided the Palečeks' two sons, Olda, about Jan's age, and Franta, six years or so older and generally regarded as a bully. Jan would rather cross the street than chance meeting him on the same sidewalk. He'd heard Grandmother say once that the town had made Franta that way, that his meanness was a rude expression of the anger he felt toward the town folk who made crude jokes about the Paleček's poverty, calling it laziness, and for having to depend on the thin charity of those he loathed. That didn't change anything—Jan still feared him.

One of Paleček's customary stops was directly across from Jan's home, and today his drumming seemed louder and more urgent than ever. In a voice that rose an octave befitting the occasion, he repeated last night's mobilization news that by now everyone already knew. People rushed past him toward the linden-lined square adjoining the town hall. The air crackled with excitement.

*   *   *

Jan had seen his father in uniform only once, the day he had fished a faded yellowing photograph out of a box of family mementos. It showed him as a young soldier, striking a dramatic pose with his rifle, face heavily retouched, impossible now to reconcile with the deep furrows and thick stubble of the father he knew. But today he was clean-shaven, adjusting the fit of his uniform, rolling the woolen leggings over his calves and tucking them into heavy spit-shined brogans that smelled of polish. The rank of sergeant—three silver half-round tacks polished to high sheen – glistened on his epaulettes. The stiff corners of his collar, bearing the red patches of infantry, propped up the loose skinfolds of his cleanly scrubbed face. A garrison cap hid the balding spot on his head.

The clock in the workroom struck seven. "Time to go." he sighed, and gulped down the last of his coffee and hard bread thinly coated with lard.

Resigned to the inevitable, Mother tried a smile, though her liquid eyes said otherwise.

"The trucks will be here any minute. Will you put out the flag when you return? I forgot to do it yesterday and there's no time now."

"I'll have the boy do it." Mother wiped a stray tear from her face. "May God bless you and keep you." Her hand shook as she drew the sign of the cross on his forehead three times.

"And you too, my dear. Please, try to understand. God willing, it won't last long and I'll be back. At any rate, we won't be too far and I'll try to get home as often as they'll let me," he said, failing miserably to sound reassuring.

* * *

Shivering, Jan pulled up the collar of his jacket, closed his eyes, and relished the rush of brisk morning air streaming past his face. Father, a volunteer fireman, had once promised him a ride in the new Škoda fire truck the town had proudly acquired, and this ride fulfilled his dream, though in a way he hadn't expected. The Škoda's long open bed, normally piled with firemen and hoses, now groaned under a heavy load of the wives, sweethearts, and children speeding to visit their loved-ones on the mountain.

The Škoda slowed down to a crawl when it reached scattered rows of triangular concrete tank traps crisscrossing the valley like the gaping mouths of hundreds of sharks. Gears whining, it turned sharply up the fresh scar of a newly cut road that rose steeply along the flank of the Boubín mountain in a series of switchbacks. The higher they rode, the more spectacular the view. At more than four thousand feet, the bell-shaped Boubín dominated the vast complex of undulating peaks known as Šumava. On a clear day, from its rocky summit, even the ephemeral peaks of the Alps could be seen far to the south, emerging eerily like a procession of ships from the underlying layers of haze. To the west lay Germany.

The roar of the motor, the biting wind, and the penetrating chill made conversation impossible, so they all huddled together under an assortment of coverings, clutching tightly their baskets of home-cooked foodstuffs, swaying in unison as the truck negotiated the hairpin turns. *Can't see how she can just sit there with her eyes closed when there's so much to see,* Jan mused, watching his mother, snuggled stoically stone-faced next to him under an old blanket, nod and rock with the sharp motion of the ride. Almost a month had passed since his father left home and this was their first opportunity to see him.

A wave of cheers rose as they approached the encampment. Showered by friendly needling of those less lucky, the fortunate soldiers greeted and embraced their loved ones with guarded, almost embarrassed emotion and quickly dispersed to various private corners among the shrubbery.

Father greeted them with an apprehensive smile. "I'm so glad. I was hoping you'd come. And you brought the boy."

"We brought a few things." Mother smiled thinly. "I had no idea all this was here." Mouth agape, she scrutinized the vast complex of bunkers and pillboxes bristling with weaponry, foremost among them massive emplacements of great Škoda artillery pieces, menacing even under their camouflage nets. Artfully shrouded under the growth of thick brush, overgrown with mosses and shrubbery, the bunkers, too, were virtually invisible. A spidery network of foxholes traversing the slopes was a beehive of activity. The great guns and other weaponry thrust their barrels westward toward Strážný, the last Czech border outpost, and beyond it, Germany.

15

"That's our little 'Maginot Line'," Father said, referring obliquely to the famed French line of fortifications, "only better—they don't have the terrain. Impressive, huh?" He put his arm around Jan's shoulder. "Do you miss me, Boy? I sure miss you. Miss you both."

"We miss you, too, Dad." Jan choked on the words.

Father took the carefully wrapped package of stuffed rabbit and bread dumplings they had brought, led them to a nearby bunker, and came out with a large blanket that he spread on a patch of grassy ground out of everyone's way. Mother uncovered the casserole, unwrapped the layers of green leaves covering the meat, and watched in silence as he hungrily attacked the meager offering. Their eyes met and she looked away.

"Still angry?" He sounded hurt.

She shook her head. "No," she said in a voice hollow with resignation.

"I'm sorry. You know I had to—"

"We're managing." She attempted a smile. "The girls are doing all they can, but I had to let some of the folks know they won't be getting their stuff until this thing's over."

"I'm sorry," he mumbled.

She shrugged. "Money has been a problem...paying the girls. But then, that's always been a problem. People don't pay and I'm not good at—" She challenged him with a hard look. "We really need you home."

He shifted his gaze off into the distance, square jaw working and lips moving, but in the end, cleared his throat and said nothing.

"The last of the hay is in for the winter, but the potatoes will be a problem. Old Man Soukup promised to plow them out

16

for us next week, but there just aren't enough hands to pick."
She sighed and hesitated. "Tomáš?"

"Hmm—"

"Remember, you promised? You said you might. Do you
suppose you could? Would they let you?"

His gaze hardened. The words tumbled out from behind his
clenched teeth and quivering lips. "Couldn't the girls? Granny
maybe? The boy? He's big enough, he's strong. You know I
can't."

She bit her lip. "Guess we'll have to manage somehow."
Her look turned vacant.

Father took her hand.

She withdrew it. "Old man Clauder stopped by the other
day."

"Clauder? Clauder came?" Father's brow furrowed. "That
bastard! The nerve! What did he want?"

Both envied and disliked, the Clauders, the only German
family in Čekaná, owned its choice fields and employed many
of the town's poorer folks as sharecroppers. Surrounded by a
towering stone wall and a massive iron gate, the picturesque and
impeccably maintained Clauder manor – a throwback to the
medieval – permitted the curious only a fleeting glimpse of their
ostentatious life behind manicured lawns and meticulously
maintained flowerbeds.

Reverently called Doctor by the town folk, the elder
Clauder, a strict taskmaster, was a daily sight, riding his horse
over the fields, often accompanied by Madame Clauder, a thin,
elegantly dressed but stone-faced blond woman, riding
sidesaddle. Swishing their crops in the air, they would gallop
past the field hands as the women would stop working, half-

straighten their aching backs and curtsy awkwardly, and the men bowed their heads and tipped their hats.

Jan both disliked and feared the Doctor ever since the day he had chased him and Jakub, cursing at them in German, crop swooshing menacingly, away from the manor creek they had been exploring.

"He brought some work," Mother said.

"After what's happened, I wouldn't move a finger for him," Father growled. The veins on his temples stood out prominently.

"He brought his uniform. A German uniform."

"That whore! What nerve!"

"I do wish you'd watch your language in front of the boy." Mother cast an anxious look in Jan's direction.

Father muttered something unintelligible and spat into the grass.

"I turned him down, of course. Not that we couldn't use the money. He's always paid—"

"I don't care, he's a German! Look what's going on! Look what they're doing to us! I don't want his bloody money. Not a damn cent."

Mother fell quiet and looked away.

"Dad?" Jan broke the awkward silence.

"Yes, Son?"

"Jakub said his uncle said that there was gonna be a war. Is there going to be a war?"

Father's bushy eyebrows arched in surprise. "That depends, Boy. Hope not, but it surely looks like it." He got up, belched, and brushed some dried grass off his uniform. "Come, let me show you something. Come, Lena. Let me show you what's really going on."

He led them a short distance to a stony outcrop where a pair of sentries manned two tripod-mounted telescopes commanding an unobstructed view of the rolling expanses. The soldiers saluted Father, gave Jan a smile, and bowed politely to Mother.

Father bent over one of the telescopes. "Anything?"

"See for yourself." The soldier stepped aside.

Squinting, Father peered into the eyepiece. "Come, have a look." He motioned to Mother. "Germany."

Straining to see, she rubbed her eyes and stiffened. "JesusMary! JesusMary!" Blood drained from her face. She recoiled from the instrument. "JesusMary! I can't believe it!"

"That's Haidmühle you're looking at, Ma'am," the soldier said. "The other scope is sighted on Bishofsreut."

The other soldier disappeared and a few moments later returned with a pair of ammo boxes. Smiling broadly, he stacked them under the telescope, so that Jan could reach the eyepiece.

Balancing on the boxes, Jan held his breath to steady the hazy image in the reticule, and gasped. Spread below him in a distant valley was a picturesque village, teeming with life. The streets overflowed with soldiers, mingled with tanks and artillery pieces, afloat in a sea of flags—red flags emblazoned with swastikas.

* * *

Slumped at the kitchen table, Jan pushed aside his homework and shifted uncomfortably. His back ached from picking and hauling the potatoes Old Man Soukup had plowed up that morning, and he tried to ignore the pain by daydreaming. His mind drifted in anticipation of the coming trip to the mountain to see his father again. Just thinking about it was a balsam for his aches. Glancing wistfully at the clock, he wished for the time to fly.

The subdued sounds of the radio, until now only an indistinct babble coming from the workroom, became louder as someone turned up the volume. The excited words gave him a chill:

"...We are sad to report that a new conference was held in Munich today, the twenty-ninth of September, at the urging of the American president Franklin Delano Roosevelt. At this conference, to which our ministers were not invited, the fate of our republic was decided behind our back, behind closed doors, against our wishes, and without even the courtesy by our allies to consult with us. The agreement that was signed by the Reichs Führer Adolf Hitler, Italian Leader Benito Mussolini, French Prime Minister Edouard Daladier, and Prime Minister Neville Chamberlain of Great Britain effectively dismembers our Republic and sacrifices our freedom, our national identity, our very existence, on the altar of false hopes and promises of world peace. With one stroke of a pen, those who purported to be our friends and whose solemn word we expected them to honor have deceived us. They readily gave away our land and our freedom for what they see as a promise of world peace. How can they so naively believe that Herr Hitler will keep his word? Are they blind to what is happening all over Europe? Are they really that naïve? Esteemed citizens, this concludes our report from the Foreign Ministry. President Beneš will address the nation sometime tomorrow as soon as he has conferred with Mr. Masaryk,

our Foreign Minister, and has had a chance to read and analyze the full text of the Munich Agreement. We will keep you posted about the time of his speech and any further developments. Pravda Vítězí! Truth Always Wins!"

The somber strains of Dvořák's *Ninth Symphony* replaced the bitter words vanishing into the ether. Mother's face turned ashen. Motionless, the seamstresses froze in confused disbelief. Grandmother crossed herself, fished a rosary out of the folds of her skirt, and started praying.

He didn't understand it all, but knew it was bad news. "Mamie? Mom? What's happening? What's he saying? What does it mean?" He tugged at his mother's arm.

"I don't know, Son." Her voice cracked as her expression darkened. "But whatever it is, it's not good." She crossed herself.

"Does it mean Dad will have to fight? Will there be war?"

She looked at him through tears and didn't reply.

"Will we still go see him Saturday?"

She drew him close and almost in a whisper said, "Hush, boy. You ask too many questions."

CHAPTER 3

Though they all knew their men would be coming home, there was no joy among the small dour-faced group huddled in the back of the fire truck speeding from the mountain toward Čekaná. The only thing worse than not coming home was coming home in disgrace. They all had read the newspaper or heard the President say that the Republic had been betrayed by its friends, and that in order to prevent unnecessary bloodshed, he would order the soldiers to withdraw beyond the new borders agreed upon at the Munich conference.

They had left the mountain earlier than Jan had expected, while the waning sun still cast long gentle rays upon the countryside, bathing it in extraordinary beauty, but he was blind to it during much of the trip. His mind was reeling.

He had never seen his father so mad. "Imagine, giving up without even firing a shot!" he ranted, barely greeting them upon their arrival to the encampment. "Those fuckin' bastards! Those whores! Those whore-lovers! We're leaving nothing here; I don't care what the President says!" Livid, face glistening with sweat, the veins on his temples bulging to the breaking point, he continued to spew venom. Even Mother, withering under his rage, didn't dare to stop him.

"If it were up to us, we'd stay here and kick their asses. Just look at them! Look what it's doing to them!" He made a sweeping motion toward the troops. "Look! Look at their faces! Nobody wants to leave, not like this. In shame!"

The men stalked about, grim and red-eyed, unabashedly shedding tears, venting their frustrations with outbursts of obscenities directed equally at the Germans, the French, and the

22

British. All along the line, shouts and cursing mingled with commands, as those not busy loading the trucks with the accouterments of war worked feverishly to knock down the emplacements and hook up the Škoda artillery pieces to the tractors.

Father continued to rant and rave. Jan expected his mother to castigate him, but she remained withdrawn, silent. Finally, he disappeared in the bunker, and when he didn't come out for a long time, she gave him a nudge and said in a voice quivering with anxiety, "Go see. Go see what he's doing in there."

Dank and dark, the bunker smelled of mold and rot. When Jan's eyes became accustomed to the darkness, he saw his father looking out of the firing slit, crying.

*   *   *

Father came home the following week. The stream of retreating armor and trucks was soon swamped by a flood of refugees clogging the main road leading from the settlements ceded to Germany. Pulling all sort of conveyances – wagons, bicycles, even prams – heaped with suitcases, boxes, rolled-up bedding, sticks of furniture, anything they could fit, the hapless hordes soon filled Čekaná to overflowing. In the fading light, they resembled a procession of ghosts. Clad in as much clothing as they could carry on themselves, they scurried up and down the streets, pounding on doors, begging for a place to stay or a handout of food.

Still in his uniform and in a seething foul mood, Father swore when hard rapping on the door interrupted his supper. "Go see who it is, Boy."

Jan cracked the door open and found himself face to face with three huddled figures, straining under lumpy rucksacks on their backs and bulging mud-spattered suitcases in their hands. A chill crawled up his spine. "Dad! I think you'd better—"

The man put down the suitcase and tipped his hat when Father appeared in the doorway. "Please, Sir, we beg you, can you take us in?" He paused for a coughing spell. "Please? At least for a while? For the night at least, 'til we can find something? We have no place to go. Our little girl is sick. An awful cough. We're afraid she'll get worse if we don't find a warm place for her. We can pay; we have some money. Please—"

Father glared at them, speechless. Sharply outlined by the shaft of light cast by the window, the stranger had the desperate look of a man at wit's end. Overcome again by a series of rasping coughs, he drew closer the collar of his coat to ward off the evening chill and shuddered. Younger than Father, Jan thought, despite his premature baldness and stubble-covered bespectacled face. Mud caked the blue uniform under his coat, crumpled from days of continuous wear. The woman beside him looked at Father with desperation. Swathed in a shawl that completely covered her face except for her pale blue eyes under thinly shaped eyebrows, she wheezed softly with each steamy breath as she tried to hold in check sporadic fits of trembling, A shivering young girl about Jan's age clung tightly to her side.

"Sir, Sergeant," the man bowed slightly in deference to Father's uniform, "you know what it's like out there; you understand, don't you? You've been up there. You've seen what it's like. You've seen it all." His voice broke. "Please, Sir, help us if you can. We've walked all day. Been on the road three days. Slept in ditches. Froze at night. And our girl, just look at her."

Mother dabbed at her eyes with a handkerchief.

"Please, Sir," the man pleaded. "Ma'am?" He turned to her.

"I don't know." Mother collected herself. "What do you think, Tomáš? Maybe Angela's room upstairs?"

"But Ma'am, please," the man protested, "we don't want to put anybody out. We just thought you might, for the night—"

"Oh, no, no, I insist. The room is empty."

She gave him a reassuring smile. "Had a girl there, an apprentice from Vienna, but she didn't come back after the Anschluss." Jan felt her sharp nudge. "Go help with the bags while I put some water on the stove so these good people can get cleaned up a bit."

The man extended his hand. "The name is Fiala. I'm Josef; this is Helena," he motioned to his wife who bowed slightly, "and that's Zlata. I was the stationmaster in Kvilda, and all they gave us was two hours. Just two hours! Imagine! Two hours to cram a lifetime into a pair of suitcases! What can you do in two hours?" His cough returned and he covered his mouth with a soiled handkerchief. "We lost everything."

*   *   *

"Heard you have somebody living with you," Jakub said as the boys settled into their favorite place on the ledge and the goats scattered among the bushes.

"Yeah. How did you know?"

Jakub shrugged. "Everybody has somebody living with them. We have somebody living with us, too."

"Oh, yeah?"

"Yeah. His name's Uncle Isaac."

"What! Another uncle?" Jan chortled.

"It's not funny!" Jakub scowled.

"Hey, I was just kidding. Did he come with all the other people that came?"

"He's not a *real* uncle, but Dad said that's what I should call him. He knew Father from somewhere. They were in the war together, or something."

"So what about your *real* uncle, the one in Switzerland? Aren't you supposed to go see him? And what about this new Uncle Isaac? Is he going, too? You told me—"

"Yeah, I know; that hasn't changed." Jakub's look darkened and he bit his lip. "I don't know about Uncle Isaac, but Father says we still can't get some papers. Some kind of permit. We got our passports, but because the Germans are in Austria, we have to wait. Father says they don't want Jews in Switzerland either, even if they have the right papers. If they find them on the train, they send them back or put them in jail…so I don't know."

"So, can't your Swiss uncle do something?"

Jakub shrugged.

"So maybe you're not going?" Jan gave him a wide grin. "I'm glad you're not going!"

"Don't know." He shrugged again.

"So how come they won't let Jews travel?"

"Father says they blame us for losing the war. The one where he got shot in the leg. And Uncle Isaac says they really hate us and that everybody's afraid of what's going to happen."

"Yeah, but how can they tell you're Jews anyway?" Jan frowned. "I can't tell. You don't look any different to me than anybody else, so how can they tell if you're a Jew or not?"

26

"'Cause the passport says so."

Jan gave him an exasperated look. "So what if you don't tell them? You don't *have* to tell them."

"You don't understand. You have to show your papers, like birth certificate and stuff, to get your passports. And besides, I'm circumcised. My father, too." He looked away, blushing. "*All* Jews are circumcised. And Uncle Isaac says they strip people naked and look them over and that's how they can tell."

The question of 'Jewness' had never entered Jan's mind. He accepted Mother's matter-of-fact tolerance the way he accepted Father's hatred of the Germans, on a hypothetical level, but without question. Still, it left him confused, particularly since Father Tlachna, the parish priest, lambasted the "infidel Jews" from the pulpit and called them Christ-killers. Hadn't he learned in the catechism that Jesus himself was a Jew? That he was killed by the Romans? And what did that have to do with Jakub anyway?

* * *

Jan dozed over a book in the back of the workroom, the largest room in the house. He liked this room. He could see but not be seen, hidden among the labyrinth of tables, Singers, stools, armoires, racks, and piles of material—an organized mayhem in which, nevertheless, everything had its proper place. It was the warmest room in the house, too, with a drum-like sawdust-fired stove glowing cherry-red in the corner.

The radio announcer commenced the recap of the daily news:

"...Reuters Agency correspondent reports that last
Wednesday, November the Ninth, in several German cities

and towns, mobs of marauding SA – Stormabtailung – and
other Nazi sympathizers plundered Jewish stores and
burned many synagogues. The raids took place during the
evening hours. Glass from the storefronts littered the
sidewalks like broken crystal. Some of the Jews, caught
either in the streets or in their establishments, were beaten
to death. Reportedly, more than ninety Jews lost their lives.
The raids reportedly occurred as a revenge for the death of
a German diplomat in France, allegedly killed by a Jewish
man. We will bring you further details as they become
available. This is Radio Praha..."

Jan watched drowsily as Father turned off the radio, slipped on an overcoat, and stalked off into the night. Middle-of-the-night visits to the outhouse were not uncommon. Minutes later, he caught a glimpse of Mr. Fiala, their new tenant, bundled in his overcoat, heading for the front door. Caught by the wind, the door slammed shut with a sharp crack that echoed through the house like a shot.

Dozing by the stove, smudged half-moon glasses perched on the tip of her nose and newspaper pages slipping from her lap, Mother lurched with a start. "JesusMary, what was *that*?" She spun around and her gaze stopped at Jan. "Did you do that? You'll wake the dead!" She gathered the paper that had spilled onto the floor. "Can't you be more careful?"

"It was the wind! The door got away from Mr. Fiala, Mom. I didn't do anything, I swear," Jan protested.

"Where's your father? What time's it anyway?" She pushed her glasses up and squinted in the direction of the clock.

"Midnight."

"Midnight? JesusMary, what *are* you doing up so late? You should be in bed! How many times have I told you!"

28

Jan cringed, expecting a tongue-lashing.

She fixed him with a withering look just as the door again swung open, sending a blast of cold air into the house. The hallway came alive with the sounds of feet shuffling on the coarse tiles and the grunts and oaths of straining bodies, someone kicked the kitchen door open—and Father, Mr. Fiala, Constable Kubek, and their neighbor Hrášek, the carpenter, stumbled in, dripping rain, more dragging than carrying two heavy wooden crates.

The constable pulled up short. "What about him? I thought you said—" He nodded severely toward Jan who stood there wide-eyed, mouth open.

"I'll take care of it," Father snapped, sending Jan scampering to bed with the harshest of looks.

Peering through the crack in the door, heart pounding with excitement, Jan saw the men put down the crates and the carpenter pry open the lids. Constable Kubek pulled aside a soiled military blanket, revealing the contents—an assortment of guns smeared with Cosmoline, wrapped in long strips of cloth. As the men checked each weapon, Hrášek, the carpenter, disappeared outside and returned within moments with a satchel full of tools. The men resealed the crates and gently slid aside the dining table. Sprawled on all fours, the carpenter took a few quick measurements and with a fine-toothed saw, cut a square opening in the wooden floor.

Father dropped a bare light bulb into the gaping opening and, taking turns, the men lowered themselves into the cobweb-infested space. Jan could hear their grunts and hushed comments, and see their shadows dance crazily as they dug a large hole in the silty soil. And then, faces twisted with strain, they lowered the crates into the hole, taking extra care not to damage the edges of the opening, covered them with the soil and detritus, and smoothed the ground to remove all traces of the dig. After carpenter Hrášek returned the wooden plug, Mother swept and washed the floor, pulled a thin rug over the cut, and Father replaced the table. Flushed with satisfaction, the men shook hands and filed out into the night.

CHAPTER 4

It was mid-afternoon of a frosty Ninth of March when the church bell began to toll. Customarily heard calling the faithful to mass and at noontime to mark the hour, it only came to life at other times when something catastrophic or extraordinary happened—an accident, a flood, or, heaven forbid, a fire.

Jan looked up at the clock, and a prickly feeling shot up and down his spine.

Peeling potatoes and humming softly one of the wordless songs from her endless inventory, his grandmother stiffened, turning pale as the melody died on her lips. Father, a volunteer fireman of long standing, tossed aside the dress he was stitching and instinctively reached for his fireman's regalia.

"JesusMary, what's going on?" Blood drained from Mother's face. "Boy, go see!'

The street, full of crusty ruts, turned slushy where the sun kissed the thick covering of last night's snow, and he skidded as he ran out. With the sound still reverberating in the air, other people began to spill out of the houses, scanning the sky for the telltale smudge of smoke, sniffing the air, milling about in worrisome anticipation.

Zlata and her parents leaned out of the upper-floor window of their room, scanning the area. She shouted and waved. "Ahoj, Jan. We can't see anything."

Jan waved back.

"Hey!" Jakub slapped him on the back.

"You shouldn't sneak up on people like that!" Jan gave him a friendly shove.

"This is Uncle Isaac I told you about." Jakub tugged at the sleeve of a tall, sallow-faced, sinewy stranger next to him. "I thought you'd be out."

"So, you're Jan, eh?" Uncle Isaac offered his gnarled hand as he measured Jan with a probing gaze. "We finally get to meet, huh?" His handshake felt like the grip of a vise.

"Yessir. We heard the bell. What's going on?"

"You mean, you don't know?" He rolled his eyes. "I'll tell you what's going on! That weakling president of ours Hácha caved in; gave in to them. That's what. And now we're seeing the consequences."

"The President? Gave in to whom?"

Uncle Isaac rolled his eyes. "Hitler and Göring, of course. In Berlin. Haven't you heard? It was all over the radio this morning. Things might have been different if President Beneš hadn't resigned last October. Hácha is a weakling. They called him to Berlin and he caved. Maybe Beneš would have, too, but we'll never know now."

Jan shook his head. "A tube's burned out on our set, so Dad couldn't—"

"Guess you're still too young for lots of it." Uncle Isaac sighed. "But someday, you boys'll understand. Just remember this day. Remember what that bastard did. I wouldn't be surprised if—"His jaw dropped as a hush, a murmur, a collective gasp rose from the crowd.

All heads turned westward to the distant bend in the road where a dark animated blob against the snow-covered hills resolved into a line of armor that slowly advanced toward the town. The sound finally reached them—a harsh roar of motors and a staccato-like clattering of tanks, filling the air and growing louder by the minute. Everyone froze, first in disbelief, and then in horror as little orange flames and the rattling of gunfire erupted from the armor. A flock of pigeons rose from somewhere, circled frantically above the rooftops and, just as quickly, dove out of sight.

"The Huns! The Germans! It's the Germans!" The cry echoed down the line as the crowd picked it up.

Cursing under his breath, Uncle Isaac grabbed the boys and jerked them close to him, shielding them with his body. "It's all right, it's all right. It's all right!" He yanked Jakub's hand until he stumbled. "C'mon, quick, let's get out of here. And you," he gave him a shove, "go home before it's too late. Go home! Go! Run!"

Panic swept the crowd. People scattered in all directions and in no time, the streets were deserted. An eerie quiet settled over everything, except for the occasional thud of a door slamming or window closing, and the gradually increasing rumble of the tanks.

* * *

"Careful, Boy." Father squeezed Jan's shoulders, as he made room for him at the window. The windowpane felt cold against Jan's forehead and his breath condensed on the glass. He wiped it with his sleeve.

The town square, spread before him to the left, and the town hall, stood deserted. Across the road, the Kohen store was dark and shuttered. Jan thought he saw a curtain move in one of the upstairs windows. *Jakub?*

At the other window, Mother and the Fialas stared glumly into the street. Trying to hold back tears, Mother dabbed at her eyes with the corner of her apron. In the back of the room, hands trembling and lips moving in silent prayer, Grandmother fingered the beads on her rosary. Zlata's whining questions about what was going on went unanswered.

Jan felt a comforting squeeze on his shoulder. "Never forget this day, Son. Never forget this day," Father whispered hoarsely.

Slipping and sliding, a squad of motorcycle troopers emerged from the outskirts and behind them tanks. The noise swelled to a crescendo. Columns of dirty exhaust rose skyward, spun there into reeling vortices by the wind. The ground shook and the windows rattled until they all recoiled in shock. The noxious smell of fumes made Jan gasp.

Three of the tanks swung into the town square and came to a halt. Swinging menacingly from side to side, their guns came to rest on the town hall. Minutes went by. Tension mounted. Finally, the town hall door creaked open and two men stepped out: the mayor, chest all but covered by a wide tricolor band, and Dr. Clauder, now hardly recognizable in a crisp German uniform. A red swastika armband emblazoned his sleeve.

The hatch of the lead tank opened with a dull clang and an SS officer rose from the turret.

Dr. Clauder snapped to attention with a resounding click of his heels, and thrusting his right hand skyward in a Nazi salute, cried out passionately, *"Heil Hitler!"*

The mayor, stared into the ground, frozen to the spot.

The man in the turret ignored the Doctor and surveyed the scene with a scowl.

Somewhat flustered now, his uplifted arm quivering ever so slightly, Dr. Clauder repeated, this time louder, *"Heil Hitler! Ich bin Doktor Clauder.* I'd like to welcome you to Čekaná."

"Sturmbannführer Fuchs. *Heil Hitler!"* the SS man shot back, as his gloved hand, holding a riding crop, came up in a lazy swipe of a Nazi salute. He shifted his glare and shook the crop at the mayor. "And who is he? Why is he not saluting properly? *Wie heissen Sie?* Who are you? What is your name?" he barked, not waiting for the Doctor's answer.

"He is the mayor, *Herr Sturmbannführer.* He doesn't speak German." Dr. Clauder shifted uneasily. "He doesn't understand."

Sturmbannführer Fuchs' pudgy face twisted in a contemptuous sneer. "Perhaps he doesn't want to. Or perhaps we must teach him?" He let out a short, hoarse laugh.

Hearing but not wanting to believe, Jan's parents and the Fialas gathered around the radio that alternated somber funerary music with pleas for calm and cooperation with the Germans. Father uncorked a bottle of slivovitz and they all lifted a tearful toast to the picture of President Masaryk, the revered founder of the Republic. It was the first time Jan's father had poured him a drink. He felt grown-up but self-conscious, aware of Zlata's gaze on him as he tried not to choke on the searing liquid. Crackling static interrupted the announcer's voice and the strains of the national anthem filled the air. They joined in, singing and crying at the same time, unashamed of the tears. Feeling his father's calloused hands on his shoulders, Jan sensed he had just become a witness to a cathartic event that would change their lives forever.

That night, Father took the national flag and the picture of President Masaryk that until now had occupied a prominent place in the house, wrapped them in a large scrap of oilcloth, and hid them in the space under the kitchen floor.

The German garrison took over one of the beer halls, while *Sturmbannführer* Fuchs installed himself in the Clauder manor. Short and stocky, almost rotund in his tight-fitting uniform, Fuchs exaggerated his height by the rakish angle of the skull-and-bones-emblazoned hat tilted up to take full advantage of its concave shape, and the thick soles of his riding boots. His pink and clean-shaven face was smooth, except for a long scar on his left cheek. A narrow, reddish mustache complemented the thin line of his lips. Rumor had it that he had received the scar during a saber duel while a student at Heidelberg. The scar had a tendency to darken whenever he became upset or enraged—often the only indication of emotion on his otherwise inscrutable face. But his eyes provided the best insight into his soul, or, as some of the folks would say, the lack of it. Pale gray, intense and unblinking, they exuded contempt for anything they rested upon. Looking into them was like gazing into an abyss. Though he wore glasses, he preferred a monocle that hung on a thin black lanyard from his breast pocket. He used it often, and when he did, the eye behind it became magnified, bulging to the point of being grotesque – not unlike that of an octopus – a hypnotic point that bore through everything it met. Adorning his chest, prominently displayed and perfectly centered in the fold of his lapels, was an Iron Cross. A red and white swastika band emblazoned his left sleeve. A Parabellum in a black holster hung from his belt, and he was inseparable from what was to become his trademark—a riding crop firmly gripped in his gloved hand and used as deftly as a conductor would a baton to punctuate the air when barking out orders.

Fuchs' heavy hand was soon felt far and wide. Every day, old man Paleček's drum roll would announce yet another edict, yet another regulation: *All political parties are henceforth dissolved. All Masaryk pictures must be destroyed within three days. Anyone caught with or displaying the picture of the former president will be severely punished. All public signs and inscriptions will be in two languages, with the German language prominent and placed above the Czech language. The country is now a German protectorate called Böhmen und Mähren—Bohemia and Moravia. Referring to it as the Republic is forbidden. The only official flag is the flag of the German Reich. All flags of the former republic will be destroyed immediately. Anyone caught with the flag of the republic will be punished. The official national anthem is Deutchland Deutchland Über Alles.*

Raiding Nazi parties that swept the town looking for illegal pictures and flags found none. Even so, the elderly schoolmaster was hauled off to jail for no apparent reason other than to make him an example of the occupiers' power and resolve.

One day, a black Mercedes skidded to a halt in front of the Clauder Manor, and two grim looking men, dressed in ankle-length leather coats, stepped out. Obviously expected, after exchanging *Heil Hitlers* and conferring with Fuchs and Dr. Clauder, they made their way to the town hall and the office of Constable Kubek, whom they summarily evicted. A new sign appeared on the door. It read: "*Geheime Stadtspolizei,*" or as it was commonly known and whispered about with great fear, Gestapo.

CHAPTER 5

Rocking gently back and forth on his heels, the new headmaster surveyed the class. His unblinking gaze shifted lazily from a list of names to the students squirming uncomfortably under his scrutiny. Young, slightly built, pale, and intense, his colorless appearance drew the eye to a large button pin displayed prominently on the lapel of his tweed coat—a black swastika in a white circle rimmed by red.

Mrs. Málek, the teacher started to introduce him, but he waved her off.

Flushed, she moved off to the side and stood staring into the ground.

"*Ich bin Hans Dietrich.* My name is Hans Dietrich," he said in a heavily accented Czech. Scanning the rows of children, his gaze rested briefly on each as though trying to burn their faces into memory, before stopping at Jan and Jakub's desk. He consulted the list one more time and his expression hardened. His piercing look lingered first on Jakub, then on Jan. A scowl swept over his face.

Jan wilted under his stare, as a sickening numbness knotted his stomach. Why was the man looking at him like this? He didn't look this way at any of the others!

"*Wie heisst du, Knabe?*" he snapped, and Jan instinctively recoiled. The scowl disappeared and his eyes narrowed in a grimace. The corner of his mouth remained upturned, baring his teeth and making him appear ready to pounce.

Jan froze.

"Your name!" Hans Dietrich barked. "Speak up, boy! Your name!"

"Jan Neuman," Jan stammered in a tiny, choking voice.

Herr Dietrich pursed his lips, and glared at Jan for a few breathless moments before his gaze shifted to Jakub. "And you there, *wie heisst du*?"

Jakub lowered his head, stood up, and stared into the floor.

Herr Dietrich's face reddened. "I said *wie heisst du? Answer me!*"

"Jakub."

Even in the suffocating silence of the classroom, Jakub's response was barely audible.

"Jakub? Jakub what?"

"Jakub Kohen."

A wisp of a smile briefly crossed Herr Dietrich's face, but disappeared just as quickly. His eyes became two slits boring a hole through Jan's friend. "*Bist du ein Jude? Ein kleine Jude? Are you a Jew?*"

Jakub swallowed hard and remained silent.

Jan felt a brief but overwhelming surge of relief that made him weak in the knees. *It was Jakub he wanted! He wasn't after me. He was after him,* flooded his brain, but his relief turned to guilt, and then to nausea. He felt like retching.

"*Bist du ein Jude?* Are you a Jew? Answer me!"

Jakub looked up and met Herr Dietrich's searing stare. "Yes! I'm a Jew!"

Jan looked at him in surprise, tinged with envy. Of the two, he thought himself the stronger one, the protector. Watching him standing there defiantly, pale-faced, chest heaving, breathing heavily, he wondered if *he* would have had the courage to do as Jakub did, had *he* been similarly tested.

Herr Dietrich stopped rocking. "So *you* are the little Jew! I should have *known*." His voice dripped with derision.

Jakub began to shake.

"Jews are the polluters of the Aryan race and the vermin of the earth," Herr Dietrich burst out in a rising staccato-like delivery. "They are not permitted in the institutions of learning in the German Reich." He swept the class with a glare. "There will be no Jews in my school! *Verstehst du? Verstehen Sie? Keine Juden!* No Jews!" His gaze devoured Jakub as he spoke.

He turned to Mrs. Málek cowering behind him. *"Keine Juden, verstehen Sie?"* He disgustedly threw the list of names on the desk and slammed down the fist. *"Keine Juden!"* His face reddened.

Almost imperceptibly, she nodded.

He spun around and glared at Jakub. "You, *Jude*, get out. Get out. Get out right now! *'Raus, Jude, 'raus! Raus!* Get out! Out! Out! *Raus gehen! Schnell!"*

Stunned, Jakub froze for a few moments and then, eyes flooding with tears, began gathering his books.

"Verstehst du mir nicht? Don't you understand me? *Raus, Jude. Raus! Schnell!* Leave those. You will not need them."

The school bag slipped from Jakub's hands and the books spilled on the floor. He made a move to retrieve them, but Herr Dietrich's scream stopped him cold.

"I'll get 'em for you," Jan whispered.

Followed by a dozen of terrified eyes, Jakub stumbled out of the classroom.

Herr Dietrich's stare followed Jakub out the door, and when it slammed shut behind him, he too turned on his heels and after a last contemptuous sweep of the class, stalked out of the room.

When Mrs. Málek dismissed the class, Jan gathered Jakub's books. Passing her desk, he noticed the list of names

Herr Dietrich had left behind. One name circled in red stood out in particular: Jakub's. The logo at the top of the stationary bore the family crest and the name *Clauder*.

That night, after supper, with Jakub's school bag under his arm, Jan slipped quietly into the street and set out cautiously for the Kohen house. The air was thick with the smell of diesel fumes, and the road heavy with vehicles streaming east. The narrow slits of their painted-over headlights resembled a procession of disembodied cat's eyes. Their motors growled rather than purred. "Toward Poland," Father had commented, "that's where they're going. And then maybe Russia, even though they've signed a nonaggression pact. You can't trust them."

Jan reached the metal gate leading to the Kohen house and was about to open it, when he sensed that something was amiss. Out of the corner of his eye, he caught sight of the store display window splattered with white paint, and a shape he was unable to make out but that clearly didn't belong there. The beam of a passing truck swept faintly across the façade and he saw what it was—a crudely sketched six-pointed star, with a single word scrawled inside: JUDE.

He knocked several times. He knew they were home—nobody walked the town streets after dark with the Germans around, especially the Jews. He was ready to give up when the key finally rattled in the lock. The door opened a crack, and Mr. Kohen appeared in the shadows. A portly but short man, with a dour face crowned by curly reddish-brown hair over a furrowed perspiring forehead and a pair of grey eyes, with shirt sleeves rolled up and trousers cinched with suspenders, he peered at Jan through the slit. "Yes, who is it?"

"Jan."

"Jan? Neuman? What do you want at this hour?"

"I have Jakub's books."

"You alone, boy?" he whispered.

"Yes, sir."

He scanned the outside briefly, and then opened the door just enough for Jan to pass through "Watch your step." He motioned him to follow up a steep dimly lit staircase above the store toward a crack of light from an open door—their apartment. Steps creaking under their feet, Jan became conscious of his pronounced limp and the aggregate smell of the contents of his store that became a part of his persona—the tang of pickles and sacs of dried goods and pungent spices, now mixed with the heaviness of his sweat.

Dimly lit by a single bare bulb, the room was the quintessence of gloom. Distorted shadows danced on the walls. The black of the blackout curtains gave it a funerary look, adding to the doleful mood of the Kohens gathered around the table, packing a large suitcase. Three other half-packed suitcases lay on the floor, surrounded by stacks of clothing. The air was sour with the smell of cabbage. A stack of unwashed dishes filled the sink.

Jakub greeted Jan with a hesitant nod. His eyes glistened as though he had been crying, and Jan noticed that his long curly locks had been clipped, in the way customary among the town boys.

Jakub's mother, a tall, angular, attractive woman, dressed in black, with her dark hair held back by a bandana, offered a sad smile. "Forgive us, Jan," she said softly. "It's been a difficult day."

Muttering thanks, Jakub took the bag from Jan's hand.

"What's going on? Are you...Are you going to Switzerland?" Jan said, and immediately froze, realizing he had misspoken.

Mr. Kohen cast an icy look in his direction. "What did you just say? Who told you about Switzerland?" His glare rested on Jakub.

Jakub turned pale.

"Was it you? How could you! You knew I told you—"

"You promised!" Jakub burst out, glowering at Jan through flooding eyes. "I'm sorry, Father."

Jan choked on emotion. "We were just talking. He didn't mean to say it. I *promised* not to tell anybody, and I didn't," he cried through sobs. "Not even my dad, not even my mom— nobody. Please, believe me. I won't tell. Please—"

Mr. Kohen's long, reproachful look washed over him like an icy shower.

"I really won't tell," he whimpered, tears running down his cheeks, when he felt Mr. Kohen's arm around his shoulder.

"I believe you, boy. Don't cry. I believe you. It doesn't matter now, anyway. It doesn't matter anymore."

"When? When will you go?"

"Tomorrow."

"Tomorrow?" Jan's chin dropped. "So soon?" He cast a desperate look at Jakub.

"It's not safe here any more." Mr. Kohen sighed. "After what they did to my boy—"

"And did you see the store?" Uncle Isaac broke in. "Did you see the window? Those bastards." He slammed his fist on the table.

"Yes, sir. The Germans—"

"What d'you mean, the Germans? No, not the Germans. I tell you, not the Germans! Someone from here, someone from this town—a Czech! Imagine! A Czech doing this to us. To us, Czechs! To *him*! He almost lost his leg for his country in the Legion, and this is how they treat him!" He fumbled for a cigarette, lit it, and blew the smoke at the ceiling in disgust.

"We can't stay here any longer." Mr. Kohen wiped his brow. "You've seen what they have done to us. What they did to the store. The business is gone. Everything's gone. We're done for. Finished. So we must get out of here while we can. You understand that, don't you?"

Jan nodded, but it didn't make sense—nothing made sense. All he knew was he was about to lose his best friend. His mind was reeling. Nothing else mattered.

"I don't really know if we can make it to Switzerland. Or, for that matter, anywhere. Austria won't let us pass since the Anschluss. But we can't stay here. So, we have to try. Maybe through Hungary. But things are changing too fast. War may break out before we know it. I just don't know." Mr. Kohen took off his glasses and wiped his eyes with a handkerchief. "I don't know. Could be we have waited too long."

CHAPTER 6

Mother stormed in, and Jan flinched as the door behind her slammed with a resounding crack. "Even if you get there early, you don't get anything!" she fumed, tossing a shopping bag on the table. "Over two hours in line at the butcher's and then at the grocer's. And for this." She spilled a bloody pack of soup bones wrapped in an old newspaper, a packet of noodles, and a small sack of roasted wheat that nowadays passed for coffee onto the table. "I don't remember any more what real coffee tastes like," she cried out. "If we didn't have the garden, and the goats, and the rabbits, much as I hate them—" She flipped through the pages of coupons in her ration booklet. "What good are these if they don't buy anything!"

"We used to give these to the dog," Grandmother muttered, poking at the bones. "Did the butcher say when he'll have some meat?"

"He said Monday. Maybe Monday. It's always Monday. You never know."

Father looked up from his work. "Guess I *could* kill another rabbit."

Mother sighed. "No, we'll have to manage. Some other time. Sunday maybe. But, guess what I saw." Lowering her voice, she paused and looked around to make sure everyone was listening. "Saw the Kohens coming back from somewhere. Must've been from the station, they were all dressed up. Dragging suitcases. Looked like they tried to go somewhere."

"The Germans check everybody at the station," Father said.

"You saw the Kohens?" Jan tried to sound nonchalant.

45

Mother's eyebrows arched and her hard gaze made him squirm. "You know something about the Kohens? You saw them last night. Did you see something? Did they say anything?"

"They were packing. Jakub mentioned something once about going to Switzerland, but—"

"Jakub told you? And you didn't say anything?" Her voice rose an octave.

Jan gave her a shrug and looked away, feeling sheepish under her glare.

"How long did you know?"

He shrugged again.

"You mean you knew and didn't say anything?"

"I couldn't; I promised—"

"What d'you mean, you couldn't? If I'd known, I could've gotten a few extra things before they closed the store. This way..." Her disapproving gaze bore through him until he shriveled.

Not until days later did Jan spot Jakub and his father out in the street. Old man Kohen looked away, clearly pretending not to see him. Jakub turned away when Jan gave him a timid wave and took a few hesitant steps in his direction. That hurt. With a heavy heart, he resisted the urge to go on, not daring to cross the great divide that had seemingly sprung between them. The next time he saw Jakub, he wore a yellow Star of David on his coat with the word JUDE inscribed on it.

There had always been Jews in sleepy little Čekaná, as evidenced by a decaying synagogue and a large Jewish cemetery just beyond the town's periphery. But even here there was a gulf between the Gentile and the Jew, with contacts limited to those civilities necessary for business. The Jewish presence was remarked upon and accepted as part of everyday life, but the people themselves were never assimilated into the fabric. Now, the gulf had become a chasm. Easily identified by the yellow stars affixed to their garments, they scrupulously avoided any contact with anyone and kept to themselves. The town folk gave them a wide berth, especially after a new Fuchs edict, dutifully hawked from the street corners by old man Paleček, forbade all contact and association with them. Having developed a fine sense of reading the wind, most people didn't have to be told anyway. The Germans, for their part, ignored them, except for an occasional snide remark and laughter at their expense when they met in the street. After some time, that all took on a semblance of normalcy.

A German administrator, ironically named Jan Czech, replaced the hapless mayor, who was jailed. One of his first acts was to demolish the town monument to the fallen legionnaires from the First World War.

In school, Jakub's seat remained empty. One day, Jan carved his initials next to Jakub's in the desktop.

Since Herr Dietrich's arrival, the mood at the school had changed dramatically. The teachers were subdued, cautious. Herr Dietrich himself made frequent visits to the classrooms, usually unannounced. He would then take over and attempt to teach the children the rudiments of being German: How to properly pronounce the title of Adolf Hitler—*der Reichsführer*—the colors and correct orientation of the swastika in the German flag, the raised hand salute with the proper intonation of *Heil Hitler,* how to sing the *'Die Fahne Hoch'* and *'Deutschland, Deutschland Über Alles.'* At times, he would expound about what it meant to be a true Aryan and how the

Jews were responsible for all the problems in the world. Sometimes, feeling particularly sentimental, he would reminisce emotionally about his days as a leader in the *Hitler Jugend*.

Feigning attention, Jan gave himself to daydreaming during his lengthy harangues.

*   *   *

The clock struck 5:00 and the BBC call sign – the Morse code letter 'V' beaten out on tympani—three shorts and a long...*ding ding ding...dong* – materialized from the crackling static. Tense with anticipation, Father and the seamstresses stopped their banter. Jan's heart skipped a beat. *Ding ding ding...dong,* it echoed, again and again, and he knew what would follow: a short musical signature of Smetana's *Moldau*, and then the grave echoing voice, "This is London, London calling," when the metallic sound of hob-nailed boots on the walkway cobblestones and a glimpse of green-gray uniforms filing past the window sent everybody scurrying. Jan had never seen Father this pale. Sweat broke out on his forehead as he leaped over the chairs and with one swoop snuffed out the radio. Jan slid down in his chair and hid behind an open book. Grandmother clutched her rosary and began praying in earnest.

"JesusMary, they're coming for us!" Mother squealed, as she retreated toward the kitchen. Crossing herself, she glared at Father. "I knew this was going to happen. What now? What have you done? You and your damn radio. I knew one day you'd get us in trouble! You never listen when—"

"Nothing! I've done nothing," Father shot back, wiping his brow with a handkerchief.

"Don't give me that. You've always been irresponsible. And you," she snapped at Jan, "get in the kitchen. Now!"

"But Mom—"

"Now!" she screeched, eyes bulging, blood draining from her contorted face.

Jan resented being treated like a child, but there was no point arguing when Mother was beyond any reason. Grumbling, he snatched the book and withdrew into the kitchen, leaving the door ajar just enough that he could at least observe the goings-on through the crack.

A heavy rap on the door put an end to his parents' spat. Without waiting for an answer, the door flew open and Sturmbannführer Fuchs, trailed by an entourage of underlings, strode into the workroom. Everyone froze.

"*Heil Hitler!*" he barked, as his icy gaze swept the room and rested on Father. His right hand went up in a flapping motion, followed by a murmured chorus of *Heil Hitlers* from his minions.

Father swallowed hard and nodded.

"*Kennen Sie Deutsch sprechen?*" Fuchs snapped, and made an impatient motion with his riding crop toward one of his aides who immediately translated, "Do you not speak German?"

"Only a little...*ein bischen*," Father lied, extending his thumb and index finger in a diminutive gesture.

Fuchs' face darkened. The scar on his cheek took on a purplish hue. "I've been told, you are a tailor."

Father motioned toward the seamstresses and forced a smile. "Yessir, you can see for yourself. Our girls, seamstresses..."

Bowing their heads, the 'girls' blushed under the probing looks of the Germans.

Fuchs consulted a notebook. "I'm told you worked in France?"

"Yes, I apprenticed at Burberry's."

"Burberry's? Hmm! A very fine house. How long were you with them?"

"More than six years." Father sent a reassuring glance in Mother's direction and cleared his throat. The tension in his face disappeared.

"Then, you will be the tailor for me and my staff. *Verstehst du?*"

"A t-tailor?" Father sputtered. "But sir, I can't just now. Too much work. But there are others—"

Fuchs' scar turned crimson. "You don't understand, *Herr* Neuman. I am not asking."

Father swallowed hard and shrugged.

"You come recommended. I want you!"

"I don't know who would. As I said, sir, you might do better with someone else, but if you insist—"

"You will be paid, but remember, my work will take precedence over everybody's. Everybody's! *Verstehst du?*" He stabbed the air with his crop and twisted uncomfortably.

"Then perhaps you'd permit me to take a quick look. Make a few measurements." Father tugged at the tape measure hanging around his neck. "If you would—"

"Of course," Fuchs said and took off his tunic. Under it, the top button of his trousers hung open as his stomach spilled over the waistband. A pair of leather suspenders kept the trousers from falling. The light grayish-brown shirt was stained under the armpits.

"I see." Father fingered the fabric. "Your uniform could use a touch-up here and there. Letting out in a couple of places. Fortunately, there seems to be enough material in the seams."

The purplish color vanished from Fuchs' scar and his manner softened. *"Sehr gut!* Excellent. I shall have the orderly bring my uniform tomorrow. I will return two days later for the fitting. It will be done, yes?"

"We will do what we can." Father gave Fuchs a tight-lipped smile. "I will do what I can."

"Sehr gut! Gehen wir, jetzt! Very good! Let us go, then!" Fuchs barked, tracing a lazy arc of the Nazi salute with his crop. *"Auf wiedersehen! Heil Hitler!"*

"Auf wiedersehen," Father mumbled, his glazed look following the Germans filing out of the house.

The seamstresses stirred in relief.

"Holy Mother of God, what are you getting us into now?" Mother pounced on him no sooner the door had slammed shut and the footsteps died out. "You fool, what are you *doing*? Working for them? Kissing their behinds? You? Tomáš? A patriot? What's the matter with you, man? Haven't you got any sense? Any pride? Any *conscience*?"

Father threw his hands up. "What choice did I have? Didn't you hear? I saw you listening."

"I was not—"

He glared at her angrily. "So what would *you* have done? Said no to them? You know I couldn't refuse. For chrissakes, be sensible, Lena. What would you have me do? I don't want their dirty work any more than you do. But at least we'll get paid for it. God knows we need the money. And besides, no telling what they'd do if I'd refused." He lit a cigarette and looked at her grimly through the smoke. "At least, this way, they'll leave us alone."

CHAPTER 7

Mother beamed when Jan passed her the stamp-encrusted envelope the postman had delivered. She tore it open, pulled out the letter, and eagerly read it to herself. Her lips moved silently as her expression darkened. A tear escaped her eye, leaving a glistening trail on her cheek. "I don't think we'll be hearing from Pepa for a while," she announced in a quavering voice, referring to her favorite brother in the diminutive. "He's been drafted." She folded the letter with a sigh, wiped the tear from her cheek, and stared vacantly into space. Josef, her younger brother, had also apprenticed at Burberry's in Paris, but unlike Father, remained in France, where he opened an atelier in Versailles. He was an infrequent visitor in Jan's home, but his letters arrived regularly to Mother's delight.

"Being sent to some place called Arras," she said.

"And Aunt Stáska? And Yvette?" Jan was fond of his younger cousin.

"Worries me just to think about them. Guess we won't see them until this madness is over. Poor dears. I told them they should've left Yvette with us. She would have been safer here. But they wouldn't listen."

"I'm afraid," Grandmother mumbled, crossing herself. "I'm afraid of wars. I've already lost one son and now this. I'm afraid." She wiped her deep sunken eyes with the cuff of her sleeve and stared blankly into space. Jan's uncle and namesake was killed in Serbia during the first days of the "War to End all Wars."

Jan ambled to Father busy with the radio. He had unscrewed the perforated cover, exposing a maze of colorful wires and glowing tubes. The pungent vinegarish smell of ozone filled the air. Contemplating the glowing maze for a few moments, he turned off the set, folded a scrap of flannel, slipped it over one of the still-hot tubes, and carefully lifted it out of its socket. He did the same with the second one, and then gently laid both in a box lined with soft cotton.

"Taking out the short wave, Son." He smiled, noticing Jan's puzzlement.

"What do you mean, taking out the short wave? Why?"

Father wiped his brow and handed Jan a small, yellow tag, slit to fit over a knob on the radio. "Here. Paleček passed these around to everybody this morning."

Jan skimmed the bold text: *Effective immediately, all radios equipped with short wave band must have the band disabled. Any infraction of this order or removal of this notice from the radio will result in severe punishment. Listening to foreign broadcasts is punishable by death.*

"I didn't know you could do that," Jan said admiringly.

"Oh, Alois showed me once."

An engineer with the Tesla Radio Works in Prague, Alois, Mother's youngest brother and Jan's favorite uncle and godfather, had given the radio to the family last Christmas.

"What's a short wave, Dad?"

"Short wave? It's a way to listen to the news the Germans don't want us to hear."

"You mean, like from England and France?"

"Even America, on a good day. The Germans don't want us to know what's going on. Don't want us to hear the truth. Remember that, Boy. Truth is hard to come by during the war."

"Dad?"

"Yeah?"

"Is it true that the streets in America are paved with gold?"

Father pulled up short. "Where did you hear that nonsense?" Trying to suppress a laugh, his face broke out in a grin.

"Grandmother told me."

"Grandmother? Boy, you shouldn't believe everything you hear. Hate to disappoint you."

"Not even Grandmother?"

"Naw! She means well but she doesn't know everything. She's old and gets confused about things."

*   *   *

From his favorite vantage point in the far corner of the workroom, Jan strained to hear stationmaster Fiala, carpenter Hrášek, and Constable Kubek discussing the war in hushed tones. Huddled around the radio, they had become regular visitors, sneaking in after dusk to listen to the BBC. Father had just replaced the two short-wave tubes and attached an antenna – coils of thin copper wire wound around a wooden frame – to the back of the set. With a resigned look, Mother jerked shut the blackout curtains, crossed herself, and glaring at Father, who ignored her, retreated to the kitchen.

"You say this is going to work as well as the old one?" Stationmaster Fiala picked up the contraption, examined it closely, shook his head, and put it down gently. "Cigarettes?" He offered all around.

"It should." Father nodded, lighting up. "I used all the wire from the one I took down. Twenty meters, all copper."

Swirling upward, the smoke took on the bluish cast of the glowing tubes, sharply outlining the silhouetted faces huddled over the set. The air filled with whistles and static and snatches of dialogue as Father spun the dial. The men scooted closer, enthralled with anticipation.

Then, there it was—a faint sound of drumbeat, *Ding, ding, ding—dong...* three shorts and a long, three dots and a dash—the letter 'V' for Victory, emerging from the crackling static.

The beats became louder, the reception clearer as Father deftly made a few adjustments. The reverberant beats sounded several more times, rising and ebbing as though riding a wave, coming through a surge of hisses and vanishing in a whisper, before a tinny-sounding voice broke through:

"Here is London, London speaking to the people of Czechoslovakia. Please stand by for an address by President Beneš who has just returned from meetings with the Prime Minister, Sir Winston Churchill, and an audience with His Majesty, King George the Sixth. President Beneš received an enthusiastic welcome at Whitehall upon his arrival from the United States yesterday, and later today was received at Buckingham with all the pomp and ceremonies accorded a head of state. Here, now, is President Beneš."

The static hum suddenly rose and the voice faded, overwhelmed by crackling and whistles. Father lunged for the knob and gave it a nudge. Flickering briefly, the glowing tuning eye stabilized in a steady glow and the words came back faint but clear:

"...just returned from meetings with the Prime Minister and members of his Government. As you know, His Majesty the King..." The words faded away and then came back again.

"...choslovak provisional government in exile. I and Foreign Minister, Jan Masaryk, along with other members of our government in exile, have been engaged in talks with the

American government officials in Washington to secure... their support of...in exile..."

The sound kept fading in and out in a slow, rhythmical fashion as the men sat entranced, straining to fill in the gaps between words, flush with excitement at hearing the disembodied but familiar voice.

Like a gunshot, the slamming of the house door brought them to their feet. Turning pale, Father lunged for the radio and in one quick swoop turned it off, tore off the antenna and threw it behind a pile of fabric scraps. The men scrambled away from the set.

A quick staccato of hard knocks, the door flew open, and there was Fuchs, his interpreter, and an orderly carrying a folded uniform.

Mouth agape, Father stood up, spilling the cigarette ashes on his trousers. His hand shook as he brushed them off. Faces pale, the men shifted uncomfortably, struggling awkwardly to maintain composure.

"Heil Hitler!" Fuchs snapped, sizing them up.

No one spoke. No one moved.

The smell of ozone mixed with cigarette smoke hung heavy in the room. Fuchs sniffed the air and glared at the group. "Perhaps I am interrupting something. A meeting perhaps?" His eyes narrowed into a pair of slits. "I thought I heard voices. A radio perhaps?" He tapped it with his crop. "A fine set. Really fine. Looks almost as good as my *Grundig*. Is it Czech?" He taunted them with a knowing smirk.

Father nodded toward the men. "My friends: *Herr* Fiala, *Herr* Hrášek, and—"

"Oh *ja, der Polizei*," Fuchs shot back. "We met before. It's a small town."

Kubek gave him a nervous smile.

"We were discussing the gasoline problem," Father said. "We're all volunteer firemen, and—"

"Firemen? You?" Fuchs cast a side glance at the men through narrowing eyes. "Gasoline problem? What gasoline problem?"

"Well, sir, the problem is, your soldiers have confiscated what little we had, and we don't have any for our pumper, *or* the truck. Luckily, there's been no fires, but should there ever be…" Father shrugged.

"So?"

"So we were just discussing how to ask you for help, *Herr Sturmbannführer.*"

"Me? Ask me?" Tapping the palm of his hand with the crop, Fuchs pursed his lips and made an amused face. "You should talk to *Herr* Administrator, *Herr* Czech. It's his problem." The smirk disappeared from his face. The scar on his cheek turned pink. "How come he didn't say anything? He briefs me every day."

Father shrugged.

"You Czechs must understand, our first priority is to support our *Wehrmacht!*" He stabbed the air with his crop. "Our men, our tanks, our *Luftwaffe*—they all need gasoline. Lots of gasoline. That's why you must sacrifice. For the *Vaterland.* For the good of the *Reich.*" He drew a deep breath and the rosy hue of his scar faded away. "But today is a very special day, so perhaps I can make an exception. I *may* be able to spare a few liters. Lieutenant, make a note of it." His aide sprung to life and hastily scribbled something in his notebook.

"You may congratulate me, if you wish," he said, brushing aside Father's profuse thanks.

"Congratulate you?"

"*Ja.* I have just had news of my promotion to *Obersturmbannführer.*" His gaze swept the men for a reaction, but they remained deadpan, purposely avoiding his eyes.

"That is why I came at this hour. I must have the new epaulettes sewn on immediately. I am certain you will oblige, *Herr* Neuman. It shouldn't take long. I will wait. Orderly!" he barked. A young private snapped to attention and, clicking his heels, presented Father with the uniform and a small cardboard box with the new insignia.

"It'll be a few minutes," Father said. "Please." He offered Fuchs a chair.

Muttering their goodbyes, the men slunk out of the room.

Fuchs sat down, but only briefly. Consulting his watch, he got up and strolled around the shop, slapping the crop impatiently on the side of his boot. Finally, he tapped the radio, slipped the monocle into his eye socket, bent over the set, and read the yellow sticker.

Beads of sweat broke out on Father's forehead.

Fuchs's eyes narrowed the way a cunning cat surveys her prey before pouncing. He let the monocle drop and sniffed the air.

Father turned pale.

"Why is the back open?" His caustic glare rested on Father.

"It's a good set but it has a flaw. Tends to overheat with all the tubes. There's not enough air. No circulation." Father swallowed hard, wiping the perspiration from his brow.

"I see. I see." Fuchs hissed under his breath. Slipping his hand inside, he touched the hot short-wave tubes and withdrew it just as quickly. *"Noch heiss,"* he growled, glaring at Father. And then he noticed Jan. His eyebrows shot up. *"Ah, ein*

Knabe!" He bared his teeth in a smile. "I didn't see you back there in the shadows. *Wie heisst Du, Knabe?* What is your name, boy?"

Heart racing, Jan sank into his chair.

"Wie heisst Du, Knabe?" Fuchs slipped the tip of the crop under Jan's chin, forcing him to look up.

An icy chill snaked down Jan's spine as their eyes met. Cold and piercing, Fuchs's seemed almost a thing apart from the anemic, scarred face that framed them. Something stirred inside, something he had never experienced before— fear.

"That's Jan, our son. He's almost ten. You have to excuse him." Father sent an anxious look in Jan's direction. "What are you doing up? Shouldn't you be in bed?"

Fuchs waved him off. "I have a boy, too, a bit older than—" He pointed the crop at Jan. "A fine boy. An *Abteilungsführer* in the *Hitler Jugend*. Makes me proud. Ready to be a soldier, just like me." His look rested on Jan and seemed to soften a bit, as if in reverie, but hardened just as quickly.

"Go to bed, Boy. Now!" Father said, a hard edge to his voice.

Muttering goodnight under his breath, Jan slid past Fuchs and disappeared into his bedroom. Lying in bed, eyes wide, staring into the darkness, straining to catch bits of the conversation filtering in from the workroom, a chill came over him as the eyes of the man he had just met materialized from his subconscious.

"He saw you, didn't he? He knows! I know he knows. JesusMary!" he heard his mother cry out after Fuchs left.

"I don't think so. I don't know," his father came back, the customary brashness gone from his voice.

"He knows. I could tell he knows. JesusMary, what have you done? You and your damn politics—you're going to get us all killed!"

He didn't answer.

No one slept much that night or the nights that followed, awaiting the sound of hobnailed boots in the walkway and the terrifying knock on the door, knowing for the first time the all-pervading force of terror.

CHAPTER 8

The goats picked up pace and broke into a run when they came within sight of the shrub-covered slope. Panting, Jan threw himself on the familiar ledge warmed by the late afternoon sun. It felt good being here, away from the world of the calamitous Germans. War here was just a bad thought, easily dismissed.

A sharp crack of a breaking twig behind him sent an icy ping up his spine. He held his breath and froze. Another crack, this time closer. His heart pounded as he slowly turned around.

Jakub stepped out from behind a bush.

"Jesus!" He felt a draining rush of relief. "It's you!"

"I had to come," Jakub said, treading carefully over the boulders littering the ledge. "Can't stay long—been already waiting more than an hour. You're late."

Jan got up, grinning awkwardly. "Never thought I'd see you here again," he blurted. "The last time I saw you, I thought you didn't want me to—"

"You know I couldn't." Jakub sounded hurt. "But I looked for you from our window. I always look for you. I saw you once, even waved to you, but you didn't notice."

"How come you're not wearing your star? Aren't you supposed to? And your hair? What happened?"

Grinning, Jakub pulled the yellow patch from his pocket. "I'll pin it on when I get back to town. Don't need it here. My Mom cut my hair."

Jan smiled. The 'old' Jakub was here, smiling and carefree. How much he had missed him. "I'm really glad you came."

Jakub's grin faded. "Can't stay long. Don't have much time. I've come to say goodbye."

"Goodbye?" Jan gaped at him, mouth open. "You mean, you're finally going? To Switzerland?"

"I wish, but we really don't know where. Uncle Isaac said, somebody told him. I don't know who, the Rabbi, somebody. Said they're taking all the Jews to a work camp, somewhere. Some place called Terezín."

"When?"

Jakub shrugged. "Not sure, but he thinks it could happen any day—today, tomorrow. Any time."

"Jesus!"

"So I had to come. Father said I could. I probably won't see you before we go." He took a deep breath. "Don't know if I'll ever see you again."

"I wish you didn't have to go." Jan struggled to keep his voice from breaking.

Jakub shrugged and wiped his eyes with the back of his hand.

The awkwardness returned, almost crushing now, paralyzing their discourse. They both fell silent, fidgeting uncomfortably, avoiding eye-contact.

"I really do have to go," Jakub finally stirred.

Jan fished in his pocket and pulled out his pocketknife. Caressing its smooth handle for a few seconds, he opened it, snapped it close, and then extended it to his friend. "Here. So you won't forget. That's all I have."

Jakub flushed. "You know I won't forget, but thanks." He reached into his pocket. "You can have mine, so *you* don't forget." He handed his pocketknife to Jan and attempted a smile, but his glistening eyes betrayed him.

"What's this say?" Jan said, fingering the raised letters of an inscription on the sheath.

"That's *Shalom*. In Hebrew. It means *Peace* or *Hello*—or, *Goodbye*."

A torrent of thoughts flooded Jan's mind, but he was unable to get the words past the dam that was the lump in his throat. Tears rolling down his cheeks, Jakub fared no better. In the end, they just reached out to each other across the gulf already widening between them, shook hands, and without saying anything at all, Jakub spun around and disappeared down the path.

* * *

It took Jan a few moments to realize he wasn't dreaming. Ghost-like in his white long johns, Father already was drawing apart the blackout curtain. The dim light of the breaking day spilled in, making everything surreal. Pale as the sheet she was clutching, Mother sat bolt upright in bed. Grandmother's pleas, "JesusMary, what's going on?" went unanswered.

The air outside trembled with the deep throbbing of motors. The nauseating smell of diesel drifted in through the open window. Excited shouts, the battering crashes of splitting wood, and then triumphant whoops as the apparent obstacle gave way with a groan, shattered the early morning quiet.

"*Raus, Juden! Schnell! Raus, Juden! Raus! Raus! Raus Juden!*" the snarling guttural commands, not unlike the baying of a pack of hounds, rose in a crescendo from the direction of Jakub's house.

Father swore and recoiled. "They're after them! They're after the Jews! They've come for the Kohens!"

Squirming in under him, Jan felt the hair on the back of his neck stand up, and a giant hand squeeze his throat until he choked. From upstairs, he heard Zlata's shriek and a muffled rebuke.

Father's jaw moved even as words failed to emerge. Finally, eyes bulging, he let out a stream of curses: "Those sons of bitches! And look over there—that's Fuchs! That's Fuchs over there! That pig! That cretin! That German whore! How I'd like to kill that Nazi bastard!"

A pair of trucks, already tightly packed with the town's Jews, idled in front of the Kohens' house. Pale, drawn, and disheveled, they stared vacantly over the gathering crowd, their unseeing eyes and stoic expressions masking the turmoil within. The gate of the last truck hung limply open. Schmeisers at the ready, guards patrolled the perimeter.

One squad of soldiers cordoned the house as others poured in through the smashed gate, flooding the courtyard and attacking the main door with their rifle buts. In the middle of it all, barking out rapid-fire orders from the back of an open staff car, stabbing the air with his riding crop, stood *Obersturmbannführer* Fuchs.

"For the love of Jesus, watch what you say!" Mother shrieked. "Watch what you say! And watch where you say it. When will you have enough sense to watch your mouth? What if they hear you? You'll get us all in trouble."

Mumbling an unintelligible response, Father hastily began to dress. Jan slid back from the window, quickly slipped into his pants, and ignoring his mother's cries, ran out after him into the street.

Prodded by rifle butts, kicks, and shoves, the Kohens stumbled out of their house, greeted by a chorus of taunts.

Bewildered and panting under the weight of their suitcases, they hesitated, not knowing which way to turn.

"Schnell, schnell, machen sie schnell!" A soldier poked at them with the butt of his rifle, herding them toward the open truck.

Jan stared at the commotion. Swallowing hard, he found it impossible to keep back the sobs. A comforting hand touched his shoulder.

"I know how you're feeling, Boy," Father said, squeezing him gently. "You must be strong."

"But why? Because they're Jews?"

"Someday, you'll understand."

Jakub swept the thin crowd of onlookers with his gaze and seeing Jan, raised his hand to wave. One of the Germans gave him a shove, and when he hesitated, hit him on the side of the head with the butt of his rifle. The hollow thud, followed by a muffled scream, sent Jakub sprawling. The suitcase flew out of his hand, spilling its contents in the dust.

"Mach schnell, Jude!" the German screamed. *"Mach schnell!"*

Jakub didn't move.

"Mach schnell, Jude!" the soldier barked again, prodding Jakub with his boot.

A second soldier joined in the prodding. *"Auf Jude, auf!* Get up!"

Instinctively, Jan lurched forward toward his friend sprawled in the dust, but Father's iron grasp kept him from moving.

Jakub staggered to his feet, straining to regain balance. He made a vague move with the back of his hand to wipe the blood trickling down his face from a gash above his ear, but succeeded only in leaving a grotesque smear.

With a wild shriek, Uncle Isaac dropped his suitcase and lunged at the German. "You bloody Nazi bastard! Fighting children now, eh? Why don't you take on someone your own size!" he screamed, face contorted by rage. He grabbed the soldier's rifle and slammed him against the side of the truck, jamming the rifle against his throat in a chokehold.

Gasping, the German let out a choking sound as the stock pressed against his windpipe, and kicking wildly, lurched to free himself. He grasped Uncle Isaac's collar, but the uncle shook him off and kept him pinned against the truck until his eyes bulged and face turned purple. It all took place in a manner of seconds.

Surprisingly fast for his heft, Fuchs unholstered his pistol, leapt from the staff car, and fired three quick shots from a point-blank range into Uncle Isaac's back. The reports reverberated among the houses. Uncle Isaac heaved upward under the force of the impact and fell away from the rifle. Grasping wildly for something and with a gurgling sigh, he slowly slid down the side of the truck as the German quickly scrambled out of the way. One more desperate lurch, one more aimless stab of the air, and then he collapsed into a dark, shapeless heap. A trickle of blood from under his body collected in a dark thickening pool.

Jakub lunged toward where Uncle Isaac lay, but his father held him back.

Fuchs holstered his pistol and spun around, glaring at the crowd. The crimson scar on his face stood out prominently—the color of the blood now pooling under Uncle Isaac's body. His gaze swept the street, fleetingly brushing Jan and his father, before he silently mounted the staff car and sank into the seat.

Prodded by shouts and rifle buts, the Kohens heaved their suitcases into the truck and scrambled in after them. A pair of guards jumped in, the gate slammed shut, and the vehicles moved out in a cloud of exhaust. Stoically, holding onto the sides of the heaving trucks and each other, the Jews stood there stunned, leaving behind a town in shock and a human heap in the middle of the street—Uncle Isaac.

The crowd scattered. Old Man Paleček carted away the body. Sickened, Jan walked over to where Uncle Isaac had lain. Staring at the dark stain and tire tracks in the dust, his mind replayed the horrible scene, inexorably stopping at Jakub. Jakub's bloodied face lingered before his mind's eye like a suffering icon of a saint, burning itself indelibly into his memory. And Fuchs's! Until now, hate was just a hypothetical thing to him, a word rather than a feeling, but all that had evaporated in an instant. He hated Fuchs! Truly hated! He knew that should the opportunity ever arise, he would seek revenge. For Jakub, Uncle Isaac, the Kohens, and all the others in the trucks. He climbed into a small hayloft above the goat shed, buried his face in the sweet-smelling hay, and cried.

CHAPTER 9

"Boy, let's stop here for a bit and rest." The grandmother nudged Jan as they crossed a gurgling stream, breached by stepping stones. "My hip hurts. Ever since I fell, it's been giving me trouble." Panting, she climbed the muddy bank, stopped by a large solitary boulder and leaned against it. With a sigh of relief, she rested the basket strapped to her back on its lichen-covered top.

Jan eyed her with concern. He recalled her murmuring something to Mother about an inflamed hip—an injury she had sustained when she tripped on the house steps and fell. Mother had tried to talk her out of the annual trek into the woods to gather moss to decorate the family grave on All Souls Day, as was the custom, but she wouldn't hear of it.

"That's what happens when you get old—you're good for nothing." She smiled wearily. "It's going to be a cold winter; I can feel it in my bones." She cinched a thin shawl tighter about her shoulders as a gust whipped the tops of the aspen and birches, and sent a swirl of leaves high into the air. Hanging low and gray, the skies threatened an early snow.

"You shouldn't have come. You're not well."

"Just a little tired. Just a little tired, my boy." She dismissed him with a wave of her hand and a reassuring smile.

"Grandmother?"

She looked at him lovingly.

"I never thought you'd tell me a fib."

She raised what little remained of her grey eyebrows. "Me? A fib? At my age? No." She shook her head.

"You told me once that the streets in America are paved with gold. Dad said it wasn't true."

An amused smile crossed her face. "Well, when I was young, I believed it myself, but I guess, if he says they aren't, they aren't. He ought to know. He's seen it. So, sorry to disappoint you, Boy."

"What do you mean, he's seen it? I don't understand."

"You mean, you didn't know? They still haven't told you?" Flustered, she pulled out a crumpled handkerchief and blew her nose. "I thought you knew. You're old enough to. Oh, I'm sorry."

"Tell me what, Grandmother?"

She began to fiddle with her basket straps, and for a few long moments disappeared into her thoughts, suddenly transported into another dimension. She looked at him with unseeing eyes, and then the wrinkles on her face came alive in a smile. "Well, guess I may as well tell you. Tomáš, your father, has been to America. We don't talk about it."

"Jesus! Why not?"

"I really wish you wouldn't blaspheme," she admonished him softly.

"Sorry. But how? When? I thought my uncle—"

"Yes, your uncle, too. But your father, when he was mustered out of the army, couldn't find a job – he was seeing your mother then – and he didn't want to farm, so he let his brother Václav, your uncle—"

"Isn't he the one we don't see? The one Mom says she doesn't want to take even one step inside the house?"

Grandmother nodded. "The same. Your dad let your uncle talk him into joining a circus. A German circus. Imagine! Joining a circus!" She sighed loudly. "It broke your mother's heart. The circus toured America, and that's how he got to see it."

"Jesus!"

She looked at him pleadingly but remained quiet.

He had often wondered about the postcard of the Statue of Liberty his father had once given him (he still counted it among his prized possessions), particularly the stamps, and the scratched-out writing, or what remained of it, over which he had puzzled. He'd always had a suspicion that it resembled his father's hand. Now he knew.

"So, how long was he there?" he asked.

"Only about six months. Not long. But with the circus, more than two years. He still has a hat stashed away somewhere, one of those Stetsons. Your mother gets furious even now when he puts it on."

Of course! It all made sense now. He'd seen his father once, long ago, before a mirror, trying on a strange wide-brimmed hat and putting it away hastily when Mother came into the room.

"So after he came back, they got married, but she never forgave him," she went on.

"What was there to forgive? He had to find work!"

"True, but not *that* kind of work. Joining a circus was like joining a band of gypsies. It disgraced the family. People talked. Your grandfather—her Daddy, my husband, God rest his soul— you didn't know him. He died while you still were a baby. He was furious. Didn't want them to get married."

"So why did they?"

"Oh, that's another story. You're still too young to understand, but I guess if I don't tell you, nobody will. So—" She sighed and wiped her eyes with the corner of her apron.

71

"Your mother had plenty of suitors. There was a nice young man who liked her a lot. Loved her. Adored her. We all liked him, too. So, after your father returned, she was going to break up with him for this other fellow, except that she still saw your father a couple of times, and turned up in a family way. Or so she thought. After that, there was no question that they would get married right away. It would have been an even greater disgrace to have a child out of wedlock than being with the circus. So they rushed to Prague to get married. Kind of quietly, of course. You know how people talk. News like that travels fast, especially in Čekaná. And they were going to come back after the baby was born. Let the word out that he—your father—got a job there. Some kind of an excuse, you understand. Except, there was no baby. It was a false pregnancy. But she was already trapped. There was no way she could leave him now. Your mother is a martyr."

"Is it why she's always sad? Why she never smiles?"

"So you noticed, Boy? You surprise me." Her eyes twinkled as she gazed at him from under the rim of her babushka. "Of course, you know that later on you had a brother. He was stillborn. And a sister. She died when she was three. Burst appendix. No way to get her to the doctor. So you came late in life. Anyway, when Pepa, that's your Uncle Josef, offered to take your father to France and apprentice him as a tailor, your mother made him go. And that's how he got to be respectable again." She looked at him lovingly through those sunken pale blue eyes that forever seemed to ooze tears, and sighed. "So, now you know. You're a big boy and you know how to keep things to yourself, don't you? Don't tell I told you."

Jan nodded, dumbfounded. She had never spoken to him this way, but then, they had hardly ever conversed at all. Until this moment, she was just Grandmother, not even 'Granny,' the diminutive that his mother deemed impolite, and never, never under pain of punishment Aloisie, her Christian name. She was a fixture, always there, a one-dimensional part of the family scenery, quiet, withdrawn, remote, more of a shadow than a presence. He couldn't conceive of her ever being young. He respected her authority and age because he'd been taught to, but beyond that, he gave her little credit for emotional depth or coherent thought. Mostly, she was just there, his refuge—someone to turn to when he hurt, calm his fears when he was afraid, extend a soothing embrace in place of words when he was scolded, someone who offered understanding rather than reproach.

Grandmother pulled an apple from one of her bottomless pockets and handed it to him. "Here, Boy, cut it, so we both can have a piece." She extended her hand after he sliced the apple. "Is that a new knife?"

He wiped the blade on his trousers and handed it to her. "Jakub gave it to me. Before he left."

She inspected it and frowned. "Be careful before you show it to anybody. That, whatever it is, these letters, could get you...could get *us* all in trouble." She wiped a tear from her cheek with the back of her hand. "Poor Jakub."

"What do you think happened to him?"

She shrugged and her gaze seemed to sink deeper behind a curtain of wrinkles. "These are awful times. People do awful things. Sometimes, they're worse than animals. I've lived a long time. Seen many things. But nothing like this. When I was your mother's age, I'd already lost one child, your Uncle Jan, your namesake, in a war in Serbia, and for what?" She shook her head. "So young, and he died for nothing." She wiped a tear from the corner of her eye with her apron. "War always hurts the innocent. Just look at your poor little cousin Yvette. God bless her soul, the war took her, too. So young, so sweet."

"Mom never said what happened."

"She and your Aunt Stáska walked all the way to Normandy, that's almost a hundred kilometers, running away from the Germans. Cold and wet. Slept in ditches. She caught a bad cold. Died a few days after they got back home."

"I heard Mother say it was Aunt Stáska's fault. Uncle Josef said so."

Grandmother sighed. "People sometime say things they don't mean when they're upset or when they're hurting. Your mother took the news hard." Putting her arm around him, she gave him a gentle squeeze. "These are hard times, Boy. God knows who else...*what* else's going to happen. The Jews, your friend Jakub, Yvette. All I know is we spend our lives struggling and struggling. Struggling for what? It can all be gone in an instant."

Jan took her hand. It was cold and the skin felt waxy. Her callused palm was rough to the touch.

She held his hand and squeezed it. "I've lived long enough to have seen it all before and I'm tired. Old and tired. It will be up to you, my little boy, you and the other children. You're the only hope I can see for the future, and God only knows what that'll be."

"I miss Jakub. I hate the Germans. I hate them. I really *hate* them!"

She drew him closer and put her arm around him. "Hate is an awful word, Boy. I know how you're feeling, believe me.

74

But not all of them are bad. Some of them are good people, same as our own kind." A shadow of melancholy swept over her face. "You're old enough to understand, so I'm going to tell you more. But it's a secret, so I must ask you—"

"I won't say anything, Grandma."

She looked at him gravely. "People don't know this; and we never talk about it. I have two sisters and they're both married to Germans."

It took a moment for the words to sink in. Jan's jaw dropped. "Did you say Germans?"

She nodded. "Let me explain. As I said, it's something else we don't talk about, especially now. Maybe you don't remember when we visited Vimperk a few years back. You were just a little boy then. Well, that was my sister's. The other lives in Stuttgart. Haven't seen her in years." She brushed off a tear with a finger. "Daddy tried to talk them out of it, marrying Germans, I mean, but they wouldn't listen. Young people never listen. So they got married, and I still remember how ashamed we all felt. How ashamed I was, ashamed for the family. Got their way but paid a price, though—Daddy never forgave them. Wouldn't let them cross the threshold of their own home." She sighed. "I tell you, they're good people. *Good* people. Not different from you and me. From *us*. Hard workers, scratching for a living just like us. You know, sometimes things happen, like this war, and people don't have any say-so. They get trapped, and all that's left is hope. Hope that the good will prevail in the end. I may not see it, I am too old. But you will— I pray someday, you will." She was out of breath and her last words vanished in a whisper.

Jan felt grown-up but puzzled. Why did she tell him all this? Why now? And what did it have to do with Jakub? His

75

mind was still abuzz when she touched him lightly, got up, and he followed.

Heaped high, the baskets creaked under their load as Jan and the old woman set out for home. As they crossed the stream, carefully stepping from one stone to the next, the old woman stumbled, slipped, and tumbled into the knee-deep water, spilling the moss. By the time they reached home, she was shivering uncontrollably. The next day, she came down with a fever and the doctor had to be called. His prognosis was grim; the remedies he administered fruitless. She died two days later. The brilliantly green moss they had collected, speckled with chrysanthemums and votive candles covered her grave.

CHAPTER 10

A heated argument spilled into the yard through the cracked-open window.

"I'm glad that butcher Fuchs is gone. But, bad as he was, at least he *paid*." Mother's voice turned shrill. "How are we to survive now, with most of the help gone, the boy growing by leaps, and you, *especially* you, spending more and more time with your cohorts than in the shop, wasting what little we make on cigarettes?"

"You don't understand. Can't you see what's happening?" Father sounded wounded. "The war has turned. Now, with America joining the fight in Africa and the British bombing Germany, Nürnberg just yesterday, the Huns have to fight on two fronts. That's why they sent Fuchs to Russia. Once he got his promotion, his days were numbered. I am surprised they let him stay as long as they did. They're running short of people. They're losing. So I say good riddance. I never wanted his dirty money anyway."

"But you took it! You took it!"

"Yeah, and they left us alone. You know I had no choice. You saw how jumpy they were after the Heydrich assassination, and what they did to Lidice. Killing all the adults. Taking away all the children. Wiping the place off the map. And, you say it yourself – they paid!"

"I can't see how we can make it. If it weren't for the Fialas' help now and then— How many times have I asked you, begged you, pleaded with you to give up smoking? And how many times have I asked you to get rid of those damn *pigeons?* All they do is mess everywhere and eat us out of the house.

Here I'm trying to make ends meet, don't know where the next meal's coming from, and you won't kill even one? I'm sick of potatoes."

"You don't know when to stop, woman, do you! I can't help it if they come back each time I try to get rid of them. They're *pigeons*." Father's voice turned reedy, and whenever that happened, Jan knew he was about to blowup. "If anyone should, *you* should understand. People don't have money. If the work doesn't come in, there's nothing I can do. Nothing!" He paused for a short, pregnant moment, and exploded. "Nothing!" Jan heard the crash of his fist hitting the tabletop and then the door slam with a crack.

Getting ready to take the goats out to pasture, Jan winced when the Fialas passed by and returned his greeting with a polite smile, pretending not to have heard. Zlata's grimace turned into a faint smirk as she hastened past him. He felt awkward and sad—and now, embarrassed, especially in front of her.

The goats sprung impatiently out of the gate and Father fell in silently beside him and gave him a nudge. Surprised, Jan answered with a strained smile. It wasn't often that Father would accompany him to pasture the goats—usually only after he'd had words with Mother and sought to escape her recriminations. Jan liked being with him; he felt grown-up in his presence. They would discuss things, adult things, often beyond his understanding, unlike Mother who seemed forever withdrawn and uncommunicative, except when she gave orders. The only time he feared Father was when he had done something wrong, like the time he got caught smoking dry potato leaves in a pipe carved out of a horse chestnut and a straw. Mother herself never disciplined him, but was quick to make Father administer the corporal punishment, which he would do with a heavy hand. On the whole, Jan preferred the hand to the words: the physical pain ended soon after the last blow, but her words stung forever.

"Dad?" Jan nudged his father. "Why do you and Mom argue so much?"

Father stopped abruptly and the smile vanished from his face. "So you heard?"

"The window was open. The Fialas heard it, too."

"I'm sorry, Boy. I really don't fault your mother." He resumed walking. "It's been hard on her these last four years, since the war started. It's been hard on everybody, but especially her. She goes out every day. Spends most of the day standing in lines, and then comes home empty-handed. If it weren't for the rabbits and the garden, we wouldn't have any food at all. All the butcher has is soup bones, when he has anything. It's hard on her to tend to the house and help keep the shop going, too."

"I heard you say that Fuchs is gone. I hope he dies!" Jan cried out fervently, as they turned onto a rutted lane heading toward the steep mountainside. "Hope they get him."

"Get Fuchs?" Father paused to light a cigarette.

"Yeah. For killing Jakub's uncle and sending the Jews to the work camp."

Father put his sinewy arm around Jan's shoulders. "The Kohens have been gone since what? 'Forty-one. That's almost two years. You may as well understand, Son, that wasn't a work camp the Germans sent your Jakub to; that was an internment camp."

"An internment camp? What's that?"

"A kind of a jail. Their regular jails don't have enough room for all the Jews and other people they're arresting. BBC said they're using prisoners as labor. That's why these camps are near their large cities. So, maybe the Kohens…who knows what happened to them."

Jan's fist closed around the pocketknife in his pocket. It felt warm and solid—a reassuring connection between him and his friend, a token of hope, and now of doubt. Father's words crushed him. He tried to hold back tears but couldn't.

Father gave him a gentle squeeze. "I know how you feel, Son."

They finished the rest of the climb in silence. Choking on the sorrow that welled in his chest, Jan conjured up the images of Jakub as he last saw him. Chain-smoking, Father paused from time to time to catch his breath. Following impassively, the goats picked up speed and scattered among the bushes when they reached their familiar grazing ground.

The valley lay below them like a giant quilt of green and ochre. Only a faint hum of distant motors and the wind in the treetops broke the stillness. A thin bluish layer of haze fueled by the exhaust from the almost incessant convoys covered everything like a scrim. From somewhere up in the valley, where the railroad followed the flanks of the mountains in a series of lazy turns and rose high above the river, a dirty plume of smoke shot into the sky. It took seconds before the sound reached them—first a muffled thud of an explosion, and then ear-jarring grinding and squealing noises of metal on metal, something heavy crashing through the trees, and finally a violent blast that sent shock waves racing across the land, rattling the windows for miles. Flickering fiery tongues emerged from the smoke, licking first the parched undergrowth and then shooting up the trunks of the pines like giant Roman candles. And then, as in a grand finale, the sky opened with an awesome display of exploding ordnance, sending arching streaks of light and smoke in all directions.

"Jesus! What's that?" Jan shrieked.

Mesmerized, Father didn't answer. "The resistance," he finally murmured under his breath. "Partisans. Looks like they got a munitions train." A satisfied wisp of a smile flashed briefly over his face.

Dusk fell by the time they got home. The usually unflappable carpenter Fiala waited for them inside, shaking and pale. Mother's eyes bulged with fear.

"Have you heard? Have you seen?" Fiala skipped the customary greeting.

"Yeah, we saw it," Father said, casting a concerned look at Jan.

Fiala moved closer and lowered his voice. "They got Kubek."

"Kubek?" The blood drained from Father's face. "Jesus!"

"The Gestapo got him. Been arresting people left and right. Don't think he'll talk, but—"

"He's a good man. Still, you told the—" Father's brow furrowed as he nodded almost imperceptibly toward Jan, standing next to him.

"Couldn't." Fiala made a face.

"Then there's no time to lose." Father whispered something in Mother's ear, and she let out a howl and grabbed his arm. He pushed her off gently.

"What's going on? What's happening? Dad?"

"It's all right, Son. Best you don't know." He gave Jan a squeeze and Mother a tentative hug. "Take care of your mother while I'm gone. I won't be long," he said, slipping with Fiala into the night.

Eyes wide open, staring at the ceiling and listening to the intermittent rumble of convoys rolling eastward, Jan lay in bed, thinking of the times his father would disappear without an explanation and be gone all night. Mother would spend those nights sitting up late and crying. When he once asked, trying to comfort her, she cradled him in her bosom and said nothing. Now he knew.

CHAPTER 11

"Didn't you hear? It's finally happening. An invasion!" Father broke into a grin as he wiped tears from his stubble-covered cheeks with the back of his hand. "There's been an invasion! The Americans and the Brits landed in France!"

Stunned momentarily, Carpenter Hrášek and Zlata' father started slapping each other on the backs, laughing and crying at the same time, overcome by glee at the news the BBC had just delivered over Father's short wave. "No wonder the convoys have been going the other way the last few days—must've sensed something was up." Carpenter Hrášek danced an impromptu jig, offering cigarettes all around in an uncommon display of generosity. "Wish Kubek could be here to hear it."

Father took a cigarette and put it behind his ear. "Speaking of Kubek, any news?

"Took him to Pankrác, the last I heard," the carpenter said. "The Prague hell-hole that the Gestapo took over."

Mother poked her head into the workroom, "Do you have to make all that ruckus? Can't you see what time it is? Somebody might hear you! And what's the boy doing up so late?" She glared at Jan through narrowing eyes.

"Aw, let him be; he's old enough." Father waved her off.

She gave him an annoyed look and drew back into the kitchen.

* * *

The goats scattered among the bushes, and Jan rolled over on his back on the familiar lichen-covered ledge and let his mind drift. Staring at the clouds, he tried to picture what the normally somber BBC announcer so excitedly described and what it all might mean, but came up blank. It was times like these that he missed Jakub the most. If only he were there so they could discuss what was happening. They would have so much to talk about, especially now that his implicit acceptance into Father's circle of friends made him privy to so many important things.

Muffled footsteps from down the trail brought him back to earth. His face screwed in disappointment at having his private world invaded. Raising their heads, the goats also took note of the intrusion. Finally, the interlopers came into view and he let out a sigh of relief. It was Zlata and another girl, a stranger, carrying bouquets of wild poppies, daisies, and bachelor's buttons they'd picked along the way. Zlata saw him and waved.

"Hey!" he greeted them tentatively. "What brings you up here?"

"Too nice to stay home." Zlata smiled, ignoring his lack of enthusiasm. "This is Inka. She's from Prague."

Inka measured him with a quick look and offered her slender hand. It felt warm, soft, and limp when he took it—*a city girl's hand.* Her probing look made him conscious of his bare feet and grubby attire – a pair of old pants patched in several places and a faded jersey – and he squirmed uncomfortably.

"Beautiful day, huh?" She forced a polite smile.

He mumbled a response. Hard to tell how old she was— definitely older than he or Zlata, but you could never tell about city girls. A colorful print dress fit snugly over her slender budding figure. A shock of flaxen hair framed her untanned face, complementing a pair of pale, wide-set blue eyes. And she wore lipstick, light but noticeable, the color of strawberries. Only city girls and Zlata's mother wore lipstick. Mother would make her scrub it off with a hard brush, if she'd had anything to do with it.

She stood flushed from the exertion. The breeze blew a strand of her hair out of place and she brushed it back with a dramatic swing of her hand and toss of her head. "You do this every *day*?" she said mockingly, making a sweeping gesture toward the goats.

He nodded, blushing under her challenging gaze. A small chuckle escaped her lips. He wished she hadn't come.

"It's nice here." Her gaze shifted to the valley. "You can see the whole town."

"That's why I asked you to come here." Zlata smiled. "I knew you'd like it. I've been coming here with Jan whenever my Mom lets me."

Jan liked Zlata. Their years under the same roof made her feel like a sister, even though their divergent interests sent them separate ways. She had stretched and matured since the day her family had sought refuge in their house, and he felt often awkward next to her in the presence of other boys. In the circumspect world of Čekaná, just being seen with a girl elicited mocking laughter from his pals, some of whom nevertheless bragged about *their* exploits, largely the figments of their imagination or stolen looks at 'French postcards' their parents hid in secret places. Facing this strange girl now and squirming under her gaze (she was pretty, he had to admit), he felt an uncomfortably delightful sensation course through him when their looks connected.

"So you're from Prague?" He tried to sound nonchalant, but his words came out hoarse and weak. "Where you're staying?" He shriveled inside.

"At the Králíčeks. They have rooms above the beer hall. Dad knows Zlata's father. They went to school together."

"Oh. Staying long?"

"Be goin' back Sunday. Father'll spend a couple of days fishing with Zlata's dad, or they'll go mushroom-hunting. Don't know." She frowned and looked away. "Prague's noisy and full of Germans. It's nice here; I like it." She took a pair of exaggerated deep breaths, exhaled audibly and smiled. And then her eyes bulged and she let out a scream as one of the goats, trying to get at the flowers, nuzzled her hand. "Aaaah! Go away!" she shrieked, recoiling. "Get away from me! Get away from me! Look what she did!" She pounced on Jan. "Can't you do something? Help me! Do something!" she screamed, wiping her hand furiously on her dress.

Jan shooed the goat away. "Don't worry. She's the friendliest of 'em all."

She glared at him. "They're dirty and they smell!" She spat the words out at him.

He shrugged, surprised at her indignation. "Hey, I didn't ask you to come."

Meeting his annoyed look for a few seconds, she responded with a pout and turned away.

He became aware of Zlata's stare. She was scowling. "I think we should go," she said, turning to Inka.

About to come back with a smart retort to put Inka in her place, Jan stopped short when a faint sound, a steady drone, not unlike a single deep melodic rumble of the church organ, reached his ear. The girls heard it, too. Cocking their heads

86

skyward, they searched the vast expanse in confused astonishment.

Far in the eastern sky, so high that it fooled the eye, fading in and out of view in the shimmering air, a tiny speck emerged from among the wisps of cirrus, becoming more distinct as it approached, and then another. And another. And another, until they seemed to fill the sky from horizon to horizon. Bombers. Hundreds of them! So high as to be practically invisible, ghostly transparent against the deep azure sky and hidden behind thick white plumes of condensed vapor, the droning formations moved slowly but steadily toward the west. The town sirens began to wail. Trucks crowding the road scattered as their occupants dove into ditches.

The sound became a muted roar. The earth vibrated under their feet. The goats scampered in utter confusion.

Crisscrossing the straight, gradually thinning contrails were other, thinner, gracefully curved fast moving lines with tiny dots at their apex. Fighters. The sky was a canvas, painted with pirouettes of dancing points tracing graceful circles around the formations, belying the drama taking place high in the sky above them. Only short staccato bursts, sounding more like drumrolls or claps of distant thunder, left no doubt, as to what they really were. Gunfire.

Spellbound, Jan and the girls gaped at the spectacle, when a sudden thunderous roar shook the earth under their feet and sent them sprawling to the rocky ground. The noise tore at their eardrums. The girls screamed. The goats bolted. The air itself vibrated as a huge low-flying bomber, white stars on its fuselage, lifted over them from the valley below, barely missing some of the treetops as it strained to gain altitude. Its three engines screamed at high pitch; the fourth sputtered in an intermittent series of backfires, emitting puffs of bluish exhaust. A faint plume of black smoke trailed from the wing. One of its wheels hung limply like a giant pendulum. It barely cleared the highest point and again dipped into the valley beyond, seeking the safety of low altitude. As it disappeared behind the treetops, its sound vanished in an instant, snuffed out by the terrain. Bewildered, Jan and the girls looked at each other as though they'd just seen a ghost.

The goats had bolted; the distant tinkling of their bells telling they'd taken off for home. Mumbling a hasty apology, Jan snatched his book bag and scurried down the path after them. From the corner of his eye, he saw the girls waving.

* * *

The planes returned the next day along with a weather change. Blotchy clouds racing the wind covered the sky, swirling about each other like wads of dirty cotton, permitting only occasional shafts of sunlight to spill onto the lush countryside. Now and then, they would part just enough to offer a tantalizing glimpse of the sky above, streaked with contrails. Again, the air reverberated with the drone of powerful engines, bursts of gunfire, and the wailing of sirens. Again, convoys lumbering down the highway spilled soldiers into the ditches.

Keeping a wary eye on the goats, Jan settled himself on the familiar ledge and sighed with regret, noticing the remains of a bouquet blown about by the wind in the dirt. She must've thrown it away. He frowned. Only a city girl would. Doesn't matter.

A rustle behind him, and then a lilting, "Ahoj again. Hope I didn't startle you." Inka walked up to him, smiling.

"No, it's all right," he lied, conscious of the blood rushing to his face. "Been watching the Germans down there, running for the ditches. Didn't hear you come up. Where's Zlata?"

"She couldn't come."

"Couldn't *come*?" His heart raced.

She tossed her head back to clear a strand of hair that fell over her forehead and lowered her gaze. "I'm sorry about yesterday."

"Doesn't matter." He shrugged, feeling off-balance, trying in vain to think of something to say.

"You said you come here every day. I had nothing else to do, so..." She sighed. "Thought you wouldn't mind."

He could feel her piercing gaze. "The goats have to eat."

"Mind if I sit down? I'm a bit tired." Without waiting for his answer, she sat down next to him on a smooth, clean boulder.

Perplexed, at a loss for words, Jan shrugged again and smiled.

She returned his smile and continued to stare at him until he overcame his distress and turned to face her. "I'm *really* sorry about yesterday," she whispered as their eyes met.

"It's all right." He looked away.

Her smile disappeared but her look softened. "I know it wasn't nice to behave the way I did, but the goat really *did* startle me. I *really* didn't expect it."

"Don't matter, I understand."

"It was the first time I was really close to one. It scared me."

"She only wanted your flowers."

"When I'm scared, I sometimes say things I don't mean, and I said some things that—"

"I told you it doesn't matter. I understand."

Her eyes clouded and she fell silent.

They sat awkwardly side by side for a while, watching the little figures scramble back into the vehicles and the convoys get underway. From the direction of the town, the steady tone of the siren announced the 'all clear.' She picked up a twig and traced imaginary designs on the rock face. This was crazy! Why had she come? And alone! What did she want? Why would she bother? What was he supposed to do? He was nothing to her! He didn't know her. He didn't even know how to talk to her. He knew nothing about her. He wished Zlata were there to help. Yesterday's contempt for her 'city' ways evaporated, as a visceral, more persistent attraction set in. It disturbed him. She confused him, made him feel off-balance.

Pretending not to notice, he watched the tip of the twig in her hand trace a random path toward him and felt an icy pulse crawl up his spine. Slowly, barely touching him, she drew a line up his side and stopped lightly on his cheek. He felt her stare.

"You're blushing!" She let out a lilting laugh.

He looked away.

Leaning closer, she puckered her strawberry lips and studied his face. He could feel her breath on him. A whiff of her sweet perfume assaulted his nostrils. "Have you ever kissed a girl?" she murmured softly.

It took his breath away and the lump in his throat made him want to gag. He swallowed hard.

"Have you ever kissed a girl?" she insisted.

His heart raced as he couldn't bring himself to look at her.

"Hey, look at me," she insisted. "Can't you talk? Have you ever kissed a girl before? Bet you haven't."

The twig twirled on his cheek. Her stare seared his skin. From the corner of his eye, he caught the sight of her amused smile. He felt trapped. "Yvette…my cousin…once or twice," he blurted, flushing. "They made me do it."

Her mocking laugh made him cringe. "You mean, you didn't *like* it?" She moved closer and let the stick drop. "Come here. Turn around," she said softly, tugging at him. "Look at me." Her voice was gentle but compelling and he hesitantly complied.

Her touch was firm as she drew him close until he felt her breath. Fleetingly, he considered pulling away, but found himself unable to resist. Face still aglow with that amused smile, she closed her eyes and gently pressed her lips on his.

He stiffened. His first impulse was to push her away,. but confused and weak, drained of all strength, he couldn't move. She held him tightly for a few seconds as he leaned stiffly against her, eyes open wide, heart racing, arms limp by his side.

She whispered, "Relax. I won't bite you."

Dizzily aware of the softness of her lips and pleasantly fresh woman-smell, he finally, hesitantly put his arms around her in an awkward embrace. A fiery wave seared right down to his belly. Torn between wanting to tear himself away and wanting more, he remained still, raked by guilt while savoring the feeling.

"Have you ever…*touched* a girl?" she murmured in his ear. Then, with a disappointing sigh, she answered herself, "I suppose not, since you never *really* kissed a girl either, huh?" She giggled.

Mind abuzz and weak all over, he looked away.

She slipped his right arm from her shoulder, and then, in a single, deliberate move, took his hand, gently placed it on the heaving mound of her bosom, and held it there, pressing down gently but firmly.

Under his clammy touch, he felt the firm rise of her breast, the hardness of her nipple, the rhythmic heaving of her chest, the pulse of her heart. Closing his fingers, he gently cupped the heaving bulge. She took a deep breath, let out a soft moan, and relaxed the hold on his hand. He withdrew in a panic.

She froze. Her eyes grew wide, flashing at him from under a furrow of her brow like a pair of sapphires. Her strawberry lips parted just enough to show the pearls of her teeth, and then morphed into a faint, amusing frown. "What's the matter? Didn't you like it? Was that so bad?" she said hoarsely.

Jan stuttered an unintelligible response.

Smiling, she again reached for his hand. "Aw, come on," she said gently. "C'mon."

He avoided her gaze but didn't resist when she again drew him close, squeezed him briefly and hard, and kissed him softly on the cheek as she took his hand and led it to her breast. They remained like that – entwined – she flushed and breathing deeply, he cupping her breast with his clammy palm, heart racing wildly, trying to deal with the flood of new confounding sensations that invaded his senses.

Finally, she gently pushed him away. "Sorry. My arm. Getting a cramp. Sorry," she whispered.

He rolled away from her and lay on his back, staring up at the sky, oblivious to the pricking of the stubble and the hard pebbles pressing into his body. Somewhere, a skylark rose from a field, showering the countryside with lilting song as it spiraled straight up in the air. It was at once a perfect moment and a source of great turmoil as she lay next to him, close but not touching, thoughtful and remote, a stranger again, lips pursed in a half-smile, eyes a pair of fountains filled with indigo. Tentatively and clumsily, he reached for her hand and she gave it without resisting. They lay side by side, silently gazing at the sky and the climbing skylark that, having reached the pinnacle of his flight and the end of his song, dove silently earthward in a stone-like finale.

They held hands as they walked silently down the steep path toward home, the goats in tow.

"Will you come again?" he finally managed to say. "Please?"

She answered with a smile.

That night, he dreamt about her. Reliving the heady moments of their encounter, he yearned for more. He ached to see her again, but waited in vain. She had left that very same Sunday without saying goodbye, or anything. He felt as badly as the day Jakub left, perhaps even worse.

From then on, she became a permanent resident of his nocturnal fantasies and an always-willing participant of his sometimes-erotic daydreams.

Counting airplanes had become Jan's favorite pastime. The rattling staccatos and thump-thump-thump volleys of air battles could be heard sporadically. The smoking stragglers increased in number, though none flew as low as the one that had skimmed the top of the mountain the day he met Inka. Now and then, pieces of airplanes would rain from above. Once a German Messerschmitt fell from the sky and burned.

Father and his friends continued their midnight meetings. Their mood was generally upbeat, except when the talk turned to Constable Kubek who had not been heard from since his arrest.

One night, after a cryptic broadcast, Father and his friends disappeared, and returned before dawn. Panting under the strain, they carried a camouflage-colored duffel bag wrapped in a green parachute. It barely fit through the opening in the floor under the kitchen table as they hurriedly buried it.

CHAPTER 12

There was something peculiar about the sheets of rain flung at the windowpanes like a series of drumrolls driven by violent gusts of wind. Jolted, Jan looked up from his book.

Hunched over a garment she was stitching, Mother shifted her gaze to the window and froze. "What was that?"

Father cocked his head and listened for a few seconds. "Aw, just the rain." He dismissed her with a wave of his hand and turned back to his work.

"No, listen. I'm sure I heard something," she insisted.

The window rattled again in a succession of distinct, progressively louder raps. Someone was banging.

She turned ashen. "I told you I heard something! JesusMary, what's that? At this hour. Who could it be?" She let go of the garment and it slid to the floor.

The pounding became louder, insistent.

Eyes bulging with terror, she let out a gasp and crossed herself. "JesusMary, the Gestapo! They're the only ones who— Oh, my God! They're coming for us. They're coming for you!" She glared accusingly at Father. "You see what you've done? You and your cohorts!? You see? You see! Kubek must've talked. How many times did I tell you this would happen! Sooner or later. How many times—"

Father dove for the switch, snuffed out the light, and cautiously cracked open the blackout curtain.

Except for Mother's soft sobs, the crackling of the fire, and the measured ticking of the clock, the room was still, the tension palpable.

"That's not the Gestapo," he finally stammered with a sigh of relief. "They always come in twos. There's only one out there." He pulled shut the curtain and turned on the light. "Can't make out who it is." He grabbed a flashlight and scurried out of the room.

Straining to hear, Jan could just make out a hushed exchange, followed by heavy shuffling footsteps in the hallway, and then a knock. The door to the workroom flung open. Mother gave out a muffled cry. Jan gasped.

Framed by the doorway was an imposing figure— grotesque and demonic. Wearing a soaked filthy green uniform of the Wehrmacht, shredded in places, covered by dark oily stains, he was faceless—literally: a pair of whitish bony protrusions stuck out where his nose would have been; a mass of lumpy scar tissue congealed where his cheeks and lips had once formed a face. A pair of bulging, unblinking eyes peered from hollow, brow-less sockets. Only a few patches of stringy, matted hair covered a reddish, blotchy head when he doffed his sweat and grime-encrusted hat. Jan shivered. *The SS skull without the bones* flashed through his mind.

On his back, the stranger carried a lumpy rucksack. In his hand, a beat-up Mauser. *"Grüss Gott,"* he addressed Mother in German and then, correcting himself, "Good Evening," in a thickly accented Czech. *"Ich bin Ludwig."*

His inquiring look was met with blank stares.

"I'm Ludwig. Ludwig! Don't you remember me? Ludwig!" he implored.

Mother's jaw dropped as she eyed him incredulously. "Ludwig?" She took a hesitant step toward him and half-extended her hand. "Ludwig. Ludwig? You mean…" Her face came alive in a flash of understanding. "Oh my God! Ludwig!

Ludwig Schreckinger! JesusMary." Her hand flew to her mouth. "JesusMary! I'm sorry! How could I—"

"Your mother, my mother...they're sisters." He grimaced, trying to smile. "Once, we came to see you. *Viele Jahre*...long ago."

"Yes, yes, I remember, of course!" she cried. "But Good God, what happened to you? You have to forgive me, I didn't recognize you. Oh my God." Tears welled up in her eyes. "What happened? How did you... I didn't know you were in the army. JesusMary! Come, come and sit down. You poor man. Come, come. Please."

He sighed. "A flame-thrower. At Stalingrad. Should've killed me, but somehow they'd managed to save me. Couldn't do much for me there, though. No hospitals, no doctors."

"At least you're alive. That's what matters. But you, a soldier?"

"*Ja*. Got drafted. Like all the others. The right age, good health. You know. Had no choice. Everybody had to. Now they're grabbing even fifteen-year-olds and old men." He gave out a short, uneasy laugh, and winced as he took off his rucksack. Grimacing, he slowly eased himself down into a chair. Father offered him a cigarette, which he snatched eagerly and lit with a shaking hand. He took a few deep drags, exhaling noisily. "And my aunt? How is she?" Squinting, he scanned the room. "Mother talked about her often. Misses her, you know. Said if I ever could, to stop and give her...give you our greetings."

"She died." Mother's eyes misted. "Over a year ago. Buried the day before All Souls Day."

Ludwig crossed himself. "May God rest her soul."

"Caught pneumonia."

He nodded and fell silent.

"Here, let me have your coat." Father helped him take off the rucksack. "And take off those wet clothes. We'll hang them by the stove. They'll be dry by morning." He raised his eyebrows at Jan, who reluctantly rose to assist.

"So that's your boy, eh?" Ludwig watched Jan wrestle the heavy rucksack off to the side. "It's Johann, isn't it? He's grown. How old is he now?"

"Almost fifteen," Mother said.

"You don't remember me," he turned to Jan, "but I saw you once when you were a little tyke. This big." His hand came down past his belt buckle. "That was the last time we came for a visit. Must've been '32 or '33. Long ago." He gave Jan a toothy smile.

Mother hung his overcoat over the back of a chair and pushed it near the stove. "Please, take off those clothes and put these on while I boil some water so you can clean up." She handed him a pair of Father's long johns and an old robe.

Jan took the uniform and hung it on the backs of a pair of chairs. It gave off a nauseating smorgasbord of putrid smells. Picking up Ludwig's boots, he noticed the hobnails gone from the soles and two gaping holes in their place.

They made small talk punctured by uneasy silences, until the hissing of boiling water spilling on top of the red-hot stove relieved them of their discomfort.

Mother and Jan carried the pot to a washroom and emptied it into a large wooden tub that took up most of the room. "The boy will help scrub your back, if you want. In the meantime, I'll heat up some soup. You must be starving." She waved off his profuse thanks and handed him a towel.

Ludwig undressed, exposing a mass of purplish scar tissue down to his waist. An ugly, brown knot stood out prominently against the pale flesh of his shoulder; another just below the shoulder blade, had turned deep purple. "Not pretty, eh?" He scowled.

Jan shrugged, trying to hide the sickening feeling in the pit of his stomach. He did not like to be left alone in the room with the German, even if he was relations.

"Got these in Bosnia, back in '41. Still have a few pieces of shrapnel in my leg, too. Give me trouble each time the weather changes."

Jan sponged Ludwig's back, careful not to touch the scars, and flinched when he accidentally scratched the hardened knots of flesh. "Does it hurt when I touch it?"

"Naw, *nein*, it's fine now. You can press all you want." Ludwig let out a deep, contented sigh, as he sank deeper into the tub until his knobby knees rose to the stubble on his chin. "My first hot bath in months. In months! Would you believe it?" Eyes closed, he let out soft groans as Jan sponged his back. *"Das ist Himmel...das ist ein echte Himmel,* this is heaven,*"* he murmured under his breath.

Ludwig was family, and therefore Jan should like him, or at least, respect him, feel sorry for him. But he was also a German. A Nazi! Recalling his last conversation with Grandmother before she died, he felt guilty for feeling resentment bordering on hatred toward this man, instead of compassion—not so much for what he was, but for what he represented. In his mind's eye, he saw other men, other Ludwigs, their faces blurred, save the one of Fuchs that still haunted him, pounding the Kohens. He saw Jakub's 'uncle' in a heap in the dust. He saw Jakub's bloody face. He couldn't like this man. He dug his fingernails into the fleshy knots on the man's back.

Ludwig didn't flinch.

"Did you *kill* anybody in the war?" he blurted, barely able to contain his hostility. "Did you? Did you kill any Jews?"

Ludwig pulled himself up to an upright position, took the sponge from Jan's shaking hand, and eyed him thoughtfully for a few moments through the slits of his eyes. His contented smile vanished. "*Ja*, I killed people. I don't know if they were Jews or not."

Jan shifted uncomfortably.

"Let me tell you something, Johann," he said softly. "There's something you have to understand." His bulging, tired eyes searched Jan's face. "Look at me, boy. Look at me."

Jan met his look briefly but averted his eyes.

"War is a terrible thing," he went on. "Terrible! Don't ever forget it. No matter which side you're on. No matter what the reason. It's horrible. It makes you do things you never imagined you could. Back in '40, when I was drafted, it was, they said, to defend our *Vaterland*." It all seemed so clear then. So beautiful. Inspiring." The scars on his face twisted into a faint smile. "Anyway, that's what they told us we'd be doing. That's what everybody believed. I believed it. Everybody was raring to fight for a cause. And I tell you, I tell you, it felt great. It was almost...almost..." he searched for a word, "...almost spiritual." His eyes lost their dullness as his gaze shifted off into space. "The parades, girls throwing flowers at us, *ach Gott*, it was beautiful. Torches burning, bands playing, everybody singing '*Die Fahne Hoch.*' Believe me, Johann, it was so inspiring, you could cry. I cried! It didn't matter how you felt about the Party. Most people loved it, loved Hitler. Adored him.

You couldn't help but feel the pride, real pride in being German. Being a patriot. Being part of history. Do you understand?" His unblinking eyes bore hard into Jan's face.

"I think so. My dad was a soldier, too. On the mountain."

Ludwig grunted gravely, gave him a smile, and slid down until only his head showed above the soapy water. He closed his eyes and, savoring the warmth, seemed to drift off.

"We used to go see him. He was going to fight for the Republic."

Peering at Jan through slits of eyes, Ludwig shook his head gravely. "You know, Johann, the idea, the idea of fighting for your fatherland is a great feeling, while it lasts. But the truth, the front, the fighting—*Scheisse...*" he swore "...that's different." He reached out, grabbed Jan's arm, and turned him until he faced him squarely. "You ask if I killed people, boy? Yeah, sure, I killed people. I did. You have to justify it to yourself, believe it. Maybe at first you think you're being a patriot, you're doing it for a cause, right cause, of course, with God's help – *'Gott mit uns'* we used to say – but soon, you realize you have no choice. You do it to survive. It's really that simple. Black and white. You live or you die. And so you kill and go on doing it, not for the pretty girls and the parades, not even for something you believe. Patriotism is the furthest thing from your mind. You've long stopped believing it anyway. You do it to save yourself, to save your own skin. You kill, because if you don't kill the other poor bastard, who's just as scared as you are and for exactly the same reasons, the other poor bastard will kill you. It's that simple. Do you understand that, Johann? Can you understand?"

Jan eyed him with confused awe. Until now, it was easy to hate the Germans, all Germans, but this wretch of man was different, and not just because he was family. His anguish seemed genuine, his tone sincere. From somewhere within, Jan felt a creeping swell of compassion.

Ludwig stood up and wrapped himself in a towel. "My esteemed father, God bless him, his name was Ludwig, too, died in the bombing last year. He tried to warn me, about the war, I mean, but I wouldn't listen. I don't know if they told you, but he'd lost a leg at Arras. That was in the other war."

Jan shook his head.

"He was a great man, but I didn't take him seriously. What did he know? He was old." He sighed. "Anyway, I always wanted to be a teacher, write poetry, do good things. I believed in the word, the elegant word. Schiller, Goethe, Keats, Baudelaire. Loved 'em all. They were my heroes—my inspiration, my world. But then the war came and I was drafted. So, here I am—a cynic. *Dulce et Decorum Est,"* he said bitterly.

"I don't understand." Jan looked at him, bewildered.

"It's from a poem by Owen. Wilfred Owen—an Englishman. Forbidden by the *Reich,* of course, unfortunately. Someday you should read it if you can, and if the war turns out the way I think it will. Talks about how men are deceived into believing that it is 'sweet and proper,' those are his words, to die for one's country." A shadow washed over his face. "I've seen it, I've seen it all. There's nothing sweet about dying."

A steamy plate of warmed-over soup and a few slices of black bread lay waiting on the table as Jan and Ludwig returned to the kitchen. The wood in the stove crackled. The air hung heavy with the sour smell of the drying uniform. Gathered around the table, they all watched Ludwig make slurping sounds with each ladleful as he devoured the soup, and methodically wiped the empty dish with a piece of bread until it squeaked.

"We were retreating," he finally said, nodding thanks to Father for another cigarette, "making our way back from house to house, when they turned the flame-throwers on us. Killed a few, hurt many others. I got it full blast. What saved me, *Grüss Gott*," he crossed himself, "I immediately buried my face in the snow. That probably saved my life. Passed out from the pain. Woke up in a field hospital, but all they could do for me was dress it. Sent me on to the rear, but they couldn't do anything, either. One night we got bombed, and the next thing I knew, everybody was gone. Everybody! Except us cripples, of course. That could only mean one thing—the Russkis! So I wasn't going to wait. Decided to go home."

"Oh, you poor, poor dear!" Mother cried out.

"You mean, you deserted?" Father peered at him sharply.

"In a way of speaking, perhaps." Ludwig took a deep breath and looked away. "Made my way back any way I could. Mostly on foot. At night. The Russkis shoot at anything that moves. Been on the road for weeks. Don't even know what I'm getting back to. Or if anyone's alive. Everything's in ruins. Haven't had news from home in months." A tear appeared in the corner of an eye and he wiped it with his fist. "Sometimes I feel ashamed to be a human being."

"And the war? How much longer do you think it's going to last?" Father leaned toward him in anticipation.

"Not much." He took a noisy drag and snuffed out the cigarette. "You see the convoys. You can see it on their faces. It's over."

He spent the night in what had been Grandmother's bed, tossing and turning, muttering something unintelligible between bouts of fitful snoring. He got up late and left after the noon meal. Mother stuffed his rucksack with fresh bread and a piece of moldy hard salami – the only meat she'd managed to squirrel away – and some of Father's underwear. After thanking profusely and embracing everyone, he hailed a ragtag convoy heading back toward Germany, gave a few waves from a truck that slowed down to let him jump aboard, and was gone.

"Boy, heard you talking to Ludwig while he was bathing. What did you talk about?" Father inquired when they found themselves alone.

Jan shrugged. "The war."

"The war? He talked to you about the war?"

"He said wars are bad; said his father tried to talk him out of it."

"Hmm. I remember the old fellow. Met him once or twice. Came home shell-shocked from the war. The First World War. They called it the war to end all wars, and look what happened." He gave a short laugh. "It gave us the Republic. So, as far as wars go, there *are* some good wars – well, good isn't the right word. Necessary maybe; yeah, that's better. Necessary wars, like defending your country. Fighting for your country."

"That's what he said he was doing."

"No, that's not the same thing when you're the invader. You remember the time on the mountain when we had to leave? When we had to leave without firing a shot? When we left without putting up a fight? Times like that, when you should've fought but didn't, you lose your self-respect." He swallowed hard and wiped his brow. "We lost our self-respect. And when you lose your self-respect, something inside you dies. You die just a little. Something heavy, like a load of stones, fills that space. And that something gets heavier with time, and the more you think about what you should have done and didn't, the worse you feel. You feel ashamed. You feel so ashamed, you can't stand it." He looked at Jan through misty eyes. "There *are* times when living is worse than dying."

CHAPTER 13

"It's starting! It's finally starting!" Father squeezed Jan's arm and flung open the window. Caught by the breeze, the long blackout curtains blew in like a pair of funerary veils. A cool but fume-laden burst of air rushed in. Outside, the road was clogged with an unending torrent of armor, trucks, motorcycles, and tanks, heaped high with grim, bedraggled, war-weary men nervously scanning the houses as they passed by, Mausers or Schmeisers at the ready. The air trembled with the drone of engines. Traveling mostly by night to avoid strafing by the American fighters, they retreated helter-skelter westward toward Germany.

"Will the war be over soon then?"

"Sure looks that way." Father nodded. "With the Russians moving in on Berlin and the Americans half-way across Germany, can't see how it can last much longer."

"Will the Americans liberate us?"

"I don't know, Son; no one knows. Depends."

"Depends on what, Dad?"

"Churchill, Roosevelt, Stalin, they're the ones that decide at Yalta who'll occupy what, how far they'll go, that sort of thing. London says it's still a secret. That's why the Huns are heading west toward the Americans. As fast as they can. They're scared to death of the Russians. Hope the Americans will treat them better."

"Hey, you two, don't forget, Alois is coming Sunday for Easter." Mother's carping voice put an end to their discourse. "You'll have to sleep together, unless you get a move-on and fix Granny's old bed."

Muttering under his breath, Father reluctantly turned away from the window.

The last time Jan had seen his favorite uncle was when Grandmother died. He'd appeared for the funeral, but only briefly, as he had to return to Prague and his work at the Tesla Works, commandeered by the Germans to produce communications equipment for the *Wehrmacht*. Mother's youngest brother and Jan's godfather, Uncle Alois was a well-read, smart but unpretentious bachelor who never failed to bring him something, usually a book, and unlike his parents, didn't mind answering the avalanche of questions Jan had, not even the ones that provoked groans and hard looks from his mother. Jan always looked forward to his visit with great anticipation and expectation.

* * *

Engulfed in a cloud of steam, the locomotive heaved a last, sooty, labored breath, sending a thick puff of smoke skyward as the train glided into the station. The great iron wheels locked, squealing to a halt. Panting like a spent greyhound, it expelled a thin shimmering breath of heat from its conical chimney. The half dozen once bright green but now smoke and grime-stained coaches disgorged a sprinkling of passengers who hurriedly made for the exit. It would have been an ordinary everyday scene, except for the menacing anti-aircraft gun encircled by sandbags mounted on the flat car at the rear of the train. A squad of Germans at the controls surveyed the disembarking passengers with scowling indifference.

"I'm so pleased you took the chance, situation being what it is." Mother embraced her brother.

"You know me. Just couldn't resist." Alois wrapped his arms around her and then around Jan, and wiped away a tear. "It's good to be home again. You've grown, Jan." He gave him a friendly nudge.

Jan beamed.

Father hoisted his heavy suitcase onto a small wagon used to haul clover for the goats and rabbits. "Thought you wouldn't be able to make it on account of the bombings and raids, and—"

Alois smiled. "They haven't bombed Prague yet, thank God, but I've seen plenty of damage. Tracks wiped out in a few places. Bomb craters. Had prisoners fixing'em. Been on the road since four this morning." He stretched and yawned, and froze, staring into the void. "Hey, wha—what is *that*?"

Squinting toward the sky, Mother blanched. "JesusMary, airplanes! Those are airplanes!"

The town sirens began to wail.

A tight group of small black dots emerged from a high cloudbank and spiraled lazily into a single file.

"My God! Fighters!" Father shrieked. "Run!"

Engines screaming like banshees, the planes hurtled themselves at a steep angle toward them. Flickering flames appeared in the nose of the lead plane, followed by staccato drumrolls of gunfire. Paralysis became panic. Screams! Shouts! Bedlam! People scattered, tripping over the rails and lumpy ground. A hail of bullets rippled the earth, splattering like giant raindrops in all directions. Expelling a great plume of smoke, the locomotive tried to gain traction, her great iron wheels throwing off sparks, spinning furiously. The anti-aircraft gun sprung into action, its ack-ack-ack-ack drowning out the screams of passengers jumping from the coaches and diving into ditches.

Pressed against the massive trunk of an old linden tree, Jan felt no fear—only a kind of awe. Mesmerized by the aerial spectacle, he was oblivious of his father pressing down on him, covering him with his body, and Uncle Alois shielding Mother, praying aloud next to him. Time slowed to a crawl. He heard every crack of the machine guns, every thump-thump-thump of the canon, every dull thud of the bullets slamming into the tree, and every sharp clang as they found their target—the train.

With a squeal, the locomotive erupted in a hissing display of escaping steam as the train jerked to a halt. What had been the antiaircraft gun was now a heap of tangled metal. Green-clad bodies—some groaning and crawling, others twisted in bizarre poses—lay scattered among the sandbags. Pulling up sharply to avoid crashing into the steep slope hemming in the railroad tracks as he completed his run, the last fighter, white stars emblazoned on its twin fuselages, dipped his wings in salute.

Jan saw the pilot's head turn and look down at them—at him, he was sure. At him. At *him*! He felt his chest expand until he had to come up for air. There and then, he resolved that someday, one day, he too would become a flyer.

* * *

"Fine dinner, Sister." Alois patted his stomach and sent Mother an appreciative smile. "Now I know what I've been missing all these years."

She waved him off, but her glowing face betrayed her delight. "I'm so glad they let you come. We see so little of you.

Easter dinner just isn't the same without family. Maybe if you'd get married…" she teased him.

He winked at Jan sitting next to him, gave her a pained look, took a long swig of beer, wiped the foam from his lips, and belched. "Would you believe Prague's already full of Russians?" He lit a cigarette and blew a thin stream of smoke toward the ceiling.

"Russians, you said?" Father looked at him skeptically. "What do you mean, Russians? I know they're coming, but they're still—"

"Really, it's true! Well, mostly Ukrainians, Estonians, Lithuanians, Latvians. Full division of them. Led by a general. Vlasov's his name. A renegade. Crossed over to the German side while they were winning and now he's trapped. They're all trapped. Don't want to fight the Americans and can't go back to their own side—they'd be shot on sight. So they're just sitting there. Waiting."

"JesusMary," Mother whispered.

"And the Germans? What about the Germans?" Father leaned forward, all ears.

"The city's still full of 'em, too, but," he yawned and belched again, "now, mostly just rushing through. Scared of the Russians like they're the devils. You can see it in their faces." Pausing abruptly, he yawned again and slumped in his seat. His eyeballs rolled upward, revealing their whites, just as his eyelids, like two shutters, slowly descended. A soft snore escaped his half-opened mouth. His head dipped limply to his chest. The stub of his cigarette lay on the edge of the table, burning a hole in Mother's finest tablecloth.

Jan accompanied Alois to the railroad station the following Monday. The railroad tracks had been cleared; the wreckage pulled off to a siding. Only the pockmarked walls of the station and hundreds of tiny craters in the road remained as witness of the mayhem two days ago. That night, Father tacitly permitted Jan to watch as he and the other men carefully dug up the boxes from under the kitchen floor and dragged them outside. Jan could hear them prying off the tops. In the morning, the empty boxes lay covered with a tarp at the side of the house. Father quickly chopped them up and burned them.

A low powerful baritone rumble, barely discernible over the ruckus of the steady stream of passing vehicles, sent the windowpanes vibrating. "Do I hear thunder?" Mother said rhetorically, eyeing the sun-drenched garden strewn with clotheslines weighed down with laundry.

Jan ran out into the street and scanned the horizon, trying to distill the special sound from the virtually continuous roar of retreating convoys. The gate of the Kohen house swung open, and a large black sedan loaded to the top pulled out and disappeared into the stream of vehicles. The thought of Jakub the day he saw him there for the last time flashed before him. Interspersed among the armor and trucks were prodigious numbers of Mercedeses, Škodas, and Tatras heaped with personal possessions, crammed with grim-looking civilians, mostly women and children—German civilians fleeing the Republic.

"The rats are jumpin' ship," Father muttered under his breath.

Mr. Fiala bounded out of the house, Zlata in tow. "Did you hear that? Did you hear?"

Zlata let out a yelp. "I hear it again, Daddy! I hear it!"

Jan heard it, too. They all heard it—a faint rolling rumble, barely audible but deep, very deep, like the waning notes of a thunderstorm but persistently rising and ebbing above the noise of the passing convoys. The two men exchanged knowing looks and broke out in grins.

"Dad?" Jan pleaded.

Father squeezed his shoulder until it hurt. "Those are guns," he whispered hoarsely. "American guns. It's the Americans, my boy. Americans!"

As darkness fell, the western sky lit up in a breathtaking display of light and sound. The gunfire became louder, more distinct, incessant. No one slept that night, and very little the nights that followed.

The convoys continued to barrel through at a frenzied pace. Out of fuel, some of the Germans drove their vehicles into the ditches if they could, or just left them in the road where their gas tanks had run dry. Those that could still move, piled high with soldiers hanging on in desperation, pushed the crippled vehicles off the road. But most of them trudged along on foot, dumping their weapons, knapsacks, anything that weighed them down, into the ditches. Their wizened, sallow, unshaven faces told the story: the war, at least for them, was over.

"You think he's out there somewhere?" Mother peered cautiously out the window.

"Who?" Father's face clouded. "Fuchs?"

She nodded.

"Hope he got what he deserved, that pig. I'd kill the bastard, if I ever saw him."

The radio fell silent and Father annoyingly reached for the tuning knob. "Damned tubes, again!" he grumbled, just as the announcer came on again, out of breath, voice quivering with excitement: *"Esteemed citizens of the Republic, please stand by for a very important announcement..."*

Father froze. "Republic! He said 'Republic!' My God, Lena, did you hear? Did you hear him say 'Republic?'" His lips trembled. "Something's going on. Boy, run upstairs and get the Fialas. Quick! Hurry!"

The Fialas rushed in just as the announcer came back, in a voice dripping with emotion:

"Esteemed citizens of the Czechoslovak Republic, this is Free Radio Prague...this is Free Radio Prague! We are happy to report that advance units of the Third American Army under General Patton have just reached the outskirts of Prague. In response, the citizens of Prague took up arms and, as we speak, are engaged in combat with several Nazi garrisons still present in the city." Sporadic gunfire popped in the background over the announcer's voice. *"We are fighting for our freedom and liberty! The radio station is ours, taken without serious casualties! We are free! Prague is in revolt against the Nazi oppressors. With the American liberators as our partners and leaders, we shall soon be victorious. Long live the Czechoslovak Republic! Pravda Vítězí! The Truth Wins!"*

The soft strains of the National Anthem filled the air—a melody they had not heard in years. Throwing all caution to the wind, Father turned up the volume and they all joined in, passionately, pouring their souls into the words, unable to contain their joy.

When the Fialas left, Father lifted the plug from under the kitchen table and lowered Jan into the opening. Jan's feet sank ankle-deep into the loose sandy soil and stumbled.

"Over there." Father pointed to a spot with a flashlight. "Just dig with your hands."

Jan scooped aside the loam and pulled out a tightly wrapped bundle—the national flag his father had buried there years ago.

Father unsealed the packet and spread the flag on the worktable. Heavily creased in several places, it showed the effects of its years in hiding. He caressed it with his fingers, and then picked up the heavy charcoal-burning iron, made sure with spittle it was hot, and pressed it. Then he pulled out lengths of red, white, and blue fabric from an armoire stuffed with remnants, and despite the lateness of the hour, set to work.

It wasn't the noise that awoke Jan the following morning— it was the quiet. An eerie, ominous quiet. *Something's not right* was his first thought. Gone was the incessant around-the-clock rumble that had for countless months permeated their lives. The sudden silence was unnerving. Throwing open the window, he gasped in surprise. The town was deserted. The Germans gone.

As far as the eye could see, abandoned trucks, tanks, and artillery pieces littered the road and surrounding fields. Piles of ammunition, grenades, bazookas, artillery shells, Mausers by the hundreds, some of their barrels bent by a blow to the pavement, lay strewn helter-skelter in the ditches. On the far slopes, high above the town, loose bands of frantically moving specks – the last of the retreating Germans – disappeared into the woods.

At first only a tentative few, but then every living being seemed to have spilled into the street. National flags, long hidden in secret places, materialized like magic. Like a field of fluttering flowers, the sea of blues, reds, and whites festooned the war-weary appearance of the town. Only on Jan's house, right next to a crisply ironed tricolor, swaying gently in the morning breeze, flew his father's toil of the night—a Stars and Stripes.

Someone pulled down the large Nazi flag from the town hall staff and tossed it in the middle of the road. Crumpled, it lay there in a heap. A roar arose from the crowd. Profanities flew, as everyone took turns stomping or spitting on the crimson fabric, giving vent to years of pent-up anger and emotions.

And then came a new distant rumble.

CHAPTER 14

The town's entire population spilled into the street. Tense faces turned westward toward where the road descended the flanks of the mountains and turned eastward toward Čekaná, and where a shimmering mirage dissolved into a caterpillar-like column of armor. A pair of armored bulldozers pushed aside the abandoned German vehicles, clearing the way for a column of tanks as they rumbled toward the town at a deliberate pace. A hushed murmur rippled through the crowd. *"Americans! Americans! It's the Americans!"* rippled through the crowd like a mantra. The tension grew to a breaking point.

Jan squeezed his father's hand and he squeezed back hard, almost cruelly.

The sound of motors grew into a crescendo as the first tank, a white star emblazoned on its turret, a small American flag fluttering from the tip of a tall swaying antenna, reached the solid wall of screaming and waving people. The crowd enveloped it, creating a path barely wide enough for the tank to pass. Behind it stretched an immense column of thundering armor, the end of which couldn't be seen. The ear-shattering sound filled the air. The ground quaked under the ponderous mass of metal.

"Nazdar! Nazdar! Nazdar...Vitáme vás! Vitáme vás... Vitáme vás... Hello! Welcome..." the crowd chanted, nearly drowning out the roar of the engines.

The soldiers began to emerge from behind their armored plates, machine gun turrets, and the bowels of the tanks. At first incredulous, not knowing what to expect, but quickly overjoyed, they reached down to the people, offering their smiles and their hands. The crowd, giddy with euphoria, seized them with a passion.

Teary-eyed men hoisted little children on their shoulders for a better view. Women cried. Blushing young girls sprinkled the tanks with flowers. Fingers forming the letter 'V' for Victory, shouting their *Hullos* and *Hiya theres*, the smiling soldiers showered the crowd with candy, chewing gum, cigarettes, and other treasures never before seen or imagined.

Surging closer to the tanks, people stroked and patted the dusty metal as if to reassure themselves what they saw was real. No one seemed to mind the dust and fumes that covered everybody and everything. The smell of the exhaust was champagne to their senses, the whine of the engines a symphony to their ears.

A roar of approval rose from the crowd as the lead tank rolled over the Nazi flag. The town hall window overlooking the road – the former office of the Gestapo – flew open, revealing a pair of familiar figures: Doctor Clauder, still in his Nazi uniform, and Administrator Czech, who had been arrested by the Resistance as they tried to flee. Forced to watch the liberating army, they stood there with faces drawn and jaws clenched, grimly surveying the elated crowd, the thundering armor, the heap of the Nazi flag being torn to shreds by the tanks.

Covered with dust and pockets bulging with 'treasures,' Jan continued to scream and wave until his parched throat gave out and he could only wheeze. Zlata wedged in next to him with yet another basketful of flowers. Father and the Fialas fared no better. Mother watched it all with unbelieving eyes, crying.

The thunderous stream continued uninterrupted for the next two days, and finally tapered off to intermittent convoys. Still, the crowds did not slacken. The town folk, lining the road shoulder to shoulder, continued to greet the Americans, offering their hands, their tears, and their hearts.

Glued to the radio, Father let out a torrent of curses. The ether cracked with the sounds of gunfire and pleas for help. "It's Prague! There's fighting in Prague!"

"What's the matter, Dad?" Jan instinctively cringed.

"The Americans! I don't believe it! Yesterday, we heard they got all the way to Prague, and now they say, they turned around and went back to Pilsen. Without firing a shot. Left the Czechs in the lurch fighting the Nazis. They're saying the Germans have two squadrons at Ruzyně and that they're going to bomb Prague." He slammed his fist into the work table.

"JesusMary, what about Alois?" Mother cried out. "What's going on?"

"Had to turn around and go back to where the demarcation line is going to be. Somewhere around Pilsen. If it weren't for that turncoat Vlasov and his army—"

"What about that Russian?"

"He's helping. Turned on the Germans. Fighting on our side, now, but don't know how long he can hold out. The bastards are desperate. They say the Russians are still at least four days away. Four days! In the meantime..." Father fell silent and wiped his forehead in exasperation.

A round of shouts, laughter, and catcalls erupted from the Clauder Manor. Sprawled on top of one of the armored cars, whiling the time away, a few soldiers amused themselves by flipping cigarette butts into the dirt and watching the boys scramble after them.

Jan tumbled in the dust, smarting from the shower of dirt someone had kicked in his face, but he didn't mind. He'd already captured the prize—a cigarette butt. Rubbing his eyes with the back of his hand, he slowly, triumphantly got to his feet, carefully put out the fire, and wiped the dirt from his pants. The other boys joshed him enviously.

"Hey, boy," a melodious voice boomed from somewhere behind him.

Jan winced. The edge in the soldier's voice made him wary. Maybe he'd tell him to empty his pocket and throw away his hard-earned 'fortune' of cigarette butts that Father would strip them, put the tobacco into an ingenious hand-loader, and push it into cigarette blanks. *That* had happened before. Or he'd be chastised for being in the compound. That had happened before, too. The compound was off limits but loosely enforced, and he couldn't resist. Stealing a look at the soldier, he felt a sense of confused relief. The soldier was smiling.

For the town folk, the Americans held an aura approaching the mythical. Coming as liberators from a distant land that to most was only an abstraction, spoken about with reverence and wonder, they were treated with almost fawning deference and awe. People, by and large, saw them as larger-than-life heroes—superhuman, bordering on godlike. Old men would bow their heads, tip their hats, and look down to the ground instead of meeting their gazes. Women would swoon. Generally larger in stature than the stocky Czechs and speaking a language no one understood, their unfathomably different manners only added to their mystique.

"C'mon, boy, come closer. Don't be afraid," the soldier insisted, waving a thick finger sporting a massive gold ring with a diamond set in onyx. Tall, fair-haired, well groomed, with technical sergeant stripes on his sleeves, jaw in constant motion, a huge pistol strapped to his waist, the soldier continued to smile.

Reluctantly, Jan approached.

"Heah, gimme that!" the soldier gently took the cigarette butt from Jan's hand, stomped on it and ground it into the ground. "No good; no good. Un'erstand? No good! These, good. Good." He reached into his pocket, pulled out a fresh pack of Lucky Strikes, and smiled. "Take this. For your father. You—give—father. Un'erstand?" He thrust a pack of Lucky Strikes in Jan's hand. "Give—Father. No—pick-up—butts. Dirty. No good. Dirty!" He shook his head in disapproval, rolled his eyes, and made a grimace.

"Děkuji," Jan whispered a thank you, took the cigarettes and, realizing that the soldier didn't understand his native tongue, repeated in German, *"Danke schoen."*

The soldier scowled. "No, boy. Say, 'Thank you.' 'Thank—you.' Watch me: 'Thank…you.' 'Thank—you—very—much.'"

Jan repeated shyly, "Tsank you! Tsank—you—veli—much."

"Okay. Okay!" The soldier grinned approvingly and gave him a pat on the shoulder.

And that was how Dick Wright became Jan's friend, teacher of English, and a regular visitor to his home. He never forgot to bring satchels full of 'treasures,' and was particularly pleased when he discovered Father spoke some English he picked up while with the circus.

"Only a little," Tomáš protested, flushing under Mother's stare and Dick's questioning.

During one of his visits, Dick pulled out a creased and stained picture of Wanda, his sweetheart, and a thin stack of her letters from a wallet he carried on a lanyard around his neck under his shirt. "She wanted to get married before I joined, but her folks wouldn't let her. Talked us out of it." His eyes misted.

One evening, he took out a piece of paper and wrote down his address in large, even letters. "Some day you must come to America and come to Albion." He gave Jan a friendly nudge. "You must come see us. You will like Wanda and Dad. Don't have a mother anymore. She died a few years back. But my dad's a fine fella. You'll like 'im. Michigan's a nice place and Albion's a fine, li'l town. You must come, okay?" Smiling, he pushed the address toward Jan.

As he pocketed the slip of paper, Jan found the idea beyond the reach of his imagination, too staggering to contemplate.

Those were halcyon days for Jan and the town's boys. With the schools closed because of the war, there was plenty of time to play, and play they did, mostly at soldiers. American soldiers, of course, shooting at imaginary Germans. They gave themselves American names, and they had guns, real guns, recovered from the wrecks that littered the landscape. Those not lucky enough to find one that worked could make one from discarded ammunition casings. Jan found his Luger inside a derelict tank. They fought mock battles among the rusting carcasses and detritus of war, and stalked the imaginary enemy—a pair of scarecrows dressed in Nazi uniforms. Hidden from public view, the boys' antics remained unnoticed until one of Jan's buddies shot himself through the head, trying to dislodge a jammed round from a chamber by poking it through the barrel with a pencil. Then one of the Soukup boys was severely burned when the exhaust flame from a German *Panzerfaust* the boys had found and fired discharged its hot recoil gasses into his face. Shortly after, the Americans sprung into action. In a sweep, they confiscated all the guns they could find, collected all the discarded ammunition, and hauled truckloads of it to an abandoned quarry where they doused it with gasoline and burned it. The explosions rocked the air like a giant fireworks show for hours.

A sharp rap on the door broke the afternoon monotony. Mother looked up at an indistinct outline of a soldier behind a milky glass pane of the salon door, and smiled. "It's Dick!" she announced.

From where he sat, Jan could see only a muscular silhouette of a soldier, not noticing he was black until he came into full view. A prickly pulse crawled up his spine as he slid down into his seat and stared at the stranger from behind his open book. He had never seen a black man before. He'd heard of 'Negroes,' even saw their pictures – crude, exaggerated drawings, to be sure – in *Robinson Crusoe*, one of his favorite books. But the man before him looked nothing like the legendary Friday.

"You a tailah, Suh?" the soldier drawled, looking around the salon, giving himself a quick, critical look in the large mirror standing to one side.

Father gave him a polite nod and a smile.

"Burst a seam in my shirt. Can you fix, Suh?" The soldier pulled a khaki-colored shirt from a bag and pointed to the split. "Can you fix my shirt?"

Running the fabric between his fingers, Father nodded. "No problem, no problem; fix okay." Extending his hands, he showed the soldier ten fingers and pointed to the clock.

"Ten minutes." The soldier nodded, smiling. "That'll be fine, Suh. My name's Jim."

Mother offered him a chair and he sat down.

Jan studied Jim's face. It was smooth and glistening, the color of polished ebony. Their eyes met and the soldier winked. Jan looked away in embarrassment.

"A fine young boy you got heah," the soldier said to Father, bolstering his words with a smile.

"Here you go, it's finished. You'd better try it on before I iron it," Father said a few minutes later, holding the shirt open for Jim and gesturing him to try it on.

"You good tailah, Suh," Jim said, pulling a large tin of something from the bag he was carrying and offering it to Mother. Peanut butter.

Jim became the second soldier to regularly visit Jan's home. He, too, never forgot to bring something, and shyly waved off any expressions of gratitude. A Red Ball Express truck driver, he would disappear for days, hauling supplies from the French ports along the English Channel to the front lines. All the soldiers in his Company were black except the commander, a ruddy-faced, chunky-looking major. The blacks soon became a source of great curiosity to the townsfolk. A steady stream of onlookers filed past the small encampment at the soccer field on the outskirts of town, gawking at the neat rows of massive olive-colored trucks and, in particular, at the soldiers with dark faces who drove them.

It was impossible not to notice that Dick became unusually quiet, hardly exchanged any words at all, and left early whenever Jim came.

CHAPTER 15

"Inka's in town, in case you're interested," Zlata remarked as she passed Jan in the courtyard.

"Oh?" His heart skipped a beat even as he tried to sound nonchalant. "Are her folks coming to see you again?"

"No, she's come with some of her friends."

"Her friends? Did you speak to her? When?"

"Yes, of course. Yesterday."

He swallowed hard. "And...did she...did she ask about me?" His spirits rose in anticipation.

Zlata shook her head.

He tried to hide his disappointment. "So why has she come?"

"'To see the Americans,' she said."

"To see the Americans? Why—"

She frowned and shrugged before he could finish the question.

"Where is she staying? The Králíček's?"

She shrugged again.

"Hmm..." His heart raced. How many times had the memories of their intimate encounter flooded his senses? Oh, how he had relished them, again and again. He would touch himself where she had led him to touch her, cupping his breasts the way she had him cup hers, pretending, and letting his imagination roam. He could still feel the chill he had felt then. And now, she was here again and he was wasting time! His chest filled with flutter. "I really gotta go," he blurted, leaving Zlata nonplussed as, propelled by anticipation, he rushed out into the street.

A clutch of nattily dressed, heavily made-up young women milled about the entrance to the Králíček's Beer Hall, which also doubled as the town's only hotel. *City girls, probably from Prague,* he thought, judging from their dress and make-up, and a certain air of haughtiness and disdain they directed at the locals who scorned them and called them vile names.

"They're nothing but harlots," Mother noted their presence, blushing at her unexpected audacity, as she watched them promenade up and down the street stalking the friendly smiling soldiers who, for the most part, eagerly welcomed their attention. At night, the town's three beer halls would come alive with the beat of boogie-woogie and the jitterbug—dances from hell as far as the locals, weaned out on waltzes and polkas, were concerned.

Jan spotted Inka from across the street before she saw him, not twenty paces away, as she emerged from the Králíček's Beer Hall. He stopped in his tracks. A searing flash shot through him like a bolt of lightning. The palms of his hands turned clammy. By God, it was her, but how she had changed! Only two years, and he almost didn't recognize her. She'd grown and matured, but there was no mistaking her: the same shock of flaxen hair, the same slender body, now even more womanly and alluring; the same smooth, pale skin. *Oh God!* Overwhelmed, he felt drained and weak-kneed, frozen to the spot.

She turned toward him and he waved. For a split second, he saw his fortunes soar as her eyes, the same dizzying violet he remembered, set wide in an ivory face with just the right touch of blush in the cheeks and red on the lips, met his in a brief, piercing look that sent blood rushing to his head. He struggled to find the right words to greet her, but no sound crossed his lips as her gaze fleetingly brushed over him and then swung past into infinity. Her expression did not change. Unsmiling, she seemed hostile, cold.

No, that couldn't be! She recognized him. How could she not? It hadn't been that long. He hadn't changed. He was stunned. What her look seemed to communicate was not hostility, but worse: indifference. Feeling foolish but ignoring his instincts, he cast aside his pride and waved again, more anxiously this time, hoping she'd at least acknowledge him. But she ignored him as though he weren't even there, as though he didn't exist. That hurt! His chest tightened the way it does before tears come, as an emptiness settled in his gut. *Why would she act this way?* reverberated through his mind.

She spun on her heels and broke out in a smile as a young lieutenant stepped out of the arched entrance, a bulging green sack slung over his shoulder, a blanket under his arm. She rushed to him and they embraced, briefly but passionately. The lieutenant's hand slipped down and rested on her sensuously rounded buttocks, pressing her close as she clung to him.

How could she? How could she let him? Out in the open in front of everybody! How could she let him do it? He felt cheated, robbed of the one precious moment he'd cherished ever since *that* fateful day he and she met, the moment he'd embellished in his mind, replaying it time and again, remembering and savoring every word, every touch, every sensation. And now she had taken it from him, soiled, stolen— gone. Robbed him. His mind flooded with pain heavy with loathing. He hated the lieutenant for being so brazen; he scorned her for permitting it. He felt crushed, diminished by the lieutenant's unfair advantage and her blatant display of boldness. He told himself he hated her, knowing in his heart he never could.

She slipped her arm under the lieutenant's, and shot a quick, defiant look in Jan's direction. Their eyes locked for an instant and her icy glare filled him with anguish. Stunned and humiliated, he wanted to run, but instead, propelled by pain and despair, he followed them.

Hemmed in by the mountains, cascading over and around huge granite boulders in a series of striking waterfalls and chutes, the river, its energy spent, finally spread its waters over the valley floor, depositing a shallow, thickly overgrown bar full or driftwood and flotsam where it reached a wide, placid bend. Clinging tenuously to drying deposits of mud and silt, patches of grass vied for the few rays of sunlight filtering in through the dazzling canopy of trees. A well-worn footpath followed its southern flank, winding through the tall pines covering the steep embankment as it traversed a spit of land on its way to the villages upriver. Carved by spring floods, the other bank formed a steep levee, overgrown with bramble and virtually impenetrable, obscuring a narrow checkerboard of meadows and fields. Long a favorite of young lovers seeking solitude and escape from the preying eyes and tongues of the town's busybodies, this wild, secluded place was where Inka and the lieutenant headed. Strolling along the narrow path, arms locked about each other's waist and his sliding lower now and then without her objection, their hips touched and swayed in rhythmic unison.

Driven by jealousy, Jan followed on the opposite bank, slogging through the tangle of waist-high grass, nettles, and bramble, bleeding from pricks and scrapes (and still more invisibly inside), occasionally catching a glimpse of them through the undergrowth. When they reached the sand spit, the lieutenant pulled Inka toward him, and tried to smother her with kisses. Giggling, she broke away and ran. He scampered after her, flinging the satchel and the blanket into the bushes. But she was too quick and he soon gave up, throwing his arms up in mock surrender. Her giggling continued to echo among the trees like the warbling of a bird. With a resigned shrug, the lieutenant retrieved the blanket, shook it a few times, and spread it on a grassy patch.

From the opposite bank, perched on his stomach behind a clump of stinging raspberry bushes, oblivious to the pain, Jan watched in silence. Was this the same girl he once held so close? The girl who permitted him – no, *enticed* him – to do things he'd never even dreamed of doing? The girl who aroused in him feelings he'd never known before and had yearned for since? *His* girl? He tried to banish that special day from his mind, but couldn't. Like scorching rays focused through a loupe on a spot, the memories seared his insides with longing and regret. He wanted to roar, roar like a wounded animal, to strike at her, at the lieutenant, at the world, but in the end, didn't dare to utter a sound.

The lieutenant shook the satchel, spilling an assortment of cans and K-rations onto the blanket. Feigning interest, Inka listened to his explanation as to what they were, pretending not to notice when his arm rested on her shoulder. Giggling, she pushed away his hand as he tried to brush her breasts. Jan bristled.

The lieutenant tried once more, and she again pushed him away, giggling. Reluctantly he gave up, took out a bayonet, and pried open some of the cans. They ate, all the while laughing and teasing, tossing the empty cans into the bushes. Each burst of laughter stung Jan like a cut of a blade. When they finished, she stuck out her tongue at the lieutenant and sensuously licked her lips. Smiling, he pulled out a flask and offered it to her. She took a swig, made a face, choked, and recovered. They both burst out laughing. He took a hard swallow and thrust it at her again. She drank more this time, still laughing and choking between gulps, still making faces, passing the flask back and forth until it was empty. The lieutenant turned it upside down and shook it as though trying to get the last drop out of it, swore, and flung it into the bushes where it shattered among the empty cans.

Inka let out a muffled laugh as she staggered to her feet. Swaying, she took a few steps and was about to stumble again, but the lieutenant grabbed her from behind and jerked her against him, pressing himself into her as his hands groped her breasts. She didn't resist. He cupped and squeezed them until she yelped. Contorted, they froze for a few moments in their awkward embrace – he pressing against her, she bent forward, thrusting her backside into him. He spun her around and clumsily fumbled with the buttons of her dress. She tried to help, but her unsteadiness frustrated him. Cursing under his breath, he tore at her clothes as she continued to thrash about and giggle. Frenzied now, he pushed her down on the blanket, yanked the dress up to her waist and, grabbing her brassiere, jerked it so hard the strap broke. Her firm breasts, alabaster-white except for the dark areolas of her nipples, freed from their confinement, spilled out toward her sides as she lay on her back, panting, eyes half-closed, a faint smile on her lips. She lifted herself, pulled down her panties, and flung them to the side.

Flushed, the lieutenant tore at his clothes, frantically tossing away pieces until he stood over her in his green undershirt and bulging shorts. She reached up to him. Still fumbling with his drawers, he let himself down on her, his hands probing her crotch. Her knees rose and she arched as he found her. She took his hand and led him in. He thrust hard and she let out a soft cry, but then fell quiet but for her panting moans, breasts pumping rhythmically up and down in concert with his lunges, faster and faster until he stopped abruptly, stiffened, rose on his elbows, let out a groan, and collapsed. They both lay quiet, spent.

Never before had Jan seen the act of love, or a girl naked. It was nothing like what he'd heard some of the older boys brag about. In vain, he tried to check the pulsing heat in his groin and the hollow feeling of frustration. It left him aroused and ashamed, and ultimately nauseated. He felt sorry for himself, angry at her. She had just been toying with him, making a fool of him. Wishing he had never met her, he cursed himself for coming.

Through bitter tears, he barely saw them get up and wash in the river. Dazed, he tore himself from the scene and quietly, slowly set out for home. Somewhere behind him, he heard her retching.

* * *

It was November when the Americans left Čekaná, the same day Constable Kubek returned from the hospital where he had been recovering from his prison ordeal. Dick was in high spirits. "Germany for a month or two, and then home. Can't wait!" he crowed, wiping the moisture from his eyes, as he shook hands all around, admonishing Jan to save his address and one day, one day for sure, come to visit him and Wanda in Albion.

Jan rushed out, hoping to catch a glimpse of Jim, but only saw the last of the Red Ball trucks off in the distance. As he watched the last of the trucks vanish in a cloud of exhaust and dust, he felt empty inside, as though something unresolved had not been put straight. With a heavy heart, he surveyed the subdued, somber crowd lining the road. Only a few people waved. Mostly they just stood there stoically, numbed by emotion, resigned to fate. Dick's armored detachment joined the stream of vehicles and Jan waved, watching his friend disappear through a veil of tears. He spotted Inka in the crowd, sobbing into a handkerchief, and averted his eyes when she accidentally glanced in his direction. When he looked up again, she was gone.

The next day, all the Prague girls were gone. Jan scoured the town for Inka, driven by yearning to see her one more time, cursing himself for being so weak. But she was nowhere to be seen. Not even Zlata could help him. The town seemed to sink into a kind of mournful lethargy, until, to everyone's amazement, one of the town's deported Jews returned from the concentration camp. Jan's spirits soared as he rushed to query him about Jakub.

The wizened old Jew looked at him sadly. "Wish I could tell you he's well, but I'd be lying. We stayed in Terezín almost a year before they shipped us out. To Treblinka. That's in Poland. An awful place. The last time I saw Jakub was with his mother the day we got there, on their way to the showers. Later on we found out…" He paused and looked somewhere past Jan with unseeing eyes. "They gassed people there."

The town emptied as the refugees driven out from the border region by the Nazis at the onset of the war began a slow exodus to their former homes. The Fialas, too, were leaving. Teary-eyed and lost for words, they embraced silently with much feeling and promised to remain in touch. Zlata planted an awkward kiss on blushing Jan's lips, and cried as an old wood-burning Škoda truck pulled up to take them away. He regretted seeing her go; she had become a sister to him. Without her, he wouldn't have met Inka. Amazing how things turn out sometimes! Now it was too late. He detested himself for squandering all his affection on Inka. He knew he would miss Zlata immensely.

A few days later, a young German Shepherd pup wandered into the yard. Matted and full of ticks, his fur barely hid his protruding ribs. A thin metal plate on the worn-out collar around his neck held a single word, *Schatzi.*

"Must've been left behind by the Germans," Father murmured, helping Jan pick off the mass of ticks covering the pup's skin and douse him with water. Taking an old belt, he cut it to fit the pup's neck and carefully scratched the word *Bojar* into the leather. In spite of Mother's protests about another mouth to feed, the dog stayed. Father and Bojar became inseparable.

Contrary to expectations, the Russians didn't fill the vacuum left by the Americans and didn't ride in victoriously after the Yanks had departed. Nonetheless, their presence was deeply felt. Usually hidden from view on the outskirts of towns, they stuck to their camps and didn't mix with the people the way the Americans had. The few who visited Čekaná, generally grim and unsmiling, just disappeared behind the doors of the town hall or the police station. Jan's heart would skip a hopeful beat whenever he spotted a jeep, only to be almost immediately chagrined, seeing the star on its side was red rather than white.

CHAPTER 16

"Am I interrupting something?" Constable Kubek poked his balding head into the workroom.

Father looked up from polishing the brass buttons on his fireman's uniform and motioned him in.

"I knocked," Kubek apologized to Mother. "Guess you didn't hear me."

They shook hands.

"Lost a button." He thrust his uniform on the table. "I know you've got plenty of extras. Gotta look right for tomorrow's parade." He sidled over to Jan. "And how are you, boy?" He gave him a pat on the shoulder. "Saw your drawing in the *Slovo*. Good job. You've got talent."

Jan shrugged uncomfortably and mumbled something unintelligible. Before he left, Dick had given him a stack of *Yank* magazines with Bill Mauldin's *Willie and Joe* cartoons, which he enthusiastically tried to emulate. The art professor at the Gymnásium had taken note of his drawings and suggested he try his skills at the newspaper.

"You never told us about Pankrác. Must've been rough." Mother made room for the constable at the table. "Coffee? It's fresh."

"Yes, thanks. What's there to tell? It was bad. Glad it's all behind me. Still get nightmares." Kubek sighed loudly and lit a cigarette. "Hard to believe it's now been what...two years since the Americans left?"

Father nodded pensively. "They were around all the time, but you hardly see the Russians."

"Oh, but they're here. I see them often. They're much more political. Don't mix with the people, the way the Americans did.

"So, what do they want?" Father said.

"What do they want? Everything." Kubek paused just enough to relieve Mother of a cup of the steaming brew and nod thanks. "They want to know everything about everything. And everybody. In cahoots with the communists. Beneš shouldn't have buckled and given them both the Interior and Defense. That was a grave mistake. What was he thinking? I always thought he'd be a strong president. Did a good job in exile. But now, he's letting 'em take over. They have all the power—the police, I mean the SNB, that's what it's called now, National Security Police, and the army. It can only mean trouble. I see it. I feel it first hand, and it makes me angry. No, it makes me sick."

"What I can't understand is why now. Why he had to give them both ministries. Why not just one?" Father fumed.

"Why not wait till the elections?" Mother chimed in.

"You know why." Kubek shook his head. "That's where the Russians come in. They got the Russians on their side. They pressed him. Put real pressure on him. They're not stupid. They know they can't win the elections. Don't have the votes. So they're grabbing all they can while they can. Now."

"Those swine!" Father's veins stood out prominently on his temple.

"Now, they have the police and the army. They have all the power. I don't like it. I don't like the looks of it at all." Constable Kubek sighed.

The air was thick with the raw smell of plowed earth wafting in from the surrounding fields. Jan shivered under his thin garb – a white T-shirt with a large red *Sokol* gymnastics organization logo emblazoned on its front, and a pair of blue gym shorts. Clenching his teeth, he tried to ignore the bite of the brisk October breeze heralding an early winter. Next to him, the Soukup brothers, Jára, his disfigured face turning purple in the chill, and Peter, sniffling into a handkerchief, fidgeted. The football field, the staging area for the parade, still bore a few bare patches of darkly stained ground, a persistent reminder of the long-departed Red Ball truckers. He scooped up some of the soil and sniffed it. Amazing, that after more than two years, it still smelled of oil! It made him think of Jim.

The band struck up a lively Kmoch march, and the milling marchers fell quiet. The Soukups snapped out of their fidgeting. Bracing himself, he instinctively threw back his shoulders the way the Sokol had taught him. A quick glance reassured him the rest of his Sokol team stood at the ready. Behind them, closing ranks, the veterans of the two world wars, the Sokol auxiliary, in their red skirts, their Catholic counterparts, and finally, a contingent of local politicos brought up the rear.

A shrill whistle split the air and everyone stepped out in earnest. Just ahead, Jan spotted his father's helmeted head bobbing up and down in cadence with the music, along with the rest of the firemen, escorting their gleaming pumper. Leading the parade was Constable Kubek, followed by the mayor, tricolor sash fluttering on his chest, flanked by a pair of Sokols bearing the national flag. The cold breeze made his eyes tear and the sea of red, white, and blue pennants fluttering in the gusts became a blurred palette of color as they turned onto the main street. A chorus of hurrahs rose from the enthusiastic crowd. Tears flowed and heads bowed as the flags filed by. Jan spotted his mother standing on the curb, and stepped out just a bit smarter and waved. She waved back and smiled.

Suddenly, a phalanx of red banners, emblazoned with gold hammers and sickles, carried by grim unsmiling men, spilled in from a side street. A hush came over the crowd. Everyone stared in disbelief.

"The communists," someone shouted. "Fuckin' communists!"

"Bastards!" The elder Soukup sent a wad of spit in their direction.

Face frozen in a defiant, contemptuous smirk, the barrel-chested Comrade Hájek, Jan's violin teacher, flanked by a squad of the local SNB police detachment, led the group in a measured lock step toward the war monument in the center of the square. A crescendo of boos and hisses erupted from the crowd, and he replied with an obscene gesture.

"Just look at that sonofabitch," Jára growled. "He's like a fuckin' peacock. Struts like a fuckin' peacock! And over there, with the SNB, that's—Jesus, that's that sonofabitch Paleček! That's Franta! What's *he* doing there?"

The band struck the national anthem just as the undulating phalanx of red flags reached the makeshift podium. Somehow, for reasons he didn't question or comprehend, singing the national anthem became the most important thing in Jan's life. He sang—they all sang, voices quivering with passion and soaring with emotion, as though their singing would become a sound barrier to ward off the communist intruders, who responded first with crude shouts and taunts, and then with a falsetto rendition of *The Internationale*. For a few moments, the two melodies merged into a dissonant cacophony, as each group grew hoarser trying to out-sing and then out-shout the other, until someone threw a fist and the two sides went at each other with everything they had.

For a few long moments, Jan watched the melee with perfect clarity but surreal detachment. He saw his father swing wildly, go down, then come up again, shouting something to him. Lost in the ruckus, the words never reached him, but from his father's bulging eyes and rage-distorted face, he understood. He quickly joined the scattering crowd and ran.

*   *   *

Father was livid. "Did you see what happened out there? Did you see?" he howled, pulling off his soiled uniform. "Those whores! Those traitors! And Hrášek was with them!" His nose was swollen and dried blood covered his upper lip. His shiny helmet had a pair of gashes left there by something hard. His blood-spattered shirt was torn at the collar. His knuckles were raw. "Those fuckin' whores," he fumed and winced as Mother, tending to him, touched a sore spot.

She was furious. "You always have to run your damned mouth, and now this! You're putting everything at risk, putting *us* at risk. Putting your *family* at risk. Your family! Your business! Everything! Don't you care, man? Don't you have any sense? Don't you think? These are our neighbors. Our customers! People who put food on our table. We need them. For once, couldn't you keep your mouth shut?"

"Dammit, I have the right!" Father slammed his fist on the table. "And besides, they're the ones who started it. You were there. You saw it. They started it!" His lips quivered. The veins in his temples bulged. "What did you expect me to do? Run?"

Her chin trembled as she glared at him through teary eyes.

"And did you see who was leading *their* fuckin' parade? Marching with the SNB? Did you see?" he spat at her.

She looked away.

"Paleček, that's who. Paleček! Franta Paleček! And in uniform. That hooligan! Didn't you see him?"

"I don't care! He's nothing to us."

"Nothing to us, eh? He's now the biggest communist in town. Bigger even than Hájek."

"So what? We never did anything to them."

Father took out a handkerchief, gently padded his bruised nose and then his glistening forehead before turning to her again. "Can't you see? Before, he was just a bully. Now he's a bully with a uniform and a gun!"

The following Monday, the two remaining apprentices didn't show up for work. Mother again savaged Father for being political. Later, Jan caught a snippet of a conversation as they counted their meager reserves stored in a tea tin hidden in the bowels of an armoire: "Never figured him for a communist. Thought he was a friend," he heard his father say.

"It's all your fault. People aren't bringing their work to us any more."

"There's still plenty to do."

"You always get mixed up in things."

"You know that's not true."

"Is this all there is?"

"Yeah."

"You haven't been squirreling away any for your cigarettes—"

"Argh, not that again!"

"What are we going to do? We can't live like this."

"Nothing we can do. Don't even know whom to trust any more. Thought Hrášek was a friend, but you saw where he was. Don't speak any more."

"He still owes us money."

"You'll probably never see it."

Within a month, Franta Paleček became the head of the town SNB detachment, and Constable Kubek was fired. They found his body hanging from a rafter two days later. Father Tlachna refused to grant him a Christian burial because he took his own life and died without an absolution. His widow and daughter left Čekaná shortly after that and never returned. Jan stopped taking violin lessons.

That October confrontation was a watershed in the life of the town. From that day on, the town divided: a chasm developed. Neighbor turned on neighbor. Old friendships vanished, new animosities emerged. The euphoria of their newly acquired freedom all but evaporated, to be replaced by the stifling intrusion of acrimony and distrust.

"It's the old curse," Jan recalled his grandmother's words. "When the Czechs are in trouble, they all stick together, but when trouble comes, they're their own worst enemies."

CHAPTER 17

"Aren't you Neuman?" a thin voice behind Jan spoke as he crammed for an exam in the school library. "The ar-teest?"

Jan had always been wary of those who praised his, as they put it, 'natural talent,' especially since their praise usually preceded a request for a favor. He cupped his hands over his ears, pretending not to hear, but relented. "Yeah. So?" Out of the corner of his eye, he could see the speaker: Medium build; thinning blond hair; high forehead; pale blue eyes; the self-assurance of a city boy. He had seen him around before.

"How about doing some drawings for the *Spirit?*" He smiled. "Our school paper. Didn't Krása talk to you? Dean Vondra finally gave his blessing. We're looking for an 'ar-teest' to spice it up with a few cartoons. Krása said you might. Aren't you working for the *Slovo?*"

Jan shrugged. "It takes up most of my free time. I'm not sure—"

"It won't be much. Once a month, a couple of sketches. That's all. How about it?"

It felt good being asked, especially knowing his favorite professor had put in a good word, but he didn't want to appear too eager.

"Aw, c'mon. How about it?" It was hard to ignore the smiling intruder's extended hand.

"And how come you're the one asking?"

"I'm the editor. I write, and a couple of other guys, too. Jarda Hofman and Martin Marek. You might know them."

"I know Hofman."

"I can type, but none of us can draw. So how about it?" His slightly trembling hand remained outstretched.

Jan shook it. Hesitantly, but feeling good inside. "And you are—"

"Daniel." The boy smiled. "Daniel Moravec."

* * *

The Almanac got it right: 1948 was indeed an exceptionally cold year. Slipping and sliding all the way, Jan arrived at the station out of breath, the frigid February air condensing hoar frost-like on the nap of his sweater, just as the six-thirty came to a squealing, jerky stop.

"Thought you wouldn't m-make it," Láďa grinned.

Jan had met Láďa, a schoolmaster's son from Hornice, a hamlet in the hills, when he first enrolled at the Gymnásium more than four years ago. Láďa would arrive every morning by bus to catch the six-thirty and they would play chess on a tiny pegboard with well-worn peg-pieces during the hour-long ride to the school. Though the same age as Jan, eighteen, he looked much younger. Slight of build, his long thin face framed by curly light brown hair, with a pair of animated grey eyes behind horn-rimmed spectacles, and with a tendency to stutter, he had filled Jakub's void.

"Got up late." Jan gave him a sheepish look. "Hey, what's going on?"

Dumbfounded, they both stared at a pair of large red flags emblazoned with gold stars over crossed hammers and sickles hanging limply in a crisscrossed fashion from the front of the locomotive.

143

Láďa made a face. "Do-don't know. Haven't heard a thing. What do you think?"

Jan shrugged.

Steamy spurts of condensed breath rose above the waiting crowd stomping around in the crunching snow to ward off the frigid cold. The coach doors clicked open and everyone rushed in, shoving and pushing, carrying Jan and Láďa with them. The inside swarmed with factory workers sporting little red ribbons on their stained blue overalls, and pulsed with rowdy conversation spiked with animated shouts amid a steamy smorgasbord of tobacco and sour smells. The windows were opaque with condensation. A falsetto voice belted out a few bars of the "Internationale," stopped abruptly with a wheeze, and died in a burst of laughter. Someone shoved Jan so hard he crashed into Láďa. It was one of his father's former customers from a village up river.

"You the Neuman boy, eh?" The man's face twisted in contempt. "Tell your old man I'm sending him a greeting. Tell'im to go to hell!" He ended with a wheezing laugh that died in his throat.

Jan tried to ignore him, but the remark stirred up his mind. The hour ride seemed much longer than usual. In the city, a scattering of red flags contrasted sharply with the February drabness of the grime-covered buildings and iced-over cobblestone streets. Except for a smattering of rowdy outbursts from the stream of workers headed for the weapons factory, the people in the streets seemed oddly quiet and withdrawn, scurrying about like scared creatures. A sense of foreboding made the chill of the morning twice as piercing.

"What do you make of it?" Jan turned to Láďa, shivering until his teeth chattered.

Láďa shrugged.

Heckling and catcalls greeted them when they entered the cavernous baroque lobby of the Gymnásium. Customarily orderly, or at best filled with the swooshing drone of students rushing to their classrooms, the halls echoed with excited cries and taunts. The professors tending to the students, normally casual and receptive, seemed preoccupied and withdrawn.

"What's go-going on?" Láďa cornered a fellow student.

"Haven't you heard?" he blurted out breathlessly. "There's been a putsch! The communists took over the government! There's trouble in Prague. Everywhere!"

A pair of surly looking police took up a position at the entrance. It was the first time Jan had seen a policeman at his school.

Later, waiting for Daniel in the closet that doubled as the *Spirit* workroom, Jan tried to make sense of it all. With the bloody communist fight during last October's town parade still fresh in his mind, he knew intuitively there was going to be trouble. He had dismissed from his mind the shove and insult he'd received that morning on the train, but now it came back, along with the memory of Father's bloodied face and Mother's laments, and the somber mood that preceded his country's spiraling descent into the abyss of war. The numbing fear he felt then returned. He cringed.

The thick stale air, pungent with the heavy odor of printer's ink coming from an antique mimeograph machine, only exacerbated the oppressive weight of the news. Jan peered through half-closed eyes at Martin and Hofman, usually chatty but now quiet and subdued, and wondered what they were thinking. Their faces told him nothing. He didn't really know them that well. What if they couldn't be trusted? Especially Hofman, the son of a policeman.

"Sorry I'm late." Daniel rushed in, flushed and out of breath. "You heard? Anybody got the paper?"

Martin tossed him a newspaper. The crimson masthead read, *Rudé Právo*. Half the front page was taken up by two giant words, 'WE WIN!' and under it, in smaller letters, 'Great Victory for Socialism and the Czechoslovak Communist Party.'

Daniel tossed it back. "I don't want this piece of trash!"

"That's all there was," Martin protested.

Daniel swore, staring at the headline.

"So, what do we do now?" Hofman stirred. "Got any plans?"

"What do you mean, what do we do?" Daniel tossed the paper into the trash can and swept their faces with his gaze. "We do what we always do. Write. Especially now. This is an opportunity. We have an obligation."

"And the Dean? Shouldn't we first check with the Dean?" Martin said.

"No. He'll let us know if he doesn't like what we do. Until then…"

"I still don't know if we should." Hofman made a face and pursed his lips. "My dad says there's going to be trouble. If we're involved…"

Daniel scowled. "Then I leave it to you. I leave it to you all. You decide. If you want to stay—stay. If you want to go— go. No hard feelings. Up to you."

It wasn't so much that Jan had to choose sides—he knew he would stay. But he worried about the reaction at home, especially Mother's.

146

An uneasy silence settled over the room. Finally, Martin stirred. "I'm staying," he said.

"So am I," Jan said, trying to hide the angst in his voice, feeling suddenly like a conspirator.

Hofman swallowed hard and cleared his throat. "Guess I'll stay, too," he croaked reluctantly.

*   *   *

"Where have you been?" Mother pounced on Jan when he walked in. "How come you're so late?"

"You knew this was my day at the school paper. I told you," he protested, hoping his father would come to his aid. But Father's head was buried in the newspaper and the silent working of his jaw and pulsing of the veins on his temples told him he was in one of his moods. "These bastards! These whores! These mammons!" he finally exploded, slamming the paper to the floor.

Bojar stopped licking Jan's hand and scurried under the table.

"Dad? I still don't know what happened," Jan said, edging up to him moments later. "There was a lot of talk at school, but…" He shrugged.

Father looked up at him through his stained glasses. Suddenly he seemed old, drawn, defeated. He wiped his misty eyes and then his brow with a crumpled handkerchief, and lit a cigarette. "Sorry, boy." He cleared his throat. "You ask what happened? I'll tell you what happened. A putsch! A coup! Everybody could see it coming. From the start, they knew, the Reds. They knew they couldn't win the May elections, so they smuggled weapons into the factories and took them over last

147

night. They say they got the weapons from the Russians. The Army knew they had the weapons but wouldn't interfere because the reds had Svoboda, the general, in their pocket. Apparently he was in on it, that bastard. Traitor! They say he confined all the commanders that didn't sympathize with them to quarters under a pretext, and so the Army did nothing. Absolutely nothing! They were the only ones that could've stopped it. In the meantime, the SNB and the secret police moved in and took over the government and the ministries. Took over everything. Forced Beneš out. Not a Russian around, mind you, but I'm sure, they were ready to jump in if things didn't go their way."

The clock struck 7, and Father turned on the radio. Sounds of martial music and excited tinny voice urging citizens to remain calm filled the room. He swore. "It's been like this all day!" He spun the dial with disgust, got up and ambled over to the old armoire. Mumbling oaths under his breath, he rifled through the contents, and with a satisfying grunt pulled out the short-wave antenna he'd rigged during the war.

"Never thought I'd be using this again," he muttered. He connected the wires and spun the dial, and broke out into a grin when the ethereal whine and static gave way to a voice—a Czech voice.

"...the resignation of President Beneš, some say, a forced resignation, seems to have cleared a way for Klement Gottwald to become the new Czechoslovak president. Clearly, this is an ominous development. Gottwald has spent the war years in Moscow along with most of the members of his new cabinet, and is considered an orthodox communist, well versed in Stalinist dogmas. The Foreign Office has not commented as to whether or not the Crown will recognize the new government.

Despite protests and isolated pockets of resistance, the Army and the SNB, the Czechoslovak State Police have been able to maintain order. The new government has lost no time in solidifying its position. We have unconfirmed reports of wholesale arrests among the former ministries, institutions of higher learning, the radio, the press, and the intelligentsia in general. Our correspondents are on the scene and we will bring you details as soon as they become available. This is the BBC world service broadcasting in the Czech language. You can hear us daily at nineteen, twenty-one, and twenty-three hours on ninety-nine fifty, sixty-one seventy-five..."

Father groaned and turned off the set.

"JesusMary!" Mother gasped, crossing herself, and then gave Jan a long look. "I want you to quit that job at the *Slovo*," she snapped harshly. "We've got enough problems without your being mixed up in anything political."

"But Mom, it's just cartoons!"

"I don't care!"

"But Mom, please, it's not much. We can use the money." He played the trump card, hoping she would relent.

"I don't want any arguments, you hear?"

"Dad?" he turned to his father.

But Father looked away, threw his hands up, and lit a cigarette without saying a word.

CHAPTER 18

The blustery wind sent swirls of powdery snow skyward. Trying to keep his teeth from chattering, Jan cast a sidelong glance at Láďa, who gave him a nervous smile and thrust his hands deeper into his coat pockets. "It's c-cold. We should be inside. What's there to see anyway? Who wants to see *him*?"

"At least we got to get out early," Jan said, gazing at a spidery platform that seemed to have sprung up overnight in front of the Gymnásium.

Crawling with carpenters making final adjustments, the skeletal structure resembled a gallows, an unsightly contraption thrown together in haste, out of character with the five-story spire-topped rococo edifice covered with Mánes' frescoes on patriotic themes, considered a jewel and national treasure. Elevated on a knoll at the junction of two avenues that formed an elongated square, the Gymnásium was the fulcrum of the city's life. Tomáš Masaryk, the first President of the Republic, had spoken here, as had, reportedly, the Hapsburg Emperor Franz-Josef during the heyday of the Austro-Hungarian Empire. Today, Klement Gottwald, the new communist president, was to make an appearance.

Cold tears prickled Jan's eyes and blurred his view of a pair of giant red flags tethered to their poles, snapping angrily in the brisk March breeze, almost completely obscuring the national tricolor and the black pendant marking the death of Jan Masaryk, the Foreign Minister, who had been found dead under the window of his office at the Hradčany Castle.

"They found him dead at the Castle," Láďa said, nodding toward the black flag. "Said he jumped."

"Dad says he was pushed," Jan murmured under his breath.

The sparse crowd around them swelled to overflowing as the workers from the *Zbrojovka* armaments factory began arriving in droves. A detachment of SNB troopers spilled out of a bus and cordoned the platform. All traffic disappeared from the streets.

The clock in the Gymnásium spire chimed noon as a line of black Škodas pulled up to the platform. The crowd erupted in shouts and whistles as a swarthy, grim-looking man, draped in an ankle-length leather coat, fleshy face all but hidden by an upturned collar and a Russian-style Kolinsky hat, emerged from one of the cars, and was immediately surrounded by an entourage of beefy-looking leather-coated men. He slipped on the icy ground but recovered, and slowly, ponderously ascended the podium. Spurts of steamy breath billowed out from the opening between the flaps of his collar with each measured step. He reached the top and turned, raised his right fist, and then just stood there, eyes glinting, scrutinizing the crowd, listening to its roar, basking in the adulation.

Finally, he brought down his fist and with outstretched arms, motioned the people to quiet down. They did so, reluctantly but obediently, and he began to speak.

A taunting shout, and then a chant rose from somewhere among the students crowding the windows: "*Svo-bo-du…svo-bo-du*, free-dom…free-dom." Just a few, scattered voices at first, but almost immediately seized upon by the rest. "*Svo-bo-du…svo-bo-du…svo-bo-du*," the students chanted, the sound of their voices drowning out the angry shouts of the crowd.

Gottwald spun around and glared at the students. He shook his fist and the chants increased. "Who do you think you are?" he barked, the tinny amplified echo of his screechy voice rebounding from the canyons of the streets. "Who do you think you are!" Trembling with anger, his tone rose an octave. "You are nothing! Look. Look!" His hand swept the crowd. "There's the future. We, *we* are the future! You bourgeois! You petit bourgeois criminals! You're nothing! You will be swept away by the tide of history! The future belongs to socialism. To Marxism-Leninism. To communism. To *us*! The future belongs to us! You are nothing but scum! Nothing!"

A shower of whistles and catcalls rained down in response. Then the students broke into *Kde domov můj,* the national anthem.

The crowd roared in disapproval. Swarming police and SNB men kicked open the entrance door and surged inside. The clatter of their heavy boots resounded from the cavernous halls as they raced up the steps and through the corridors. The crashing doors sounded like the cracks of pistols. Floor by floor, the heads vanished from the windows. One by one, the windows slammed shut. And then all went quiet.

Jan trembled. Surrounded by the hostile crowd, he felt naked—an interloper, fearing that someone might read his thoughts, might find him out, might do him harm. He fought panic.

"Tha- tha- that was," Láďa swallowed hard, staring at the troopers spilling out of the building, "close," he finished in a whisper. "C'mon, let's get out of here."

*　*　*

"What do you suppose the Dean wants?" Jan sidled up to Daniel, as they made their way slowly up to the fourth-floor Dean Vondra's office.

"Don't know." Daniel shrugged. "Nothing good, I guess. I have a feeling."

"You think it's the demonstration? The thing you wrote in the *Spirit*?"

Daniel shrugged again and nodded toward the long bench next to the Dean's office, already occupied by slumping Martin and Jarda, looking gloomy. "Must be, if he called all of us."

"Hey, what's going on?" Martin greeted them as they approached.

"I warned you. I told you we'd get in trouble," Hoffman whined, looking at Daniel darkly. "But you wouldn't listen."

"Hey, you had your chance," Daniel snapped. "This is not the time to argue."

Hoffman sank back in his seat and sulked.

Muffled sounds of a sharp exchange could be heard from behind the massive door. Finally, it swung open and an SNB officer stalked out, cast a cold, sideways glance at the boys, and disappeared down the stairs. Moments later, the door opened again, a bald head popped out, and a gravelly voice summoned them to enter. They filed in.

"Dean Vondra sent for us," Daniel said, scanning the dark-paneled office for the dean.

The balding man before him was a stranger. Young, stocky, and dour-faced, dressed in a rumpled dark suit brightened only by a red ribbon pinned to its lapel, he glared at the boys through a pair of heavy-rimmed glasses. His jaw moved up and down behind his tightly closed lips as though gnawing at the words before spitting them out.

"Dean Vondra isn't here any more, and won't be back. I'm Professor Kaček. I'm the new Dean. Interim Dean for now, 'til they find a replacement. I'm the one who called you." Without breaking eye contact, he slid behind the massive mahogany desk and slowly let himself down into the heavy padded chair. He continued to stare.

Daniel's jaw dropped. Jan felt an invisible fist squeeze the air out of him and fill him with nausea. Martin and Hofman turned pale.

"Who's responsible for *this*?" Kaček hissed, holding up a copy of the *Spirit*.

"Guess we all are." Daniel stepped forward. "I'm the editor."

Kaček continued to glower. "This piece of bourgeois crap doesn't belong here. This piece of revisionist trash has no place in a people's institution of higher learning!"

"But, Sir—"

"And who's responsible for the cover? Who drew this picture?" He shook the *Spirit* in front of their faces.

"I did, Sir," Jan croaked.

"You? And what's your name?"

"Neuman, Sir."

"Neuman, huh? How dare you! How dare you insult our great Communist Party! How dare you insult the patriot workers who fought so hard to bring us socialism, by tacking their glorious symbol on the tail of an ass! How dare you! What's the meaning of it? Who put you up to it?"

"Nobody, Sir. I just did it to—"

"Did Vondra have anything to do with it? Did he approve this? Did he see it? Did he read it? Answer me!"

"He didn't seem to mind," Daniel said.

"He-didn't-seem-to-mind," Kaček mocked him. "Did he, or did he not read it? Did you submit the copy to him before you printed it?"

"No, Sir, he said he didn't—"

"He didn't read it?"

"No, Sir."

His pig eyes bore a hole through Daniel. "Then I hold *you* responsible. I hold *all of you* responsible, understand?" He stood up and slammed down the copy of the *Spirit*. A wispy cloud of dust exploded from the desktop. "As of right now, there is to be no more of this…this…" he searched for a word, "…bourgeois rubbish! Do you understand? You're closed down! You're finished!"

Daniel shifted his gaze to the floor and didn't respond. Jarda and Martin stirred uneasily.

"Have you made distribution yet?"

"No, Sir."

"I want all the copies on my desk immediately. Do you understand?" His voice barely rose above a whisper, but his contorted face turned purple. "Your arrogance! Your attitude! People like you don't belong in this institution." His jaw again worked silently as he glared at them and then nodded toward the door. "Get out! For now. I will deal with you on individual basis. Later. The key!"

Daniel fished the workroom key out of his pocket and he snatched it from his hand.

After they filed out of his office, Jan noticed the door of the workroom wide open and all copies of the *Spirit* gone.

Having to quit his cartooning job was a low point in Jan's life, and the remorseful feeling returned as he got closer to the *Slovo* regional office. He was late, on purpose, halfhearted to face the editor again. He loathed good-byes. He liked the old man who had always treated him fatherly and kindly, and who got teary-eyed when he tendered his resignation the day before.

"I understand," the old man said, nodding sadly. "You have to respect your mother's wishes even if you don't agree with her. We'll miss you. I'll miss you. Stop by tomorrow; I'll have the money due you ready."

He was almost there, and was ready to cross the street when two black Škoda sedans pulled up in front of the *Slovo* offices. Something was terribly wrong. It stopped him cold and set his flesh to crawling as he watched four burly men dressed in identical trench coats and wide-brimmed hats spill out and knock, and immediately without waiting for a response kick in the front door of the office. His first impulse was to turn around and run, but a sense of foreboding kept him riveted to the spot. He joined a small crowd of gawkers that began to gather.

Chaotic voices, shouts, and crashing sounds spilled from the *Slovo* office. Finally, the door flew open and the men emerged, half-dragging and half-pushing the editor. They slammed him against one of the cars and held him there as one of them fumbled with the door. The old man's wild look rested on the onlookers, and on Jan. Their eyes met, fleetingly, but there was no overt sign of recognition, only a silent scream of terror. Two of the men spun him around, shoved him into the back seat of the car, and slammed the door. One of the men slapped an official-looking placard on the door and padlocked it. Stoically, without a sound or change of expression, the people began to scatter as the Škodas roared off in a cloud of exhaust.

Stunned, Jan found himself weak in the knees, unable to move. His guilt at trying to avoid the old man vaporized. A few minutes! Five or ten, no more! What if he *had* been on time?

156

What then? He shuddered, haunted by the old man's look, but then felt an uncharacteristically selfish flood of satisfaction wash over him, that he had been spared, that being late had saved him, that were it not for a stroke of luck, he, along with the old man, would be in the back of the black Škoda. The palms of his hands sweated. He wiped them on his trousers as he started to shake. He felt exposed, naked, vulnerable. Mother was right. Damn the money! Should have never— No! What was he thinking? It was the right thing to do. He did the right thing. He did the right thing! Who could have known? He had to get out of there.

The few passers-by ignored him, rushing by self-absorbed, staring at the ground like hounds following some invisible scent. He had to stay calm. Lowering his head, he pulled up his collar and fixed his gaze on the pavement, all the while feeling cold eyes staring at him from everywhere, from every shadow, from every doorway, from behind every curtain, as he scurried to the safety of the railroad station and home.

CHAPTER 19

When Jan told his mother he had quit his job at the *Slovo*, her eyes misted and she uncharacteristically pulled him close, not gently, but in a desperate bear-like grasp. He felt the strength of her arms, the bony inserts of her corset pressing into him, her matted hair on his cheek. He didn't remember her ever hugging him like this. "I was so worried," she bawled as he stiffly returned her smile, all the while avoiding her eyes.

He had mentioned nothing about what had happened to the editor or about his problems at school, and deceiving her, even by omission, weighed on him heavily. Still, he managed to act nonchalant, though his pretense was shattered the moment he stepped out of the house.

Ever since the debacle in the Dean's office and, in particular, the day the editor of the *Slovo* was arrested, he couldn't shake the feeling of vulnerability. He felt himself being watched, standing out as though his innermost thoughts were there for everyone to see. He conjured himself a marked man, and looked for the telltale ill-disguised glance of an eye indicating that he'd been noticed, singled out, and followed. He tried to remain rational and calm, but the waiting, and most of all the fear and uncertainty, frayed his nerves.

He hadn't seen much of Daniel during the past three weeks, nor had he spoken to Martin or Jarda, though he had seen them a few times. Other than a furtive look, they were consciously avoiding a face-to-face encounter, and he was only too glad of it.

And so he was startled when Daniel fell in next to him as he walked to the train station one afternoon after classes and gave him a friendly jab with his elbow. "Got to talk," he muttered.

They turned off the main avenue and onto a side street leading to a park along the river. It was deserted at this time of the day.

"Kaček's got Dean Vondra's job," Daniel finally said after a quick glace over his shoulder.

"Yeah, I heard. It worries me. You think we'll get suspended?"

Daniel shrugged.

"My dad might understand, but my mother..." Jan rolled his eyes.

"Mine, too. What did your folks say when you told them?"

"I didn't. About the Spirit, or the editor's arrest, or anything."

"Jesus!" Daniel bit his lip. "You know they're jailing everybody and people are scared. Running away. Crossing the border into Germany. One day, they'll be after us." He scanned the empty park nervously and then looked away as though something else weighed on his mind. "What would you say if I told you I've decided to go, too?" he finally said.

"What do you mean? Escape? What are you saying?"

"I don't want to wait for them to get me. To be kicked out of school. Or go to jail. And besides, did you know there's a Czech army forming in the American Zone? In Germany? A patriot army, kinda like a legion. Like what they did in England during the war. Did you know?"

Jan felt a chill. Of course, he had known all about the four Czechoslovak squadrons that fought in the Battle of Britain, that had come home as heroes with their Spitfires and Liberators.

But an army? "What do you mean, an army?" His stomach twisted into a knot.

"To come back and liberate the Republic from the commies. They say hundreds have already gone. *Hundreds*. In fact, a couple of guys I know are going this Sunday."

"This Sunday? And you? Are you—"

"Naw, but in a couple of weeks. After Easter. Martin's going, too."

"You talked to Martin?" Jan felt his heart skip a beat. "Does Hofman know?"

Daniel shifted uncomfortably. "Haven't talked to him yet. Not sure I can trust him. His father's a cop."

Jan swallowed hard. It was so audacious! The knot in his stomach made speech difficult. "And you said there's an army?"

"A legion, actually. It was on the BBC. I didn't hear it myself, but one of the guys that's leaving swears he heard it." He looked at Jan squarely.

Though he had sensed the drift of Daniel's conversation, the question, when it came, made him gasp.

"How about you? Would *you* want to come?" Daniel's unblinking gaze turned hypnotic.

Jan's first panicky impulse was to turn him down, but the words stuck in his throat. The very idea made his head spin. He froze.

Daniel took his hesitation as a sign of indecision. "Aw, c'mon. They've got our names. I'm sure Kaček's already reported us. Dean Vondra's gone. He can't help. You worked for the *Slovo* and the editor's in jail. You're a marked man. It's just a question of time."

Jan's mind screamed yes, but his conscience rebelled. The enormity of the idea held him in check. He had to think. "Yes, I know. But I really can't say right now. I need some time."

"We may not have any time." Daniel shook his head. "I'm serious."

"I know, but I need time."

"Then let me know, and soon? One way or another? And not a word."

"Yeah, I promise."

"We need to find a way to stay in touch over the Easter break, just in case. I can call you. We have a telephone."

"We don't. Nobody in Čekaná has one except the police and the one at the railroad station, and there's one at the post office. You have to pay to use that one and anybody can hear what you're saying." He felt a twinge of frustration. "Wait! Do you know Láďa?"

"You mean Havel? Your pal?"

"Yeah. I see him most weekends and they have a telephone. You can trust him. His father's a schoolmaster."

Daniel's idea was all Jan could think about. It would be a way out of his dilemma—an honorable way. There was no question that one day soon either *they* would come for him or he would be expelled and publicly shamed, and his parents dishonored. Most likely both. Daniel was right. Waiting made no sense. By then, it would be too late to do anything. Take the bold step now and make the move. If there really was a legion, if there was an army and they took him, perhaps he'd even get to fly. The opportunity might not come again. Of course, they'd win—righteous causes always win. And then they all would return heroes, the way the Spitfire pilots had when they came back from England only three short years ago. How he admired

161

them. How he envied them! And now the chance to do the same was his for the taking.

But what about Mother and Father? They knew nothing. Telling them now would hurt them deeply. Dad might understand, but Mother? Never. No way could he talk to them. No way could he tell them. He shuddered as he considered the pain and turmoil his departure would cause them. His conscience hit a wall. An impenetrable wall.

The clock struck 11 and Jan anxiously spun the dial until the familiar BBC voice came on. Heart pounding, he heard news of communist purges, jails filling with the so-called 'enemies of the people,' hundreds escaping into the American Occupation Sector, the regime rushing soldiers to seal the border. But nothing about the legion.

"You? Listening to BBC? Why the sudden interest?" Father jabbed him gently as he slid into a chair next to him.

"Oh, just curious," he lied.

"About the only news that means anything these days." Father padded him approvingly on the shoulder and lit a cigarette.

"Dad?"

"Yeah."

"Have you heard anything about a legion? A Czech legion? Daniel said there was something about it on BBC a few days ago."

"A legion? No, haven't heard a thing. But then, I don't listen all the time. Why do you ask?"

"He said there's a legion being formed in the American Zone from some of the people that escaped."

"A legion, you say?" Father's eyebrows shot up until his forehead filled with wrinkles. "Haven't heard, but it wouldn't surprise me, given the situation. But it could be just a rumor, too. People say things all the time. Can't believe everything. As I said, I don't listen all the time." His gaze shifted as his face lit up in a half-smile, the kind that comes with reminiscing. "Like I said, it wouldn't surprise me. Kind of reminds me of '38, up on the mountain, after we got the word about Munich and before the Germans invaded. There was talk then, too, and many of my men left, to France first and then to England." He sighed. "You know, Son," his voice broke and he blew a column of smoke toward the ceiling, "there was a time I too wanted to go."

"You? Wanted to go?" Jan was dumbfounded.

He nodded. "There were four of us, from my squad. We thought of going to Austria. The border was right there, only a few kilometers away. Then on to Switzerland, France, England…"

"So why didn't you?"

"Lost my nerve. Couldn't do it." He smiled sadly. "It's different when you're single. The other fellows were. But when you're married, when you have obligations, a house, family that depends on you, business…you understand, don't you?" The distant look returned but he caught himself, gave Jan another pat on the back, and wiped his eyes with the palm of his hand.

* * *

"Guess I'd do the same thing if I had your concerns," Láďa said when Jan spoke to him about the telephone and confided in him. "The way t-things are right now…" He sighed.

"So why don't you? You could come with us."

"Me?" He pursed his lips and frowned. "I could ne-never do that to my parents, especially my mom. You know she's not well. She n-needs me. If I did it, don't know w-what would happen to her. Maybe if *they* were after me, if I *had* to, but they've got no-nothing on me, and I…I don't think my folks would go along with that. In fact I know they wouldn't. What do your folks say?"

"They don't know."

"They don't *know*? You mean, you haven't told'em?"

Jan shook his head, wishing he hadn't brought up the subject. "Can't."

Láďa's accusing look made him feel rotten. They both tried to sound upbeat as they parted, but Láďa's moist eyes gave him away. "Don't worry about the t-telephone. In a way, I envy you, but I really wish you w-wouldn't go. Maybe you w-worry too much. Maybe you're overreacting. Maybe they w-won't do anything. Maybe you're not that important. And your parents…I couldn't do it to them. In either case, will you let me know?"

Later that night, unable to fall asleep, staring at the void that was the ceiling, Láďa's words came back to haunt him. For the first time, he realized the true enormity of what he was contemplating. And for the first time, his conscience rebelled against his selfish impulses of self-preservation. Láďa could be right. Probably *was* right. Fear amplifies things. The longer you think about something, the worse it seems. Your mind plays tricks. He was imagining things. He wasn't *that* important. Deep down he felt he couldn't do it to his parents, either. He was amazed at the clarity of his decision. He'd tell Daniel he would not go.

CHAPTER 20

Dawn still covered the countryside in a bleak monochrome when someone rapped loudly on the front door. Jan felt a chill crawl up his spine. Bojar let out a low growl. Mother put down her coffee cup and cast Father a questioning look. Father shrugged and shook his head, and when the rapping resumed, walked over to the window and pulled apart the heavy curtain. "It's Láďa Havel." He sighed with relief.

"JesusMary, what's he doing here so early? And on Saturday!" She crossed herself and looked sharply at Jan. "What's going on? Is there something I should know?"

"It's probably about school work. It's nothing." Jan lied.

"I hope I'm not intruding," Láďa apologized as he walked in, and cast a quick glance in Jan's direction. Usually ebullient, he seemed withdrawn and somber. The color had gone out of his face and dark rings under his eyes spoke of a lack of sleep. Jan felt his chest tighten.

"No, of course, not. It's just that on a Saturday, at this hour, we didn't expect..." Mother smiled. "We were having breakfast. Have you eaten? Would you like to join us? What's going on? Is everything all right?" She motioned him to a chair.

"Not so good right now, I'm s-sorry to say." Láďa's face clouded over. "It's my Mom. Had to call the doctor last night. Gave her an injection. Said to get this prescription filled right away. So I'm here to catch the pharmacist as soon as he opens."

"Her heart again?"

Láďa shrugged. "That, or her nerves. Probably both." He fidgeted uncomfortably. "They fi-fired my f-father yesterday," he stuttered. "It really upset her."

165

Mother's hand flew to her mouth. "JesusMary, what are you saying? Who'd do such a thing? And why? He's been the schoolmaster there ever since I can remember. All through the war. Such a good man. JesusMary!" She crossed herself.

Láďa sighed. "T-the police. The SNB. Paleček. Came to the school yesterday. D-dragged him out in front of everybody. Called him bourgeois traitor and t-things like that. Awful things."

"Did they take him? Is he in jail?"

"No, thank God. B-but wouldn't even let him go back and get his things."

"JesusMary!" Mother gazed at him with compassion.

The clock struck the hour and Láďa shifted uneasily. "Guess I'd better go. Reason I stopped, I need to ask Jan about something." He looked at the clock and fidgeted. "Can he come along?"

"Of course," Mother said. Is there anything—"

"No," he shook his head, "but thanks for asking."

"Sorry you had to go through all this for me," Jan apologized outside, out of earshot.

Láďa shook his head. "You don't understand. Dad *was* fired and Mother *is* sick. It just worked out that way. Coincidence. I didn't have to lie."

"Sorry."

"I'd have had to come anyway, because that fellow Daniel you said had a phone called." He quickly looked around the empty street. "He said to tell you t-they got Hofman." His words came out in a raspy whisper. "Said the StB got him. The secret p-police. That's what he said. Last night. Said they dragged him right out of the theater. You knew he was in an Easter school play?"

166

"Yeah."

"Anyway, this f-friend of yours said to tell you there's no more time, so he and the other fellow, f-forgot his name, are going, and if you'd decided to go, to be there tomorrow. They'll be on the eight o'clock train t-tomorrow morning, the one that gets here at 9."

Jan felt a jolt, and then a peculiar sickening numbness invaded his gut. His heart raced.

"You're not going, are you?" Láďa cleared his throat as his eyes took on a sheen.

Jan shriveled under his probing look. "I wasn't going to after we talked yesterday, but now I don't know. I have to think. What I don't understand is why they would take Hofman and not Daniel, since Daniel was the one in charge. It doesn't make sense. He was the editor, and yet, he must be free since he was able to call. That means nobody's bothered him. So I wonder if there's some other reason they took Hofman. Something that doesn't have to do with us."

Láďa's face lit up. "You're right, and if that's the case, then you have nothing to worry about, at least for now. You d-don't have to panic. You d-don't have to go."

Jan felt a modicum of relief. "Could be, could be." He welcomed Láďa's reasoning, finding it plausible, even comforting, for deep down he was torn, still hoping for a way out, for an excuse not to go. What Láďa said made sense. He'd never made a firm commitment to Daniel, so if he didn't show, he wouldn't be missed. Wouldn't be thought a quitter or a coward. Nobody could accuse him of reneging. And once *they* were gone, no one would ever know. Láďa would understand and there'd be peace at home. A crisis averted. So, why did he still feel so unsure, so sick to his stomach. So rotten?

167

That evening, as dusk fell and as she had always done, Mother walked over to the windows to pull close the heavy curtains and let out a muffled cry. "JesusMary! Tomáš! Tomáš! Come quick! Hurry! Have a look! My God! What's going on? What do you make of this?" Transfixed, she stared into the street.

Jan overheard, and was at the window two leaps ahead of his father. Blood drained from his face. Father took one look, swore under his breath and drew back. Headlights snuffed out but their engines idling, a pair of sedans sat in front of the house like two dark heaps silhouetted in the fading light. Only a thin wisp of exhaust and a glow of a cigarette hinted of someone inside. Then the motors fell silent, the doors of one of the cars swung open, and four uniformed men slithered out into the street. One of them moved quickly to hold open the door of the other sedan, and saluted as two more stocky men in bulky overcoats and wide-brimmed hats slid out. They exchanged a few words and silently moved toward the house.

"JesusMary, they're coming here!" Mother's eyes grew wide with panic. "What's going on? What have you done now?"

She glared at Father and he at her, and then they both took notice of Jan, pale and frozen to the spot. "You?" Father whispered hoarsely, beads of sweat breaking out on his forehead. "Was it you? Was there something you didn't tell us?"

Mother let out a howl. "What have you done?" She turned to Father. "JesusMary, what has he done?"

Jan stared at her, stunned. "Nothing. I swear. Nothing! I can explain."

In one swoop, Father leaped to the kitchen table, swung it to one side, and jerked aside the rug. Grabbing a kitchen knife, he slid the blade into the seam of the opening cut into the floor years ago by carpenter Hrášek and, prying feverishly, yanked until the plug gave with a groan and sprung open. "Get in! Get in!" He grabbed Jan by the arm and shoved him into the opening.

A thick tangle of spider webs enveloped Jan's head as he dropped down onto the soft soil and he brushed them off frantically. Above him, the plug fell back into place with a thud. He heard the splat of the carpet, the scraping noise of the table being slid back into place, and the shuffling of the chairs just as sharp pounding on the door sent an ominous echo through the house.

He rolled over on his back and wiped the remaining cobwebs off his face. His heart pounded. The fetid smell of stale air laced with the rancid odor of rodent droppings made him want to retch. The crawl space was pitch dark but for a single thin line—a seam that had opened between two floorboards, permitting a razor-thin shaft of light seep through. He heard the door bang open and the scraping of hobnails on the floor.

"Where is your boy?!" someone barked.

He couldn't make out his father's response, but heard Bojar growl, and his mother's wailing. The thick boards above his head muffled all sound. Only an occasional sharply spoken word filtered through, fueling his imagination magnified by fear. Heavy footsteps directly overhead sent thin streams of powdery dust down on him. He wanted to sneeze, but stifled the urge. Something crawled down his neck and under his shirt. *A spider!* He dared not swat it.

Pounding boots rushed up the stairs to where his room was. Fainter noises trickled in from the outside. Outbursts of cursing. The yelping of Bojar. Pleading voice of his father. And then the slamming of car doors, revving of engines, and finally…silence. He was drenched in sweat, but now felt a chill and began to shake, at first lightly, then uncontrollably. The wet warmth in his crotch made him realize he had soiled himself.

It seemed like hours before the plug slid open and Father's face appeared in the opening. "Come up, Son," he said sternly, offering a hand.

"I can explain," Jan croaked. "They shut down the *Spirit* and the *Slovo* editor got jailed, but I couldn't—"

Father put a finger to his lips and nodded toward Mother, collapsed in a chair, rocking gently back and forth, staring vacantly into space, sobbing softly, repeating like a mantra, "My son a criminal…my son a criminal…my son a criminal…"

"I had nothing to do with it. I can explain!" Jan's eyes filled with tears.

"Not now, Son." Father stopped him. "Not now. We'll talk later. Leave her alone."

"Who were they?"

"Who else? That bastard Paleček and his goons. Don't know the other two. Must've been from the District."

"What did you tell 'em?"

"That you were in Prague for Easter. Visiting your uncle. I don't think they believed it. You're safe for the moment, but they'll be back, I'm sure. They'll probably watch the house, too. So, why don't you get yourself cleaned up and try to get some sleep. We'll figure something out tomorrow."

"And Mother?"

She was still rocking, still sobbing, still moaning softly, "My son a criminal, my son a criminal…my son a criminal…"

"Let her be. Say nothing," Father growled. "You'll only make things worse."

Lying on his bed in the darkened room, unable to sleep, staring into the pitch-black night, his nerves on edge, listening for any telltale sound, Jan saw his decision not to join Daniel evaporate. The urgency to survive and the exigency of leaving home overwhelmed him.

CHAPTER 21

Though tired and emotionally drained, Jan slept fitfully. After he finally drifted off, he would sit up at the sound of the slightest noise, real or imagined. Heart pounding, he would listen for the rumble of motors, telltale footsteps, a knock on the door—anything that could send him scampering to the hole in the floor.

It seemed only minutes before he felt a hand on his shoulder. It startled him. He leapt out of bed with a shriek, before realizing it was his father.

"It's all right, Son," Father said softly, "it's all right, but you need to get up. It's Easter. Mass is at 8. Mother's getting ready. But I don't think you should be seen with us, they might be watching." His eyes narrowed. "I want you to stay home. Better yet, get back down under the floor while we're gone. We'll be back in a couple of hours so take a blanket or something, and stay there till we get back. You never know what *they* might do."

From the kitchen came the sounds of Mother fixing breakfast. Red-eyed and grim-faced, her brisk movements hinted at pent-up emotions. Jan greeted her, but she ignored him. He had hoped for a sign of absolution or at least a hint of reconciliation, anything, but other than briefly piercing him with an accusing look, she looked past him and went on with her chores. He would have preferred her tongue-lashing to being ignored, for while her words stung like the slashes of a whip, they lasted only moments, ending inevitably in catharsis. She might have even forgiven him. Her silences, however, could last for days, culminating in a slashing torrent of verbal reproofs only when complete capitulation brought him, or on rare occasions his father, to his knees. There was nothing worse than being shunned and vilified by her.

They ate in silence, and as he descended into the opening, her anger and sadness-laden gaze brushed over him. Was that a tear betraying her true emotions?

The plug above him slid into place and he was enveloped in darkness. Sounds of Father admonishing Bojar to stay, Bojar's whining as the door closed, and the rattle of a key in the lock were replaced by heavy, oppressive silence. He felt strangely detached, almost numb. But his mind was sharply clear and focused. In a way, he was relieved that he no longer had the luxury (or was it burden?) of choices. There was only one thing he had to do.

The clock struck 8. He had less than an hour.

He stooped under the opening, pressed his back against the plug and heaved. It gave, but just. The rug, weighed down by the table and chairs, kept it from coming loose. Summoning all his strength, he heaved again. The raw wood bit into his shoulders but he sensed it move, until finally the rug gave, forcing the table and chairs to the side just enough for the plug to pop open. Bojar, whining, greeted him with a lick and a wag as he climbed out.

He dressed quickly in his warmest winter clothes, and stuffed a rucksack with a few precious cans of meat – the last of Dick's largesse that Mother had stashed in the larder almost three years ago – as many changes of underwear as he could fit, a topographical map of Šumava, a notebook, and a small flashlight. He hesitated, but then took a fifty-*Koruna* bill from the tin on top of the dresser, feeling like a thief. It would be missed. How often he'd watch his parents count the meager take, juggling what could be bought and what would have to wait until some customer paid. How embarrassed he'd felt watching his father hide a few *Korunas* in his own secret kitty for his cigarettes.

He tried not to think of the reaction his leaving would trigger, but couldn't escape the overwhelming crush of guilt. Moreover, he was leaving without making peace with Mother— the rift between them would remain forever, the chasm never breached. He took a piece of paper and tried to write a note, begging her and Father's forgiveness, but the words seemed hollow, trite. *The less they know, the less they can tell if someone asks,* he tried to convince himself as he tore it up, knowing it was a self-serving act of cowardice.

He peered out through the crack in the curtain. The street seemed deserted and safe, but he didn't dare to take the chance. Bojar nuzzled him, whining and heading for the door in anticipation. "No, not today." Jan pushed him back gently as he closed the door behind him and stepped out into the yard, almost in a daze. The crisp air made him gasp. Caught emotionally between two irresistible forces – to stay or to go – he knew there would be no turning back, whichever he chose. He shook off the feeling that held him fast and without looking back, lest he succumbed to the pull that made him hesitate, set out across the orchard behind the house, slipped open a plank in the fence, squeezed through, and taking a roundabout way through a tangle of back streets, struck out for the railroad station. He arrived at the main street and hesitated before crossing it. His home was just visible behind the bend. And then something else caught his eye. A short distance away, not readily visible from but facing his house, sat a black Škoda, idling.

The railroad station was empty; hardly anyone traveled on Easter Sunday. The stationmaster, an old mustachioed man who knew Jan well, pushed up on the bill of his red cap and gave him a long, knowing look. "Going to Lenora for Easter, eh? Know somebody up there?"

Jan had not anticipated a question from the taciturn old man, whom he had been seeing almost daily for the past four years without ever exchanging two words with him. His mind went blank. The stationmaster's look bore into him, and then Jan saw what he thought was a twinkle in his eyes. The old man leaned closer and whispered hoarsely, "*They*'ve already been here. Good luck to you, boy."

The train, a small commuter, was on time. Except for a small group of soldiers arguing loudly in the front of one of the two coaches and a few solitary passengers, it was empty. Some of the soldiers gave Jan a cursory look as he boarded but quickly returned to their banter. He slid in a corner seat, pulled the collar over his face and, pretending to be dozing off, scanned the scene. One of the slumped figures stirred and turned toward him. It was Martin. Daniel was nowhere to be seen.

The train moved sluggishly past the grain elevator, still pockmarked with bullet holes, and the freight dock, still laden with rusting debris from three years ago to the day they were strafed by the Americans. It picked up speed, and clattered staccato-like over the tangle of switches and rails that converged into a single pair of silver ribbons stretching westward. Like a curtain drawing closed on a scene, one by one, the red roofs of Čekaná disappeared from view. Down below, he caught a glimpse of the river path where he saw Inka and the American lieutenant three years ago, and then the racing scenery dissolved into a horizontal blur, turning the window into a mirror, reflecting his ghost-like face back to him. He didn't like what he saw and averted his eyes. When he looked up again, Martin's face materialized next to his.

"I didn't think you'd come," Martin whispered, settling himself down next to him. "Daniel said you might, but since he didn't hear from you..."

"Where is he? Isn't he coming?"

"Didn't show." Martin winced. "Don't know what happened. Saw him yesterday. Everything was set. Said he'd called you. You know, they got Hofman?"

"Yeah, Daniel called. They came after me, too. Last night."

"They *did*? Then something must have happened to him. We've been lucky."

The soldiers and most of the passengers got off at Vimperk, a garrison town. Kalashnikovs at the ready, dogs at their heel, a pair of guards strolled up and down the platform, scornfully scanning the disembarking riders. Jan's chest tightened. He didn't figure on patrols. "Guards," he scowled and nudged Martin.

Martin cringed.

The train began a slow laborious climb up the steep flanks of the mountains, still snow-bound on the shaded slopes, but turning raw brown and muted green where the sunlight could reach them. Streams, heavy with snowmelt, cascaded precociously down the ravines. The pale rays of the sun did nothing to soften the bite of the frigid air.

"Lenora, last stop. Lenora," the conductor cried out in a singsong voice, and disappeared in the service compartment.

The train approached a switching station and slowed to a crawl. Just ahead, a red semaphore light glowed like an enormous unblinking eye. Another train, full of soldiers heading in the opposite direction, awaited their arrival on a siding. Further down loomed the brown dilapidated hulk of the Lenora station, seemingly deserted, except for a pair of sentries with dogs at their heels, surveying the scene with wearisome detachment.

Jan met Martin's telling look. Deliberately, so as not to arouse suspicion, they strolled out on the boarding platform between the two coaches, gave a quick look, hesitated for a moment, and jumped.

The thick growth of bramble and stunted evergreens quickly swallowed them, tearing at their skin. Jan buried his face in the wet green cushion of mosses and leaves, trying in vain to keep his teeth from chattering. *What if the guards or someone saw them?* He flattened himself against the raw ground, stomach in knots. Next to him, Martin clawed at the sodden ground as though trying to bury himself in it. Behind them, among the hissing and clanging, the troop train began to move. If anything were to happen, it would be now!

Shaking from the cold and fear, they lay like that for minutes that seemed like hours, listening for telltale sounds, footsteps and shouts, steeling themselves for the worst. It did not come, and they were overcome by the nausea of release. Behind them, the train full of soldiers moved out and their train left the station. The platform was empty. The guards gone.

Sticking to the cover of the forest, they slowly climbed up the steep slope. Deep shadows still held the remnants of last winter's snowdrifts, and the raw earth smelled of rotting leaves. Avoiding open spaces, they paused frequently, listening for anything out of the ordinary, but all they heard was the rustling of the trees and gurgling of melt water. Below them lay

Lenora—a scattering of chalets dotting the slopes that hemmed in the railroad station, a weathered log-and-shingle church, and a narrow lichen-covered wooden bridge over the Vltava. Most of the chalets were empty, abandoned when the Czechs drove their German tenants out of the Republic at war's end. It was easy to spot the ones occupied by soldiers.

Nearing the crest of the steep hill, they broke into a clearing and quickly drew back as a massive chalet came into view practically on top of them. Its typical high-pitched moss-covered roof almost touched the ground to ward off the heavy snows of winter. The small shuttered windows looked down on empty flower boxes that once almost certainly had overflowed with geraniums. The walls, holding up the ornamentally carved eave, were thick and solid. It seemed deserted.

They lay silently under the cover of low-slung branches, gazing at it, watching for signs of life. There were none.

The door, hanging by a single hinge gave an unpleasant squeal when they forced it aside and crossed the threshold. The inside was bare. The wooden floors creaked in places where the planking had come loose. The whitewashed walls, decorated with flowery motifs, were smeared with graffiti—obscenities and names of soldiers who had passed through. The few sticks of furniture that had escaped looting lay smashed next to an old iron stove where someone had used them for firewood. The faint smell of burned wood mixed with a much stronger putrid odor of body wastes permeated the air. Jan touched the stove. It was warm.

"Someone's been here." He nudged Martin and looked around in earnest.

Martin touched the stove, drew back, and they both held their breaths, listening.

A faint, barely audible scraping sound from somewhere above made Jan flinch. "Did you hear that?" he turned to Martin.

"There. There's a door. In the corner," Martin whispered, pointing to a small trap door barely visible among the roughly hewn blackened boards and beams of the ceiling. It was closed. And then, in the shaft of sunlight pouring in through the windows, a faint flicker of tiny flakes of gold—dust particles colored by the streaming sun – trickled down through the cracks in the boards. "Someone's up there," he hissed.

They froze, staring at the shimmering flakes.

"What do you think?" Jan's palms began to sweat.

Martin shrugged.

Jan picked up a board and rapped hard on the ceiling.

The scraping stopped, and moments later, resumed. Louder now, too loud to be an animal.

Jan followed with his eyes as the sound moved toward the trap door.

Terrified, they scrambled to the door ready to bolt.

The trap door sprung open and someone shouted down, "Don't worry, I won't shoot." A ladder slid down with a thud, and then a foot – a bare foot – groping for the rungs, then the other, and finally the rest of the lanky figure, a soldier, not much older than they, sallow-faced, blue-eyed, reddish-brown hair protruding from under a flight cap, wearing a soiled Czech Air Force sergeant's uniform, holding a pair of sneakers in one hand and a pistol in the other. "I won't shoot, don't worry!"

Jan and Martin stared at him, slack-jawed.

"Tonda Suk. Saw you come up from up there." He nodded toward the ceiling. "Been there since last night because of the patrols." He smiled, noticing Jan's stare at his sneakers. "Didn't even have time to put on my shoes when they came after me. Had to run barefoot. Got scraped. Finally stole a pair of tennis shoes. Bastards! Almost got me. I came this close." Wincing, he measured the air with his thumb and index finger. "Didn't figure they'd be that fast. Got soaked climbing up here. Shoes, socks, everything's wet. Built a little fire last night to dry them. Gawd, my feet hurt!" He sighed.

"How come they were after you? Jan asked.

"You ever heard of Panák? Captain Panák?"

"Panák? You mean the ace? The one on the postage stamp?"

"The same." Tonda nodded. "Served together in Budweis. I was his mechanic. Helped him get out. Escape."

Jan looked at him in awe.

"Naturally, you didn't see it in the papers or hear anything on the radio. They wouldn't admit to anything like that. But last week he took a Spitfire and flew it into the American Zone. I and a couple of other fellows got the plane ready for him. You know, they're jailing all the 'Spit' pilots. He was sure he'd be next, so he decided not to wait."

"I've heard there was a legion forming in the American Zone. Do you suppose?"

"Yeah, I heard it too." Tonda shrugged. "I don't know."

"So how'd they find out about you?" Jan said, staring at Tonda's bloodied feet.

"Somebody talked."

CHAPTER 22

Darkness fell, and the valley below became a void, with only a few solitary points of light revealing the presence of life as Jan, Martin, and Tonda filed out. They had ceremoniously added their names to those covering the walls of the chalet with a stick of charcoal from the stove, and, shielding the flashlight beam with their coats, for the last time huddled over the map, fixing in their minds the layout of the terrain. A sliver of a moon, barely visible through the treetops, cast muted shadows over the landscape. The stars shone with piercing brightness.

The going was arduous from the start. Bringing up the rear, all Jan could see of his friends were two opaque forms moving in concert, occasionally outlined in wispy clouds of exhaled breath, stumbling over the uneven terrain, stopping now and then to listen for sounds of danger. The biting cold made him wish for the comforts and security of home, his bed, the warmth of the crackling fire in the stove, his parents. The thoughts filled him with guilt.

The deep forest covering the steep flank of the mountain swallowed them, obscuring the moon. Thick canopy of evergreens made it difficult for their eyes to adjust to the softer indigo of the sky and the inky darkness at their feet. Driven by fear and anticipation, they stumbled on like robots, bumping into trees, tripping over rocks, too numb to feel the pain from cuts and scrapes. The frigid air pricked Jan's face, turning his breath into buildups of frost on his upturned collar. How he regretted forgetting to bring a pair of gloves.

The ground rose sharply, in places vertically, as they reached the summit. All around, the occasional blotches of snow became a solid icy mass, glistening faintly in the moon glow. Throwing caution to the wind, they scrambled up hand over foot, slipping and sliding, emboldened by the prospect of success.

Trees at the summit were sparse—stalwart survivors of high winds and bitter cold. Twisted into bizarre shapes, they resembled a lamenting gathering of ghosts, raising their skeletal arms skyward in silent protest. Remnants of mammoth-sized snowdrifts covered the rocky outcrops and crevasses. There was no wind—the stillness was perfect. Somewhere below them, a faint sound of gurgling water spoke of a stream flowing out of the melting snow mass.

Exhausted and out of breath, they collapsed on an upturned tree and exchanged smiles.

Tonda peered into the darkness, rubbing his feet. "Should be all downhill from here," he said.

Behind them, far below in the distance, a few points of light betrayed the presence of Lenora—another world. To the west, an inky abyss beckoned—Germany.

With Jan cupping his flashlight, they huddled under the coat and rechecked the map. Tonda's finger stopped at a symbol straddling a purple line. "That's the border. All we have to do is follow the water." He reached into his rucksack and pulled out a paper sack. "Here, put some of this in your pockets."

"Smells like pepper." Martin smelled it and sneezed.

"That's what it is. Ground pepper. A little insurance. Got if from my buddy in the Quartermaster. Almost a kilo. I heard they've got dogs, so sprinkle it behind you as you go."

From ahead to their right came the gurgling of the stream. To the left lay a sea of boulders—the remains of some primordial upheaval. Directly ahead, straddling the crown of the ridge, a barely visible path wound through patches of dirty snow into the darkness. Jan noticed a few faint footprints. *Someone like us.* The thought of kinship warmed him.

"Goddammit!" Tonda swore under his breath as he took a bad tumble that sent him sprawling. "Hey, what the— What *is* this?" He held up a thin black wire, stretching taut as he lifted it.

Jan fished the flashlight from his pocket, cupped the beam, and carefully followed the wire into the darkness. Stretched just a few inches above ground, supported lightly in places by twigs to keep it at just the right height, it crossed their path at a right angle and disappeared somewhere down the slope.

"Shit! Do you know what this is?" He threw it down as though it were a snake. "A trip line. A fuckin' trip line! And we just tripped it. Those bastards! Put out that light!"

Jan quickly snuffed the flashlight. "What do you mean a trip line?"

Tonda didn't have to answer. Down below the boulder field and slightly to their rear, a bright harsh light exploded in the darkness and immediately began sweeping the boulders, the steep flank, and what appeared to be a narrow road the map didn't show. Barking of dogs and excited voices shattered the silence. An engine sputtered to life. Muffled shouts. Voices. Meshing of gears. Dogs baying. A second beam of light swept the forest from atop the vehicle as it gathered speed along the road.

They ran. Behind them, the light seemed to follow them. Like in an echo chamber, the barking of dogs came at them from all directions.

"The pepper! Use the fuckin' pepper!" Tonda screamed, tossing out handfuls of the powdery stuff.

The beam of the searchlight traced a path along the ridge and brushed them.

"Down!" Tonda barked, and dove headlong behind a clump of bushes. Too late. The light swung back jerkily and stopped, turning night into day all around them. Everything was still. And then, like tongues of fire, muzzle flashes sparked in the darkness as a volley of shots rang out, resounding among the trees in a cacophony of echoes. The zing and splat of the bullets hit all around them.

"The gulley!" Tonda screamed, scooting backward on his stomach down the embankment toward the gurgling stream.

Jan and Martin tore after him, sliding down on their backsides. Above them, the ridge, outlined in a silvery halo by the searchlight, stretched like a spine of a great elongated beast. Down here, among the boulders, they felt safe in the darkness of the gully. But not for long. Out of nowhere, two soldiers appeared on top of the ridge, silhouetted sharply in the glare of the light. With Kalashnikovs at the ready and flashlights sweeping the forest, they moved cautiously in their direction. Between them, a barking dog strained at his leash. One of them made a move. The dog quit barking and was gone.

Tonda swore and thrust the bag of pepper at them. "Grab a handful of this, and if he gets here, let him have it. Aim for the head." He barked at Jan, "Get your flashlight. We'll need to see him."

Clutching the flashlight in one hand and a fistful of pepper in the other, Jan half-hid behind a tree. His heart thumped like a drum. He felt no fear, only a kind of detached tension. Time slowed to a crawl. Every action became crystal-clear. All his faculties were focused on a single thing—the pressing of a switch and tossing a fistful of pepper.

The crashing of the dog got closer in the darkness. Then it was there.

"The light!" Tonda screamed.

Faced with three targets, the dog pulled up short. Jan tripped the switch and it lunged at the light—at him. The next moments were a blur. The dog flying through the air. Everyone tossing pepper at him. Being knocked down. The flashlight flying out of his hand. Tonda firing three quick shots point-blank into the dog.

"You all right?" Tonda extended his hand to help Jan to his feet. "Got to get out of here. They know where we are. C'mon, run! Run!"

They crashed through a tunnel of low-slung branches. A gauntlet of ghostly arms and spidery fingers clawed at their skin and tore their clothes. From the slope above them, the flashlight beams swung in their direction. A volley of shots sent a spray of bullets to where Jan's flashlight lay among the boulders.

Treacherous, slippery, and strewn with rocks and boulders, the stream was barely visible in the darkness. The icy water shocked them as they jumped in and ran for their lives.

The stream widened as the dense growth gave way to a clearing. In the center, overgrown with moss and lichen, a massive stone marker thrust its obeliscal shape skyward. The border! A newly bulldozed road skirted the spot.

Stumbling out of the water, out of breath and lungs on fire, Jan raced for the marker. Next to him, Martin let out a series of retching sounds. Tonda, a few steps ahead, face twisted with exertion, turned to urge them on just as a truck, full of soldiers, emerged from around the bend. The spotlight swung in their direction, trapping them in its beam. Desperate, driven by a chorus of shouts and cries of "Halt! Halt!" they plunged into the thick growth on the other side of the border. Volleys of shots rung out. Bullets tore into the branches all around, zinging over their heads. They ran, recklessly now.

It was not until they halted before a large farmhouse looming dark against the moonlit sky that they realized the shooting, the voices, and the barking of dogs had ceased. They stared at each other, cold, wet, bleeding from cuts and bruises, breathing wheezily. They'd made it!

A light came on in the farmhouse, and a dog barked when they approached. They froze. The door creaked open, and a burly man, holding an oil lamp over his head, cautiously stepped out. *"Wer gehts darin? –* Who goes there?" he called out, peering into the darkness.

Hesitantly, they entered the flickering circle of light. The dog's barking increased.

"Wer gehts darin? Wer sind sie? Was wollen sie? Who goes there? Who are you?" The man peered at them, and then with a sigh of recognition, let out a short, chortling laugh. *"Ach, noch einmal die Tchechen, die furflügtene Tchechen!"*

For the first time in his life, Jan was glad he had learned German, mandatory at the Gymnásium under the occupation. Now it came in handy. "He says he's seen other Czechs," he translated for Tonda. "He's seen this before."

The man sharply admonished the dog and motioned them inside.

They filed into a great room, dominated by a huge black stone cube abutted against two walls—an oven that provided heat for the entire house. The top, the warmest place and large enough to accommodate the entire family, was where they slept: a bony, sallow-faced middle-aged bleary-eyed woman, clutching a shawl modestly over her torso, peered at them over the edge; a pair of half-naked children, rubbing their eyes, gawked at them with unabashed curiosity.

The whitewashed walls of the room were spotless. In one corner, under an ornately carved crucifix, a flickering votive candle cast a light on a collection of family photos and of the man as a soldier. A picture of Adolf Hitler adorned one side of the crucifix. On the other, a swastika flag hung suspended from a pair of nails. A military decoration – an Iron Cross – dangled from one of the nails; a small, fancy dirk of an SS officer, from the other.

The German motioned them to a long rough-hewn bench next to the table. *"Bitte, setzen sie. Es ist zu spät. Sie müssen bis Morgen warten."*

"Says, it's late. We'll have to wait till the morning," Jan translated for Tonda, taking off his rucksack.

The woman climbed down from the oven, poured some warm water into a tin basin, and without taking her gaze off them, gestured them to use it.

The German scrutinized them as they washed the blood and mud off their faces and hands, and wrung out their wet clothes. *"Sie sind ganz glücklich gewesen,"* he mumbled under his breath. "You were lucky…"

The woman reappeared with a half-loaf of black bread, laid it on the table, and retreated to the stove, where she sat and glared at them. "Don't have anything to offer you except bread," the German apologized, gesticulating with his hands as he sliced off a few thin morsels.

Jan's chest tightened as a wave of relief and gratitude washed over him. He unsnapped his rucksack, pulled out the three cans of meat he had taken from his mother's larder, and laid them on the table. "*Bitte*," he motioned to the cans and smiled.

Stone-faced, the German stared at him through half-closed eyes, and then hesitantly returned his smile, slit the cans open, nodded to the wife and the children, and they all ate, forgetting, at least for the moment, the differences that had once made them enemies.

CHAPTER 23

The dog barked and Jan woke up with a start. Outside, an engine sputtered to a halt. Footsteps on the icy ground. Voices. Someone slipping and letting out an oath. For a few moments Jan lay disoriented, before realizing where he was and what was happening.

The door swung open and the German walked in, trailed by two men. Wearing rumpled civilian clothes under green army-style parkas, their closely cropped hair and crisp demeanor left no doubt as to who they were: Americans.

"Hier, wieder noch drei." The German nodded toward the trio, now on their feet.

The Americans sized them up in one quick look. "We're the CIC," one of them said in a thickly accented Czech. You must come with us immediately. Please get your things and let's go, okay? Let's go. Right now."

A jeep with a white star emblazoned on its hood, covered with grime and frozen mud, waited outside. The Czech-speaking American held open the canvass flap as they squeezed into the tight space in the back of the jeep, zippered closed the opening, lit a cigarette, and slid behind the wheel.

No one spoke during the short, bumpy ride. They reached a town, or what was left of it, reduced, for the most part to piles of brick and rubble. A sign, bearing a single word, *Freyung,* virtually obliterated by bullets from its tiled face, flew by as they turned toward the square and skidded to a halt before a relatively undamaged two-story house. An American flag hung limply above the entrance.

"Follow me. Bring everything," the Czech-speaking American ordered and led them into a room, bare except for a desk and a few chairs. He offered them a cigarette, shrugged when they declined, lit one himself, and collapsed into a padded chair next to the desk. "I will translate for you," he said, blowing a thin stream of smoke in their direction.

"Take everything out of your rucksacks and pockets, and lay it on the table," the interrogator, an older, stockily built, ruddy-faced, mustachioed man ordered in a tone that conveyed neither kindness nor dislike. His eyebrows rose when he saw the pistol. He reached for it, sniffed it once or twice, and examined it closely. "That yours?" he turned to Tonda. Tonda nodded. "Not anymore." Chuckling, he slipped it in his pocket. He sorted through the small pile of their possessions with the blunt end of his pencil and came up with Jan's pocketknife. He opened it, tested the blade with his thumb, closed it, fingered the raised inscription, and studied Jan through the slits of his eyes. "You a Jew?"

"No, Sir," Jan croaked. "Got it from my Jewish friend. Died in a concentration camp." He was sure the man would take it, but he grunted twice and tossed it back on the table.

The interrogation lasted most of the day, mainly because of the ineptness of the translator. The CIC man methodically wrote down everything they said, often asking the same question more than once. In the end, he confiscated their compass and map, and when Tonda surprised him with a question about Captain Panák and the Czech legion, answered with an annoyed look and stalked out of the room.

* * *

190

The jeep's mesmerizing whine and the freezing air whistling in the ill-fitting zippered seams of the canvas top made conversation impossible. Jan's senses were dulled. Still tired, but mentally deflated the way one finds himself after a sudden release of tension, his feeling of loss was smothered by a sense of inevitability and resignation. His misgivings were crushed. Home seemed only an abstraction. Next to him Tonda and Martin rocked drowsily with the motion of the jeep, self-absorbed, seemingly lost in thought.

They reached Regensburg just before dark, and saw that the seemingly undamaged city's real wounds lay beneath the surface, behind the crumbling façades, under the piles of bricks and trash swarming with silent, shabbily clad Germans scavenging through the rubble, oblivious to the honking of horns and rush of military traffic.

The jeep came to a halt in front of a well-preserved building bearing a crisply incised inscription, *Göthe Schule.* An improvised sign on the ornate iron gate read, *Sammlung Lager.* "Just a holding camp. Shouldn't be here more than a few days," the translator reassured them as he led them inside, past a long line of people greeting them with curious looks. A few smiled and waved.

A German in a faded Wehrmacht officer's uniform, discolored except where the insignia and rank had protected the fabric from fade and wear, met them at the door and gestured to the shrinking line of people shuffling toward a table piled with cubes of black bread. A steaming drum perched over a hissing gasoline field stove stood nearby. A pair of uniformed Germans dispensed the food. *"Sie haben noch Zeit...gehen Sie zu Essen,"* the German said.

"He says we can still eat," Jan translated.

"I see you met Herr Oberst," someone behind them spoke softly.

The voice belonged to a middle-aged gray-haired woman, clutching three empty tin cans.

"Forgive me for intruding," she said, "but I noticed you're new. Probably hungry. I know we were when we got here. You'll need these if you want to eat. They don't provide any dishes here. You can borrow them for now, but tomorrow you'll have to get your own. They're hard to come by. The Germans snap them up as soon as the Americans throw them away." She smiled. "My name is Olga Beranová. I'm here with my husband. We're from Prague."

They thanked her and introduced themselves.

Her face clouded. "We call him Herr Oberst," she nodded toward the German, "because that's what he wants to be called. That was his military rank—Colonel. Don't really know his name. Don't care. And why they put him in charge is beyond me. It's not right! It's demeaning to be ordered around by the Germans. Especially him. Look at him! Makes you feel like they're the ones that won the war. This is supposed to be an American camp but you won't see any of them here. They let the Germans run everything. It's not right." She sighed. "Just look how they look at us. How they treat us. It's a shame!"

"Been here long?" Jan asked.

"Five days."

They reached the hissing stove. Smirking, one of the Germans splashed a ladleful of thin colorless gruel into Jan's tin and the other thrust a bite-size cube of black bread into his hand.

"They call it *Eintopf*, and it's awful. We ate like kings during the war, compared to this," Olga lamented. "It's been the same every day—*Eintopf* and bread. Bread and *Eintopf*. *Eintopf* and bread."

Jan looked suspiciously at the greasy liquid. "Hard to tell what's in it."

"Not much more than salty water with a few sticks of vegetables—beets mostly, a few potatoes, heavy grease. They throw everything in the pot. Never clean it. Just keep adding water and whatever. It's not that the Americans don't give them plenty of decent foodstuffs and things, but they steal it. Steal everything. Steal it and sell it." She sighed. "Never thought I'd be eating such awful stuff from a tin can scavenged on a garbage pile. Not even during the war. But one has to survive."

The gruel was hot and the cans burned their hands.

"There aren't any spoons." Olga frowned, watching Tonda pass the hot can from one hand to the other and then lick his finger where he'd scalded it. "We made ours out of wood. Pavel – that's my husband – made them with his pocket knife. He'll let you borrow it if you need to. I'm sure the Americans gave 'em *some* silverware, but..." She shook her head in dismay.

What Olga Beranová called the trash pile was a vacant lot, not far from the camp. Several times a day, American army trucks would arrive and dump trash. No sooner would the garbage hit the ground that throngs of waiting Germans would descend upon it like vultures, stuffing huge shopping bags with whatever they could snatch. Sporadic arguments and even fist fights would erupt during the dump. In a matter of minutes, everything would be gone.

Pushing and shoving, they each managed to grab a can, along with a scrap of wood from a crate, and using Jan's pocketknife, fashioned crude spoons.

"Never thought it'd be this bad." Martin sighed.

"Beats jail," Tonda admonished him.

Olga introduced them to her husband Pavel. "We weren't really political," she said. "He was just a professor at Charles University. Taught History. But they came after him anyway—anybody who wasn't one of them. Who wasn't a communist." She looked away and her eyes flooded. "Oh, it was so terrible!"

In the coming days, the population of the *Göthe Schule Sammlung Lager* swelled to overflowing. The new arrivals told horror stories and brought sparse and confusing news. Rumors abounded. Nights resonated with the snoring of men and crying of children. Fully expecting to see Daniel, Jan and Martin searched incoming contingent for his familiar face, but to no avail.

Herr Oberst's answer to the continuing influx was to add more water to the *Eintopf* and make the cubes of bread smaller. For the first time in his life Jan felt hunger—not just the pangs and stomach cramps he'd known during the war, but a constant gnawing at his gut that gradually took over his mind to the exclusion of everything but food. He even dreamt about it. The watery gruel didn't satisfy, passing through his body in bouts of cramps and diarrhea. The only food of substance – bread – was gone in a single swallow. The thought of the canned meat he had shared with the Germans at the border made him wince with regret.

"The professor's wife says that people are selling things on the black market to get food," Jan said, watching people come and go. "I have fifty crowns, but she says it's worthless over here. They want dollars or something of value."

"I don't have a thing." Tonda shrugged, turning his pockets inside out.

Martin took off his shoe, lifted the insole, and fished out two American dollars. Tonda and Jan watched in astonishment.

"Bet this place never sleeps," Tonda said as they entered the cobblestone plaza surrounding the cathedral in the old part of town. Hawkers, barterers, whores, and pickpockets mingled with the crowd. Lining the side streets, tiny cardboard and trash-wood cubicles displayed a variety of goods—shabby clothing, furniture, war memorabilia, cigarettes, olive-green wax-covered K and C rations, even a few American tins of foodstuffs.

With a heavy heart and a pang of guilt, Jan traded his watch, a graduation gift from Father, for a ration coupon worth two loaves of bread. Martin's two dollars paid for the bread at a nearby bakery. They found a quiet corner in a nearby park and gorged themselves on the still-warm loaves. When they returned to the camp, they saw that someone had stolen the cans they had left on a windowsill next to their bunks.

"Just look at those fools," the professor cried out, glaring at a small straggling knot of Czechs walking grimly out of the camp, lugging their suitcases, women clutching their children.

Olga's eyes misted. "Pavel dear, don't be so hard on them." She took his hand. "With children and all, I don't know what I'd do in their situation. I feel sorry for them."

"I still say they're fools. They've risked so much. Made it so far. They're *here*, for chrissakes!" The professor's lined face turned red and he had to pause for breath. "Forgive me, but I get a bit emotional," he apologized, taking note of Jan.

Jan shrugged. "What's going on?"

"They're going back. Can't take it. Cowards!"

"But why? Why would they go back?"

"Mostly because of the children, I suppose. Still—"

"You can't blame them, Dear." Olga put her hand gently on his shoulder. "Just look at us. Here we are, living worse than gypsies, eating swill that we wouldn't have fed our pigs, out of rusty cans picked up in a garbage dump. We're alone and coping, but what if we had children? What if we couldn't feed them?"

"I understand. I really understand." The professor's brow furrowed as he shook his head in dismay. "But do you think, just like that," he snapped his fingers, "they can go back? After what they've done? Hah! They'll use them for propaganda and then they'll throw them in jail, or worse. Damned fools. If only they could have waited just a little longer. Few more days."

Jan couldn't take his gaze off the bedraggled group. "But will the Americans let them go?"

"The Americans don't care." The professor threw his hands up.

"But it's fifty, sixty kilometers to the border."

"They'll take a train, I suppose," the professor replied angrily. "I hear some are still running. A train to some place near the border, and then..." He shook his head and looked away.

Overwhelmed by admiration and sorrow, Jan watched the small band of Czechs turn the corner and set out toward the railroad station. Something inside him moved—a longing, a pang of remorse, even a smidgen of envy. How he missed home. The professor's harsh judgment saddened him. It took at least as much courage, if not more, to go back, to sacrifice their lives for the good of their children, to return to a nightmare that most assuredly awaited them.

CHAPTER 24

"Get up, boys." The professor flung himself into the room. His voice trembled with excitement. "The gods have smiled at us, boys. We're leaving! We're finally leaving!"

All around them, rushing footsteps, doors slamming, and excited voices mingled with Herr Oberst's and his minions' guttural shouts, as they poked their heads into the rooms, shouting at the top of their lungs, "*Schnell! Schnell! Machen Sie schnell! Sie ziehen heute aus. Machen Sie schnell!*"

"What's going on?" Tonda sat up, still groggy. "What's the bastard yelling about?"

"We're leaving!" Jan cried and began to dress. "C'mon!"

"Leaving? Where? Did he say, where?" Tonda skipped around on one leg, pulling on his trousers.

"He wouldn't say," the professor bawled, "and I don't care. An American camp, I hope. We're getting out of this hell hole, boys! Make haste!" He danced out of the room.

A line of American trucks idled alongside the curb. The drivers – all Germans – stood by lethargically, smoking cigarettes, casting scornful looks at the lines of Czechs forming at the rear of each vehicle. The orderlies thrust a pair of C-Rations into each one's hands. Others pinned yellow tags to their clothing. Smiling toothily, Herr Oberst took the final count before permitting them to board. A short ride deposited them at a row of shabby rail coaches, still bearing the *Deutsche Reichsbahn* banner with the eagle and swastika hastily painted over, waiting on a siding, away from the main Regensburg station.

The mesmerizing staccato of the rails opened a floodgate of memories, making Jan melancholy. Next to him, Tonda and Martin slept fitfully. Tonda snored. Outside, the countryside slid by, changing off and on from pristine purity to scenes of devastation: Munich, Augsburg, Ulm—once proud, now largely reduced to rectangular heaps of rubble, swarmed over by ant-like chains of Kafkaesque human beings silently passing bricks and stones to one another, robot-like, stacking them into neat piles.

At long last, as dusk began to turn everything to gray, the train came to a halt in a shabby, nondescript town nestled under a steep sugarloaf of a hill. A long line of army buses awaited them just outside the deserted station.

Tonda pressed his head against the window and stiffened. He rubbed his eyes with the back of his hand, looked out again, and let out a breathless oath.

"See something?" Jan slid beside him and peered out.

Milling about the busses and cordoning the train were soldiers, but not American soldiers. Everything about them was black—their crisply ironed American-style uniforms, their belts, their shoes, even their helmets, except for a red and white band each man wore on his left sleeve. There was no mistaking them—their facial features and stocky, squatty appearance clearly gave them away as Slavs.

Tonda's face lit up and he babbled something, barely able to contain himself.

Jan nudged him. "What did you say?"

Tonda was in a trance. "I can't believe it. The legion! This is it! Can't you see? The legion," he whispered breathlessly. "The fuckin' legion!"

The door swung open and a soldier walked in smartly. *"Prosze pani,"* he commanded, pushing the door open and indicating with his hands for them to hurry. *"Prosze pani."*

"What? What's he saying?" Jan's mouth fell open. "That's not Czech!"

Tonda flushed. Grimacing, he threw down his rucksack and swore. "That's Polish! I should've known! The ribbon. Red and white. That's Polish. They're fuckin' Pollacks!"

A squad of black-uniformed guards waved them on as they slowly passed through a bullet-spattered gate still incongruously displaying at its top an elaborate *Waffen SS - Panzerbrigade* wrought-iron sign, and under it, in smaller letters, *"Wasseralfingen."* Rows upon rows of low wooden barracks lined the streets teeming with shabbily dressed swarms of people – mostly men – milling about seemingly without purpose. Thin columns of smoke drifted skyward from a forest of stovepipe chimneys, enveloping everything in bluish haze.

The buses came to a halt on a grassy sports field in the center of the camp, ringed by a crowd of curious onlookers. The guards checked off the new arrivals' names as they tumbled out, stiffly, stretching their limbs and contorting their bodies to shake off the effects of the long ride. A cluster of stucco-covered buildings surrounded by coils of barbed wire formed one side of the perimeter, with just a narrow opening, barred by a cantilevered beam, permitting entry. A pair of American MPs hovered at the entrance. An American flag, faintly illuminated by a single spotlight, hung limply from a flagpole.

A shaft of light shot into the falling darkness as a door of the closest building flew open, disgorging a group of Americans. With a pop, the overhead lights came on. The MPs snapped to attention and saluted smartly as a major, trailed by a small group of aides, strode onto the field. Strutting stiffly, a large pistol swinging from the belt of his jodhpurs, swooshing a riding crop rhythmically against his thigh with each step, and surveying the scene through a pair of yellow aviator glasses perched high on his nose, he cut an imposing figure.

He glared silently at the Czechs and nodded to one of the guards.

The guard stepped forward and cleared his throat. *"Prosze pani, mowi pani po angielsku?"* he called out. He scanned the crowd, and when no one responded, tried again. Finally, sputtering in frustration, he bellowed, "You speak English?"

A hesitant hand went up and a familiar voice answered. "I speak a little English." It was the professor.

"Prosze pana." The guard motioned him to come closer. *"Prosze."*

The major acknowledged the professor's bow by touching the brim of his hat with the crop. "I want you to translate," he snapped. "Can you do it?"

"I think so." The professor shifted uncomfortably. "Please, you must speak slowly."

The major gave him a thin smile. "Tell 'em this: I am Major Palletti. Pa-let-ti. United States Army. Go ahead; tell 'em!"

The professor translated.

"Tell 'em, I'm the commanding officer of this camp. As refugees you have no citizenship status. No rights." He stabbed the air with his crop for emphasis. "You will be issued German identification cards, but you will be under the authority of the U.S. Army." He paused, making sure that the words sank in, as the professor translated.

"You already met my assistants, the Polish patriots." He made a vague motion toward the men in black uniforms. "Their orders are my orders. You are to obey them at all times. Do you understand?" He took the crowd's silence for an answer, and glanced at his watch. "The mess hall will remain open for another thirty minutes if you wish to eat, so I will not keep you. My assistants will direct you." He dismissed the professor with a nod of his head and a flip of his crop, spun on his heels, and briskly retired into the compound.

"These are Anders' men," the professor said, easing himself behind the long mess table.

"Anders? The Poles?" Jan perked up. "I remember hearing the name when we listened to the BBC during the war."

The professor nodded. "The same. Been here three years. Since the war. Three years! Imagine!"

"My God, three years!" Olga looked at him darkly. "How did you find out?"

"I asked one of them." The professor smiled.

"Who's this Anders?" Tonda looked up from a steaming mound of macaroni.

"Ah, I knew you would ask." The professor smiled. "A general. Polish general." He reflected for a moment. "Fought the Russians during the First World War, and both, the Germans and the Russians again during the Second, in 1940, when they attacked Poland. The Russians captured him and jailed him. Sent his troops to gulags in Siberia. But later, when Hitler attacked Russia and Stalin joined our side, he found himself on the side of the Allies and the Russians had to let him go. Let' em all go. So, Anders gathered his men and organized a Polish brigade. Naturally, there was bad blood between the Poles and

202

the Russians because of all that, so the Russians released him to the British to get rid of him. Fought in Africa. Italy. Monte Cassino. A big hero. But they never let him, never let *them* return to Poland. You remember Yalta. Churchill, Roosevelt, Stalin. Let the Russians take over Poland. So here they rot. Except Anders. He's in England. The English took him. But not his men."

"And they've been here three years. Three fuckin' years! Like this! Just waiting!" Tonda swallowed hard. "Do you know what that means?"

They all looked at him silently.

"Can't you see?" he said hoarsely. "They rot—we rot. There isn't any Czech legion. There never was any Czech legion. There isn't *ever* going to be any fuckin' legion."

Stacked three-high, wooden bunks filled the graffiti-covered bay of the single-story barrack. The rungs of the ladders leading up to the top tiers were worn smooth from years of use. The inside was damp and cold. Someone started a fire in the two rusting potbelly stoves on either end of the building and the cavernous room soon filled with the acrid odor of smoke. Too tired to care, without even bothering to undress, Jan collapsed on a soiled mattress reeking of disinfectant, pulled a thin musty-smelling blanket over his head, and slept.

* * *

From atop his bunk, shivering under a thin blanket, Jan watched the professor, Tonda, and Martin busy themselves with a game of cards to while away the time. Pelting the roof, heavy rain tapped out drum rolls of watery plops, turning the streets into a quagmire. Whistling plaintively, the wind sent narrow but piercing jets of cold air into the cavernous room through tiny crevices around the ill-fitting windows. The acrid smell of burnt firewood mixed freely with heavy odor of stale air, cigarette smoke, and humanity.

"Do you know who really runs this fuckin' camp?" Tonda slammed down his cards on the table. "Not the Americans. Not the fuckin' major. The fuckin' Poles."

"I'm afraid, you're right." The professor sighed and laid down his cards. "I tried to talk to the major yesterday, since I am supposed to be a spokesman," he rolled his eyes, "but he brushed me off."

"Did you ask him about us?" Martin inquired. "What's going to happen to us? America?"

"Yes," the professor sighed, "and he laughed in my face. 'Everybody wants to go to America,' he said. Said, it wasn't up to him, that he had other things to worry about. Said to talk to his Polish assistant and not bother him with trivial things."

"That sonofabitch!" Tonda sneered. "And did you ask this as-sis-tant about the food?"

"He wouldn't discuss it." The professor shrugged.

"Those bastards! They're as bad as the Germans." Tonda fumed. "You saw all the American stuff in town, on the black market. All the food. Probably *our* food. With the Poles in charge of the mess halls and warehouses, it doesn't take much imagination to see how it got there."

"But, to change the subject," the professor broke in, "there's one thing that bothers me even more." His brow furrowed. "You know, here, besides the Poles, there also are the Vlasov men. A few hundred of 'em. You remember Vlasov, don't you? The Russian general. Joined the Germans. Turned against them in Prague? And then, there are a few more hundred Ukrainians. Bandera people. Partisans. Sided first with the Germans against the Russians, and now the Russians are after them. These two hate each other. Always have. It's in their blood. The Poles hate'em both. And now the Czechs are added to the mix. Remember what the Poles did to us when the Germans invaded? How they stole some of our land, like vultures? This place is a tinderbox. I wouldn't be surprised if one day..." He looked away and shook his head.

The climb to the top of the sugarloaf hill – an immense slagheap, Jan discovered, as Wasseralfingen had been a mining town long before the war – was hard and he had to pause to catch his breath. Full of ruts and gouges from years of footsteps and runoffs that carried away the thin layer of soil, the path made the going difficult. In a way, it reminded him of home— of the countless times he had climbed a similar path with Jakub at his side, the goats in tow, to the overlook that was their private world, a perch providing an unobstructed view of their valley and their town, its red-tiled roofs so familiar, so secure, so reassuring. He missed Jakub, missed it all. It all seemed so remote now, so distant. So surreal. He traced the pale zigzag line of the path snaking down the precipitous slope, drawing the eye to a sprawling scar upon the otherwise unsullied landscape—the camp. Reality!

He wanted to be alone, to think, to find a solitary place where he could give vent to his emotions. Time had not been kind. More than a month had passed since he had left home and each day his depression deepened. He was desperately homesick. For the first time, he found himself doubting his decision to leave. Rotting for years in a camp such as this one, the way the Anders people have, was a daunting prospect. It would have been so much better to be rotting at home. And so he sat there, feeling sorry for himself, letting the warmth of the sun and coolness of the breeze soothe him, draw the pain out of him, and replace it with a kind of dullness—detachment from it all.

When he finally got up to return to the camp, he saw a convoy of buses approaching the gate. By the time he returned, they were already lined up on the grassy field, disgorging their human cargo.

CHAPTER 25

"Jan? Is it you, Jan?"

A crawling sensation raced up Jan's spine. His mind drew a blank as he tried to place the familiar voice. Slowly, he turned around and gasped. Not two steps from him stood Jára Soukup, his childhood buddy.

Jára's scarred face widened in a grin. "Almost didn't recognize you. You've changed."

Stunned, Jan mumbled an incoherent greeting. They shook hands, politely, almost like strangers, and then, overwhelmed, embraced and patted each other on the back like children.

Jára shook his head in disbelief. "I was hoping…I never thought…I thought you'd be gone. It's been so long. I'm so glad!"

"Still here." Jan sighed. "But what about you? Your dad? And Peter? Your mom?"

The scars on Jára's face flushed. "Father's not well and Peter's in jail. We lost our farm. The bastards took it."

"Who took it?"

"Who else? The communists! Stole it. Peter got into it with that sonofabitch Paleček when they came with the papers. Insulted my mom. Pushed her around. Called us names. So he got in one good lick. Gave the bastard a bloody nose, but it cost him. They beat him up right there and then took him away. Let us keep the house, but the farm is gone. Horses, cows, chickens, the fields, everything. Gone."

"And your mom?"

Jára pursed his lips and looked away. "She begged me not to go."

"But you left anyway."

"Dad made me go. Convinced her I should get out before they got me, too."

They both fell silent for a few awkward moments, and finally, both craving and fearing the news, Jan could wait no longer: "And my folks? Mother? Father? Did you have a chance to see them before you left?" he asked.

Jára didn't answer, but instead, fumbling with the buttons of his shirt, reached down into the folds, pulled out a small flat sweat-stained packet, and took out an envelope. "For you," he said. His hand trembled as he handed it over. "From your dad."

Jan stared at the ceiling atop his bunk, caressing the stained envelope, holding back the urge to tear it open. For the first time, he was afraid of words. Yet, however harsh and painful, the words also might bring catharsis by exposing a long-festering emotional sore to the light of day, and bring a measure of solace to his troubled mind.

With hands trembling in fearful anticipation, he carefully slit open the top with his pocketknife and pulled out the folded sheets of paper. He sighed with relief when he saw that only Father had written. At least he wouldn't have to face Mother's scathing words. But then, if she had not written, she was surely still angry at him. The thought sickened him.

A small holy picture of the Infant of Prague and a tiny bouquet of pressed flowers – violets and four-leaf clovers – fell into his lap as he unfolded the pages. Heart pounding, he devoured the lines:

*My Dear Son, It is with a heavy heart that I write this
letter and pray to God that it will reach you in good health,
wherever you are. Most of all, I hope you are well and not
in any danger. You are still young and not experienced in
the ways of the world.*

*It saddens me beyond words to have to tell you that your
beloved mother is no longer with us, having died of a stroke
about a week after you left.*

He stared at the words, slowly dissolving into
unintelligible blobs as his eyes flooded. An invisible hand
squeezed his throat until he felt like retching. An unintended
moan escaped his lips.

"You all right?" Martin looked up from below.

Jan waved him off, holding back sobs, fighting the
heaviness in his head, wishing he were alone so he could cry.
Forcing himself to read, he returned to the letter:

*You can't imagine how hurt we were when you left
without saying anything, not even a good-bye. I knew right
away that something had happened when we returned from
church and found you gone. You know how sensitive
Mother was—she became very distressed. At first we had
suspected the police, but late that afternoon, your friend L.
came by and told us what you had done and why. That you
didn't say anything made us very sad. Dear son, I want you
to know we would have understood, if only you had
confided in us. Had I known, I could have made it easier on
your mother. You can imagine how hard she took it. She
cried for days.*

*We spent all night waiting for news of you, hoping you
might change your mind and come back, but most of all,
fearing that you would be caught and brought back in*

chains, or, worst of all, dead. We felt relieved when we heard nothing.

I don't really fault the town people, but as soon as the word got around that you left, they stopped talking to us. It didn't surprise us. Sunday night, the police paid us a visit. We were already asleep when they came. I expected something like that to happen, and we had discussed it. Nevertheless, it was so traumatic, your mother became physically ill. I tried to help her but they would not let me. Because I had to go with them, I don't know exactly how or when she died. The doctor told me she had had a stroke.

They took me to the police station and asked all kinds of questions, mostly about you. Maybe you still remember F. P., the one that became the police chief. Next day, they took me to the district StB in Prachatice and questioned me again. I could not tell them anything because I did not know anything. But then the word came that your mother had died, and they let me go because there was nobody to arrange for the funeral. They made me sign a statement that I would tell them immediately if I heard where you were. Alois came and helped, too. I must say, I was surprised how many people attended her funeral.

I don't think I'll reopen the shop. People don't come around any more the way they used to, so I have decided to do just a little on the side for the few friends that still come.

My dear son, I wish I could have given you better news, but I think it important that you know the truth. We both must now find the strength to go on. It is how life is.

I don't know your plans, but don't forget your Uncle Joe and my sister Stáska in France. They are family and will help you with whatever you may need.

I hope Jára will be able to deliver this letter. Forgive the sloppy writing, I had to write it in a hurry.

I found the flowers and the holy picture in Mother's prayer book. She picked them herself in our garden. As for me, know that you are held dearly in my heart and that my day begins and ends with thoughts of you.

Your Father

Mother's dead. Dead! Because of me! He closed his eyes, trying in vain to shut out those damning words that seared his conscience like fire. Drowning in guilt, he pulled the pillow over his head and wept.

"You know, your dad didn't tell you the whole story." Jára looked up, slipping the letter back into the envelope after he had read it. "He left out a few things. What happened after they took him. It's possible, he didn't know."

Jan gave him a blank look. "So, how do *you* know?"

"Everybody knew. People talk. It's true your mom was scared when they came for your dad, but she was all right until they tried to arrest your dad. When they grabbed him, your dog—"

"Bojar."

"Yeah, Bojar. Wouldn't let them get close. Your dad tried to control him but he wouldn't obey. So, Paleček shot him. Shot him right there on the spot. And that's when your mother collapsed. When the bastard started shooting. Guess it was too much for her. So she lay there on the floor and your dad tried to get to her, but those bastards wouldn't let him. They dragged him out of the house and just left her there. I'm sorry, Jan."

"Go on!"

"As I said, they just left her lying there. And what's worse, didn't tell anybody. Didn't call the doctor. Didn't do anything."

"Jesus!"

"So, they finally found her a week later. Dead, of course. Somebody noticed the lights burning all night, night after night, so they went in and checked. Found her on the floor beside the dog. Doctor said it was her heart. Figured she must have died the day they took your dad. The house was full of chickens when they found her. Those sonsofbitches left the door open as they left. Some of the other animals died, too. Rabbits mostly. Starved. The place was a mess." Jára averted his eyes. "Maybe I shouldn't have told you."

"No, I need to know the truth!" Jan cried. "I need to know everything."

"They beat your dad, too."

"What!"

"Beat him. Hurt him. I know Paleček did, your dad said so. Now he's walking with a cane. Showed me his bruises. Scars, actually. They'd begun to heal."

"So how's he taking care of himself?"

"A couple of friends still drop by now and then, he said. Usually after dark. Everyone's afraid."

CHAPTER 26

"So this is your old friend?" Olga smiled, turning to Jan.

"That's Jára. Known him all my life. Brought a letter from home," Jan said.

"Oh, a letter? You didn't say anything about a letter. Is everything all right?"

Jan looked away, wishing he hadn't mentioned it.

"Sorry," Olga said, "didn't mean to pry." She touched his arm gently. "How fortunate you were able to meet again." Her gaze rested on Jára. "And you came through Regensburg, too?"

"Yes. Ours was the last shipment there, they told us. They're opening a new camp somewhere. A place called Burg, I think they said. Just for the Czechs. The Regensburg camp filled up in four days."

"So they're still coming."

"Oh, yeah," Jára nodded, "but it's going to get tougher, everybody says. They're clearing a wide strip along the border. Cutting down trees. Building guard towers. Stringing barbed wire. Even planting mines, somebody said. A guard that escaped said they were told to shoot without warning. So guess I was lucky that—"

Out of the blue, fast-approaching blare of horns and wailing of sirens cut him short. Everybody rushed outside, just as a line of jeeps full of soldiers in combat gear raced by at breakneck speed. Sounds of fighting punctuated by screams erupted from the Polish Sector of the camp. A thick column of black smoke rose skyward.

As though drawn by a magnet, crowds mindlessly rushed toward the source of the ruckus. In a place where boredom was the principal commodity, anything out of the ordinary was a welcome diversion. "It's the Pollacks and the Ruskis!" someone shouted. "The Pollacks and the Ruskis!"

The professor tugged at Jan's sleeve and stopped, trying to catch his breath. "Didn't I tell you? You could see it coming. Why the Americans herded them all in here, I'll never understand. Cats and dogs! Oil and water! No understanding. No sense of history. I hope the Czechs stay out of it." A pair of MPs, carbines at the ready, barred their way. Behind them, a riot raged as men clawed at each other with their fists and anything they could find. Smoke poured out of one of the barracks.

"Return to your quarters!" a booming amplified voice rose above the fracas. *"Stop the fighting! Return to your quarters That's an order!"* it commanded, alas, without success.

A volley of shots rang out. Then another. And another. Instinctively, Jan ducked, for a fleeting moment transported cerebrally to the border, running for his life. The sound of the reports reverberated among the buildings. For a pregnant moment, the brawl stopped, but then, like a flash fire, flared with ever greater intensity, until a barrage of popping and hissing teargas grenades enveloped everything in a wispy white layer of gas, and the fighting stopped. Clutching handkerchiefs to their faces, running shadows scattered in all directions. Others wandered about aimlessly, squatting on the ground, burying their faces in their clothing, gasping for air. Sounds of retching replaced the din of fighting. Soldiers in gas masks rushed in.

A faint breeze carried the misty cloud toward the onlookers. Reeling, the crowd dispersed. Eyes smarting, choking on the noxious fumes, Jan and his friends retreated to their barrack.

Olga, who had remained behind, handed Jan a wet cloth and another one to Martin. Tonda refused. Jan found the cold water soothing.

"That's some welcome you had," she said to Jára, wiping his eyes with a wet handkerchief. "If they don't move the Czechs out, this could be just a prelude to more trouble."

The professor groaned and let out a soft sob.

"The teargas still bothering you, dear?" She gave him a concerned look.

"It's not the tear gas, my dear. That's gone." A tear rolled down his cheek.

She took his hand and lowered her voice. "So what is it? Are you turning sentimental?"

The professor took a deep breath and sighed. "Just thinking what a place like this and time does to perfectly rational human beings. Watching those Poles and the Vlasov people and the Bandera Ukrainians trying to kill each other…I wonder if it all was worth it."

"What are you saying? I don't understand."

"There's no future here. There's no future."

"Oh, Pavel," she said softly. "I never thought I'd hear you say that. It's bad, I know. But we're coping. We're alive. We're free."

"Yes," his attempted smile turned into a grimace, "but when we left, abandoned everything, we had no idea. Now that we're here, looking at it all, I can see there's no future. We have no future."

"But, my dear, that's not fair to say. We didn't have time to think. To plan. To consider the 'what ifs.' We had no choice."

"Yes, of course. And I know I should be grateful. But still, it seems we've exchanged one unbearable situation for another. A dismal future there for what looks like a dismal future here. No difference. We're isolated. Cut off from our own. Cut off from the world. We don't belong. What can we do? Where can we go? How can we survive? Who wants us? Can you see us three years from now? Or five, or six? Here? Or some other place like this? At the mercy, at the *whim* of others? Maybe if we were younger. But at our age, who needs us? Who's going to take us? Who'd want us? We're old."

"Maybe America."

"America?" He snickered. "If they wanted us, this camp wouldn't be here. The Americans tolerate us, but they don't really want us. They've got their own problems in Berlin. Nobody wants us, because we don't belong. We make others uncomfortable. We're here at the world's mercy and the world doesn't care. We don't belong."

"But dear—"

He shook his head. "Looking at those two, the Poles and the Vlasov people, and even the Ukrainians, at least they have something that binds them together. Common purpose, common past. Perhaps even common hatred. They're all soldiers, partisans. They all fought for a cause. But what do we have? There's nothing to bind us. All we have in common is our misery. The legion might have done it, if there had been one. But there's no legion. No purpose. Nothing. We're being swept away. Swept under. Submerged. The world will drown us in its problems and ignorance."

"So what are you *saying*?" Olga cried out. "That you want to go back? That you regret—"

"No, of course not." The professor swallowed hard and made a choking sound, trying to contain his emotion. "But I do miss my home. Miss it terribly. Prague, my lovely Prague. Our friends. My work. I'd be lying if I said I didn't."

She took his hand and caressed it. "You must be a realist."

"But I *am* a realist. All I am saying is that there's a terrible price to pay. A terrible price."

The professor fell quiet but his words continued to resonate in Jan's mind. Though surrounded by friends, he, too, felt alone. Privately, in his deepest thoughts, despite his guilt, he wanted – no, ached – to return home.

* * *

Martin nudged Jan. "Hey, what's that mean? *Liberté, Egalité, Fraternité.* You *par-lay français*, don't you?"

"Yeah, some. That's, Freedom, Equality, and Brotherhood, I think. Comes from the French Revolution," Jan said, scanning a new notice, fringed in tricolor, on the camp bulletin board. I'm pretty sure, it's a recruiting poster for the French Foreign Legion. It says something about adventure, patriotic spirit, *gloire*, that's glory. 'Preserve the peace in the world by serving alongside the brave men and women of France.'"

"I saw a movie once about the French Foreign Legion." Martin sighed.

"What do you think?" Tonda turned to them. "Serious."

"What do you mean?" Jan gave him a puzzled look.

"Joining. Would be one way to get out of this fuckin' place. Been here almost a month now and—" Tonda spat in the dust.

"I wouldn't mind signing up," Jára said.

They all turned to him in disbelief.

"I think, Tonda's right. I keep thinking about what the professor said the day of the riot. He was right. I look at the Pollacks and the Ukrainians and all the rest, and see us sitting here. Rotting. So, what have we got to lose? Can't be any worse than this. At least we'd be doing something worthwhile."

"I'd hate for us to break up," Martin said.

"Why *would* we, if we all join." Jan frowned at him.

Tonda nudged him. "I thought you said you had an uncle in France somewhere."

"Versailles. But I don't really care. Really."

The small circle of friends had become his 'family,' their friendship the sustenance that gave him strength. Furthermore, he'd never liked his uncle, remembering him only as a small but overbearing and argumentative man who almost incestuously favored his mother and showed indifference and even disdain toward his father.

"So I say, let's do it," Tonda said.

"It says here, the recruiter's gonna be here the day after tomorrow." Jan translated.

That night, letting his mind wander, Jan kept turning over the three magic words, *Liberté, Egalité, Fraternité.* He liked their sound, their cadence, their purity. And most of all, he liked the fact that they provided a substitute, however imperfect, for the cause that drove him from home, infusing a breath of new life into his tattered ideals.

When they told the professor about their decision to join the Legion, he was taken aback at first and then, much to Jan's surprise and chagrin, rebuked them. Was there a trace of envy in his reproach? Olga cried. In the end, they both wished them luck and embraced them as they boarded a bus to take them, and a small contingent of other recruits, to the train station. Still, it was with some trepidation that Jan watched first the professor's and Olga's fluttering handkerchiefs, and then the camp disappear from view.

Jan's chest filled with a peculiar heaviness. Absurdly enough, the now-familiar Wasseralfingen camp seemed like home to him – a poor surrogate, to be sure, but a momentary safe harbor nevertheless – while ahead lay a turbulent sea of the unknown and uncertainty.

CHAPTER 27

There was no joy among the ragtag group of Russian, Ukrainian, and Polish recruits swaying with the movements of the train speeding toward Freiburg, a French garrison town straddling the banks of the Rhine River under the purplish fog-shrouded flanks of the Black Forest. Their faces were stoic, a trait they had learned in the camps to mask inner turmoil.

"Guess we're the only Czechs." Tonda scowled, scanning the lot. "I thought there'd be others."

"*Faites vite! Dépêchez-vous,*" their escort, a grizzled French lieutenant, barked, herding them to the door as the train pulled into the station. "*Allez – allez! Vite – vite!*"

A truck and a smartly dressed but gruff and unsmiling French soldier in a white *kepi*, mark of the legendary Foreign Legion, met them as they disembarked, and motioned them to board. The lieutenant joined him in the cab, and they sped off toward an imposing yellow-stuccoed grime-covered complex of massive buildings surrounded by a tall masonry wall pockmarked by bullet holes—the French caserne. A huge tricolor flew from a stubby flagpole projecting skyward from the roof of the main fortress-like edifice.

The guards saluted smartly as the driver spun the truck through an ornate wrought-iron gate and halted in front of a building identified by a sign and a flag over its entrance as the headquarters. The place was a beehive of activity. Gone was the casualness of the Americans. Here, the French moved about in military formations, walking stiffly and ramrod-straight even when alone. Many wore the white *kepis* of the lower ranks of

220

the Legion. Others more ornate and different colored ones—the officers.

"At least the food's better." Tonda wrapped his arms around himself, shivering, as they fell in line, stark naked, waiting to be examined. "Half a liter of wine, good bread. Could use some of the wine right now to keep me warm."

The scrutiny by the doctor, clad in a white smock over his uniform and assisted by a similarly dressed pair of orderlies, was cursory and quick. Humming to himself as he checked off a long list of particulars, he ceremoniously signed and stamped the form each of them was carrying, and with an airy flit of his hand and a surly, "*Allez!*" dismissed them one by one.

As Jan started to dress, a thick voice behind him spoke. "You fellows Czech?"

It was one of the orderlies—a stocky balding man of nondescript age, with a puffy pockmarked face furrowing around the temples. He eyed them curiously.

"I heard you talking," he addressed them in the lilting dialect of a Slovak.

"We're Czechs," Tonda said.

"My name is Jurka. Doctor Ivan Jurka. From Bratislava." He offered a limp handshake all around.

"Haven't seen any Slovaks in the camps," Martin said. "Not one. You're the first."

"Yeah. Those that made it out got out through Hungary and Austria. That's how I got out. Back in '46."

"Forty-six?" Tonda's eyebrows shot up. "Why, that was—"

"Yeah, before the coup. I was with Tiso during the war. You remember Monsignor Tiso?"

"Yeah, that priest sonofabitch that betrayed the Republic and delivered Slovakia to Hitler," Tonda snarled. "I remember.'

"But I was never political, I swear. Never! Not a Nazi. Not even a sympathizer. Just a doctor on his staff. Doing my job." His face turned ruddy and he wiped his brow, looking at them for empathy. Finally, his gaze rested on Jan. "I swear."

Jan shrugged "What's done is done."

Tonda's hint of a smile put him at ease. "After the Russians came," he went on, "they started jailing everybody in any way connected with the regime. Even people like me. Innocent people. So I got out. Made it all the way to France. I'm a doctor and there was a shortage, so I tried to find work. But nobody would hire me. Not even to sweep their goddamn floors. I was desperate. So, in the end, I signed up with the Legion." He sighed. "And you?"

They gave him a sketchy reply.

He took a quick, nervous look around and motioned them to come closer. "Listen, let me tell you something. You'd better think twice about this Legion thing before it's too late. Take it from me."

Tonda's smile faded. "I'm not sure I heard you correctly. What do you mean think twice? Why?"

"Why? I'll tell you why." He lowered his voice. "It's because the Legion's ninety-percent German. That's all you see. Fuckin' Krauts. That fuckin' doctor is a Kraut. A Nazi, probably. *Merde!*" He spat on the floor. "That's what I see every day. Makes me sick. They've been signing up in droves."

A sickening feeling filled Jan's craw. Joining the Germans in any scheme would be nothing less than betrayal—betrayal of his principles, betrayal of Jakub, his best friend, betrayal of his country. Long dormant hatred bubbled up to the surface, and he bristled. "But don't the French care? After what they did to them during the war, how can they cozy up to…"

The orderly laughed hoarsely. "Shit, they'll take anybody. They'll take you. They don't ask any questions. They don't care. All they want is a healthy body. Especially now that they have their hands full in Indochina."

"So are you saying that we're making a mistake?" Tonda growled.

"That's exactly what I am saying. Don't be damn fools. Can you really see yourselves taking orders from the Krauts? After what they did to *us*? What they did to the Republic?"

"But, *you're* doing it!"

"Yeah, and that's why I'm telling you. I'm trying to save you from making the same stupid mistake I did. Once you're in, you can't get out." His voice took on a hurtful edge. "I'm trying to do you a favor."

Tonda glared at him. "Can't. We're already signed up. And besides, they won't let anybody out of the caserne. We're stuck here."

The orderly drew a deep breath, let out a wheezing sigh, and shook his head. "Then you haven't got much of a choice. Maybe if you knew somebody, but—"

"Hey, wait a minute!" Tonda broke in. "Jan's got a family in there somewhere. Didn't you say you had an uncle in France?"

The orderly's pudgy face lit up. "You have family there? Where?"

"Versailles." Jan bristled at Tonda for mentioning it.

"Hmm. Then things could be different if they could help. I didn't know anybody. Didn't have any connections. In life, you got to have connections. Could they help?"

223

Jan shrugged.

"They'll be sending you to Perpignan. Trains are always crowded. So, once you cross the border, pick a large city, jump the train, and make your way to wherever you said your relatives are. Everything's still screwed up from the war. Lots of confusion. They won't know where to look for you."

*　*　*

A week later, clutching military-issue satchels with a day's ration of bread, cheese, and wine, with a hundred-franc note in their pockets and shepherded by a taciturn, white *kepi*-hatted legionnaire, a group of about thirty recruits boarded the train in Freiburg for Perpignan in the south of France, the Foreign Legion training camp. Jan watched with mixed feelings and a touch of nerves as the picturesque city faded into the greenery, the Black Forest disappeared in a haze, and hours later the Rhine passed under them when the train crossed a long trestle and sped into France. The coaches became crowded after a stop at Strasbourg.

"We'll do it at the next major stop," Tonda whispered as they huddled in the corner of the compartment. "Don't make a move until people begin to disembark. One at a time. Blend in. What's the matter with you?" He turned to Jára, noticing his sour look. "You don't like it?"

"I'm sorry, but I've decided not to go with you," Jára said, burying his head in his chest and staring at the floor. "I'm going to go on."

They all stared at him flabbergasted.

"I've decided to stick with the Legion. I thought about it hard." He fidgeted uncomfortably.

"But why?" Jan felt a sickening stab of distress. "I thought we'd be together. You don't know how happy I was to see you when you showed up at Wasseralfingen." He choked on the words.

Jára shrugged. "You have something to look forward to in France. A family. But I have nothing."

"You have us. We're friends. If my uncle'd help me, he'd help you. You're my friend. I promise. I swear!"

"It wouldn't be right."

"Are you crazy?" Tonda snarled in his ear and grabbed his arm. "We'll be all right if we stick together. Why would you want to have anything to do with the Germans? You heard what the Slovak had to say, didn't you? Shit, man, don't be a fool!"

"*Fuck* the Germans!" Jára shot back and jerked free his arm. "I left home to fight the communists. They stole our farm and that's what I have to do and that's what I'll do, even if it's in Indochina, or wherever. I'll take my chances."

Disheartened, Jan scribbled his uncle's address on a scrap of paper. "Then, would you at least write? If you can? if you need something? Anything? You can always reach me through this address."

Eyes glistening, Jára carefully folded the paper and slid it into his pouch.

* * *

Squealing and careening over switches that tossed Jan and his companions from side to side like puppets, the train pulled into Reims. No sooner it came to a hissing halt in a cloud of steam, it was enveloped by surging masses, some pressing

225

anxiously, trying to disembark, others equally eager, struggling to board.

A quick handshake with Jára, a look at the dozing legionnaire escort, and they were off amid the bedlam of shoving and pushing stream of passengers, shouts of '*Merde!*' and '*Oh zut!*' and '*Allors, Monsieur, s'il vous plaît*', forcing their way out into the cinder-smelling air. The crowd swallowed them immediately. Glancing over his shoulder, Jan saw Jára at the window, holding up his hand with the index and middle fingers spread out in a sign of victory.

Another train from the opposite direction pulled in and blocked their view. The crowd again surged and they had to fight to break free. Through the narrow gaps between the coaches, they saw their train move and slowly gather speed, permitting one final glimpse of Jára—still at the window, still holding up his hand in a 'V.' Then he was gone.

Jan joined a line of people at the ticket window and bought their tickets. Wary of a pair of gendarmes hovering near the exit, they ate the last of their meager rations and discreetly threw away the telltale military bags in a trash bin. Two hours later they were on their way, unnoticed, mesmerized by the cacophony of sounds, the uncertainty of expectations, and the pungent mixture of body odor, stale wine, strong cigarettes, and cheap perfume in the overcrowded train as it charged toward Paris.

CHAPTER 28

"JesusMary!" Blood drained from Aunt Stáska's face. "JesusMary!" she cried out, thrusting her hand over her mouth as though seeing a ghost. "Is it you? It's really you?" She embraced him until he gasped, planting kisses on both cheeks. "JesusMary! I can't believe it," she whimpered, and pulled up short, seeing Tonda and Martin behind him in the semidarkness of the hallway. She blushed. "Oh, I didn't realize…" She motioned them to come closer. *"S'il Vous plaît, messieurs…"*

Jan made the introductions and they shook hands.

She led them in. "Excuse the place. It's small. We didn't expect you. If we had known…"

The second-story flat was dark, facing an equally dark and narrow cobblestoned courtyard. Situated in a relic of a house predating the revolution, covered by layers of grime and history, it showed the effects of centuries of continued use and benign neglect.

The aunt led them past a miniscule workroom reeking of cigarette smoke and occupied by an attractive black-haired girl, hunched over a garment. *"Mademoiselle* Lili," she said.

The girl raised her head and smiled. *"Enchanté,"* she murmured in a mellow, breathy voice, blushing slightly under her velvety complexion.

They followed the aunt past a pair of Singers and a large worktable that nearly blocked the way into a tiny sitting room dominated by a large, ornate fireplace under a massive, equally ornate mirror that made the room appear larger than it actually was.

She slipped a crocheted covering from a small but bulky round table and begged them to sit down. "Are you hungry? There's still some *bourgignon*. You must be starving!" She sighed, and with an apologetic smile disappeared into the kitchen.

It took only minutes before she re-emerged, the twins in tow. "You remember Jean-Paul and Josephine?" she nudged them toward Jan as she filled their bowls with the steaming *bourgignon*. "They're four now. Born in '44. Just before the war ended."

"I only saw them once, when you came for a visit after the war," Jan said. "They've grown."

"Go kiss your big cousin and the *Messieurs*." She nudged them again and smiled.

They did, reluctantly, and retreated behind their mother.

"They're a bit shy with strangers," she said, rewarding them with a smile.

"And Uncle Joe?" Jan tried not to show his anxiety.

"Been gone to Paris since early morning to pick up an order from Burberry's. Should be back any time now. Don't know when." She gave him a reassuring smile. "Will he be surprised to see you!"

Propped up against the door with the twins by her side, a half-smile on her face, she watched them as they ate. "You must be dead tired," she finally said, and turned to the black-haired girl. "Lili, do you suppose you could take the children for the night?"

Lili blushed. "Of course, *Madame, avec plaisir*."

The twins shrieked in delight.

"You have to forgive us, but there's not enough room for all three of you. But that's all right. Tomorrow, we'll figure what to do." She quickly silenced Tonda's and Martin's protests.

The hallway door slammed shut and Uncle Joe, a package under his arm, walked in. Short, sallow-faced, and gray-haired, he looked different from the way Jan remembered. His deeply lined face covered with short gray stubble seemed more pallid, his appearance disheveled. The only thing that hadn't changed was his eyes, pale blue like Mother's, intense and wary under bushy gray eyebrows. A tiny cigarette butt hung from a nicotine-stained corner of his mouth.

He laid the package on the worktable and mashed the butt in an overfilled ashtray, where it continued to smolder. "Ah, what do we have here?" he growled, fixing Jan with a cold, piercing look. "Thought you might show up one day." He embraced him diffidently, brushing his stubble against Jan's cheeks in a feigned kiss. "How did you get here? Who are your friends?"

Jan introduced them and they shook hands, and then, under the uncle's probing questions, gave a sketchy account of their experiences.

"*Merde!*" he swore under his breath as they told him about Freiburg, jumping the train in Reims, and stumbling through Paris until a cabby took them to the Versailles train station. "*Merde!*" he swore again, this time more loudly when they finished. "You know you're in lots of trouble, don't you? With the *flics,* with the police? *Merde!*" He lit another cigarette, and blew a cloud of smoke in their direction. "Did you give them your real names?"

He blanched under the stubble. His bottom lip trembled. "*Merde!* That was stupid." He glared at Jan. "Stupid! The police already *have* your name on file. Had to give it to them when I applied for our visa to travel to the Republic to—" He swallowed hard and his eyes flooded. "When I had to get a visa for Lena's, my sister's, your mother's funeral. All they have to do is check their files. And believe me, they *will* check their files. *Merde!*" He took several deep, wheezing drags until the stub glowed so hot it burned him and he swore again, put it down with a sigh, and blew a cloud of smoke at them. "One day, you can be sure, they'll be here looking for you. And then, what do I do, huh?" His clenched stained teeth showed through slightly parted lips as his face screwed into a dark, contemptuous glare.

Eyes liquid with apology, the aunt gathered up the empty dishes and withdrew. Tonda and Martin just stood there, rooted to the spot, staring into the ground. Jan wished he hadn't come.

"Did anybody see you walk up?" he pressed.

"I don't think so. Except the woman that let us into the house."

The aunt reappeared. "That was Madame Boulanger, the *concierge*. She won't say anything," she said.

"I don't *care*," he snapped. "I don't want them in this house. Can't afford any trouble." The beads of his half-closed eyes riveted each of them to the spot.

"They're tired. Let them get some sleep," she pleaded. "Tomorrow we'll see what we can do."

He fixed her with a glare, put out the cigarette, gave them one more disdainful look, and stalked out of the room.

* * *

Daylight was already streaming in through the shuttered window of the tiny room when Jan awoke to the slamming of the hallway door, Lili's warbling *'Bon Jour,'* and the twins' excited prattle.

"Sorry, but there's water only in the kitchen. We take turns washing. As I said, this is a very old house," the aunt said, handing each a towel. "There's a public bath house down the street. We try to get there at least once a week. Costs just a few centimes."

Taking turns in the tiny kitchen, the boys splashed water on their faces.

"*Merde.*" Uncle Joe announced his arrival with an obscenity, yawning and stretching. "A person can't even get a decent night's sleep."

"Pay no attention," she murmured, setting a basket of fresh croissants on the table and pouring the coffee. He's like that whenever he gets up early. Likes to sleep late, because he usually works way past midnight and then still goes for a walk before going to bed."

The uncle lit a cigarette and took a swig from his cup. "That was a stupid thing you did, leaving home." He glared at Jan. *"Stupid!"*

"Oh, Joe, please, let him be." Aunt Stáska touched him lightly on his arm, and he jerked loose.

"That was a stupid thing you did! Stupid! Leaving home. How *could* you?" He blew a whiff of smoke in Jan's direction and glared at him with an unblinking stare. "Didn't you think about the consequences?"

Tonda and Martin stopped chewing and stared blankly into their cups.

"Joe, please, not now. Not here. Please. Leave him alone," the aunt pleaded. "Please, Joe."

He ignored her and turned on Jan with slashing, unmitigated rage. "If you'd stayed home, none of this would have happened. *Merde!* Your old man in jail! And your poor mother..." His voice broke and he paused for a moment to collect himself. "She'd still be with us."

"But Uncle—"

"If you'd have kept your snotty nose out of politics, none of this would've happened. None of it! And you have the nerve—"

"Joe, please..."

He spun around and turned on her with such a fury she reflexively covered her face. "*Tais-Toi!* Shut up!" he snapped, droplets of saliva flying out of his contorted mouth. "How can you! After losing my Yvette." He glared at her as she burst into tears. "My sweet, innocent, beautiful Yvette. Dragging her all the way to Normandy. Making her sick. Doing nothing to help her! And now you're trying to defend this dim-witted jerk's stupidity? Cost me my sister! *Merde!*" He took a deep drag on the stub of his cigarette. "Couldn't even see her face for the last time. Was already buried by the time I got there!"

Jan was crushed. This was not the uncle he'd expected. Nor were his cutting charges concerning Yvette, a wound of which he had not been aware. He remembered the murmurs and the acid tones when Uncle Joe and Mother had commiserated about Yvette's death during their last visit, but back then, he didn't understand. Now he knew.

The aunt's face knotted in anger as she struggled to find the right words. "You. You! How could you ever think I could harm my own child! I'd have given my life. You went off and *left* us! *I* had to be the one to take care of the house. *I* had to be the one to take her and run, with the Germans on our heels. Everybody running. Panic! Cold! Hunger! Sleeping in ditches!

No wonder she got sick. *That's* what killed her. The *war* killed her. And *you*? You were gone! When we needed you, you were gone! And now you have the gall to say—"

"I had to go!" He shook his fist in front of her face, but she didn't flinch. "That was war! *Merde!*"

"Yeah, that was war. There's still a war. It will never be over!" Her eyes filled with tears. She started sobbing.

"Excuse me, Uncle, but you don't understand—"

"Understand?" The uncle spat at him. "Understand *what*? That my sister would still be alive? That your *mother* would still be alive? I know what happened. I know *exactly* what happened. They told me everything. There's nothing you can tell me that will change things! What you did killed your mother. *You* killed your mother."

Shaking, Jan stared at the uncle. The guilt and remorse, suppressed since he had read his father's letter, seared him like fire. He wished he had gone with Jára. He wished he had never come.

Satisfied with his rant, Uncle Joe turned to his breakfast and ate with gusto. No one spoke. A few minutes later, he got up, wiped his mouth, shot an icy look at Jan, and without a word stalked out of the room.

Tears in her eyes, Aunt Stáska begged and ultimately persuaded Jan and his friends not to leave. "He's not all that bad, when he's calm," she pleaded.

Still, the confrontation set the tone for the days ahead. The pall remained, though the tension eased somewhat. The aunt cleared one of the rooms for Jan and Martin by having the twins share the other, and Madame Boulanger, the concierge, brimming over with kindness and empathy, put up Tonda in a small windowless storeroom off the hallway with just enough room for a cot.

Jan seldom saw his uncle who slept late, often until noon, and took his meals separately. Though Jan and his friends consciously avoided him, they couldn't avoid his obvious disdain, manifest in his eyes and the tone of his voice whenever they couldn't evade him. Discussing their plight among themselves, they came face to face with the crushing reality that they were unwelcome guests in a divided house, dependent on the charity of a man who detested them and a woman who paid a price each time she showed them kindness, and that they had become stranded in a totally self-absorbed land where the fate of their country and their own meant absolutely nothing. For the first time since leaving home, they reluctantly raised the issue of going their separate ways.

With tension at a breaking point and much to Jan's surprise, Uncle Joe greeted them one day with the news that, through the intercession of some of his customers, he had found them work. Relieved, they absorbed the news gleefully and even shook his hand in gratitude. Tonda was to be a jack-of-all-trades on a farm, Martin was to work as a helper for Truffaut, the largest gardener in the city, and Jan was to assist in the day-to-day needs of a summer camp.

CHAPTER 29

Oblivious to the brisk wind whipping the salt grass around his ankles and the grains of sand stinging his skin like pin pricks, Jan stood atop a sand dune, captivated by the sight that until now had been only a figment of his imagination, lifeless and unmoving, gleaned from postcards and magazines.

Before him lay a vast expanse of a sparkling beach widening under a receding tide, and beyond it the sea, alive and moving like a great living thing, its blue skin continually wrinkling into undulating white-capped furrows, spilling row upon row of waves onto the corrugated sand. Flocks of seagulls cavorted noisily above the tide pools that reflected the sky like mirrors. A few solitary figures dug in the sand looking for clams. Farther out in the water, odd, spindly, black triangular shapes – landing craft traps – set in neat but staggered rows as far as the eye could see emerged eerily from the receding water—relics of the Great Invasion. And among them, the boxy rusting specters of wrecks.

He took off his shoes and walked down the steep embankment. The air was pungent with the salty, chlorinous smell of decaying seaweed lying in scattered lumps along the indistinct meandering line left there by the ebbing tide. Tiny ridges of the surprisingly hard sand pressed against the soles of his feet as he walked past the clam diggers to the edge of the receding water, and then into it, until the waves licked at his ankles. He waded in a few more steps and stopped. The sea stretched before him into infinity, the shimmering azure of the water ultimately merging with the blue haze of the sky, wiping out the horizon and making him feel as though he were standing on the edge of the world.

He was grateful for the job at the *Colonie Vacances La Pommeraye*, a summer camp for city children, almost hidden from sight behind the dunes. It consisted of a collection of tents set in a meadow behind a Norman farmhouse, a stone's throw from Villers-sur-Mer, one of a string of seaside hamlets hugging the windswept coast. His job was easy—chaperoning about thirty children in their daily visits to the beach and helping around the camp.

The farmer, who provided milk for the camp, took a liking to him and they held long chats about the war, the glory of France, and the state of the world, often at his rustic farmhouse after hours over mounds of steaming mussels, oozing morsels of ripe *Camembert*, and mugs of a pale searing liquid they called Calvados.

The easy pace of the colony was a godsend. Chaperoning the children on the beach while they swam, explored the pools of water, played volleyball, or wandered among the abandoned bunkers and gun emplacements that lined the shore provided Jan with ample time to reflect. It gave him a chance to rid himself of the embarrassment he felt each time he faced his friends, to come to terms with his predicament. He was sure of one thing —he would leave his uncle's house on *Petit Carré* when his time at the colony came to the end. He must.

He tried to think no further, but a small voice in his brain wouldn't be stilled. Then what? Germany again? Or perhaps turning himself in and rejoining the Foreign Legion, taking his punishment and meeting Jára? And then the intruder he had consciously tried to ignore clawed its way to the forefront of his mind—heeding his uncle's urging and returning home. Home!

But at what cost? The prospect of returning home in disgrace knotted his stomach to the point of retching.

Wearily, he resolved to put off any decision until he returned to Versailles, until he and his friends could discuss it. Perhaps together they could think of something. So long as they stuck together, they could support each other and endure. Somehow, they would find a way out of the morass —a way to survive.

* * *

The vacation time came to an end and the camp closed. Half-heartedly, Jan returned to Versailles. A sinking feeling gradually slowed his brisk pace to a crawl as he turned the corner to the old house on *Petit Carré*. His heart skipped a beat and he felt a rush of nausea as he reluctantly climbed the rickety stairs to his uncle's apartment. Recalling his acid tongue, he sighed with relief when one of the twins opened the door.

"It's Uncle Jan!" Josephine shrieked in delight.

Aunt Stáska emerged from the kitchen, wiping her hands on a dishrag. "JesusMary, I didn't expect you so soon!" she cried out, throwing her arms around him and kissing him tenderly on the cheeks. She seemed tense. Her face was furrowed and drawn. And then he noticed the two bluish blotches standing out prominently on her cheek and forearm.

She saw he noticed and forced a smile. "It's nothing, just my stupidity. Slipped and fell down the stairs in the cellar, fetching coal. You know how dark it is down there. How narrow the steps are. Nothing serious. Really. Looks worse than it feels." Smiling, she patted the spots with her hand. "See, it's nothing."

She poured two glasses of Beaujolais and listened attentively as he recounted his experiences. The twins, captivated at first, began to fidget, but yelped with delight and kissed him on the cheeks when he surprised them with a bagful of seashells.

"And Uncle?" Jan finally broached the subject.

"Still the same. Still asleep. You know how he is." She smiled weakly but avoided his eyes. "He'll be up soon."

"And Lili, not here yet? Is she sick?"

"Mademoiselle Lili doesn't work here anymore," Jean-Paul, the other twin, interrupted.

"Hush!" Aunt Stáska admonished him sharply. Flushing, she swiped at him half-heartedly as he ducked. "Mind your manners." She gave Jan an apologetic look and, in a hard-edged tone that thwarted any further inquiry, added, "She won't be coming today."

"And Martin? Still working?"

"Afraid, not. There were problems. I'm sure he'll tell you all about it. He has moved out to Madame Boulanger's room. The one Tonda used to have. It's a tad bigger and more private. I'm sure, he's there now." She sighed.

"So what about Tonda?"

"You don't know? I guess you wouldn't." She gave him a sad smile. "He's gone. Showed up here a couple of weeks ago. Didn't expect him. Looked awful. Stayed one night and…" She averted her eyes. "You'd better let Martin tell you. I don't know all the details. He knows the whole story."

"You have a letter! You have a letter!" little Jean-Paul burst into the room, waving an envelope above his head. "Can I have the stamps? Please? Please? They're so pretty."

"This boy! I don't know what to do with him." Aunt Stáska snatched the envelope from his hand. "He just won't mind."

"Of course, you may have the stamps," Jan said, taking the letter. "But after I've read it."

"Came the other day. A post card, too. Meant to give them to you myself." The aunt cast a stern look in Jean-Paul's direction. "And I saved something else for you, too." She reached out to the fireplace mantle and handed him a folded piece of paper. "Don't know if you'd be interested."

Incredulous, Jan stared at the letter. The envelope, addressed in vaguely familiar handwriting, bore an Italian postmark. He flipped it over and stared at the return address. It was from Daniel. Daniel! Jesus! He'd made it. He'd made it! His hand shook as he fought the impulse to tear it open, but instead slipped the envelope in his pocket and unfolded the paper his aunt had handed him. It read:

COMITÉ D'AIDE AUX REFUGIES TCHÉCOSLOVAQUES
58 Rue Maubeuge
PARIS 9

ANNOUNCEMENT AND INVITATION
This is to notify all democratic Czechoslovaks that the
COMMITTEE OF HELP FOR THE CZECHOSLOVAK REFUGEES
has opened an assistance office at the above address
where you can register and obtain valid
INTERNATIONAL REFUGEE ORGANIZATION (IRO)
documents recognized as legal credentials by the FRENCH EPUBLIC
until such time as you are able to satisfy official residency requirements
and obtain official residency and work permits.
Everybody welcome. We are located five minutes from Metro
Maubeuge and open from 8:00 – 16:00, Monday through Friday

His stomach knotted as he read it. "How did they... You mean, someone already knows we're here?"

"Oh, no! No! Nothing like that," his aunt reassured him, smiling. "It's from a Czech club. A fraternal organization. Most of the local Czechs and Slovaks belong. People like us. We belong, too. They have dances. Sokol. Get us our tickets when we visit the Republic. They have our name. I threw the envelope away, it wasn't addressed to you. So don't worry. There's no problem. You're safe here. But may be a way to get your papers."

From somewhere came the sound of the uncle coughing, lighting a cigarette, and clearing his throat, followed by his shuffling steps as he approached. They greeted each other coolly, politely, without emotion. A palpable tension filled the room. The twins' jabbering lowered to a whisper. The aunt, stone-faced, rushed out to fix his breakfast. They made small talk as he ate.

Excusing himself at the first opportunity, Jan retreated from the table and in the privacy of his room, slit open Daniel's envelope. His heart pounded as he devoured the words:

Ahoj Jan!

First, my greetings and apologies for not having written sooner. Seems like years since we last spoke back home. Sorry we couldn't leave together, but the StB came for me that Saturday and I barely got away. I hid at my sister's for almost a week. Later I found out that Martin had left that Sunday anyway as we had planned, probably thinking I had lost my nerve. Were you able to see him in Germany?

In case you wonder, your father gave me your aunt's address before I left. I telephoned your friend Láďa to let you know about my problems, but he said you had already left. So, I sent word to your father when I was ready to go and he met me in Vimperk. We talked a bit, and he gave me a letter for you and a couple of packs of American cigarettes. I still have the letter, but smoked the cigarettes.

I hooked up with a couple of other guys from the Gymnasium to cross the border. The Americans took us first to Freyung and Schalding, and then to Regensburg, where we waited a couple of weeks. The food there was really bad, so I ended up spending the few dollars my dad gave me. Then they sent us to our permanent camp in Burg. It was alright except for the food and smokes—not enough of either. I spent the rest of the money I had on the black market. They also gave us official papers and let some of us apply for emigration to the USA. There is some kind of quota that lets in about two thousand, depending on when you left. I qualified and I think you would have, too, had you been there. Anyway, after a few weeks, they loaded us onto a train and shipped us down here to Italy. This camp is very large. Thousands of people. It's mainly a processing center for those that will immigrate to different countries. I hope to go to the USA. To pass the time, I am learning Italian, which is relatively easy (the Italians refer to their language as 'dolce e facile' – sweet and easy).

As he read the next paragraph, he felt his chest tighten and a pricking sensation spread through his body. He read and re-read the passage:

A couple of days before we left Burg, a new shipment came in from Regensburg, about a hundred. I recognized old Březina, the pharmacist—surely, you remember him from school. Amazing, but his whole family made it, all five of them. He introduced me to a couple of people, a girl and her mother, he had met in Regensburg, and after a while it came out that they used to vacation in your town. Your name came up in the conversation and the girl said she knew you. Her name was Inka. She asked about you, but all I could tell her was that I didn't know much, except perhaps that you were in France. We didn't get to talk any more because I shipped out two days later. As far as I know, they are still there. Anyway, I thought you might be interested.

Inka! She had long since faded from his memory, until now. Flushed, he tried in vain to recall her likeness, but while he clearly recalled his feelings for her, the ghost that floated up in his inner eye was unclear, except for the color of her eyes and the frozen cast of her smile—a mere shard of remembrance. His initial rush of elation quickly dissolved into bitterness, the old bitterness he'd once felt toward her, bitterness she herself had heaped upon him. But by now, his feelings for her were muted, almost sweet, a mixture of sorrow and regret, a mere shadow of what he had once felt. It had been too long. Time had ablated the sharp edges of disappointment. He had mellowed. No longer a flame, she remained only a warm glow that shimmered briefly in the far recesses of his mind, passing across the dark vault of his memory like a shooting star that came and went, leaving only a wisp of a trail where there once was light.

He put away the letter and went to see Martin.

CHAPTER 30

Seeing Jan in the open doorway, Martin sprung to his feet and tossed aside a magazine he was reading. "I don't believe it! They didn't say anything about your coming. Am I glad to see you!" He rushed at him and smothered him in a bear hug. "You didn't write?"

"Would have, but everything was so confused—say, what happened to Tonda?"

Martin's smile froze on his lips. "Your aunt didn't tell you?"

"She said you better do it. Said he's gone. Where? Why?"

"He's gone back."

"Gone back? Back where?"

"Gone home. There's some kind of amnesty. It was on the radio, your uncle said. So that's what he did. Decided to go home."

"Jesus! But why? He was always the strong one. He was the one who said that we could make it if we stuck together. And on top of it he's a deserter. They'll—"

"I know. I was with him when he did it. Tried to talk him out of it, but…"

"Jesus!"

"In a way, I don't blame him. He told me all about what happened. I understand."

"So what did he say?"

"I'll tell you *exactly* what he said. Some relative of Lili, that's how the uncle got him the job. He got there and there was nothing. A little place out in the sticks. *Port de Pic* it was called, or something like that. In Normandy. Tiny beat-up heaps-of-stone farms, the place gets huge windstorms from the sea. Anyway, he's the only one that gets off, and the only person waiting for him is a hunchback with a bicycle. He tells him to get up on the handlebars. Had an old blanked wrapped around them for him to sit on. Straps Tonda's bag to the carrier and they ride to the farm.

"They get there and the farmer leads him to a long stone building. The pig sty. No windows, only rickety doors. Dutch doors. Full of pigs, except for one room that the farmer cleared out and threw some whitewash on the walls to cover the stains. And that's where he put him. Just a dirt floor, a bed, and a crate in place of a table. An iron spike in the wall and a pair of clothes hangers to hang stuff on. The mattress just a burlap sack full of straw. And the smell…you can never get rid of the smell. Said he ate well and there was plenty of wine, but that first evening, when he got back to his room, the smell got to him so bad he puked it all out.

"A woman would come every day from someplace and cook. Never spoke a word. Fact is, there wasn't much talk at all. The farmer didn't speak Czech and he didn't speak French, so the hunchback would talk to him with gestures. Imagine!"

"Jesus!"

"So the hunchback shows him what to do. They give him some old rags to wear and a pair of shit-covered brogans, and he has to get up at four and take care of the pigs, haul the shit out and put the new straw in and feed them, and then, after breakfast, go work in the fields and plant cabbage. Said, they used a short stick to do that. You made a hole with the stick, dropped the cabbage in, squeezed the dirt, made another hole two stick-lengths away, stuck in another cabbage, and so on. He was on his knees all day, in the wet dirt, with only the hunchback jabbering at him and replanting what he just did. Day after day. From dark in the morning till dark at night. Said he was so tired he almost passed out at night, stink and all. And that's when he started thinking about getting out of there. Said he'd be looking at the tatters of his uniform and thought, what the hell am I doing here? Got so homesick he cried."

"I can understand that."

"So one night he was laying on his bed, half-drunk to ward off the stench…it was completely dark, the moon was not out…when he thinks he hears the door open. He hears somebody breathing. And before he can do anything, *that* somebody's on him."

"The hunchback?"

"No. That sonofabitch farmer! Pinning his hands and going for his crotch. So Tonda manages to free one of his hands and starts hitting him. Somehow he finds one of his brogans and hits the bastard over the head. The farmer lets him go just long enough for him to jump up and, butt-naked, run out into the field. Said he nearly froze to death. Was surprised the farmer didn't hear his teeth chattering. When he heard the door slam, he knew the farmer had gone back to the house. So he snuck back, put on his uniform, got his things, and got the hell out of there."

"So he came back here?"

"Yeah, he showed up one afternoon. Looked like shit. That's when we heard about the amnesty and he decided to go back. I tried to talk him out of it and he tried to talk me into it. So, in the end, I went with him. Told him, begged him, that he should at least wait till you got back, but he wouldn't have it. We took a train to Paris and a cab to get to the embassy, it's not far off the Champs, on a side street. And I tell you, I was tempted seeing our flag over the entrance and the sign, *Le Consulat de la République Tchécoslovaque*. It gripped me right here." Martin tapped his left breast with his fist. "I tell you, I was tempted."

"So he rang the bell, and the door opened, and this guy shows up, smiling, you know, that kind that smiles all the time. Like a cat watching a bird, you can never figure them out. He gestures for us to go in. So Tonda goes in right away, and I…I just couldn't. And now I wish I had."

"What do you mean, you wish you had?" Jan pulled up short. "What are you saying?"

Martin thrust his face closer and grimaced. "Just look at me." He glared at Jan. "Can't you see the bruises?" His face was covered with fading pink blotches and a shadow under one of his eyes, the remains of a shiner. "And I am still black and blue under my shirt."

"Jesus! What happened?"

"You know the job at Truffaut's your uncle got me? Knew the *chef* there. You can't tell from the outside, but the place is huge. An old place. Been there probably since they built the chateau. Supplies all the flowers and greenery for the gardens.

"So we got there late and the *chef* is fuming. A short guy with a *mego* in the corner of his mouth like your uncle. I knew right away that he and I wouldn't get along. He takes me to the rose field. Rows and rows of roses. Immense. He tries to show me how to prune them. He don't speak Czech and I don't *parlay Francay*, so you can imagine how it went. He was right behind me most of the time, cussing me out and doing it over. People everywhere, all hunched up over their work. Nobody talks or anything. Later I found out they didn't have time 'cause there was a daily quota. Took me until late at night to get mine done. You should've seen my hands.

"It got better a few days later. The pay wasn't bad, so I bought myself a bicycle. It's a long hike and the buses are expensive. So about a week ago, I get back to where I park, and see my bike in a heap. Completely smashed. Frame bent. Spokes in a knot. Tires slashed to pieces. And in the middle of it a sign, *La Peste Capitaliste à La Porte!* Get out, you capitalist pig."

"So did you say anything? Complain?"

Martin frowned. "Of course, but the *chef* only threw up his hands and swore, and spat out a bunch of gibberish I didn't understand, except for *merde* and *magot* and *communist*."

"And my uncle?"

"Your uncle? Hah! Got furious that I got him involved. Said the communists probably did it. Told me to keep my mouth shut."

"I am sorry."

"Yeah, me too. But that's not all. The next day, the day after they trashed my bike, they put me on a far side of the field. About as far as you can get. A few fellows were there already, closer to me than normal, but it didn't occur to me at the time. But before I knew it, they were on top of me. Somebody pulled my shirt over my head and somebody pinned my arms behind my back. And then they beat and kick the shit out of me. I couldn't move. Tried to roll up into a ball, but that didn't work. Kept hitting and kicking me until I passed out. When I came to and pulled the shirt down from my face, they were gone. My face was a mess. I think they broke my nose. I could smell my own blood. I puked allover myself. I passed out again, and when I woke up, it was dark. So I never went back. I'll say again, had I known that would happen when Tonda left, I would've *gone* with him. Gladly!" His face screwed up in a grimace. "But I'll tell you, I'm so happy I'm here and not up there." He nodded toward the apartment.

"Why? Did something happen?"

He scowled at Jan from under his wrinkled forehead. "Haven't you noticed her bruises?"

"Yeah, I saw them. Said she had fallen fetching coal from the cellar. I can understand that. It's a dark hole, and the stairs—"

"That's not what happened. I only know what I saw, but I swear to you, I'm telling the truth. I walked in on them one day last week and your uncle was slapping her around pretty bad. Beating her up. Don't know why, but she had her hands in front of her face and he was hitting her all over. She didn't scream or anything. Just took it. He quit when I walked in, and gave me this look. Right then, I knew I had to get out of there, so this thing about Tonda quitting came as a blessing. I got his room."

Jan stared at him, mouth open.

"She ran out crying, and he just stood there glaring at me, so I got myself out of there. Haven't talked to him since."

"I always knew he had a short fuse," Jan croaked. "Quick temper. You saw what he did to me when we got here."

"Frankly, it's none of my business, but I think it had something to do with that girl, Lili. She came running out of there a few minutes later like she was on fire. Crying. I haven't seen her since."

"And the kids? Did they see it?"

Martin shrugged. "Didn't see them around. Just your uncle and aunt. And the girl."

"Jesus." Jan looked away, avoiding Martin's probing look.

"So, what do we do?"

Jan pulled out the flyer and handed it to Martin. "My aunt gave me this. I think we should at least get our papers," he said. "It was a mistake coming here."

Martin studied it for a few moments. "Yeah. We've got to get out of here. But where?"

"I heard from Daniel."

"You heard from *Daniel*!" Martin's jaw dropped. "You mean, he made it?"

Jan pulled out the letter. "He's in Italy. Here, read it yourself."

Martin grabbed the letter and his grin widened as he devoured the words. "That sonofagun! Italy, eh?" He laughed out loud and slapped his thigh. "Italy! That sonofagun!"

CHAPTER 31

"You haven't been quite honest with me," Jan chided Aunt Stáska, giving her a hurtful look.

She looked up flushed. "Not honest with you? I don't know what you mean, my boy. I've *always* been honest with you. Always. It hurts me to think that you should—"

"You know what I mean. The bruises."

She stopped short. "Martin told you?"

He didn't reply and she continued to gaze at him, unblinking, a pair of tears trickling down her cheeks, until she finally turned her head and buried it in her apron. Her shoulders heaved.

He took her hand and stroked it, not knowing what to say. "Please, Auntie, please," he whispered, feeling awkward."

She stopped sobbing and let the apron fall from her face. Her pale eyes, red and tired, sunken in their sockets, spoke of pain and sadness as she made a vain attempt to dry them with a crumpled handkerchief. "It is true. *He* did it. He did it to *me.*" Desperately, she dabbed at her eyes, as though shifting the force of her wrath to the crumpled piece of cloth. "That bastard!"

She reached behind the great mirror hanging over the mantle and pulled out an envelope. "Here. Look at this. See for yourself." She thrust the envelope on the table. "See what that bastard's done!"

A thick stack of photographs spilled out and Jan's jaw dropped. He stared at them, unbelieving. Crudely shot. Lili, in various poses. Naked. Reclining, smiling seductively, legs spread wide revealing a bushy crotch and rounded buttocks, arms outstretched, inviting, tongue sticking out like a triangular spear. Her breasts, surprisingly firm, barely spilling to the side, projecting like two symmetrical mounds from her contorted enticing lithe body.

"That bastard!" The aunt let out an anguished cry. "That *putaine*!"

The photos had been taken in the workroom, some on the great cutting table, others on the rickety work stools gathered in the middle of the floor strewn with snippets of fabric and her hastily shed undergarments. The shabbiness of the setting clashed with the alabaster luminosity of her almost perfect body which seemed to float above it all—ghost-like, detached, surreal. A porcelain mannequin floating in a cesspool. Flushing, he flipped through the stack, feeling like a voyeur.

"But how *could* they," he blurted out. "Right here in the house?"

"Oh, very easily. I was a fool." She let out a harsh laugh. "You know, I have to go to Paris now and then. We do contract work for Burberry's, so I am the one who has to go to pick up the work. I keep the account going. If I didn't go, we'd lose it. He almost never goes. He sleeps too late. Usually takes me all day."

"So, that's when they—"

She nodded. "The other day I was looking for some material in the closet we use for storage in the hallway. Nobody ever goes in that closet. Most of the stuff is old and good for nothing. Takes up space. Should have been thrown out long ago, but he never throws anything away. Anyway, as I was rummaging through the stacks, an envelope fell out. At first, I thought nothing of it and was going to put it back. There were other old papers, too. But then, on impulse, I opened it." She sighed and made a vague motion with her head toward the pictures. "That's where he hid them. He was clever. That bastard!"

"So you confronted him?"

She shook her head. "That was my first thought. I was so angry! I was *so* angry I could have killed him, killed them both. But I didn't. Instead, I put the envelope back and said nothing. But the next time I had to go to Paris, a few days later, I went to the park instead. Stayed a couple of hours until I knew he'd be up, and then went back. I was prepared to make an excuse, tell him I got the days mixed up or something, but I didn't have to. I let myself in, quietly, and found them in bed. My bed! Together in my bed! Fucking! He was fucking her in my bed! That *putaine*!" Face twisted in anger, she gave Jan a furious look.

Jan stared at her, speechless.

"She was naked, not a stitch on her, and he in his long johns – you know he wears them all the time – with his slimy worm sticking out. But I got'em good! You should've seen them! They both got white as sheets. There wasn't a drop of blood in their faces when they saw me."

"Jesus!"

"I didn't say a word, just stood there for a few moments and watched them scramble." A faint twisted smile crossed her angular face.

"And then I left. I can almost laugh about it now, but then, I was too angry even to cry. I quickly grabbed the pictures – they were still where I had left them – and hid them behind the mirror. A few minutes later, I heard her rush out of the house, and then he stormed in like a wild bull, demanding that I give them to him. He must have realized I found them and that's how I knew." She sighed. "Anyway, I wouldn't give'em to him, so for the first time in my life he hit me. *Hit* me!" She paused, touching absently the bruise on her face, and shook her head in disbelief. "He beat me…" Her eyes flooded and she wiped them with the back of her hand. "It was Martin's walking in that made him stop."

Jan took her hand and squeezed it. It trembled.

The lines and furrows on her face stood out prominently, reflecting all the pain and sorrow she'd had to endure. Her eyes turned opaque. "So now I know what's been happening—and you know. He's not a nice man. He's never been a nice man. I was blind. You know, his late evening walks, sometimes he's gone way past midnight? He goes to her place and—you know what I'm trying to say. She doesn't live far, just a couple of blocks. That bastard," she murmured under her breath. "I have no idea how long it's been going on. I suspected nothing. I was such a fool."

"But she's so young, so pretty, and he—" Jan caught himself in time, remembering his mother's admonishment about criticizing his elders.

The aunt smiled sadly. "Yeah, I know. I don't know what she sees in him except maybe money. He's the one who controls the money. Gives me only a small allowance. I'm sure he gives her money. That *putaine*. That bastard!"

* * *

"What's the matter with you?" the uncle growled, peering at him over the rim of his glasses, as he took a deep drag and mashed the *mego* in an overflowing ashtray. "Why are you looking at me like that? Didn't you get enough sleep, or is something bothering you?"

Jan met his cold stare.

253

"Lost your voice?"

"Yeah, you should know!"

"*I* should know? I should know what?" His eyes narrowed under his bushy eyebrows.

"I saw the pictures."

"*Merde!*" Uncle's face puffed up in rage. He slammed his mug on the table so hard, the coffee spilled. "So *she* told you! *Merde*! Damn her! *Merde*!"

"How *could* you? How could you do that. How could you hit her? If I'd been there, I'd have—"

"You'd have what? What? Are you threatening me? You ungrateful little bastard! You come to my house with a pack of strangers and have the gall... You want to fight? Is that what you want? C'mon then, fight. Fight me! C'mon, you."

Jan didn't budge.

"You little prick. What gives you the right talking to me like that? I'm not one of your pals. I'm your uncle. Your uncle, *understand*! Your mother's brother! Don't you ever forget it, you snotty-nosed bastard! I was already making money; I was somebody when you were still in diapers. And here you come, uninvited, all high and mighty!" He stuck a fist in Jan's face. "So c'mon, you ungrateful little bastard! Fight, if you're so damn high-minded! C'mon, you!" The uncle moved closer, so close Jan could smell his foul breath.

Perhaps if he'd been there as it happened, Jan would have reacted reflexively in the heat of the moment. But now the impulse was lost. Sickened, he broke off the stare and looked away.

"You thankless bastard, you come here begging and I give you shelter and food. And this is how you repay me? This is your gratitude? And you have the gall to preach to *me*? You, who are to blame for the death of your mother? You stupid twit. What do you know about life to lecture anybody? To lecture *me*? Nothing! You know nothing. But you *do* have a nerve! *Merde!*"

Jan didn't budge.

"*Merde* is what you are, you little hypocrite. And a loser. Just like your old man."

"Leave my father out of it!" Jan snapped.

"Hah, you don't like to hear it, huh? Let me tell you! If it weren't for me, he'd never amounted to anything. Never become a tailor."

"You're lying!"

"Oh, yeah? He didn't bring anything into the marriage except his dirty clothes. Not even a *sou*. Bet you didn't know he had to marry her because he got her pregnant, huh? I was the one who had to take care of him. Prod him to become something. Save the family from embarrassment. Save your poor mother from grief and ridicule. Me!" He slammed his fist on his sagging chest. "I was the one who did it! Understand? *Me!* And you have the nerve to judge me?" He jabbed Jan's chest with his finger. "Who do you think you are? You're nobody. Nobody! You understand? If you have an ounce of respect left in your body, an ounce of conscience, you'll crawl to the consulate and beg them to let you go home. Beg them to take you back. And when you get there, go to her grave and beg her forgiveness. You little hypocrite!"

Jan's anger welled up to the point of robbing him of thought. His sole impulse was to strike the twisted spitting face glaring at him from only inches away, but he found himself unable to move. Something held him back, squeezing his chest, draining his resolve, leaving him weak and, ultimately, crushed.

His uncle scowled. "I want you out of here, do you *understand*?" He shoved him until he stumbled. "I don't have to take this from you, you ungrateful bastard. I want you out! Your buddy, too. Get out and stay out! Leave us alone!"

Aunt Stáska stood off in the doorway with the twins hanging onto her, crying.

Without saying a word, Jan went into his room, and started packing.

CHAPTER 32

A short, wizened, officious man greeted Jan and Martin at the door of the *Comité d'Aide aux Refugies Tchécoslovaques* at 58 Rue Maubeuge in Paris. His pale watery eyes set deep in a bony, lined face measured them with tired indifference. "Please, have a seat," he said, "if you can find one. It'll be a while." He sighed. "Sorry we don't have more room, but this is all we could get. Office space is so hard to find in Paris these days." He took their names and disappeared.

The anteroom was crowded. The air was thick with cigarette smoke and the peculiar sour smell typical of unwashed flesh, dry sweat, and dirty clothes. Small groups of Czechs, mostly men, loitered about stoically while others sat on their suitcases, talking in low, hushed voices, sucking on cigarettes— waiting. A few looked up when they entered, but mostly just ignored them, staring without seeing, their glazed eyes and taut expressions betraying their inner turmoil.

It was midafternoon before the same little man called their names and ushered them into a sparsely furnished office dominated by a large desk that took up most of the room. Piles of neatly stacked papers lined one wall. Four chairs crowded the front. A pair of French and Czechoslovak flags hung limply over a framed picture of the late president Masaryk. A long shaft of sunlight poured in through a single narrow window, giving substance to a bluish column of air adrift with a universe of dust particles afloat in faint billows of smoke. The well-worn parquet floor creaked under their feet.

The man motioned them to sit down. "Mister Minister will be with you shortly."

A few minutes later, a short, rotund, balding gentleman in a rumpled pinstriped suit rushed in and slid behind the desk. His jowl hung over a starched ill-fitting white collar that pinched his fleshy neck, giving his face a ruddy appearance that almost matched the color of his stained purplish tie. "Minister Chrabal," he said. "And you are?"

They gave him their names and he grunted in response.

"If you're looking for a room at the *Maryša*, we're full." He glared at them over his pincer spectacles.

Jan pulled out the sheet of paper Aunt Stáska gave him. "It says that it may be possible to get papers here. Refugee documents," he said, handing it to the Minister.

The Minister sighed in relief and smiled. "I assumed...beg your pardon. Everybody wants to go to the *Maryša*. Been only open a month. Forgive me; it's been a long day. You tourists?"

"No, Sir. Refugees" Jan replied. "Got here from Germany."

"Should've stayed in Germany." He nodded toward the outer door. "Most of 'em out there are tourists. Trapped here by the coup. Like me. I was here visiting the consul. He's here, too, and some of his staff. Wouldn't go back when they recalled him." He shook his head in dismay.

They told him their story and he looked at them scowling over the rim of his spectacles. "You know, you may be in trouble with the police," he said, rummaging through one of the stacks of papers and pulling out an official-looking document. "This is what the *Sûreté* passes around. Here, see for yourselves. I hope you're not on it." He pushed it toward them.

Jan unconsciously recoiled seeing their names. Martin swore under his breath.

"So you *are* there?" The Minister pursed his lips. "Then, there's nothing I can do. The moment I turn in your names...

You understand." He studied their dejected faces for a few moments. "Perhaps I can get you some other papers – not French, mind you – but at least you'll have something. Takes about a week. You'll need pictures. You know the kind, just the head and shoulders. Cost you a few francs. There's a place two doors down. Can't miss it. Do you have a place to stay?"

His scowl returned when they confessed they didn't.

"The Cardinet, er, *Maryša,* is out of the question. The gendarmes come all the time. And besides, it's full. I wouldn't advise you to stay at *any* hotel. You look too suspicious." He shook his balding head. "Got any money?"

"Some. Not much." Martin tapped his pocket.

"Hmm." He bit his lip. "There is only one other place I can think of. Some of these folks stay there. Have to. But it's not nice. In fact, it's so dreadful, I hesitate. But that's all there is right now."

"We really have no choice," Jan said, looking to Martin.

Martin shrugged.

"Do you know how to ride the Metro?" the Minister said.

"Yes," they lied.

"Then go and take it to Porte de la Chapelle—it's the last stop on that line." He wrote the name on a piece of paper. "When you get out, you'll see a fountain. Can't miss it. Many of the people you saw here stay there as well and know the way. Follow them. But frankly, I have to warn you, I don't like to send people there. That's why we've rented the *Maryša.* But…" He threw his hands up.

* * *

259

The Metro reached the Porte de la Chapelle and disgorged a thin stream of passengers. Jan found it reassuring when he overheard them conversing in Czech. Some carried raggedy shopping bags filled with foodstuffs. All seemed to be headed in the same direction. Jan and Martin followed.

They passed a small square dominated by an ornate fountain, entered a cobblestone side street, and stopped cold in their tracks, totally unprepared for what lay ahead—a gaping mouth of a tunnel. The street plunged steeply into its bowels where it disappeared in the darkness. It was a Kafkaesque sight. As far as they could see, the glistening walls were lined with boxes, cartons, valises, bags and rubbish of all kind—meager possessions that narrowly defined habitable spaces in a community of squatters. Wispy columns of smoke rose from behind the barricades, forming a bluish haze plainly visible against the dark abyss. Judging from the stacks and variety of refuse – old mattresses, piles of rags covered with blankets made into beds, and crates, trunks, or odd pieces of lumber contrived into makeshift tables and chairs – many of the castaways had been here a long time. Jan gazed in amazement at the mass of milling people, the flicker of fires, and the columns of smoke that resembled the gypsy camp he once saw under a bridge in his town, or better still, Dante's infernal path into the underworld.

"Your first time?" Someone behind them spoke.

A young, sallow-faced Czech, clutching a stained bag cinched at the top so that only the end of a baguette stuck out, had come up behind them, and hesitantly offered his hand.

"Sláva Turek," he said. "Saw you at the *Comité* this morning, so I knew you were Czech. My family's over there." He pointed toward a woman busy over a small fire and two children playing on a mattress in one of the enclosures. "I could tell from your reaction." He chuckled slightly. "You can always tell strangers from the way they react the first time they see this place. I was the same way." His smile faded. "Can you believe this? Can you believe people living like this, in the so-called civilized West? In Paris, the 'City of Light,' of all places? Living in sewers? In sewers like rats?"

"What do you mean, sewers?" Jan said.

"The famous Paris sewers. Better than the celebrated labyrinths of Arsinoe and Knossos, they say. You know about them from school, don't you? Still, they are just sewers. This is where they come out. Here's where they go in to work on them."

"We had no idea." Jan shook his head.

"It goes on like this inside for over two hundred meters. Poles, Arabs, beggars. Street people. And now Czechs. Living like animals. Like dogs out in the alley, sleeping on trash and eating garbage. And the French? Hah, they pretend we're not here, except for the gendarmes. They snoop around now and then. And they call themselves civilized?"

Speechless, they took in the incredible sight and the pulsing of the faint, indifferent hum of the city somewhere beyond the confines of the encompassing high walls. So this was it. They had finally hit the bottom.

*   *   *

"This is Marie." Sláva introduced them to a slim, blond woman hovering over a contraption of a stove.

She acknowledged them with her liquid ash-grey eyes that projected despair even as she attempted a smile. "These are our

261

children," she said, pointing to two girls busying themselves with magazines on a makeshift bed. "Will you stay for supper? You must be hungry. We're having stew tonight," she said as a spark flashed in her eyes. "Find a place to sit, if you can. It'll be a while yet."

The girls shook their hands politely and withdrew to their magazines.

"It's so hard on the children here." She looked at them lovingly. "Just look at them. How fortunate that they don't fully understand. They would have been in school if we were home. I try to teach them here, but it's so hard. It breaks my heart. Should've stayed in Germany."

"You came through Germany?" Jan's eyes widened. "I thought you were tourists."

"Yeah, Germany." Sláva put his arm around his wife's shoulder and squeezed her affectionately. "I was a fool believing the French. They made us promises – a job, better life – so I signed up. But none of it happened. They shipped us to Tours. That's where the French iron industry is. Worked in the smelters. Back home I was a mining engineer, but they put me on the floor. Furnaces. Killing work. Dawn to dusk—ten, twelve hours a day. Mostly Arabs. Nobody else would take the job. And no spending money. Took most of it for lodging and food. One filthy room with a bed and a table. Hole in the ground for a toilet. One small bed for the four of us, not much better than this," he nodded toward the children, "and it took all we made to pay for it. Marie washed dishes in the kitchen. Had to keep the children with her with no one to watch over them. No school." He flushed, as his voice grew angrier. "Mind you, I am not afraid of hard work, but—" Marie put her hand on his arm and he stopped. "Forgive me for getting emotional."

"We understand. We're also disappointed with France," Jan said.

"Couldn't take it any more, so we finally quit and left. And here we are. The little money we had didn't last long, and the *Comité* won't help either. Can't. All they have is this little hotel. You heard about the *Maryša*?"

Jan nodded.

"It filled in less than an hour. We never had a chance." He looked at Marie busying herself over the fire. "I don't know what else to do," he said dolefully. "The little money we had is gone. We're broke. I can barely scrape the few *centimes* to get to Les Halles for some food. Been selling off our personal things. And when they're gone..." He shook his head and sighed.

"So what are you going to do?" Jan asked. "What *can* you do?"

He shifted uneasily and looked into the ground. Then he wiped his eyes with the back of his hand before meeting Jan's gaze. "Go home, I guess. Go home, and take my punishment. Whatever *they* can dish out, whatever they do to us can't be as bad, as degrading as this. Go home and at least have a roof over our heads. Children in school. Family. Friends. We will survive. They may not be as hard on us as they say. I hear there's an amnesty."

Dusk descended, and the flickering fires painted the walls with abstract shadows. They sat self-absorbed around the makeshift table eating the stew out of cleanly washed metal cans salvaged from some trash heap, savored the baguette, and sipped weak tea from scavenged chipped cups.

Sláva finally stood up. "It's not that we don't want you to stay," he said, "but you need to find a place to sleep before it's too late."

They bid their good-byes to Marie, gave a wave to the girls, and followed him into the gaping chasm.

"Food's not a problem," Sláva said as he led them deeper into the tunnel. "We all go down to the markets every day. You've heard of Les Halles? It's the biggest one in Paris. It's huge. There's everything. Plenty of scraps. So people go there, take the Metro – it's only a few *centimes* – and pick up scraps, stuff that's thrown away or left behind at the end of the day. Sometimes they steal, too, but that's stupid. Unnecessary. There's enough of everything just for the taking. If you're not fussy, of course. Some of them, the French, I mean, the merchants, some of them even take pity on you and give you something gratis. Even meat—that's how come we had the stew today. So, at least in theory, a person could survive here indefinitely."

"But what about water?" Jan asked. "And where do you *go*. I don't see any *pissoires* around or anything."

Sláva smiled. "You have to go deep into the tunnel, past all the people—it's good to have a flashlight. You'll smell it before you see it. Be careful where you step. As far as water goes, we go to the fountain and fetch it. Some even try to wash in there, but the gendarmes get real nasty about that. They do look the other way, though, when we just take it. I think they understand. But as I said, washing is a real problem. Haven't had a bath in weeks. We all stink.

Deep in the tunnel, in a dark alcove under wet, glistening walls, they found a place that had somehow escaped the attention of the roaming plunderers—a pair of crates and a damp, stained mattress splitting at the seams. Proximity to the privy part of the tunnel made the air acrid, but too tired to care, they were soon asleep.

The next day, when they stopped by Sláva's cubicle, he was already gone scavenging for food. The following day it rained hard and the tunnel flooded. When Jan stopped by to see if Sláva needed help moving deeper inside, he and his family were gone.

*   *   *

"This is the best I can do for you," Minister Chrabal said a week later, tapping a pair of gray official looking booklets. "Did you bring the pictures?"

The Minister handed them to the short man who carefully glued them to the blank spaces on the inside pages, put a large rubber stamp close to his mouth, breathed on it deeply a couple of times, and brought it down with a solid thud. The Minister smiled approvingly.

Hands trembling, Jan and Martin caressed the booklets. They were impressive, with official looking '*IRO*' circled by '*International Refugee Organization*' inside a stylized ring buoy, and below it, in large letters, *International Passport* emblazoned on the cover.

"Don't get too excited," the Minister said. "Actually they're worthless. All they do is say that you are refugees. Most countries don't recognize them. The French certainly don't. But they are better than nothing. That's all I can do for you under the circumstances."

CHAPTER 33

Jan and Martin stepped up to the central SNCF ticket office window in downtown Paris, flashed their new 'passports,' and bought two International Second Class tickets from Paris to Naples. It took nearly all the money they had saved from their jobs.

Elbowing their way through the shoving crowd at the *Gare de Sud*, they managed to find a window seat in a fast-filling coach. The soft velour seats were heaven after a week of wet, bone-chilling cold and spasmodic sleep on the smelly remains of a mattress in the hellhole of a sewer. They hurriedly hoisted Martin's heavy suitcase and Jan's rucksack into the rack, and moments later, drifted off into an abyssal sleep. Paris was just a bad dream.

A gust of warm salty air startled them when someone opened a window, leaving them gaping at the landscape rushing by at a dizzying pace. The sky was cloudless. Towering cliffs bathed by morning sun wore hues of pastel under massive clumps of cacti and a cascading expanse of bleached shrubbery spilling into a shimmering bowl of azure—the Mediterranean. A palm-fringed road snaked along the shore, where exploding waves smashed against the rocks in a frothy flurry of spray. Marseilles, Cannes, Nice, Monte Carlo flashed by as though in a dream, until the singsong voice of the conductor broke the spell, "*Menton, Menton, Mesdames and Messieurs, Menton, Menton.*" With a steam-laden sigh, the train came to a stop. The border!

A blast of hot air greeted them as they stepped out onto the sun-drenched platform. Jan gasped. Beads of perspiration broke out on Martin's forehead. The few disembarking passengers quickly disappeared, leaving them alone, uncomfortable in their winter clothes, feeling exposed and vulnerable.

An agglomeration of pastel-colored houses clung to the flanks of rocky cliffs, separated from the narrow strip of the shore by a highway. Beside the faint swooshing sound of waves lapping onto a sandy beach, nothing stirred.

Martin pulled out a Michelin roadmap. "We take Monti, cross over here, at Mont Grammonds," he tapped on a peak well inland, straddling the border, "come down on the other side, and pick up the train in Ventimiglia."

Jan gauged the precipitous flanks of the Maritime Alps soaring high over the town and disappearing in a dusky layer of clouds. "Looks steeper than I imagined," he mused.

Martin shrugged, grimaced, and picked up his suitcase.

A short squiggle on their map turned out to be an all-day journey. They never got to Monti. Taking turns carrying the suitcase, they rested with increasing regularity as the deserted dusty road turned into a succession of rutty rock-strewn switchbacks, and finally played out altogether at a rocky wall hemming in the first in a series of terraces, each higher than a man's reach, climbing the flanks of the mountains like a giant Cyclopean staircase. Stubby stones, protruding randomly from the rocky walls, served as steps leading from one level to the next. Barely a few meters wide, each terrace contained a narrow winding field of lumpy rock-hard soil strewn with stubble from some past meager harvest, and the droppings of sheep.

"Either the map is wrong, or we took a wrong turn." Martin spat disgustingly into the dust.

A tinkling of bells followed by bleating sounds sent them scurrying for cover in the thin underbrush. Jan flattened himself into the dusty soil. A flock of sheep moved past them, snatching bits of grass from the rocky crevasses, followed by an old shepherd puffing on a pipe and humming to himself as he passed. He brushed them with his gaze, but after another cursory look in their direction, moved on.

They tackled the first terrace. Jan climbed the stony steps as Martin, sweating profusely, lifted the heavy suitcase one stone at a time until Jan could reach it.

"Don't know what made me take this fuckin' thing," Martin swore, hoisting it to the top with one last heave.

Dismayed, they surveyed the procession of terraces stacked above them like the folds of a giant accordion, vanishing out of sight.

The sun dipped abruptly behind the ridges and the countryside dissolved into deep bluish shadows. They became aware of a dilapidated shack topped with a rusty tin roof and a gaping opening for a door a couple of terraces above them, and with renewed vigor, reached it just as darkness fell. Exhausted, they collapsed on the hard dirt floor, drenched in sweat, light-headed, too tired even to speak.

Considering the searing heat of the day, the night was bitterly cold. Jan slept fitfully, waking at odd times to see Martin staring at him bleary-eyed, teeth chattering. In the end, they pulled Martin's overcoat over their heads and huddled together for warmth.

A drum roll of rain on the tin roof awoke them just as dawn broke. The sky had opened up, sending torrents of water earthward. Gusts of wind rattled the corrugated metal, blasting an occasional shower through the gaping doorway. The damp cold numbed them to the bone. A stream of muddy water made its way inside and they had to scramble to move the suitcase and rucksack out of harm's way. Outside, yesterday's parched, bone-dry terraces had turned into a sea of mire with dirty waterfalls cascading down their sides. Huge raindrops, splattering in the soft muck, covered the ground with a carpet of coffee-colored geysers. Dismayed, they watched the sheets of rain fling themselves earthward with a vengeance. They were trapped.

The rain stopped around noon and they resumed their climb, one terrace after another. Slipping on the now slick ground, they were soon caked in mud. With each hoist the suitcase seemed heavier, and they both cursed it as they progressed ever so slowly and painfully upward. Spotting another shack, they rushed to it with the last of their strength and collapsed on the dirt floor in utter exhaustion, even ignoring what was left of the salami.

It rained again the third day, just as they reached yet another rock-strewn ridge devoid of any vegetation, intercut by more terraces. Soaked to the skin, the only thing keeping them warm was the climb—the sheer exhausting physical effort of slipping and sliding, hoisting and pulling, one terrace after another, after another, after another. As they wrestled the cheap rain-soaked cardboard suitcase, it finally gave during one of the heaves and exploded, literally, spilling its contents into the mud.

In disgust, Martin flung the handle and straps dangling from his hand into the mud. "That's our food and my clothes. They're gone! Shit!"

Jan watched the aggregation of boxes and clothing quickly sink into the quagmire. "I'm not really sorry." He sighed in relief. "It's been holding us back."

Martin cast a sneering look at him and then at the soaked pile of disintegrating cartons "Shit! Can't you see? Our food's gone! Can't even make fuckin'tea." He fished out what remained of the dry salami from the mud, wiped it clean, and with one big kick, sent the sodden foodstuffs and bundles flying down the hill. "The hell with it!" he roared, face twisted as he continued to stomp on the pile of remains, sending mud flying in all directions. "The fuckin' hell with it! I wish Tonda were here. He'd know what to do. He's probably home by now, sleeping in a fuckin' bed, and we..." He spat in the direction of the debris.

"What do you think we should do? Are we lost?" Jan looked at him with concern.

"Shit, I don't know. Can't go back, even if we wanted to. Can't afford it. We're broke." He returned a hostile stare. "And we don't know anything about where we're going. Your buddy, what's his name, Daniel, I have a feeling. Can you trust him? What if he's just bragging?" We're doing this on one guy's word. Shit! How well do you know him?"

"Daniel wouldn't lie. I know him!" Jan snapped, realizing that beyond the goings-on in school, he really didn't know him at all.

It alternately rained, sleeted, or snowed the next two days. They shivered under their wet clothes and spent the nights in the open, huddling with only Martin's overcoat over their heads for shelter. Dismayingly, Jan found himself longing for the filthy mattress in the tunnel. They smelled foul of earth and sweat, and sucked water from their sodden handkerchiefs to quench their thirst. Their conversations became monosyllabic, when they spoke at all. They seemed to grow apart, immersed in their thoughts, moving mechanically like robots, up, always up, tired to the core, shivering when they stopped, driven on by some inner reserves and desperation. Snatches of disembodied visions paraded before Jan's mind. Mother, Father, Lád'a, even Fuchs and Jakub, Uncle Alois, Jára, Inka—he relived his past and ached for it.

On the sixth day, the thick cloudy soup that had engulfed them parted just enough to reveal a sight they had longed for— the summit. Forgetting their exhaustion, they scampered up the last few hundred meters, slipping and sliding on the blotches of snow-covered ground. Before them loomed the remains of an old bunker –an observation post, Jan guessed – a relic from the war, surrounded by tangled coils of barbed-wire. A rusty assortment of weaponry, shell casings, and hand grenades lay strewn all around. In the middle of it all stood a tall, weathered, lichen-covered obelisk, bearing the faint remains of a red, green, and white tricolor. Italy! Buffeting in the wind, a weathered sign hung from a post on the far side of the perimeter. Beyond it, the remains of what once might have been a road dropped from view below the rim.

They rushed across the slippery ground to the drop-off on the far side and pulled up short, totally unprepared for the sight that opened before them—a vast churning sea of clouds, broken now and again to reveal breathtaking snapshots of the lush landscape below – way, way below in the abyss – and beyond it, vanishing in the distance, azure splotches of finely rippling water. The sea.

On the verge of tears, grinning and laughing, they slapped each other on the back in an impromptu jig. Jan felt as light and weightless as a cloud. Oblivious to the penetrating cold and biting wind, they stared down the ridges in awe until the weather again closed in and erased it all.

With renewed strength, they set down what once used to be a road. Jan stole a last look at the gaping slits of the bunker and caught the bleached letters of the flapping sign that now faced them. The sign read: *ACHTUNG – MINEN*.

*   *   *

It took them two more days to reach Ventimiglia, the little town on the Italian side of the border. Much to Jan's relief, they encountered no terraces, but the terrain was much steeper. The bleached ribbon of the road wound itself down in what seemed an infinite series of folds. The air turned warmer as they descended. Birds sang. The clouds lifted, revealing a living palette of colors as a breathtaking canvass spread before them in full majesty, culminating in a shimmering wash of the Mediterranean beyond a tiny collection of pastel-colored dabs—houses rimming the shore. They found a lone persimmon tree and gorged themselves on the bittersweet, overripe fruit. Then, for the first time in days, they slept soundly under the stars.

The next day, as the sun reached its zenith, they stopped at a stream and washed themselves as best as they could, before setting out for the town and the railroad station.

CHAPTER 34

Jan and Martin were momentarily blinded by the intense sun as the train emerged from a tunnel into an immense circular bay ringed by a sprawling metropolis and dominated by the majestic caldera of Vesuvius. Parasol-like pines shaded the tops of the surrounding hills. A vibrant medley of colors, smells, and sounds assaulted their senses. The sky glowed like burnished mother-of-pearl.

Jan was tense. He had written Daniel about their coming, but unable to provide any particulars, worried about the last leg of their journey—finding the refugee camp Daniel had described in his letter. With an overwhelming sense of relief, he spotted Daniel running along the platform as the train pulled into the Napoli train station.

"Dammit, you made it! Can't believe it. This is a miracle!" Daniel bawled, grinning broadly. "Been coming here every day now for a week. Didn't want to miss you." He held Jan at arm's length before embracing him like a long-lost brother, and then, noticing Martin, patted him on the back. Tears welled in his eyes. "Can't believe it," he kept saying, choking on his words. "Can't believe it!"

They elbowed their way onto a streetcar through a mass of shabbily dressed men of every shape and age hanging precipitously from its sides, clinging to the running boards, grasping any protrusion that might give them hold.

"They get to ride free." Daniel answered Jan's bemused look. "Do watch your pockets. Seems like every other guy's a pickpocket. Been robbed twice already."

The streetcar air was pungent with a cocktail of smells, mostly from the fishermen returning from a market somewhere, tending to their buckets full of fish, octopus, and squid, and street vendors with their wide flat baskets overflowing with fruits and flowers. It careened noisily westward along the rocky shore toward a tunnel that pierced a jutting cape separating the great shimmering bay from a smaller one, fringed by a collection of ochre-colored houses clustered around a compact harbor, and an imposing array of sun-bleached massive concrete structures hugging the steep flanks of the surrounding pine-covered bluffs.

"The camp. Bagnoli." Daniel made a wide sweep with his arm. "Used to be the Italian naval headquarters during the war. Now it's the IRO main processing center. Everybody from everywhere passes through here. People come and go all the time. A bunch of Czechs shipped out already—Australia, Canada, Brazil, Argentina, New Zealand. *America.*" He lingered on the last word, pronouncing it with an almost religious reverence. "Anybody who'll take 'em."

"Many Czechs here?" Jan asked.

"Hundreds, and more arriving almost daily. The camp holds thousands. Told you, everybody ends up here, sooner or later."

A swarthy scruffily uniformed guard barred their way at the gate – a low bunker-like structure spattered with bullet holes, abutting a tall wire fence topped with massive coils of concertina wire – as another checked the papers of a steady stream of equally shabbily dressed people making their way from the direction of the town.

"Albanians," Daniel muttered and spat into the dust. "All the guards are Albanians. Been here the longest. Got all the police jobs sewn up. Bastards."

"*Documenti!*" the guard said harshly.

Jan and Martin handed him their IRO passports. Daniel flashed an ID card.

The guard gave him an approving nod, but frowned seeing the passports. He leafed through the pages and stared at them dumbly before snapping them close and fixing the boys with a hostile stare. "*Aspetta qui,*" he growled, and disappeared into the guardhouse.

"What's going on?" Jan's stomach tightened.

Daniel shrugged. "Don't know Wants us to wait."

The guard emerged several minutes later with a scowl. "*Documenti no sono buoni.*" He shoved the passports in Martin's hand. " *No posono entrare!*"

Martin stared at the passports. "What's the matter? What's he saying?"

Daniel's face stiffened. "Says they're no good. Won't let you pass. Bastard."

The guard's sneering look instantly evaporated Jan's elation—the feeling of relief and the clutching breathlessness of anticipation that had built up as they approached the camp. As if stripped to the core, he became suddenly aware of a nauseating emptiness in his stomach and the shooting pain in his swollen feet. He had not been able to take off his shoes since they left Paris. And now this!

"What does the sonofabitch mean, they're no good? They're IRO! Look. I-R-O!" Martin glared at the guard as he waved the documents in front of his face.

Daniel pulled him aside. "For chrissake, don't piss him off. Sometimes they do this. Let me talk to him." He motioned the guard off to the side, took out a pack of Lucky Strikes and offered them to him. The guard lit one and put the rest in his pocket. Daniel then pulled a stack of lire out of his billfold, but the guard shook his head and pushed him away with a scowl and an obscene gesture.

"That bastard!" Daniel snarled, face livid. "Probably can't even read, but won't budge. That bastard. Thought I had him. Took all my cigarettes. That bastard!"

"So what do we do now?" Jan felt nauseous and suddenly very tired.

"Don't worry. I think I can get you in." Daniel smiled thinly. "I know a way. It's a bit risky, but…" He shrugged.

Panting heavily, they followed him down a side street skirting the perimeter of the camp, and then up a steep dirt path snaking through heavy undergrowth and clumps of prickly pear to the top of the bluff, thick with a grove of shrubbery and pines.

The ground around them was tamped down, and the massive chain-link fence ringing the camp bore signs of tampering. The coils of concertina wire affixed to it had been pulled together sloppily in one place where they had been cut.

"Have to wait for the guards to pass. They know about this place," Daniel whispered, motioning them behind a clump of bushes. "You never know when they'll show up. Sometimes they hide, trying to catch some poor slob just for the fun of it. Mean sons-of-bitches. Get nasty if they catch you. Gotta be careful."

The lights began to flicker around the bay before they finally heard voices and heavy footsteps on the gravel perimeter road. A pair of guards passed in front of them, stopped briefly to examine the fence, tugged at the wire and twisted the loose ends together, urinated on it and, laughing, disappeared into the thick brush.

Minutes later, Daniel carefully pulled aside the concertina wire, pushed open the cut in the fence, and they squeezed through the jagged opening, cursing under their breath as they snagged their clothing on the barbs. Daniel quickly reclosed the breach, and, stumbling over rocks and ruts in the fast-falling darkness, they followed him down an almost invisible path to the bottom of the bluff and the sprawling complex of buildings lit sharply by glaring lights, where they merged with the colorless crowd milling in the streets.

"Most of us Czechs stay in Block A," Daniel nodded toward a massive three-story stucco building, "but they're scattered in all the blocks. There are four—A, B, C and D blocks. Each holds a couple o' thousand. They bring in refugees from all over Europe: Albanians, Poles, Croats, people from Trieste, from the Balkans. And of course, Czechs. And ship them out just as fast. Australia, New Zealand, Canada, South America. All over. The consulate people have their own village. Recruiters, interrogators, you name it." Daniel pointed to a scattering of villas beyond the main area of the camp.

"You didn't say Americans," Martin reminded him.

"Oh, they're here, too. You can see their flag from here. Not much action yet. There's talk about a special quota."

Daniel led them to one of the buildings, a pink-stuccoed multistoried structure with a large sculpted "A" affixed by the entrance. "They separate the families from the single guys like us," he said, nodding toward a cavernous bottom-floor bay subdivided into hundreds of tiny corrugated cardboard cubicles, open at the top and in full view of the gawkers streaming up and down the centrally located staircase. Some of the cubicles had blankets stretched over the gaping top openings by the occupants in a vain effort to escape the eyes of the curious. There were no doors. "Call 'em paravans. Noisy. Things go on all the time. Fights. Mix all the nationalities in there. Big problem. Not so much the Czechs, the others. Like cats and dogs. You'll see. Go right through the walls when they fight." He chuckled.

The wide balconies, running the entire width of the building, one on each floor, teemed with activity. Designed to catch the fresh cool breezes wafting in from the sea during the summer heat, they were wide open to the inside, providing easy access.

"It's always crowded," Daniel said. "I sell peanuts here. Brings in a few coins. You can buy anything. Or sell anything, 'cause there's no work. People need cash. Some will sell the shirts off their backs, or steal. Steal everything. There are no lockers of any kind, and if there were, they would steal them too and sell 'em. Most of it ends up on the black market here in town or Napoli." He shrugged. "People get desperate."

Graffiti covered the walls of the huge open bay, full of row upon row of closely spaced steel double-bunks. Odor of sweat and urine mixed with the fresh air wafting in from the balconies. "There may be close to a thousand people here, just on this floor," Daniel said, as he led them to a corner and an empty bunk standing next to one occupied by a lanky blond young man reading a magazine. He sat up and swung his spindly legs over the side.

"Here's my place." Daniel pointed to a picture of President Masaryk tacked to a wall under a small Czechoslovak tricolor. "And this is Vladimír."

Vladimír cleared his throat and smiled.

"We watch each other's stuff. I was able to save you a bunk, but you'll have to sleep on the springs until I can find you a mattress. It's not much, but…"

CHAPTER 35

"You'll have to get proper papers." Colonel Gregor frowned, casually inspecting Jan and Martin's bogus passports. "The sooner, the better." A graying serious man of around fifty, still dressed in the fading remains of a once resplendent uniform, Colonel Gregor had been the military attaché of the Czechoslovak Consulate in Rome. A much-decorated Spitfire pilot during the Battle of Britain, he was revered after his return, rose quickly in rank, and was ultimately rewarded with a consular position. But rather than face persecution and almost certain imprisonment after the coup, he refused to return when the communist government recalled him and turned himself in to the local authorities instead. They had sent him to Bagnoli. When his presence in the camp became known, he immediately became the impromptu head of a swelling Czechoslovak contingent.

"For now, we can get you meal cards," he went on, "that's not a problem. But without papers, eventually you'll be caught, and that will be the end for you. You won't be able to emigrate. You might even end up in Lipari."

"Lipari?" Jan gave him a questioning look.

"A penal colony. A hell hole. On an island near Sicily. A couple of Czechs got sent there. For nothing." He sighed. "This camp's a temporary thing. Two, three years and it'll be gone. And then what? You may as well give up on returning home. The way things look, you may never be able to. Your only future is emigration. Making a new life for you somewhere else. For that, you must have proper papers. Do you have any money?"

"Not much. Don't know how many lire it is." Jan reached for his wallet.

"A few francs," Martin said.

"Never mind." The Colonel waved them off. "You must somehow get to Rome, as soon as possible. Can you travel?"

Jan shrugged. "My feet are still sore. Full of scabs. Can't even take off my socks. Could use a few days."

"We have a contact in Rome, a fellow refugee. In the Vatican. A priest. His name is Father Janáček. I know him well. He'll help. I'll write to him and give you a letter to carry. He'll help you get your papers."

* * *

The December air had a cutting chill to it as Jan and Martin got off the train at the Rome central station—an immense glass-enclosed, smoke-stained dome resounding with a crescendo of noises and blaring loudspeakers. Jan shuddered, wishing he hadn't had to sell the jacket his father had made him from an American blanket and a piece of soft leather. Giving it up had been like severing a nerve, one last bond that had tied him to home. It hurt. Next to him, Martin pulled the collar of his coat tighter about his neck.

"You must be Jan and Martin," a soft voice behind them said.

Spinning around, they found themselves face to face with a smiling friar, clad in a brown cassock cinched at the waist with a thick rope, and sandals over his bare feet. "I'm Father Janáček. Welcome to Rome."

More than thirty minutes later, the old Fiat taxi deposited them in front of a vast complex of windowless buildings fronted by an ornate gate with a single word, *Cinecittá*, embossed on its massive façade. The driver, an aging taciturn Italian, swung the doors open with a graceful motion and bowed deeply as they stepped out. Father Janáček blessed him as he bowed his head, and with a polite smile and profuse, *"Buena note, signori, buena note...buena note, molte grazie,"* sped off in a cloud of smoke.

A steady procession of shabbily dressed people streamed in and out of the gate, manned by a nattily dressed squad of *carabinieri*. Inside, an immense collection of decaying film props, from medieval catapults to mockups of airplanes and antique cars, lay heaped between the buildings.

"This is *Cinecittá*." Father Janáček nodded toward the sign. "The Italian Hollywood. A bit shabby now...an IRO processing center. Everybody from the Balkans comes through here. Mostly Croats and Slovenes now. People from Venezia Giulia. Trieste. The detritus of Europe uprooted by the war." He paused briefly as a group of shabbily-clad refugees passed by and bowed, and answered with a smile, a sign of the cross, and a whispered benediction. "Not political like the Czechs," he continued. "Displaced. Driven from their homes by the Russians, or the ethnic reshuffling that happens after every great war. I've seen Serb *cetniks* and Croatian *ustashi*. *Blue Division* Hungarians. Even a few Vlasov men passed through. You see it all."

An olive-skinned dark-haired boy greeted them at the desk with a *"Buena sera, Padre, buena sera, signori"* and a broad smile.

"This is Pietro. He'll take care of you. He's our friend." Father Janáček shook his hand and murmured something in Italian.

Smiling, Pietro retreated to a large bin in the corner of the room and pulled out two sets of blankets, sheets, and pillows.

Father Janáček glanced at his watch and sighed. "I'll be by tomorrow to pick up whatever documents you have. In the meantime, Pietro will fix you up with a temporary pass so you can get around a bit. There's much to see." He took a few steps toward the door, hesitated, and turned around. "Oh, I almost forgot to tell you—we've been blessed. The Holy Father has granted us an audience. He will see us this Sunday."

Their blank expression turned his glee into a frown "You have to understand, we've been asking and praying for this a long time. He's such a busy man. He's very much interested in refugees. He's committed to help, but we feel he needs to meet them in person. See their faces. Help him appreciate the enormity of the problem. Meeting them will make a statement. Provide focus. We've been praying for months for some recognition. Anyway," he crossed himself, "he will see us this Sunday at 11, after the High Mass."

"I'm a Protestant. I don't want to see your Pope." Martin made a pained grimace after Father Janáček vanished into the night.

Jan shrugged. "That's up to you. I don't think he'll mind."

* * *

"This is what it's like every day, now. A flood. Bring 'em in by truckloads," Father Janáček said the next morning as he emerged from a milling crowd of new arrivals.

Jan gaped at a long line of men with bewildered expressions on their drained stubble-covered faces, women with babies crying irritably in their arms, and children of all ages clutching little satchels or holding onto their mothers' skirts. Apart from the babies, they all had something in common—the hollow, distant look of desperation he had seen before, of people uprooted cruelly from their homes and cast into the tumult that was post-war Europe, reconciled with but uncertain of their fate. Weighed down by mountains of baggage, even articles of furniture that they shoved awkwardly along as the line advanced, they slowly snaked past a row of tables where officious-looking clerks checked tags attached to their clothing, passed out bedding, and stamped sheaves of documents.

"It's tragic." Father Janáček sighed. "It tears the families apart. Only the lucky ones will make it. The others...they'll have to stay behind. The countries that take them, they only want the young ones, the healthy ones. Not the old and infirm that can't work."

"So what's going to happen to them?" Jan asked.

"God will provide, I hope," Father Janáček replied in a voice lacking conviction.

At the stroke of 11, a rotund priest, wearing the purple toque of a Monsignor, led the ragtag group of refugees up a marble Vatican staircase to a large anteroom dominated by an ornate, gilded double-door guarded by a colorfully dressed Swiss Guard. He disappeared inside but emerged almost immediately, mumbled something sotto voce to Father Janáček, and then in a somber sonorous voice made an announcement to the group.

"The Holy Father has been delayed so we have a few moments," Father Janáček whispered to Jan. "I will tell you what to do once we get inside."

The door finally cracked open, just wide enough for a two-fingered wave beckoning them in. Richly decorated with ornate tapestries, the room was empty except for a pair of long narrow velvet-covered benches along two of the walls. Inside, a thin somber-looking priest dressed in a black tight-fitting floor-length cassock stopped them with an outstretched hand and wordlessly motioned them to spread out into a single file. Then, never taking his gaze off them, he retreated into a far corner.

Finally, a small, virtually invisible door in the far wall swung open and a pair of Cardinals and at least a half dozen Monsignors in flowing robes and colorful toques glided in, followed by a thin, white-clad man, a white toque framing his sallow face dominated by a beaked nose and an enormous pair of sunken eyes made even darker and larger by a pair of thick spectacles. His robe was cinched at the waist by a wide sash; a large gold crucifix hung around his neck. The thin priest sprung into action, signaling with a wave of his arms and downturned palms of his hands that he wished them to kneel. Upon reaching the center of the room, one of the Monsignors whispered something into the Pope's ear. The Pope gave a slight nod and, turning to them, indicated with his outstretched arms and upturned hands that he wished them to stand. The priest duplicated the motion with much more verve and upward thrusts of his head. Turning from one end of the group to the other, the Pope extended his right hand and made several signs of the cross as his eyes seemed to rest on each of their faces, but only fleetingly, all the while silently saying something, for Jan could see his lips move but heard nothing. And then, just as quickly as he had arrived, he was gone.

"It all happened so fast, my head's still spinning," Jan said, squinting into the bright sun as the small band of refugees emerged from the audience onto the steps of the broad colonnade overlooking St. Peter's Square.

"Yes, regretfully, it was rather brief." Father Janáček smiled sadly. "The Holy Father is an extremely busy man, and that he would see us at all..." He shook his glistening bald head in disbelief. "By the way, in case you're interested, His Holiness comes out at 3 to bless the crowd. It's a thing to see."

"Do you mind then if I don't go back with you?" Jan said.

"Of course not. It's such a beautiful day. You do remember how to get back, right?"

The square filled to overflowing as the hour approached. The crowd surged forward and the hushed crescendo turned into a roar as the window decorated with an ornate white mantle opened and the miniscule white-clad figure of the Pope appeared in the dark rectangle, arms outstretched, just standing there like a statue, letting the crowd have its way, then raising the right hand in the customary blessing.

Jan stumbled as the press of bodies thrust him forward, carrying him against his will. An old man almost fell against a priest elbowing his way across the human stream. "*Mi scusi, padre,*" he cried out, apologizing, just as the priest spun around, glaring at the old man. A thin scar on the priest's left cheek turned crimson.

For a split second, Jan didn't absorb what he saw. But then, staring at the priest facing him, he felt the rush of recognition and a creeping, choking sensation that made him gasp. That face! How could he ever forget? The reddish mustache was gone, the head shaved. He was thinner, almost slim in the tight-fitting frock. But the scar and the eyes—hard, cold, pale, chilling, freezing everything in their path. No. It couldn't be…No! Not here, in Rome. In the Vatican. A priest! No way. It wasn't possible! But he *knew* he wasn't mistaken. Klaus Fuchs!

For a split second their eyes locked, but there was no sign of recognition, only an icy, disdainful glare. Just as the priest started to turn away, unwittingly, barely loud enough to be audible above the din, Jan cried out, "Fuchs?"

The priest hesitated in mid-stride, and then plunged into the crowd. A man with a boy on his shoulders momentarily blocked Jan's vision, and when the view cleared, only the priest's bobbing hat was visible above the crowd as he rapidly scurried away.

Jan took off after him. Pushing aside bodies, offering breathless apologies at angry looks and protests, squeezing through breaks in the human tide as they opened and closed, he dove into the crowd, all the while keeping in sight the bobbing hat frantically moving away from him. To his dismay, it was gaining.

The bobbing hat reached the edge of the square where the crowd had spilled into a side street, paused for a few moments, and just as Jan broke clear, vanished. A small pedestrian door within an imposing gate slammed shut.

Once ochre but now covered with soot, pigeon droppings, and crumbling plaster, the building was one of several nondescript edifices ringing the Vatican in fortress-like fashion, the ornate gate with its door and a hinged peephole covered with heavy iron grating being the only thing that set it apart from the others.

Jan stared at the massive portal. *He had to be in there!* Yanking at an iron ring, he pushed, pulled, and knocked. But the door failed to yield. Frustrated, he battered it with his fists. Still no response. He turned away in disgust.

The peephole swung open and a bearded face of a monk filled the opening. *Si?*" he said harshly.

Taken aback by surprise and the monk's unfriendly tone, Jan stood there, open-mouthed.

"*Si? Che voi?*" The monk glared at him.

"A man, *uomo, monsieur…entrare qui…ici, un prête…*priest…*compri?*" Jan blurted out, angry at being unable to make himself understood.

The monk's upper lip curled, revealing his stained teeth. "*No capisco niente. Vai via!*"

"Klaus Fuchs! German! Nazi! Klaus!" Jan's voice shook with anger.

The peephole door slammed shut in his face.

He continued to stare at the gate, weak-kneed, frustrated, and upset. *If he went in, he must come out!* For Jakub's sake, he must wait! He had to! For Jakub! And his conscience.

Feeling like his mind was about to explode, he crouched out of sight behind a round kiosk smelling of urine and plastered with old posters and remnants of wartime propaganda. His mind raced, filled with images of Jakub and Fuchs. It was all so bizarre! So unbelievable! And yet, he was sure of what he saw. He'd know Fuchs anywhere. *Anywhere*!

He forgot about time as his gaze bore into the windows set deeply in the thick walls, but they blankly returned his stare. His heart skipped when he thought he'd detected movement behind one of them, but with the passing of time, he wasn't sure his eyes weren't playing a trick on him.

Dusk covered everything with a scrim. The street emptied. The crowds in the square had long dispersed. Lights began to flicker in some of the other buildings, but the house across the street remained dark, mysterious, unyielding. Cold, hungry, and mentally drained, he reluctantly decided to quit.

* * *

"What you say is impossible. The Holy Father would never allow anything like that. It's simply inconceivable." Father Janáček puckered his brow when Jan confided in him the next morning "Surely you didn't think Holy Father— you were mistaken."

"But I know what I saw." Jan shriveled under his severe look.

"Just think what you're saying. What you're *implying*. That's blasphemy!" Father Janáček's solicitous tone disappeared. "The Holy Father would never allow… It's simply unthinkable. I don't deny you saw someone. Someone who you *thought* looked like a man you once knew. But you must've been mistaken. Right?"

Surprised by the fervor of Father Janáček's reaction, Jan didn't answer.

"Right?"

Jan nodded, feeling foolish for having mentioned it.

"I know what I saw. It *was* Fuchs," he later told Martin, as he recounted the experience. "I saw that bastard! I'm absolutely sure it was Fuchs!"

* * *

Two days later, new papers in hand, Jan and Martin bid good bye to Father Janáček, who accompanied them to the station. "God bless you and be true to what you are and who you are, wherever you are," he said as they shook hands for the last time. "Don't lose hope and don't forget your mother country."

CHAPTER 36

"I really saw him! I swear!" Jan burst out, exasperated under Gregor's hard look. He didn't count on being challenged and felt foolish for having listened to Daniel, who had talked him into telling Gregor about Fuchs. Rocking gently back and forth, Gregor leaned back in his chair, blew a cloud of smoke skyward, and shifted his gaze into infinity. Finally, he stopped rocking. "Oh, I believe you. I'm sorry if I gave the wrong impression." He smiled reassuringly. "I was just trying to recall something. Came across my desk at the Consulate. A memo about how they'd found Nazis dressed as peasants. Some were even posing as Jews from the concentration camps. So being dressed as a priest isn't all that far-fetched. What surprises me is the coincidence."

"Father Janáček didn't believe me, either. Said I must be mistaken."

Gregor smiled. "What did you expect him to say? What you're saying, what you're implying… You have to understand. He's a priest." He bit his lip, and then his face lit up. "Ah, I remember! The memo I was trying to recall had to do with something called Odessa."

"The Russian city?"

"No, of course not." He snorted. "It's a name of an organization. A very *special* Nazi organization. O-de-ssa. Note the two esses. Doesn't it tell you something?"

"I am sorry. I don't follow."

Gregor exhaled loudly and leaned toward him. "SS! The SS! It's an acronym. It stands for '*Organization Der SS-Angehörigen*'—ODESSA. Organization of people belonging to the SS. It's an outfit that helps the Nazis evade justice. Leave Germany. Hide in other countries like Spain, South America, Africa—anywhere."

Jan considered his answer. "Father Janáček mentioned he'd seen the *ustashi,* too, and the *cetniks,* the Hungarians, the *Blue Division.*"

"You see? They all fought with the Nazis. So why not the Nazis themselves? They have the most at stake. War crimes and all that. So Odessa fills the bill. Europe is still in turmoil and this place is like a giant vacuum. It sucks in everybody. Nothing is settled."

"Can't we tell somebody? Report it somewhere?"

Gregor scratched his greying head. "Don't know where. And even if we could, I doubt anyone would listen. Or believe us. I doubt anyone'd care."

"The Americans?"

"The Americans have enough problems now that Stalin is blockading Berlin. This is nothing."

"But it's not right!" Indignation swelled in Jan's gut.

Gregor gave him a bitter smile. "Right? What's right? Ten years ago, I left home to fight for the Republic. Went to France, from there to Spain, Africa, England. Fought for the right cause. Did the right things. And look at me. What did it get me?" He shrugged. "At least, back then, they kept us together. Common purpose. Common goal. Four squadrons, Spitfires and Liberators. Fought together. Came home together. But look at us now. Look what's happening to us here. We are being scattered. Ignored. Erased."

"There was talk about a Legion when I left."

"Oh yes, I've heard." Gregor's bushy eyebrows shot up. "A pipe-dream. Any opportunity, if there ever *was* such a thing, was lost when they began to separate us. Ship us out to places like this one, and then God knows where. As political refugees, at least we had an identity. Something in common. Common goal. The Legion, perhaps. Our country. Liberation. Future. But now we're being thrown in with everybody. Diluted, so to speak. Marginalized. We're no longer considered political refugees, but displaced persons. Thrown in with everybody from anywhere. Displaced persons. DPs! A semantic trick, but an important one. So yes, I'm bitter. Yes, I'm disappointed. Yes, I'm angry. But I'm not giving up, and you mustn't, either."

"But Fuchs—"

"The world's full of Fuchses. People do strange things to survive. All *you* can do is be true to yourself. Make a future for yourself somewhere else. We'll never be able to go back." He paused and looked at Jan sadly. "You will find life a great burden if you don't accept that."

The imposed idleness of the camp was demoralizing. After the first few days of registering at the various "desks" and "commissions," filling out sheaves of immigration documents and sponsorship applications, there wasn't much else to do but lie around and worry.

Christmas came, and for the first time in his life Jan wished it were over, as he and his friends gathered around a decorated cactus spear in place of a Christmas tree and sang familiar carols and patriotic songs to the tune of Vladimír's harmonica. Tears and *Marsala* flowed freely, loosening tongues and opening a flow of long-suppressed emotions. Jan thought of his father, equally alone. In the privacy of his bunk, he took out the only tactile object connecting him to the old man, his letter, fragile now, stained and falling apart at the creases, and stared at the faded words, painfully conscious of how much he missed home. He cried.

* * *

"When we came through at night, it was too dark to see it," Daniel said, veering off toward two enormous tunnels cut like two huge scars into the face of the bluff. "Used to be gun emplacements. The biggest coastal guns the Italians had. Never got to use them."

The surrounding bluff was littered with twisted and rusting metal. The guns were gone, but the remains of two massive steel doors that once concealed them and rails that moved them into position still lay there by the entrances, warped and shattered.

"Hundreds of meters deep. Used to be shelters and ammo storage," Daniel said.

Their footsteps echoed inside, littered with stacks of rebar, rusting pipes, and human refuse. Stale sour odor permeated the air. The walls, covered with graffiti and pockmarked with bullet holes, dripped water that pooled on the concrete floor. Jan tossed a rock into the darkness and heard it land with a splash.

"The floor must've shifted. All this 'round here is volcanic. There's a little town just up the road, Pozzuoli, and a place called *Solfatara*. You can stick a dry branch into the ground and when you pull it up, it'll be burning."

They walked up to the breach in the fence, slid into the bushes, and fell quiet. When the guards passed, they carefully squeezed through the opening.

"Most people don't know about this," Daniel said, pulling apart a thick clump of branches in a clearing and revealing a gaping fissure. "A cave. My business contact in town, the fellow I buy peanuts from, showed me once."

Completely hidden from view, the cave was narrow at the entrance but widened quickly, becoming round and smooth, high enough for a man to stand.

Daniel led Jan inside. "They say it's an old lava tube."

The walls were smooth and black. Slightly sloping at the breach, the cave dropped off sharply and disappeared into the dark bowels of the earth. A smattering of bones, bleached white by time, littered the silty floor. A skeleton of a larger animal, a dog perhaps, lay almost intact at their feet.

"Don't bend down!" Daniel cried out as they progressed a short distance down the steep slope and Jan stumbled.

Jan jerked upward, bumping his head on the rocks.

Daniel sneaked past him and stopped a short distance from where the floor broke downward. "Now bend down, but carefully. Carefully. Slowly!"

Jan bent down and took in a gulp of something, odorless and tasteless, which instantly flooded his lungs and took his breath away, choking him and sending him reeling. Eyes bulging, coughing and gasping for air, he staggered out into the open and collapsed on the ground, fighting the urge to heave.

"Interesting, huh?" Daniel laughed. "Don't know what it is. Some kind of gas. Stays close to the ground. Reaches the lip of the cave and spills out. It's clear, but you can almost see it ripple. No smell, but it can kill. You saw the bones."

* * *

The passing of winter into spring was hardly noticeable at the Bagnoli camp's latitude, except for the searing brilliance of the sun, and the calendar, reminding Jan that a year had passed since he left home. It made him melancholy and he dwelled on it as he approached his bunk where, to his surprise, he saw the normally sedate Daniel skip and twirl in an impromptu jig. Daniel greeted him with a wide grin. "Hey! Got a sponsor! Going to America!" he crowed. "Michigan!" He punched Jan playfully in the shoulder.

"America? That's great!" Jan croaked, feigning delight as his gut filled with nausea of foreboding. "Does it…does it mean then you'll be leaving soon? Now that we finally got together, and—"

"Nah, don't worry. They say it'll be weeks, maybe even months before anything happens. But I hear that they'll be sending most of the Czechs to other camps. There have been rumors ever since I got here, but now it's official. Looks like it's going to happen. So, you may be going."

"Me? And what about you?"

"Gotta stay here. Few others, too. Those that have sponsors."

"But why? Why now?"

"They need room for the people from the East. Venezia Giulia, Trieste. Coming in by the hundreds. Mostly families. Clogging the system. Australia's taking them as fast as it can, but—" He made a face. "Most of the Czechs are single, no families, so they're easier to move around. Don't have to break 'em up."

"For how long?"

Daniel shrugged and looked away.

Jan fought a sudden tightness in his chest. "Guess I won't see you again." The words came out strangled. "We barely got to see each other, and now you'll probably ship out to America and—"

"Anything can happen." Daniel tried to sound reassuring." I may still be here, but just in case, I'll give you my sponsor's address." His voice broke and he cleared his throat.

They posted the lists the next day and a week later, a convoy of trucks delivered several hundred Czechs to the Napoli railroad station for a trip to a relief camp in a place on the Adriatic called Senigallia.

Overwrought, Jan shook Daniel's hand and they hugged each other with emotion. He was sure they would never see each other again.

CHAPTER 37

Nothing's changed, Jan reflected, looking out the back of the truck as it careened toward Bagnoli. The sameness of the iridescent hues of the bay, the lofty cone of Vesuvius shrouded in haze, and the pungent Napoli air filled with aromas of flowers, fruits, and the sea was reassuring. Time can play tricks on you, he mused. He and the sizeable Czech complement had been gone only a year, and it had seemed an eternity. To his surprise, he saw Daniel running along and waving as the truck pulled up to a stop at the camp's cavernous processing center.

"I don't believe it!" Jan cried, elated to see him. "I thought you'd be in America by now!"

"Told you I'd be here when you got back." Daniel grinned, helping him and Martin off the truck.

"Can you believe it's been over two years since we left home?" Jan scanned the crowded square and the blocks teeming with life, and shook his head. "If we'd stayed, we'd be getting ready to graduate. Be somebody. Have a life. I miss that. Instead here we sit, and you're still here."

"Or we'd be in jail. Probably worse. You having regrets?" Daniel scowled.

"Sometimes. And you?"

Daniel shrugged. "I think now that the Berlin question's been settled, American emigration's going to pick up. Your time will come."

"Berlin? What about Berlin? I haven't heard. We were completely out of touch."

"Yeah. The airlift's over. The Russians backed down. Anyway, there's movement. The Czechs are leaving. Vladimír's gone. Tasmania. And Benáček, the basketball player, left for New Zealand. Some place called Ruakura Animal Station." He rolled his eyes and knitted his brow. "But Gregor's still here. And many of the others."

"Gregor? Wasn't he supposed to go to England? Wasn't he in the RAF, and—"

"I know, but the Brits wouldn't take him. Cancer. Nobody wants sick people." He made a face. "I managed to save you your old bunk. Made it look like it was occupied, and Martin can have Vladimír's. So where did you go?"

"Took us to Senigallia first, for three months. On the Adriatic. Somebody said Mussolini vacationed there. Remote and small, but I liked it. Right on the beach. Not fifty meters from the water. Quonset huts. Said it was an American rest camp or something. Could've stayed there forever, except one night in March we had a giant storm. Huge! You can't imagine. They said it was a fluke, never saw anything like it, but it washed away everything. The huts, our things, everything. So, they had to evacuate us. They drove us to a place called Grugliasco, all the way across Italy not far from the French border in the Alps, near Torino, and put us in an old manor that had belonged to a local Fascist *capo* or something. Anyway, that was fine, too, except for the cold, and the fact that that part of Italy is mostly communist. All the big factories and stuff. So the communists started to demonstrate in front of the camp. Huge crowds. Loudspeakers. Throwing rocks. Smashed most of the windows. Had us trapped. Nobody could get out."

"Didn't you have guards? The *carabinieri*?" Daniel looked at him in disbelief.

Jan shook his head. "Watched it all, but didn't move a finger. So, one night, way past midnight, the trucks showed up and drove us to a place called Jesi. Quonsets again. On a mountain top, in the Apennines. Completely isolated. Spent the last six months there. And then, yesterday, the trucks showed up again, and...here we are."

*   *   *

Returning to his bunk one evening, Jan was surprised to see Martin waiting there, distressed, face pale, staring vacantly into space.

"You look like a ghost. Something's the matter?" He nudged him.

Wordlessly, Martin handed him an official-looking piece of paper. "They want me to go to Chile." His eyes glazed. "Chile! Do you know where that is? The asshole of the world. I'd have rather gone to Australia than Chile. And all the while, I thought...I hoped... Shit!"

Jan scrutinized the document. "It says here, you're going as an architect. An architect? You're not an architect."

"I never really said I was an architect. I did what you did on your application, on all the applications. Put down 'student,' technical student, and architecture as the goal. I was sure one day we'd be going to America together. All three of us." He flung the piece of paper on the bunk in disgust.

"But, there's no guarantee. There never was any guarantee."

Martin looked at him blankly. "I have an uncle in America."

"In America? You never said anything about an uncle!"

Martin flushed and remained silent.

Jan shook his head in disbelief. "Didn't you give 'em his name at the Commission? At the American Desk? Write to him? Ask him?"

"Yeah, I wrote to him, and he wrote back and sent me some dollars. He was going to be my sponsor. But the last letter I wrote came back." His look darkened. "He died."

Though shared hardships drew them together, Jan never felt as close to Martin as he had felt toward Jakub, particularly after the trek across the Alps. Martin's habitual aloofness and secretiveness never permitted a deeper emotional involvement. There always remained a distance. Nevertheless, Jan had grown fond of him. Along with Daniel, Martin represented a slice of his past—a link, however tenuous, to home. And that link was about to be severed. With emotions welling up inside, Jan instinctively reached out and embraced him, amazed by an overwhelming feeling of kinship he had not experienced since they had left home. Somehow, a whiff of Martin's body odor – a sour mixture of dust and sweat – reminded him of the freezing nights crossing the Alps when they huddled together under Martin's sodden overcoat. They had shared so much in such a short time, and yet, it all seemed so long ago. And now this!

"Maybe later, someway," Jan murmured, knowing the futility of his response. "There's got to be a way."

They both fell silent, overwhelmed by the oppressive weight of inevitability.

"When?" Jan finally spoke.

"Two weeks. Get my first physical tomorrow."

"Two *weeks*? Jesus! You told Daniel?"

"Yeah. But I swear to you, one day...one day I'll be in America!"

A scruffy Albanian guard barred Jan and Daniel's way when they tried to board the bus to accompany Martin to Naples where the Chilean freighter was moored. Almost frantic, they rushed to town and took a Naples streetcar, but by the time they reached the harbor, Martin had already boarded.

Breathless and filled with a heavy dullness, Jan stood on the long stone pier as the ship, without ceremony, weighed anchor, and after a blast from its horn, accompanied by a pair of tugs, slowly eased into the open water. There was no drama, no emotion—only the starkness of the moment. No bands played and no people waved the way he used to see in the movies. The last he saw of Martin was a small waving figure standing on the fantail, getting smaller and smaller, until he finally became one with the indistinct shape that was the ship.

The few people that managed to witness the departure dispersed and Jan realized how very alone he was. He thought of the transitory fragility of human bonds and relationships, sucked dry by the places conducive to shredding and destroying them—the camps. He mused how some of the most momentous events in life pass by inconspicuously, cloaked in indifference, and how the world, callously preoccupied with itself, hides beneath its veneer of concern a seething repository of drama on a scale that defies imagination, yet passes by virtually unnoticed. Next to him, Daniel stared silently into the void where the grey shape of the ship had merged with the silvery gray of the horizon and vanished like a ghost.

CHAPTER 38

"Give it to me, you fuckin' bastard!" someone screamed up above the second floor balcony, almost directly above where Jan and Daniel tended to Daniel's peanut stand.

More thrashing and groans, more shouts and moans, a dog's painful yelp, until finally something fell past them and landed with a dull thud on the concrete down below.

"I told you to keep that goddam dog quiet when I'm asleep! I told you! Don't say I didn't warn you!"

Jan leaned over the edge to see. A small pup, now lifeless, lay splattered on the pavement, a pool of blood slowly spreading from under its broken body.

"You sonofabitch, you killed my dog! You sonofabitch, I'm gonna kill *you*, you sonofabitch!"

Daniel hurriedly threw the few remaining bags of peanuts into an old beat-up suitcase and they both rushed upstairs, where a crowd had already gathered round the two staggering men.

"That's Jánoš," Daniel said. "He buys peanuts from me. Don't know the other."

They both knew Jánoš, a Slovak and a former commando, who prided himself on being tough by sticking pins in his arm or burning it with cigarettes without flinching a muscle. The other man stood fast with his back toward them, legs spread apart in a boxer's stance, weaving from side to side, fists clenched, waiting for Jánoš to come at him.

"I'm gonna kill you, you bastard! I'm gonna kill you!" Jánoš lunged at him, grasping him in a headlock with one hand and pummeling him with the other.

Each hit lifted the hapless figure flailing and kicking off the floor, eliciting a wheezing sound like air being forced out of a deflated bag. Wrapping arms around him, Jánoš made a move toward the ledge of the balcony as the other man desperately dug in his heels.

"I'm gonna kill you, you sonofabitch!" With one heave, he lifted the battered figure onto the ledge. "I'm gonna kill you the way you killed my dog!"

The crowd closed in around the men and pushed them back.

"Let the bastard go, Jánoš. Let him go," someone pleaded. "He's not worth it. You'll end up in Lipari. You'll never get to leave here."

"But you saw what that sonofabitch did! He killed my dog! I loved that little dog! And this sonofabitch—" Jánoš grabbed the straining man by the collar and gave him one final crushing blow to the face that sent him flying backward into a post. It propped him up momentarily and then he slowly slid to the floor, blood oozing from his nose and mouth. Quiet now, he lay there in a heap, breathing heavily, staring vacantly at the ceiling.

Jan finally had a clear view of his face. Even under a covering of blood, there was something familiar about it. A slow chill crept up his spine as recognition set in. The bloody face staring blankly into space belonged to none other than Franta Paleček.

"You getting sick or something?" Daniel nudged him. "What's the matter?"

"That…" Jan nodded toward the man on the floor, "that's Paleček!"

"Paleček? Who's Paleček? You know him?"

"I told you, remember? He's the bastard that beat up my father! Sent him to jail. Left my mother dying. Head of the SNB. A communist!"

A pair of friends led Jánoš away, still cursing and fuming. Paleček spat out a wad of bloody sputum, wiped his mouth with the back of his hand, and stood up looking around groggily, swaying in place like a drunkard. His gaze met Jan's, but there was no recognition as he slowly spun around and stumbled out of the balcony toward the washroom.

"I think you need to tell Gregor," Daniel said.

"Gregor?" Jan frowned. "He can't do anything."

"Still—he should know. I think he should know."

Face puffed up and bruised, but now clear of blood, Paleček staggered from the washroom and disappeared behind a door at the back of the open bay.

"Where is he's going? Do you know what's up there?" Jan stared at the closing door.

"Looks like private rooms. Offices or something." Daniel scowled. "Don't see how he gets to stay in there, though. Must know somebody."

"Sorry to bother you, but Daniel thought you should know," Jan said, as Gregor carefully folded Jan's letter, and slipped it back into the tattered envelope.

"Are you absolutely sure he's the one?" Gregor's forehead furrowed under his hard look.

"One hundred percent!" Jan detected a sickening measure of doubt in Gregor's voice and wished he hadn't listened to Daniel.

"And what you said your friend Jára told you—"

"Jára was there. He saw it with his own eyes."

"And where is your friend now? Can he corroborate?"

"French Foreign Legion. We got separated."

Gregor leaned back and closed his eyes, and Jan took his silence as a confirmation of his doubt. "Jára wouldn't lie about that. I believe him." His voice trembled just a bit.

Gregor sat up and cautiously looked over his shoulders. "I believe you." His eyes narrowed. "There's only one explanation. He might be a spy. A communist spy. Never thought I'd see a Czech do it. It's really very clever." He gave a short tense laugh. "Really, this would be a perfect time. With all the turmoil and confusion, thousands escaping, camps overflowing with all kinds of people, no papers, no way to check them out thoroughly, pressure to get rid of them—it's clever. It's not difficult to get documents. Just look at you. And he surely would have had a good cover story to tell to whoever questioned him. There's no way to check. As I understand it, the German camps were full of them. They'd pretend that they'd escaped, and then blend with the real refugees. Spy on them. Get information about them. Names, addresses, that sort of a thing. And then disappear, re-cross the border, pass the information to the SNB, and you know what would happen next to their families back home." His eyebrows shot up and his face screwed up in a scowl. "Except, this one's different. This is Italy. The border's hundreds of kilometers away. So I don't think he's going back. I think he's in for the duration."

"Are you saying, he wants to emigrate?"

"That, and more." Gregor sighed. "It happened in England during the war. Germans. Spoke excellent English. Infiltrated and settled among the Brits, and then passed information back to the Nazis. Most of them got caught, but not before they caused a lot of damage."

Jan felt a sudden chill. "I had no idea. So you think he would—"

"No question in my mind. It's easy for him to pass himself off as a political defector. Here, he blends with everybody. Nobody knows him. Your meeting him was a fluke. Just think. If it hadn't been for the fight, you might have never known he was here. And once he'd immigrate, he'd disappear in the local population like a mole, settle down, and wait. A communist spy with a perfect cover. Do whatever he's told to do. Do you understand what I'm saying?"

Jan sat silently for a few moments, contemplating Gregor's words. "Can't we do something? Report him?" he finally said.

"Report him? To whom?"

"The Americans."

Gregor shook his head. "I wish, but this is Italy. An IRO camp. The Americans aren't the occupiers any more. They're here to screen people for immigration, that's all. The worst that could happen to him would be that they would reject him. Assuming, of course, that they'd believe us, which they might not. Remember, he is not stupid if he made it this far."

Jan looked at him painfully. "I'd do anything!"

Gregor gave him a reassuring pat. "I know how you feel. Give me a few days. Let me do some checking. I have contacts. But in the meantime, under no circumstances let on that you know him. And don't let him see you. Understand?"

In the days that followed, Jan and Daniel took turns watching the door of Paleček's room from a safe distance, hoping to catch a glimpse of him. When he emerged, Jan followed him, blending seamlessly into the crowd, but in the end, fearing discovery, decided to heed Gregor's advice and wait.

* * *

"There's no Paleček registered anywhere," Gregor said when Jan met with him again almost a month later. "I rather expected that. But there's Palec—Martin Palec. Paleček is a diminutive of Palec, so there's the connection. Gives his home as Prague. A big city. Hard to trace. And occupation as a guard at a publisher that was shut down by the communists and the records confiscated so they can't be traced. I told you he was smart and ingenious. He's applied for an American sponsor. And that's not all. He's got a job."

"A job? Here? He had to know somebody."

"Don't know," Gregor shrugged, "but he's working in the old UNRRA warehouse, distributing packages."

"Packages?"

"Yes. Toothpaste, toothbrushes, combs, soap, cigarettes. Stuff they give out to people that are leaving. Everybody gets it. You'll get one, too, someday. We searched his room and found nothing. He covers his tracks well. What we did find was a lot of UNRRA stuff; mostly cigarettes, conserves, everything. I think he steals it. He steals it and sells it. So, he's a thief, too!"

"That bastard!"

"I had him followed. He's in cahoots with one of the Albanian guards. The Albanian waits for him at the breach in the fence, and even helps him get the stuff out."

"Up where we got in?"

"The same." Gregor nodded. "Then, on the other side, he meets a local. An Italian."

"That sonofabitch! Can't we do anything?"

"As a matter of fact, we can." Gregor leaned closer until Jan could feel his breath on his ear. "Here, let me tell you what I want you to do."

CHAPTER 39

The sun shot a dying burst of color through a slit in the leaden clouds hanging low and thick just above the horizon, before sinking into the sea. The cicadas fell quiet. The breeze came up, rustling the dry grass and crowns of the tall pines, now only a swaying black mass above Jan and Gregor sprawled behind a clump of bushes. Below them, falling darkness all but obliterated the faint trace of the path leading to the breach in the fence.

"Do exactly as I told you and you'll have nothing to worry about," Gregor whispered. "You sure you can do it?"

Jan nodded, fingering the flashlight in his pocket, and swallowed hard, trying to overcome the shakes and nausea settling in the pit of his stomach.

"There's still time if you don't want to. Gregor looked at him anxiously. "We'll do it some other time, or I'll get somebody else."

"I can!" Jan whispered, hoping that Gregor wouldn't hear the pounding of his heart.

"Don't worry. The others are already there." Gregor nodded toward the bushes and gave him a reassuring smile.

Unable to stop shaking, Jan held his breath until he felt the blood pounding in his temples, and snugged the thin jacket around his shoulders to ward off the chill. He scoured his mind for all the ruthless things he knew about Paleček. The nagging rage he had felt at him for days had subsided, supplanted first by doubt and then resignation. He felt strangely deflated. He wanted to *hate* him, hate him the way he once hated Fuchs, but hating someone in the heat of the moment was not the same as arbitrarily commanding hate—it seemed to reside in a realm of its own, apart from his will, like a festering toothache. Now, the only thing that drove him on was a sense of righteousness and his conscience. A moral obligation. He shuddered, and felt Gregor's reassuring hand on his shoulder.

Somewhere behind them a series of scuffling sounds briefly disturbed the rustling of the wind: a muffled howl of an obscenity in singsong Italian; a cry cut short; indistinct pummeling noises; the sound of running footsteps—then silence.

"That was Paleček's Italian contact coming to meet him," Gregor whispered. "Got rid of him. Scared him off. That tells us, *he's* coming tonight. He's coming for sure."

Jan heard the guard before he saw him, or rather just the glow of his cigarette and an occasional flicker of his flashlight as he stepped up the rutted perimeter road. Treading carefully, he paused to listen every few steps until he reached the hole in the fence, looked around, stomped on the cigarette, and snuffed out the light. Swallowed immediately by the darkness, only his heavy breathing, an occasional grunt, and a gurgling sound as he relieved himself gave away his presence.

Minutes passed. Finally, the guard swore under his breath as he checked his watch, switched on the flashlight, and quickly sent three flashes down the hill into the inky void. A few seconds later he signaled again. And again. Then, cupping his hand over the flame, he lit another cigarette and settled into the grass. Time passed.

From the darkness below the rim of the hill came the heavy scraping sound of footsteps. The guard snuffed out the cigarette and became one with the night. Laboriously measured, the footsteps drew near until they resolved into a barely visible outline of a man against the faint glow of the sky.

Jan drew back and Gregor squeezed his arm.

The man's wheezing breath came in short spurts as he stood there, a pair of bulging bags slung over his shoulders, peering into the darkness, listening. Finally, in a raspy voice, he called out a name. The guard shot a quick flash of light in the man's face. Barely a blink, but long enough for Jan to see even at that distance that it was Paleček.

The guard showered Paleček with a foul torrent of words as he cupped his hand over the flashlight, and as they both climbed up to the fence. Paleček untangled the wire and quickly wiggled himself through the opening. The light went off, and all Jan could make out were vague movements of the two men, the scratchy sounds of cloth snagging on the barbed wire, and the cursing of the guard as he pushed the bags through the hole to Paleček on the other side. More cursing, a few whispered words, and it was over. The guard shut the opening and without a word, vanished into the darkness.

Paleček picked up the bags and climbed the short grassy embankment to a narrow clearing just below the bushes shielding Gregor and Jan. He dropped the bags, let out a soft whistle, and cocked his ear.

The silence was profound.

He swore under his breath and whistled again.

A loud crack of a breaking twig spun him around. "Guido?" he barked hoarsely. "Is that you?"

No answer.

"That you, Guido? Don't play games with me, you fuckin' fascist, come on out! I know you're there. Guido?" Paleček raised his voice above the rustling of the wind that suddenly flattened the heads of the palmetto thickets and scattered the dry grass in a gust.

Gregor squeezed Jan's arm and gave him a nudge.

Trying to hold in check his now uncontrollable shaking, clutching the flashlight, Jan stepped into the clearing.

Paleček spun around. "Guido, you sonofabitch, you trying to play fuckin' games with me?" he groaned.

Jan became numbingly calm. His heart still pounded, but the fear left him. The shaking stopped. The only thing he saw was the bobbing hulk not ten steps away from him.

"*Guido?*"

"Hey! Paleček!" Jan cried out and shot a beam of light at the figure in front of him.

Paleček recoiled. "Hey! What the—" The beam of his flashlight slashed the darkness. "Who the fuck?" He glared at Jan, as his face contorted in startled recognition. "Shit! Neuman? You! Neuman! They said you were in France. What the fuck are you—" He took a step back and quickly looked around. "You sonofabitch!"

The darkness came alive with moving shadows.

He whipped out a knife. "You sonofabitch!" he snarled, dropping into a crouch, knife in one hand, flashlight in the other, and lunged just as a club hit his outstretched arm. The blade flew out of his hand.

He swore and stumbled over his bags. The moving shadows jumped him. His flashlight flew to the ground, bathing the scene in a surreal display of struggling phantoms. He fought back fiercely. A pair of burly hands pinned his arms. Someone cinched a belt around his kicking feet, permitting only fitful thrusts. Someone else threw a blanket over his head, stifling his cries. It was over in a flash.

"You did fine," Gregor muttered reassuringly.

Jan didn't respond.

Half-carrying and half-pulling, the men dragged Paleček toward the cave. His feet sporadically found the ground and he dug in his heels, only to be jerked upward and given a shove that sent him flying. The heavy blanket muffled his screams and curses.

His thrashing increased as they reached the opening. With one final heave, he freed one of his hands and snatched the blanket off his head. His eyes bulged like a pair of giant glistening marbles. Gasping for breath, he twitched with rage. He spat at Gregor, but missed. The men pinned his arms again and dragged him inside.

Flashlights bathed the dark interior of the cave in ghostly lights and shadows.

"Do you know why you're here?" Gregor said.

"Fuck you!" Paleček spat back, straining to free himself.

"Is your name Paleček? František Paleček?"

"Fuck you!"

"You *are* a spy and a thief!" Gregor said.

He didn't flinch. "I don't know what the fuck you're talkin' about."

Gregor turned to Jan. "Is this the man your father wrote about in the letter you showed me? Is he the communist SNB chief from your town?"

"Fuck you, you sonofabitch. He's fuckin' lying! I never met him before!" Paleček exploded.

"Yes," Jan whispered, meeting Paleček's glare.

Gregor gave a slight nod and the men swarmed over Paleček, forcing him downward—down into the invisible layer of gas.

"You're fuckin' making a mistake!" he screamed. "I got dollars…"

He fought desperately, spouting threats and obscenities, until he finally crumbled and sank to his knees. Someone pushed his head down toward the ground. His face stiffened as he held his breath. His darting gaze fixed on a point and he turned crimson. Bulging as though ready to burst, the veins on his temples stood out like ropes.

He continued to struggle, but a dozen hands pressed him firmly into the invisible layer of gas. With one last heave, he let out a hoarse groan as his mouth gaped wide and took a deep breath. A stream of vomit gushed out as he recoiled in a series of spasms. His eyes, still bulging, froze in a wide, glazed look. He continued to thrash, but gradually his convulsions grew weaker, until they stopped altogether and he lay still, vomit continuing to ooze from his mouth, pooling on the ground. He was dead.

The men quickly untied the belt from his legs. Someone produced a bottle of Marsala and stuck it in his mouth, forcing in the liquid until it gushed and mixed with the vomit under his body. It was Jánoš. "That's for my dog, you bastard," he growled, tossing the bottle next to Paleček's hand.

Just as furtively as they had appeared, the men melted into the darkness. Horrified and sick at his stomach, Jan staggered out of the cave and found the enfolding thickness of the night comforting. He had not expected murder. Gregor never said they would kill him. Collapsing against a boulder, he threw up until dry hives replaced the foul vomit. His mind screamed that he had done the right thing. *The right thing!* So, why was he so overwhelmed by guilt? After all, he hadn't even touched

Paleček. Or had he? He trembled, weakly at first, then uncontrollably. Someone put an arm around him and stuck a cigarette in his mouth. He took a deep drag and choked on it.

CHAPTER 40

Though Daniel's leaving was only a question of time, the announcement still took Jan by surprise. He stared at the calendar on the wall where Daniel had been crossing off the days, and where he had gleefully circled in red the date, 1 April 1950.

"Going to America! Michigan." Daniel's smile turned into a frown. "Hey, what's the matter? Aren't you glad for me?"

"Of course I am. But you can't blame me if I have a feeling we'll never see each other again. When?" Jan tried to sound nonchalant.

"The first of next month. From Germany. By boat, I guess. Hey, you gotta believe your turn's coming. Just a question of time. C'mon." Daniel gave him a friendly nudge.

Forcing a smile, Jan shook his hand. "I'm truly glad for you," he muttered and meant it.

"Dammit!" Daniel withdrew his arm. "I'm so excited I almost forgot. Do you want a job?"

"Huh? What are you talking about? A job? Here?"

"Yeah! The fellow I spoke with at the American Desk. Not the chief, another one. Pretty high up. We talked. I practiced my English on him. He wanted to know if I knew somebody who can draw. They have Italians do all the clerical stuff, but he said they could use somebody to spice up their reports. Draw pictures. Graphs. Statistics. That sort of a thing. He showed me what he meant. Naturally, I thought of you."

"A *real* job? I don't believe it."

"Shiiit! For you, it'd be a piece o' cake. So, I gave him your name and he wants to see you. Interested?"

The palms of Jan's hands began to sweat. Was his luck finally turning? He surely could use the money. "Sure, but—"

"Maybe I should have asked you first." Daniel shrugged. "Hey, I don't care. You can still have my peanut business when I'm gone."

"No, no, it's not that. Thanks," Jan stammered. "When?"

"Tomorrow, at nine. His name is Smith. Mr. Smith."

Shifting his weight nervously, Jan awaited some sign of acknowledgement by the deeply tanned blond-headed young American, slouched in a large chair behind a massive mahogany desk that dominated one corner of the windowless room at the American Desk. The secretary's worktable, a tidy metal affair, all but taken up by a typewriter, occupied the other. Between them, a door bearing a small rectangular brass plate with a single word, *Chief,* hinted at a private sanctum.

Taking deep drags on a cigarette, Mr. Smith ignored him. The chair squeaked gently each time he rocked back and forth, tilting precariously until his feet, decked in fancy but scuffed cowboy boots, came close to sliding off the edge of the cluttered desk. *About my age,* Jan guessed.

Mr. Smith's gaze brushed over Jan but did not rest there. His expression remained blank, self-absorbed. His focus shifted past Jan's head into space as he continued to rock, engrossed in blowing smoke rings and following their wispy path toward the ceiling, where they dissolved in a bluish haze high above a large American flag, flanked by posters of American scenes and a somber picture of President Truman.

The young Italian secretary shrugged and gave Jan a thin smile.

"Speak English?" Mr. Smith finally growled, addressing the spiraling smoke and following it with his eyes before shifting his gaze to Jan.

"No, sir."

Mr. Smith sighed. "Don't matter., Carmelita can translate. But you *do* speak Eye-tah-lian, right?"

Jan shrugged and smiled uncomfortably, not fully understanding the question.

"Parla Eye-tah-liano?" Mr. Smith's curled upper lip revealed his teeth.

"Si, signore," Jan replied.

"I don't, but that don't matter. You'll be working with the Eye-tah-lians most of the time anyhow." He swung his legs off the desk. "That there's Carmelita." He made a vague motion in the girl's direction.

"Con piacere, signorina." Jan bowed slightly in her direction.

She responded with a shy nod.

So, can you draw? Are you an ar-tist?" Mr. Smith's brow knitted. "Carmelita, please."

"Oh yes, *si, signore*, yes sir," Jan answered as she translated. "I drew cartoons for a newspaper and—"

"Never mind." Mr. Smith waved him off and proceeded to rummage in one of the stacks of papers. "Can you do something like this?" He pointed to some simple graphs in a business magazine. "Or this? What did you say your name was?"

"Jan. Jan Neuman, sir."

"That's John, right?"

"Yes, sir."

"And you ain't leavin' anytime soon?"

Jan shrugged. "I don't know, sir."

The door swung open and a portly, distinguished-looking man, a shock of wavy gray hair framing his ruddy face, dressed in an elegant gray suit and carrying a leather briefcase, strolled in. "Good morning, folks, *buon giorno*, Carmelita!" he bellowed melodically, smiling.

"*Buon giorno, signor* Carmine." Carmelita blushed.

His quick gaze swept the room and rested on Jan. "And who's this, Bob?"

Mr. Smith jumped to his feet. "Morning, boss. This is...what was your name again?"

"Jan. Jan Neuman."

"Yeah, John Neuman. He's the artist I told you about."

For an instant, Mr. Carmine's gray eyes bore into Jan's, who bowed slightly and whispered hoarsely, "*Signore...*"

Mr. Carmine's stern look disappeared and he smiled. "Welcome aboard, John. We surely do need you. Bob getting you all fixed up?"

"Oh, yes sir," Mr. Smith broke in before Jan could answer. "He'll be startin' tomorrow."

Jan found the job easy. He had his own desk right next to Signor Brilli, a graying bon vivant of a man who delighted in war stories and office gossip when not compiling data or explaining the rudiments of statistics. "No good. Be careful," he warned Jan, nodding toward Mr. Smith. From Brilli, Jan had learned that Mr. Smith, the son of a high State Department official, though lacking the ability, had been given the position at the intercession of his father to secure a career in the consular service.

Others in the office shared Brilli's low opinion of Mr. Smith. Even Mr. Carmine's exasperation was clear under the thin veneer of civility when he questioned Mr. Smith's coming and going at will, usually at odd times, often without leaving a word. Mr. Carmine's normally gentle face would redden, grey eyes narrow, and mustachioed lips tighten as he queried Carmelita about Mr. Smith's whereabouts.

He would then usually call out, "Bob," when Mr. Smith returned, and they would disappear behind the closed door of his office, with only muffled sounds of raised voices hinting at the nature of their discourse. Thereafter, Bob Smith would stalk out, quickly light a cigarette, and throw himself petulantly into the padded chair behind his desk, all the while casting sneering looks in the direction of the Chief's office. With Jan, he was curt and distant, making him glad their contacts were few and brief.

*   *   *

A line of *carabinieri* held back the boisterous crowd of onlookers as a line of buses pulled up at the Napoli railroad station, disgorging their human cargo. With an array of large colorful tags attached prominently to their clothing, they shuffled along, pushing their meager baggage, ready to board the train for Germany. Jan scanned the small contingent of departing Czechs for Daniel and when he saw him, waved. Still slightly hung over from last night's farewell celebration, he elbowed his way through the surging crowd and they shook hands for the last time. It all seemed surreal, like floating in a sea of fog while looking at the world through a thick, distorted lens: the embraces, the crying and the laughing, the silent set of jaws, feelings held in check, glistening eyes set in stoic faces masking a flood of emotions. The shrill sound of whistles. The unrelenting march of time.

Daniel disappeared into one of the coaches, and moments later, opened the window and leaned out, grinning broadly. "See you in America!" He waved. "See you in America!" he shouted, as the train got under way.

His words felt like stabs.

CHAPTER 41

Waiting in lines was one of the constants of camp life, a daily ritual, Jan reflected, arriving for work one morning and scanning the usual snaking line of refugees in front of the American Desk offices, waiting for the doors to open. He dodged a few as others moved out of his way, when a woman's voice behind him called out softly, "Jan?"

He felt an icy chill.

"Is it you, Jan? Jan Neuman?" the woman said in that lilting unforgettable sort of way he'd never forgotten.

An invisible hand gripped his chest and squeezed it until he gasped. There was only one person who possessed that kind of a voice—Inka! A thousand pins pricked his skin, deluging his senses with tender pain as a wave of panic washed over him. His knees buckled.

"Jan?"

His heart raced as he turned around.

At first he saw no one fitting the iconic image in his memory, but then she waved and he recognized her. The five years since their last encounter had been kind to her: her slender body had blossomed. Cinched with a bright scarf, her flaxen hair spilled down to her shoulders, longer and thicker than he remembered. The strawberry lips that had once brushed his, sending shivers through him, seemed even more sensual. Her skin, no longer the shade of alabaster, was now the color of wheat. But it was her eyes that hadn't changed at all—still forget-me-not blue, penetrating, disarming, melting his defenses. He fought to regain composure.

"Jan? It *is* you, isn't it?" She extended her hand.

Jan took it hesitantly. "Inka? My God!" he blurted out, trying to hide his anxiety.

Half-smile on her face, she squeezed his hand and held it, gazing at him. His heart raced.

"You've changed." She smiled, revealing the pearls of her teeth. "Never thought I'd ever see you again." She cupped her other hand over his, holding him captive.

He sensed she was toying with him, taking pleasure in his discomfort. Her easy way confused him. He wanted to withdraw, but his mind rebelled. For years, he had vainly tried to repress the thoughts of her, purge his mind of her image. But instead, he selfishly relished the memories of their awkward encounters, more sweet than bitter under the mollifying patina of time. And now she stood before him—a fata morgana—the last tangible contact with home.

"Been here long?" He reluctantly retrieved his hand.

"Uh-huh. Two weeks. Got in from Germany. Murnau. Kept us there over a year. And you?"

"Oh, it's a long story." He waved her off. "Heard your mum was with you in Germany."

A cloud crossed her face. "She went back to Daddy. Back to Prague. Last year. There was an amnesty." She sighed deeply and brushed off a tear. "They finally let Daddy out of prison. Naturally, his job, his position, everything was gone. Got a letter from him in Germany. One of his students smuggled it out. So when she found out he was out of jail, and with the amnesty and all, she decided to go back. Said that's where she belonged. But she didn't want me to go. Begged me to stay here. Make a better life for myself. In America. Somewhere. So here I am." Dabbing at her eyes with the corner of her scarf, she gave a quick sad smile.

The door of the American Desk opened and the line of waiting people came alive.

"Sorry, but I have to go," Jan said, wishing he didn't have to. "Don't want to be late."

"Oh." She made a long face.

"I work in there." He nodded toward to door. "At the American Desk."

"That's where I'm going. Fill out more papers."

Jan swallowed hard. "Maybe we could meet again?" He immediately regretted his words, recalling the fiasco of their last encounter. "I mean, if you want to. I don't know when. I work all day."

"She smiled, took his hand, and squeezed it.

Jan's pulse quickened when he saw her there, waiting, as he walked out with Signor Brilli, Carmelita, and a throng of others shortly after 5.

She greeted him with a smile, but seemed melancholy.

"I didn't think you'd come." He tried to hide his inner turmoil.

She giggled. "Silly! Why wouldn't I? I'm *so* happy to see you again. Really." She squeezed his hand and the electric feeling returned.

A large sedan, an American flag fluttering from a short staff on its fender, slid by them and stopped at the curb. The chauffeur jumped out and smartly swung open the door for Mr. Carmine and Bob Smith. The car made a wide turn and sped toward the villas. As it passed, Mr. Carmine smiled and Bob Smith gave them a limp wave through the open window.

Inka waved back. "Who was that?"

"The chief, Mr. Carmine. He's nice."

"And the other one? The one that waved?"

"Oh, that's Mr. Smith. His deputy. He's my boss."

Down in the square, long lines of Italian workers began to board a line of buses to take them back to their homes.

"Hungry?" Jan said, trying to hide his anxiety, wishing his words didn't come out so reedy.

She nodded.

A spate of catcalls from a boisterous gaggle of customers surrounding a belching *espresso* machine greeted them as they walked through the time and grime-encrusted *trattoria* to the back, where a bead curtain over a doorless opening led to a stone terrace overlooking the bay. Wisteria covered the walls, its pale lavender blossoms spilling onto a pair of orange trees, weighed down with ripening fruit. The strong aroma of coffee drifted in from the inside. A few round tables, topped with faded umbrellas, crowded the tiny enclosure. From below came the murmur of the sea breaking on the rocks. A slight breeze brought in the pungent cocktail of smells of the harbor. Somewhere, a plaintive voice belted out a few bars of an aria. Dipping below the horizon, the sun painted the landscape with melancholy.

A dark-skinned barefoot girl led them to a table with a clear view of the bay, and brought their order of *frutti di mare* and wine. Jan found small talk difficult, but Inka's relaxed manner put him at ease. Their eyes locked and she took his hand and held it, and they reminisced about the old days: she begging his forgiveness for the hurt she had caused him, he feeling guilty for ever thinking ill of her.

The harsh glare of a string of bare bulbs ringing the terrace almost obliterated the darkening bay, and she shuddered as a chill blew in from the water. A shadow brushed her face.

"Something the matter?"

She sighed and her eyes filled with tears. "They won't let me go to America." She started to sob. "Said I couldn't...something about a quota. I didn't really understand."

"Is that what they said?"

She nodded.

Inka's distress made Jan painfully aware of his helplessness. Watching the tears roll down her exquisite cheeks, he thought of Daniel opining once that all women are more beautiful when they cry. So true. He felt heartbroken.

"Said I could go to Australia. But I don't *want* to go to Australia." She dabbed at her tears with a napkin. "I don't know what to do. Oh, Jan." She reached out to him. "Isn't there some way? You work there, at the American Desk. Couldn't you..."

He held her trembling hand, mindful of his impotence.

"Please," she implored over her sobs. "Please."

"You know I'd do anything." He sounded hollow, knowing he could do nothing. "I'm just a clerk."

"Can't you at least ask? Ask somebody? Please. That nice man that was talking to you—"

"You mean, Mr. Carmine? I can't do that."

"Why not?"

"He's the big boss. I never talk to him. I wouldn't dare."

"Please, try, just once. Just ask him. Ask somebody, that's all I ask. Please. Just ask." She squeezed his hand.

Jan felt trapped. Refusing her meant losing her again, and he desperately didn't want to lose her. "All right. But I can't promise anything," he conceded, mindful of the futility of it.

327

"I know, I know." She wiped the last of her tears and smiled.

A cool breeze wafted in from the bay and she snugged her collar around her neck.

"Perhaps we should go?" he suggested.

She nodded and stood up.

"Do you need anything? Money? Anything?" He reached for his wallet and pulled out a wad of Lire.

She shook her head, but her eyes told him it was only an act of pride. He thrust the bills in her hand and closed her fingers on them.

She resisted briefly, but then relented. "Someday I'll pay you back, I promise." She planted a soft kiss on his cheek.

Her warm gaze filled him with joy.

* * *

"They split the families. The men are upstairs, so we're all women and children down here," Inka said, leading Jan through the maze of flimsy corrugated cardboard cubicles in the basement of her building. "They're short of space, so they put us here with the Slovenes and people from Trieste." She stopped at a cubicle.

The blanket that passed for a door was pulled back, exposing three cots and an inverted cardboard box serving as a table. A young woman sat on one of the cots, doing her toilette. Seeing Jan, she quickly pulled a sheet over her bare shoulders.

"Sorry." Inka smiled sadly. "I'd ask you in, but..."

Disappointed, he extended his hand. "That's all right. I understand. Good night, then."

She let the blanket drop, took his hand, and drew him gently toward her. Lurching awkwardly, he didn't resist. She closed her eyes and offered him her lips, and as he kissed her, pulled him closer, pressing herself into him with unexpected strength. Her hungry kisses hurt as her darting tongue probed his mouth. Awkwardly, he reciprocated.

Throbbing in the pit of his stomach sent waves of heat to the tips of his nerves. He felt light-headed. His resolve melted. Dizzy with her woman-smells, feeling the searing firmness of her body and the pricks of a thousand needles with each brush of her hair, he surrendered to the moment.

Finally she gently pushed him off. "I really must go." She sighed deeply. "Sorry."

He reached for her, but she moved away.

"Sorry," she whispered, smoothing her dress. "Good night, Jan. Don't forget." She slid under the blanket and disappeared inside.

CHAPTER 42

"*Mi dispiace, Giovanni.* I'm sorry." Brilli sighed. "I'd like to help your friend, but I just can't think of a way...a regular way. But that doesn't mean there's no way. *Capisce?* Regulations are regulations, but all regulations have exceptions. American regulations, Italian regulations, IRO regulations— makes no difference. Does your friend have any special skills? Qualifications? Relatives in America? Friends? Anything at all that might help?"

"I really don't know." Jan gave Brilli a sheepish look.

Brilli nodded gravely and bit his lip, as his face crinkled in a grimace. "Can't think of anything, *Giovanni. Mi dispiace.*"

In a strange way, Jan felt relieved. Inka had insisted and he had promised, though he knew the futility of it. Now his conscience was clear. She would understand.

Brilli nudged him gently. "*Aspetta!* Wait! There may be other ways I don't know. There always are ways, if there is a will. Always. Perhaps if she would talk to *Signor* Smith or *Signor* Carmine. I could try to arrange that, if you want. I'd be happy to do it. Just for you."

Jan stared at him, open-mouthed.

Brilli squeezed his shoulder and with a reassuring smile, disappeared into Mr. Smith's office. He finally emerged an hour later, with a frown. "*Mi scusi, Giovanni,*" he apologized profusely, "*Signor* Smith and I always seem to get sidetracked, but he will see your friend tomorrow around 10, if she can come."

Overwhelmed, Jan grasped and shook Brilli's hand, unable to get the words of thanks past the lump in his throat. Grinning, his mind leapt ahead to the end of the day when he would tell Inka, watch the smile come over her face and happiness stream from her eyes—and perhaps even feel the touch of her gratitude.

She was there waiting when he walked out, and ran to him, seeing his grin. "You have news?" Her eyes sparkled.

"Yes, very good news, I hope." His voice trembled with emotion.

She squealed and threw herself at him. "Tell me. Tell me what happened," she pleaded. "Oh, please, tell me. Tell me!"

"Tomorrow at 10! Mr. Smith will see you tomorrow at 10." It felt great to be the bearer of good news.

She showered him with kisses. "Yes, of course I'll be there! Oh Jan. Oh Jan! how can I thank you? I *knew* you could do it. I knew you would help. Oh, Jan."

He relished her closeness, until she pushed him gently away and took a few short steps backward, spinning around. "See my new dress?" She curtsied. "Bought it off my roommate for the money you gave me. Didn't fit her, but it's just perfect for me, don't you think?" She swirled around again and took his hands. "You like?"

They held hands as she led him down toward the bustling square.

"Would you like to go somewhere? Eat something? Have a drink? Whatever?" He was flushed with anticipation.

She smiled sadly. "Do you mind if we don't? I really don't feel well today."

He felt a stab of disappointment. "Is there something I could—"

She shook her head. "Nothing serious. Just female things." She gave him a reassuring smile. "But if you want, you could

331

walk me back to the paravan." She squeezed his hand gently. "Please?"

She pulled the blanket open and beckoned him in. The paravan was empty.

"I *really* don't feel well." She smiled softly and extended her hands. "We have a few minutes."

His stomach knotted and his palms turned clammy as she drew him to her. The world spun wildly as they melted into each other. She kissed him passionately, and then savagely as he strained to return them. Gasping, he felt her fingernails digging into his back.

Shuffling awkwardly, they collapsed on her bed. She took his hand and drew it to her breasts. *The way she had done long ago, when we first met,* flashed through his mind as he relished the thought. He grasped them tenderly, then eagerly, and she moaned as he kneaded them, feeling the hard prominence of her nipples against his sweaty hands. She arched to press herself against him. Her kisses hurt. Her fiery tongue lashed at him in provocative thrusts. Letting go of her lips, he caressed her breasts. Her soft moans urged him on. Tracing searing paths all over his body, her hands dug into him as he lightly bit her nipples. Her touch was electric. The pounding in his brain grew relentless. The roar in his ears obliterated all sound. The pulsing inside strained for release. He reached down with his free hand and jerkily, desperately yanked at her panties.

"No!" she cried out sharply, as she stiffened and pushed him off her, closing her thighs.

Jan was on fire. His entire being focused on one searing, pulsing point of unstoppable energy demanding release.

Yanking furiously, clumsily, desperately at her panties, he slid his hand past her quivering belly to the moist heat of her crotch.

She shrieked and pushed him off so violently he nearly fell off the bed. "No!" she cried out. "Please...Ple-ease..." Her last plea dissolved into sobs.

He jerked his hand from between her legs and rolled on his back. No longer able to restrain himself, he yielded as the spasms found release, gushing out in uncontrolled spurts, coating his bare thighs and abdomen with sticky semeny warmth.

And then he just lay there, embarrassed, spent, and frustrated, overwhelmed by a sudden chill and debilitating weakness. He raised his hand and stared at it in shock—it was covered with blood.

She lay next to him, tugging jerkily at her dress, trying to cover her bloodstained legs, crying softly

"Oh God! Oh, God! I'm sorry!" he blurted out, but she covered her face with her hands and remained mute, leaving him full of remorse and pain.

He wiped his hand on his trousers and touched her lightly to comfort her, but she recoiled.

"It's not you, it's me," she whimpered. "We shouldn't have...I shouldn't have let you." She continued to cry, softly, her body heaving with each sob. "Better go before they show up," she said, dabbing at her red-rimmed eyes, and then turned away from him and just lay there, staring into the corrugated cardboard wall, as he hastily dressed and scurried out of the paravan.

* * *

Tossing Jan an appreciative look, Brilli greeted Inka with his usual aplomb. Brushing against Jan, she touched his hand and whispered an apology. He gave her an uneasy smile.

"Better go in with her, *Giovanni*, in case you need to translate." Brilli glanced at his watch. "*Signor* Smith should be ready for her about now."

"Hiya, John," Mr. Smith bellowed as they entered. "So this is your friend Brilli mentioned yesterday, huh?" He measured Inka with his eyes.

"Brilli told me about your problem. Of course I'll see what I can do. That's what we're here for, right? To help y'all good people emigrate, if we can. That's our job. But," a bemusing smile crossed his face, "haven't we met somewhere before? I could swear..." He turned to Jan. "Ask her, will you, John?"

Before Jan had a chance to say anything, Inka extended her hand. "Hello sir. I'm so happy to meet you," she said, smiling. "You perhaps saw me the other day from your car. Outside in the street."

"Ah! You speak English!" Mr. Smith's face lit up. "Brilli didn't tell me—how wonderful. Of course! I remember."

Jan flushed. "You didn't tell me you spoke English," he muttered.

"Didn't have a chance," she apologized tersely. "Sorry."

"And where did you learn English, Miss...Miss..." Mr. Smith turned to Jan, pleading silently for help.

"Inka." She smiled. "Inka Šimonová."

"Inka Shim-oh-hoh— Ah, of course!" He laughed out loud. "May I just call you Inka?"

"Of course. I learned English in school. We all had to. And when the Americans liberated my country, I met a..." She cast a

334

sideways glance at Jan. "I met a friend who helped me a little. A soldier."

"So, then you do know somebody in the States. I mean, the USA?"

She blushed. "Yes. I have his address."

Her prickling words washed over Jan like a cold shower. He didn't really know her at all. The things he had conjured up about her were just figments of his imagination. She had played him for a fool…again.

"Guess we won't need you after all, John, since your friend, ah, Inka," Mr. Smith gave her a smile and she smiled back, "speaks English. You can go now."

She averted her gaze as he stumbled out, devastated.

He didn't see her leave and she wasn't waiting for him when he walked out at the end of the day. He didn't see her the next day, either. In a way, he was relieved—he preferred solitude to tend to his wounded ego. While he ached for her, deep down he feared seeing her. Most of all, he feared her rejection—he found living in doubt more tolerable. Still, he found the uncertainty crushing. When she didn't show the third day, and then the next, he screwed up his courage and decided to see her. Quaking inside, he went into her paravan, but she wasn't there. Only the girl he saw during his first visit was in, sitting on the bed, talking to another young, statuesque girl in a Slavic tongue he didn't understand. He apologized for the intrusion, and when he asked, his question was met with a shrug. He decided to wait outside.

He finally spotted her emerging from the shadows, and the iciness of her gaze gave him a chill. She greeted him coolly. "What are *you* doing here?"

"It's been four days…" A knot slowly twisted his gut.

She frowned.

"If you're still angry about the other day—"

"Forget it!" she snapped and looked away.

"I'm sorry. I had no idea."

"I said, forget it!" She shifted uncomfortably as a couple of passers-by gave them a curious look. "I need to go."

"What about Mr. Smith? Can he help?" Jan pressed.

"I think so. I certainly hope so." Her tone warmed somewhat and the twinkle returned to her eyes. "Bob...Mr. Smith said he'll do anything he can to help." The wistfulness disappeared. "Look, Jan, I really have to go." She took his hand and gave him a weak smile. "Please."

Reluctantly, he let her go. "When will I see you again?"

She sighed. "I don't know. I have things to do."

"Things? What things?"

"Things."

He watched her disappear into the building.

* * *

First one out the door of the American Desk when the day ended, Jan felt the sting of disappointment when he didn't see her. He lingered, unwilling to accept the futility of it all. Nor did she show the next day or the next. Finally, late one evening, he spotted her from a distance. Even from afar, the blue of her dress and gold of her hair gave her away.

She strolled out of her building, a large handbag swinging from her shoulder, heading away from him, past the administration building, toward the compound of consular villas clinging to the palmetto, cactus, and pine-strewn slope. Fighting a mounting unease, held back by intuition but driven ahead by a force beyond his control, he followed.

The guard at the gate to the compound barred her way and she stopped, dug in her bag and held up something. Apparently satisfied, the guard saluted and lifted the long white barrier, letting her pass. She strode down the manicured road and then up the steep hillside, until she reached a villa not far from the one with the large American flag. She mounted a few steps, stopped at the door, and rang the bell. Fidgeting, she looked around uneasily until the door opened and a man emerged to greet her. Even from this distance, Jan could see who it was—Bob Smith.

CHAPTER 43

The next time Jan saw Inka, she was again heading toward the villas. This time, he didn't follow. Days later, she strolled out of Mr. Smith's office just as Jan and Brilli reached the door. Jan blanched. Brilli raised an eyebrow in surprise. She blushed, caught off guard, and hesitated ever so slightly, but then defiantly and without even a nod of recognition scurried past them toward the exit. A few heads turned as she passed, swaying sensually in what Jan surmised was a new dress.

He rushed after her.

"I need to talk to you. We *need* to talk," he plead under his breath when he caught up with her.

"Not here. Not now," she snarled, not missing a stride.

Pushing angrily through the crowd milling around the entrance, she stormed past the snaking line of people where he had first seen her, and up an abandoned road leading to a parapet at the mouth of one of the tunnels.

Jan touched her arm.

"Don't!" Eyes flashing, her face twisted with disdain. "What do you want of me?"

Her ferocity stopped him cold.

"Can't we just talk? Please? Why do you ignore me?"

"Ignore you?" She mocked him. "Huh! What's there to ignore?" She gave a short, sarcastic laugh.

"You know what I mean."

"No, I don't. What *do* you mean?"

"You and Bob Smith. I saw you." Sick inside, Jan wished he hadn't come.

She glared at him for a moment, speechless. "You followed me?" Her face drained of color, but then her fierceness came back unabated. "You *followed* me? Spying on me? How dare you!" Her face turned crimson. "Whoever gave you the right?"

"I thought we were, we might have—" He saw the futility of his words and stopped.

"Might have what?" she sneered.

He didn't answer.

"It's none of your business, but Bob's been good to me. I want you to know. He'll help me get to America. I know he will. He promised. Can you understand that?"

"But what about us? What about—"

"Us? Did you say, what about *us*? Us?" She let out a shrill little laugh. "Where did you get the idea? We've only been friends. That's all. And now, *you*'ve destroyed even that. Spying on me!" She shook with anger. "I don't trust you any more. You're nothing to me, understand? Nothing! I don't owe you a thing. I don't *want* to owe you anything. Understand?" With trembling hands, she snatched a roll of lire out of her handbag, unpeeled a wad, and flung them at his feet. "Here! I don't need your charity!" He felt the piercing stab of her glare as she spun on her heels and stalked away.

Caught by the breeze, the bills scattered among the bushes.

* * *

"*Che é succeso*? What's the matter? Don't you feel well? *Stai malado*?" Brilli wrapped his arm around Jan's shoulders in a fatherly fashion.

Jan looked away. He had spent the night mentally wading through yesterday's confrontation, trying to come to terms with the reality. He hadn't slept much.

"*Che é succeso, Giovanni?* Is it the girl? It *is* the girl, isn't it?"

"She wants nothing to do with me." Jan motioned with his head toward Mr. Smith's office. "*É finito*…it's finished."

"Oh?" Brilli raised his eyebrows. "Carmelita told me something was going on. But I didn't realize…she seemed such a nice girl. *Mi dispiace*, but I can understand. Such a *belezza*." Grunting appreciably, Brilli touched his lips with his cupped fingers and made a kissing sound, a gesture reserved for only the prettiest.

"Should have known better. I was a fool." Jan forced a weak smile.

"*Mi dispiace, Giovanni. Mi dispiace, sinceramente.*" Brilli put his arm around Jan's shoulders and gave him a fatherly squeeze. "*Sta sera*…this evening, after work, you come with me, okay? We go out and have good time. Drink a little. Talk. Okay?"

Unlike Via Carragiola – the antiseptic stuff of the postcards – rimmed by grand hotels and towering palm trees circling the bay against the dramatic backdrop of Vesuvius, Via Roma, that paralleled it, was where the real life of Napoli coursed like the life-giving blood in the veins of an amorphous giant, where it could be seen, heard, felt, and smelled. Day and night, its sidewalks teemed with people, flowing like two rivers of life past shops, *trattorias*, bordellos, and espresso bars, now in the waning light casting shafts of brilliant glow onto the glistening cobblestones.

Deposited at regular intervals by clanging streetcars, droves of workers of all stripes spilled out like ants and disappeared into the hovels lining the dark, narrow sidestreets emanating from it like fissures in the solid cover of man-made labyrinth, crisscrossed by a helter-skelter maze of electric wires and webs of clotheslines laden heavily with laundry, giving them the appearance of some Brombignanian relic. Music blared from the bars as plaintive voices belted out Neapolitan songs.

"Watch out for pickpockets," Brilli cautioned as the flow carried them along. Buoyed by the alcohol in their veins, they ignored and fended off the pleas of beggars, pimps, and hawkers trying to sell them everything from young sisters to watches and American cigarettes. Earlier, they had exchanged life stories over Chianti and a sumptuous meal at Brilli's favorite restaurant.

Having learned English as an American prisoner of war in Africa, Brilli, a graying bachelor in his late forties, felt himself fortunate in having found work at the American Desk. The war had interrupted his plans to marry, and when he returned, he found the girl of his dreams married to someone else. It left him sad but philosophical. "*Force un giorno... qui sa?* Who knows? Perhaps one day." He shrugged when the conversation veered toward the direction they both consciously tried to avoid. Liberal servings of Chianti dulled but did not erase Jan's hurt, and he was appreciative of Brilli's tactful demeanor.

"*Ecco qui...*here we are." Brilli pulled Jan aside in front of a tall brownstone building, nondescript except for a large statue of the Virgin Mary adorning the entrance, a red light flickering at her feet, fresh flowers festooning the pedestal.

Jan's eyes widened. "You live here?"

341

"Practically." Brilli smiled, knocking on the door.

With a clang, a peephole slid open and closed. The door silently opened, letting them in. An elegantly dressed matronly woman met them in a small foyer. "*Ah, signor Brilli, buena serra,*" she greeted him, smiling.

"Not very busy tonight?" Brilli returned her smile and kissed her hand.

She shrugged. "It comes and goes. People don't have the money for quality, so they go down to the..." She nodded toward the door. "But we're okay. *Siamo bene. Venga. Venite.*"

"*Mio amico, Giovanni,*" Brilli introduced Jan.

She took Jan's hand and caressed him with her eyes. "*Que bel ragazzo!*" She smiled. "*Con piacere.*"

They followed her up a short flight of velvet-trimmed stairs into a large, discretely lit, ornately decorated sitting room. Beautiful paintings of medieval scenes and noble women adorned the walls. Small tables overflowing with freshly cut flowers complemented the elegantly stuffed furnishings. An immense gilded mirror dominated the facing wall. The scent of fine perfume hung in the air. A gathering of scantily clad Reubenesque young women, lounging around in various airs of repose, stirred as they entered.

"A little drink perhaps? A little Marsala?" she murmured, leading them to a comfortable sofa.

A girl in a black servant's outfit appeared out of nowhere with a pair of goblets.

Smiling, one of the girls approached and rested her hand on Brilli's shoulder. "So nice to see you again, *amore.*" She stroked him gently. "*Mi piace vederci.*"

"My favorite, as you can see." Brilli smiled and put his arm around her waist. "But, *Giovanni,* all the girls here are nice." He touched his lips with his fingers and made a kissing sound. "Clean and healthy…no need to worry." He put down the goblet and got up. *"La Donna* will take care of you." He bowed to the smiling older woman hovering discretely in the back of the room. *"Buona fortuna,"* he quipped over his shoulder.

La Donna took Jan's arm, squeezed it reassuringly and led him to a tiny room, barely large enough to accommodate a small settee and a table. The back of the door was a mirror. *"Aspetta qui, carino…*wait here and just relax." She gave him a caressing stroke. "More Marsala?"

The black-clad girl refilled his glass.

"Que bel ragazzo." *La Donna* pinched him playfully on the cheek as she waltzed out the door.

One by one, the girls came in and performed their tender routines. Discomfited, reeling under the stupor of too much Marsala, he allowed himself to be touched and kissed and caressed, all the while vaguely conscious of an ambivalent feeling of betrayal. One girl stood out from the rest. It was not that she was beautiful – though she seemed younger than the others did – but there was something about her, an air of sadness, which struck a chord. Her smile could not erase the melancholy in her eyes. Her caresses were soft and tender, yet she seemed withdrawn, distant. When their eyes connected, it was as though a finger had plucked a solitary chord inside his hollowed-out soul. He'd found a partner in misery—a soul mate.

She took Jan's hand and led him upstairs to one of several rooms fronting a hallway. Softly lit and tastefully decorated, the room, with its brocade-covered walls, was just big enough to accommodate a large bed and a small loveseat. A brass coat rack stood in one corner. A porcelain water basin and a pair of ornate pitchers rested on a short mantle. A trace of perfume lingered in the air.

In a fog, Jan's world swirled around him. Murmuring sweet nothings, the girl, brushed herself against him and stroked him gently as she undressed and washed him. He found her tenderness soothing, and the pangs of remorse fading from his conscience. She gently pulled him down on top of her and helped him enter. But as he sank into delirium, it was Inka's twisted face that floated up from the depths of his consciousness. He stiffened.

"Something the matter, *carino*?" the girl whispered. "Your first time?"

Stroking him gently, her lips brushed against his skin. Her gaze was on him as he lay next to her, spent, confused—guilty. She wore a wedding ring. He touched it.

She withdrew her hand and sat up abruptly. Her eyes misted. "*Mio marito.* Didn't come home from the war. Have no family. There is no work. Have two children. They have to eat. Please *signore*, please, don't tell Madame you were not pleased."

She washed him again and helped him dress. "You pay Madame," she said, as he fumbled for his wallet.

He laid a sheaf of bills on the mantle and she thanked him with her eyes.

Each time he returned to the brownstone house with the statue of Virgin Mary by the entrance, the image of Inka, the impostor who would hijack his mind, grew fainter. One day, the girl wasn't there. "Not been here a few days, *mi dispiace.*" *La Donna* shook her head and shrugged when he asked. "Don't

344

know why. Didn't say. She was *such* a nice girl. But there are others. Would you like—"

Jan thanked her, walked out, and never returned. For a time, the sad girl's eyes followed him until they, too, faded. He never knew her name.

CHAPTER 44

Jan's senses had dulled over the nearly two years of endless waiting. Most of the Czechs he knew had left—even Gregor was granted asylum by Sweden, the only country that would take him because of his tuberculosis. And so his mind didn't immediately grasp the meaning of Brilli's excited words when he saw him waiting by the entrance with a thin sheaf of papers and a wide grin. "*Mi scusi, Giovanni*, but I couldn't wait. *Que buona fortuna!* I'm *so* glad for you. Here it is!" He waved the papers in front of Jan's face. "You are going to America!"

Incredulous, Jan stared at the documents. Printed on coarse yellowing paper, the mimeographed forms bore the logo *Minnesota Commission for the Resettlement of Displaced Persons*, and an official stamp over an illegible scrawl. His hands shook as Brilli helped with the translation. He read and reread the line, *Name of Person, Relative, Firm, or Family Offering Opportunity*, and the name typed in the last box, Sophie Kostka, a complete stranger to him but a godsend—his sponsor. An improbable, incomparable rush of emotion left him cotton-mouthed and weak all over, but Brilli's slap on the shoulder brought him to his senses. "*Sta sera*, we must celebrate," he said, smiling. "I'll see if Carmelita will come too, if it's all right. *Bene*? I know she'd want to."

"*Si*, of course. *Con piacere*. We'll go to the *trattoria* down by the harbor. I'd like to treat, if you don't mind."

A few catcalls greeted Jan, Brilli, and Carmelita as they entered the bustling *trattoria*. The owner gave him a friendly nod. Squeezing past the bar crowd, they made themselves comfortable at a table on the terrace. The barefoot girl brought Marsala and food, and they all toasted his fortune.

Surrounded by his friends, Jan was suddenly seized by a feeling of isolation—a foreshadowing of a widening gap between him and them. His life had suddenly taken a leap while theirs remained rooted. One day, he would leave, they would stay. It was the way of the camps—lives touched and friendships formed, only to break. The risk of making friends was having to lose them, with the pain of separation the only certainty.

Darkness began to fall and the string of bare lights came on, bathing the surroundings in a harsh glow. Brilli glanced at his watch, put down his glass, and nudged Carmelita. "Sorry but we have to—"

"*Si*, I have to get home," she sighed, "or they'll be worried. Couldn't let'em know I'd be late, *Giovanni. Mi dispiace.*"

They walked out into the night just as a large sedan pulled up at the curb. The chauffeur opened the door and two people slid out, a man and a woman. In the shaft of light streaming through the open doorway, it was easy to see who they were— Bob Smith and Inka. Engaged in a spirited conversation, oblivious to Jan and his companions, they quickly disappeared inside the *trattoria* as the sedan roared off. Brilli squeezed Jan's arm in consolation.

"*Fa niente,*" Jan lied, unwilling to admit he was overcome with jealousy. It gnawed at him like a sore that never heals and he hated himself for it.

"Did you notice something peculiar about the girl?" Carmelita nudged Brilli. "She's not been around the office for quite some time now so I couldn't be sure, but there's something different about her. She looks pregnant."

"Carmelita tells me that your friend had been trying to see Mr. Smith a few times at the office," Brilli said to Jan a couple of weeks later.

Jan shrugged, pretending not to care.

"But he's gone. Will be gone at least two weeks. Your friend seemed in distress. Carmelita says, she tries to hide her belly with a scarf, but that definitely she's pregnant. Guess girls can tell such things. Thought you'd like to know."

"I don't care," Jan lied, wishing Brilli hadn't brought up the subject.

*   *   *

All heads in the office turned as Inka walked in, unannounced. Carmelita looked up in surprise. "Signor Smith is in a meeting right now, but you can have a seat and wait, if you want." She motioned to a chair. "He shouldn't be too long."

Inka thanked her and gingerly sat down with a sigh, uncomfortable in a dress that pulled at the seams. She ignored Jan as though he weren't there.

The door swung open and Mr. Smith strolled in.

She tried to get up, and as she did, the color drained from her face. Grasping her abdomen, she doubled over and slid to the floor. A crimson stain began to spread on the back of her dress.

Mr. Smith stopped dead in his tracks, blanched, and turned away.

Brilli called the ambulance.

Jan followed it to the hospital and stayed the night, and was the first thing Inka saw the next day as she emerged from a deep, sedated sleep. She didn't recognize him at first and looked at him vacantly, but then extended her hand.

"Where am I? What happened?" She looked around, bewildered.

"In the hospital." He took her hand. You lost a lot of blood. Don't talk."

"So sorry...so sorry...so—" She began to cry, but then her grip relaxed as she drifted off again.

"Are you a relative?" The nurse tapped him on the shoulder.

"No, just a friend."

"Are you Bob?"

Jan shook his head.

"Can you tell us who she is? She didn't have anything on her. No ID card. No papers. Nothing. She tried to say something about her purse when she came to, but she wasn't coherent. All she did was moan something about a tunnel and someone named Bob."

Cool and dark, the tunnel was empty except for piles of rusting rails and iron rods—the detritus of the war. The guns were gone. A carpet of debris covered everything. Water dripped onto the concrete floor, glistening where it seeped through the rough-hewn rock and forming pools that, from within, reflected the light of the entrance like shards of a shattered mirror. The deeper Jan moved, the dimmer the light, the cooler the air. Apart from the mesmerizing plunk-plunk-plunk of droplets hitting the pools of water and the buzzing in his head, it was eerily quiet.

A faint, sickly odor assaulted his nostrils as he reached the far end. He gasped. The ground around him was covered with dark splotches of dry blood. Her scarf, still wet, lay crumbled on top of a pile of metal rods and under it, her purse. As he reached for it, he tripped over something and stumbled. It was an old coffee tin, full of foul-looking brew that splattered his feet. He swore in disgust—and froze in horror: floating in the muck was a tiny dead fetus. *Her baby!*

The thought made him ill. Staring at the lifeless form, he instinctively crossed himself, the way he was taught as a little boy, and whispered a prayer. The tiny wrinkled head tilted upward, as though crying out to him. He felt like retching, but couldn't tear himself from the sight. There was nothing he could do—nothing to be done. Nothing. He grabbed Inka's purse and rushed out, sick at the sight of it all.

Slouched in a chair next to her bed, he watched her drift in and out of delirium. She dreamt wild dreams, called out for Bob, and cried. At times, he could tell she seemed vaguely aware of him but kept her eyes closed, pretending not to be awake. He decided to leave.

"I see Signorina Inka is going to Australia. Leaving for Trieste tomorrow," Brilli commented a month later, looking up from a sheaf of papers. "Signor Smith will be pleased. And you?"

"I thought she was a friend." Jan shrugged. "I was a fool. I feel sorry for her."

"*Mi dispiace, Giovanni*, but there's nothing we could have done. Perhaps if she had known that Signor Smith was married, but there was no way to warn her."

"She probably wouldn't have listened anyway."

"The guard told me what happened. He is an old friend of mine from the war. From where he works, he has a good view of the villas. She went up and a woman opened the door. Must have been Signor Smith's wife. Remember when he took a leave to pick her up in Cherbourg? Came in on the *Queen Mary?*"

"Maybe that's why Carmelita said he wouldn't see her when she asked for him."

"No doubt. Anyway, there was a huge argument, Signor Smith rushed out, pushed his wife back inside, and then savaged your friend. By the time she returned to the gate, crying, he had called and ordered the guard to take away her pass. He said he saw her walk toward the tunnels."

"She must have been desperate."

"She told the doctor that she found those heavy metal rods, the Americans call them rebar, and lifted them until a sharp pain made her pass out. She apparently bled a good deal, but somehow made it back to the paravan when the bleeding stopped."

"I saw what happened in the tunnel. I'll never forget it. Never! But in a way, I'll miss her."

"Miss her?" Brilli's eyebrows shot up.

"Whatever she was, she was my last tie to home."

Several days later, Jan received a postcard from her:

Dear Jan!
Today, I am finally boarding the ship "Dundalk Bay," which will leave Trieste at midnight. They kept us shut up in the barracks for the entire time like in a concentration camp. Other than that, it is one of the best camps in Italy.

I didn't have the courage to tell you how much I appreciate what you did for me, and how sorry I am that things between us didn't work out.

    With sincere regrets,

Inka

CHAPTER 45

It was noon before the 'American' train, crowded with displaced families from the Balkans, Venezia-Giulia, Trieste, and a contingent of Czechs, finally left Bagnoli. The mood was upbeat as the camp vanished from view. Like the ablated vertebrae of a gigantic spine, the procession of jagged peaks of the Apennines, clad in purple in the valleys and fall colors at the crests, and cradling medieval towns in their crags, slid by like apparitions. The train picked up speed as it reached the great verdant floodplain of the Po, and began to labor after leaving the villa-encrusted shores of Lago di Garda behind the rising flanks of the Alps. The singing and merriment subsided as the last vestiges of Italy vanished into the falling night and fatigue set in.

The outside temperature dropped steadily as they climbed toward the high peaks looming above the Brenner Pass. The air inside the coaches grew stale, reeking with body odor, cigarette smoke, and the heavy aroma of their last meal—military K-Rations. Sprawled out in grotesque poses among their baggage on the hard wooden seats, tossed to and fro by the lurching train, the refugees stirred fitfully.

Snuggled in the corner of his seat, buoyed by the gentle swaying of the coach and the metallic staccato of the rails, Jan closed his eyes and mused over the last few days—a whirlwind of processing, briefings, medical examinations, and goodbyes.

"I don't know how long I'll be here, John," Mr. Carmine had said, as he gave him a friendly slap on the back and handed him a letter of recommendation, "but you can give my name if you need any kind of reference." Even Bob Smith showed up, offering a limp handshake and a "Y'all have a nice trip." Carmelita cried, and Brilli, trying to hide his envy, took him to the cantina and wished him luck over a bottle of Marsala.

Jan had lived for this day, but now he felt choked up, inexplicably reticent, almost fearful of the impending change. He had grown accustomed to camp life. It had been his home for nearly two years, giving him a certain degree of normalcy. Still, the constant comings and goings, with most of the Czechs leaving almost daily for places like Australia, New Zealand, Brazil, Chile, or Canada, had made him feel lonely.

He found solace in Daniel's letters describing in superlatives the New World, and read and re-read them until he knew them intimately. Still, he held his elation in check, mindful of one of his mother's favorite homilies: "Don't ask for too much and don't expect too much, and you'll never be disappointed."

Late the next day, the train reached the fog-cloaked flatlands and marshes of northern Germany, and came to a stop in the vast North Sea port of Bremerhaven. Military buses, white stars emblazoned on their sides, whisked them to a complex of compact red buildings, seemingly untouched by war, surrounded by a high brick wall. A large sign on the gate read:

INTERNATIONAL REFUGEE ORGANIZATION

INTERZONAL
EMBARKATION CENTER
CAMP GROHN

An American flag hung limply from a flagpole in the center of a manicured square, now alive with the new arrivals.

Martial music blared from the loudspeakers. Scurrying officiously from bus to bus, waving their arms and shouting orders, black-clad German guards directed the tired and bedraggled travelers to their quarters.

Jan heard his name called, and a guard, pointing to one of the buildings, thrust a packet of papers and a card with a room number into his hand. A blast of warm air welcomed him as he swung open the door. Though small, the room was clean and comfortably appointed, and he collapsed on the bed without even undressing.

The regimented urgency of the coming days, filled with medical checks, vaccinations, lectures, films about America, and classes in introductory English served only to fan everyone's anticipation. Even the weather, full of morning fogs that rolled in from the North Sea like giant walls of dirty cotton and drizzle that pricked the skin like a sprinkling of needles, failed to dampen the general feeling of euphoria. They were going to America. To America! Scuttlebutt had it they would leave in two or three weeks, as soon as the transports got in.

* * *

The day had been long and the lesson tedious. Jan's mind wandered. He stole a look at the clock at the back of the room and suppressed a yawn, as a strange creeping sensation, a pressure—an almost tactile contact at the back of his head, made the hair at the nap of his neck stand up. Someone was staring at him!

He fought the urge to turn around. Perhaps he was imagining things. Perhaps it was just someone's innocent glance he had caught out of the corner of his eye. He tried to dismiss the thought but the feeling persisted. He turned just enough to see, and felt a chill. Someone at the back of the room gazed intently in his direction—a girl.

He didn't immediately recognize her, but then recalled she was the one he encountered the time he had looked for Inka. He squirmed. Surely she remembered how foolishly he had acted that day. He discreetly stole another look. Her gaze hadn't changed. He felt himself flushing. Unable to resist the impulse, he met her stare.

A faint wisp of acknowledgment brushed over her face. It was the first time he really noticed her—he had been too emotionally distraught back then in Inka's paravan to notice much of anything. Tall and statuesque, she was the archetypal Slav. Her round tanned face was framed by short, reddish-brown curls. Her pale blue-gray eyes, intense under her arched eyebrows, bore through his carefully constructed layers of emotional armor and touched his heart. Their tender eloquence disarmed him, stripped him of his defenses. He felt exposed and vulnerable before her—emotionally naked. She smiled.

Confused and unnerved, he broke off the contact and turned around. Focusing on the lecture was useless. All he could think of was the piercing feeling in the back of his head and the language of her eyes. The desire to look again became overpowering.

She was no longer smiling, but looked at him intently, face flushed, lips parted, eyes pleading. His resolve melted. He felt irresistibly drawn to her.

He lingered until everyone filed out before walking out into the street, his mind in turmoil. Drops of heavy drizzle reflected like diamonds in the harsh glare of the streetlights. She stood there, waiting—a solitary silhouette among the blurry stream of shadowy figures scurrying in all directions. She averted her gaze, lowered her head, and stared at the ground, tense and ill at ease, giving him a free pass should he wish not to acknowledge her.

A faint voice inside his head urged him to do just that, but something far stronger turned his feet to clay as he approached. Tense, unsure of himself and, most of all, unsure of what she might do, he stood there speechless.

She looked up and smiled nervously. "*Non ci ricordi? Don't you remember?*"

He nodded, unable to get the words past the lump in his throat.

"We only met once…briefly. In the camp. In the paravan. You were looking for someone."

"Yes, of course. I remember. *Con piacere!* I remember you very well."

"*Mi chiamo* Majda. Majda Maruk." She hesitantly extended her hand.

He introduced himself and took her hand, and as he met her gaze, a breathtaking feeling overwhelmed him. The force and purity of the emotion staggered him. It was as though he had known her forever.

Her breath came in shallow bursts, sending thin streams of vapor into the air. Her pale blue eyes probed his, speaking volumes. Spellbound, they held hands, until a gust of wind drove the rain in their faces, breaking the spell.

She shuddered, withdrew her hand, and snugged a thin shawl about her shoulders. "The rain…" She smiled apologetically.

He offered his coat but she refused it. Instead, she cradled his hand under her arm and led him toward the row of buildings across the square. He felt her shiver again and slipped his coat over her shoulders. She slid her hand around his waist and drew him closer, pressing herself gently against him. "It's cold," she said. "Not used to it after Italy."

He hesitantly wrapped his arm around her, fully aware of her firmness as they strolled rhythmically, step in step, across the grassy expanse, sharing the electric warmth flowing between them. Light-headed, nerves tingling, he wanted this moment never to end.

"I am a Slovene," she finally said. "From Trieste."

"A Slovene?" Jan shook his head. "Had no idea. I'm a Czech."

"Yes, I know. That pretty Czech girl in the paravan told my friend, and my friend told me."

Inka was suddenly thrust between them like an intruder.

"Your girl?"

"No." He blushed.

She puckered her brow and smiled. "I was born in Trieste," she said, "but my parents are Slovenes. They're both teachers. Lived there all their lives. I've never even been to Slovenia."

"So why did you leave? What happened?"

"The war. First the Germans and, after the war, Tito and the communists. You know Tito?"

Jan nodded.

"We lost everything. My parents lost their jobs when they closed the school. Then we lost the house. Had no place to go. Couldn't return to Slovenia, not even if we'd wanted to. There was nothing to go back to. No family. No relatives. No place to live. Nothing." She looked at him through misty eyes. "Wouldn't have gone to Slovenia even if we could, because the

Russians were there, and people feared them even more than the Germans. And you?"

She listened intently as he gave her a sketch of his life.

They reached the entrance to her building and she pulled his coat off her shoulders. "*Grazie, grazie tante.*" She smiled. "I am so glad we met."

"Will you...could I see you again?" He hoped she didn't notice his nervousness.

"Yes, of course. Tomorrow, at breakfast. I'll wait for you." She touched him lightly.

Flushed, he fought the urge to reach out to her, to spill his heart to her. Face glowing, lips parted, she returned his look, and he knew she understood.

Finally she shuddered, outstretched her hand, and said softly, "*Buena note.*"

CHAPTER 46

Jan collapsed on his bunk and let his imagination soar. Whispering Majda's name, he tried to recall her face. The thought of their extraordinary encounter staggered him, but a small voice inside his head wouldn't be stilled. His mind was in turmoil. Could he trust his reactions, or was he deluding himself? Was it just a fortuitous coincidence that she appeared when his self-esteem was at its lowest? Did she offer more than just sympathy and compassion, seeing that he was emotionally vulnerable, trying to salvage his ego? It was all so incredible, it defied rational thought.

He didn't expect this onslaught of feelings. Until now, 'love,' as he knew it, was a hypothetical mystery, fueled by romantic fragments from movies and awakening manhood, by the pleasurable anticipation of conquest and the pain of reaching and not touching, of anticipation and fulfillment—of Inka who personified all that, having catapulted him to the emotional zenith and then letting him fall. He had been infatuated by her. She was so beautiful, so exciting—so unattainable. She awakened in him sensual desire and carnal passion. She challenged him, hurt him, humbled him, angered him, used him, and yet, through some strange chemistry, taught him. He grew emotionally, if only to prove he could survive the calamity of her. He tried then to convince himself it was love, but now saw he had been only a willing accomplice in her deception, blinded by her beauty, taken in by her cleverness, vanquished by her passion. What she had awakened in him was visceral. What happened to him today was an epiphany.

When he rushed out the next morning, Majda was already waiting by the entrance to the mess hall. Her face lit up when she saw him.

The vast hall was crowded with people milling about, looking for vacant places. A table, already occupied by an elderly couple, two empty chairs tilted against the sides, showed that they were expected.

"Papa...Mama..." Majda made the introductions.

The father, a gaunt, graying man dressed in a once-elegant gray suit that now hung loosely on him over a wrinkled shirt without a tie, stood up and smiled. "Maruk." He offered his hand. "Please, sit down and join us. Majda has told us all about you."

Majda's mother, a slight sweater-clad woman with pale blue eyes set in a wrinkled face and long hair twisted in a braid neatly coiled at the back of her head, gave him a shy smile.

They touched briefly on their lives, the mother looking at him kindly, Majda giving him reassuring smiles whenever their eyes met.

A faint frown crossed the father's face as his gaze hardened. "So, you left without your family?"

Jan told him about the coup, his involvement with the Spirit, and his escape into Germany.

"An idealist, heh?" He chuckled lightly. "That's the disease of youth, my boy...idealism. I was a boy like you once, an idealist, and what did it get me? Just look at me. At us." His tone grew bitter. "I thought I would change the world by going into teaching, and here I am. Here we are. Irrelevant. We had a good life there, but they forced us out. Lost it all."

"We're too old for all this. They don't want idealists, they want workers. They don't want brains, they want brawn. All they want is young, strong people like you—not old schoolteachers with soft hands and flabby muscles like us." He lifted his hands and turned them mockingly palms up. "You have somebody in America? Relatives? Somebody?"

"No, sir."

"And where are you going?"

"Minnesota."

The father nodded pensively. "We're going to some place called Virginia. Richmond. Know absolutely nothing about it. Have some distant relatives there that we've never even met. If they hadn't vouched for us, I don't know where we would end up."

"Everybody wants to go to America."

"Yes. All things considered, we were lucky, I suppose. I hear we'll be leaving in about a week, if you can believe the rumors."

"A week?" Jan's voice cracked.

"Heard people talking. Just this morning, before you came. A week, ten days at the most. Seems they had word about the ships. The lists should be up in a couple of days."

* * *

Paying scant attention to the droning of the instructors, Jan couldn't wait for the day to end. He heard nothing, intent instead on Majda's nearness, feeling the occasional electric rush when their bodies touched and a wondrous flutter when their eyes met. The whiff of her perfume, a faint scent of lilacs, made him dizzy.

362

She took his hand as they walked out of the classroom late in the afternoon. "There's a small park not far from here. Shall we go for a walk? Please?"

"Of course, but your parents?"

"They know." She squeezed his hand.

Shrouded in drizzle and fog, the park was deserted. Once beautiful, it was now overgrown with vines and strewn with debris of a pair of blown-up bunkers. Their crumbling hulks and twisted metal seemed incongruous among the pastoral setting and ancient trees towering above the winding footpath. Shorn of their leaves, their bare limbs reached skyward in silent lament as drops of water, collecting on their tips, fell to the ground like giant tears, splattering noisily among the detritus. From somewhere ahead came the sound of waves lapping the shore.

She clung to him as they walked in silence. He held her tightly, oblivious to everything but her presence, and the feel of her against him as they brushed. Despite the penetrating cold, he felt flushed. He sensed the tension in her as her pace slowed, until finally she stopped and turned to him and reached out to him, eyes pleading, face aglow, lips parted. They embraced, at first gently and tentatively, then desperately. Moaning softly, she showered him with kisses until they hurt. Locked in an embrace, they rocked gently from side to side, pressing their bodies together until they staggered, holding desperately onto each other like two souls about to drown.

"Do you believe in fate?" Jan touched her ear with his lips. "We've only just met, and—"

"I believe in fate."

"It scares me. What's going to happen to us?"

She snuggled closer and he kissed her tenderly, brushing his lips against the velvet of her skin.

"Oh, Majda…*carina*…"

"Shh," she touched her finger to his lips and lay her head on his chest.

He buried his face in her hair and they just stood there, wanting the moment never to end, all the while mindful of time tearing at them. Finally, she nudged him and they went on, alone with their thoughts, stopping every few steps to embrace and kiss, heedless of the drizzle, impervious to the cold.

The path terminated in a grassy belt bordering a narrow beach exposed to the tides. At its widest point, a few moss-covered cement benches formed a semi-circle around a weathered statue of a mariner gripping a wheel, pockmarked with bullet holes, gazing seaward. Protruding from the sediment, a soldier's helmet rocked gently back and forth with the rhythm of the waves. Jan picked it up with a stick and hoisted it out of the water. Rusted through in places, the metal was jagged where a bullet had pierced it.

"If it weren't for the war, we wouldn't have met," she reflected. "Isn't it ironic? And now that we have, we don't have much time." Her eyes flooded.

Jan tossed the helmet back into the surf. "What will become of us?"

"I don't know. I never imagined. I'm afraid." She kissed him gently.

"We only have a few days. Two, three weeks at the most, if you count the voyage. And then—"

"Let's not talk about it now." She clung to him as he held her closer.

In all his life, he was never more sure of anything than his feelings at the moment. He had to say it—he *had* to tell her.

"You may think me presumptuous and you may not believe me, but I think I love you! *Ti amo! Ti amo.*" The words came out in a hoarse whisper and he felt immediately guilty for not being more eloquent.

Her breath came up short and she stiffened under his touch. He felt himself sinking. "Please, believe me."

She looked away and he felt her tremble.

"I know it doesn't make sense. I know we've just met, but—"

She pulled away and faced him, smiling faintly. "But you...what about the other girl? The one you looked for that day back in the camp? What if you are deceiving yourself? What if you are seeing what you want to see and hearing what you want to hear? What then? I don't want you to be hurt. I don't want you to hurt me."

An icy stab took his breath away, leaving him speechless. "It wasn't love," he stuttered.

"But I saw you."

"Whatever it was, it wasn't love. I swear. I know it now."

"She was very beautiful."

"Yes. I'd known her since the war. Came from the city. Used to come to my town for summer vacations. Used to flirt with the boys. Flirted with me. I was naïve, then. Stupid. I was taken with her, but she wasn't what I saw, she was what I *wanted* to see. She was very skillful at using people. She hurt me. She hurt me every time we met and I kept coming back for more each time she smiled. I was a fool. Anyway, I finally saw her for what she really was. She paid a horrible price. Someday, I'll tell you the whole story."

She fell silent for a few moments and then snuggled closer to him. "Forgive me, *carino*, but I have to be sure." Her voice had a rasp to it. "Can't you see? I feel the way you feel. Felt that way ever since I first saw you, when you rushed into her room and didn't even notice me." She kissed him tenderly. "Oh, *carino mio, ti amo, ti amo*, but we have so little time, so little time. I'm afraid." She began to sob.

The drizzle stopped. The fog lifted just enough to reveal the horizon and a tumultuous, steel-gray sea crashing against a long jetty stretching far out into the bay. Bashing themselves relentlessly against the rocks, great trains of waves shot gobs of spray and foam over the top. At its far end, a light beacon flashed intermittently. Off to their right, in the distance, bristling with cranes and warehouses, was the harbor. Two large ships lay alongside a long deserted pier.

CHAPTER 47

"We're leaving Monday. *Mi dispiace*." Majda's father put his hand on Jan's shoulder when he joined them at the bulletin board, surrounded by a swarming crowd trying to get a look at the shipping lists. *"Mi dispiace.* I'm sorry." He pulled out a crumpled handkerchief and wiped his glistening eyes.

"But, but we're not going together," Majda cried out over her sobs. "There are two ships…"

It took him a moment to grasp the full impact of her words. A sickening feeling spread through his gut.

Off to the side, the mother gazed at them sympathetically, holding back tears.

"At least we're going to the same place, to America." The father tried to console them.

Jan stared at him in anguish.

"I know what it means to her." The father looked at her affectionately, and then at Jan. "She's very fond of you."

She came to Jan and put her head on his shoulder, crying softly, and he held her, feeling awkward in front of her parents. Four days! Four days was all they had. In four days they would part and he would lose her. The thought overwhelmed him. He felt cheated.

"Could there be a mistake? With so many names of the lists," he cried out in desperation, knowing full well the futility of it.

"See for yourself." The father stepped aside. *"Mi dispiace."*

Jan pushed to the front of the milling crowd and stared at the words: *The following individuals will depart Monday, 13*

November 1950, on the USAT General Sturgis, destination New York. Below it, alphabetically, the names, beginning with the A's and ending with the M's. Maruk was nearly at the end. The second list, identical in appearance except for the name of the ship, *USAT General Harry S. Taylor*, and the date, 14 November 1950, listed the names from N to Z, with his name, Neuman, near the top.

He stared at the names, rereading them as though he could wish them away, until the jostling of those behind him forced him to withdraw.

Majda cried softly and he held her, feeling hollow, helpless. "I am so sorry. I am so afraid," she whispered between sobs.

His mind reeled. He'd do anything to change that! But what?

*　*　*

The administration building, the tallest structure in the camp, was abuzz with people streaming in and out of its gaping entrance like ants. The classrooms took up most of the ground floor, while the administration occupied the second. The American offices were on the third floor.

"*Dritter Stock.*" The sentry at the door motioned vaguely in the direction of the wide, polished granite staircase when Jan inquired about the commandant's office.

The guard, a wizened dour-faced German occupying a small table in front of the Commandant's office, greeted Jan with a smirk. "*Ja? Was wollen Sie?* What do you want?"

"*Bitte*, I must see the commandant. It's very important."

He shook his head. "The commandant is busy. *Beschäftigt!* Come back tomorrow."

"But tomorrow is late. I must see him! Now! It's important. It's *very* important. Please."

"I told you he's busy." The words came out in a growl.

Jan wouldn't be deterred. "I *really* must see him. Please."

The guard stretched back in his chair, measured him for a few moments, and then leaned towards him across the table. *"Hast du Geld?"* he snarled.

Money! Oh god! The bastard wants money! Jan felt a bit of relief. With trembling hands, he pulled out his billfold and fished out a handful of Marks.

The guard's scornful gaze darkened. *"Amerikanishes Geld! Nur amerikanishes Geld! Hast du keine amerikanishes Geld?"*

"Dollars? You want *dollars*?

In a secret compartment of his billfold, Jan had hidden a ten-dollar bill, one he had exchanged in Italy for his last pay, hoping to save it for his first days in America. It was all he had. Reluctantly, he pulled it out.

The guard snapped the bill out of his hand, slipped it into his breast pocket, and nodded toward the commandant's door.

"Ja! Herein!" a man's voice answered when Jan knocked.

The office Jan entered contained only a typist's table and a large desk next to a door marked *Commandant*. Monotonous sounds of someone dictating filtered in from within the commandant's office.

A stocky German rose from behind the desk and scowled. *"Ja? Was wollen Sie?"*

"I must see the commandant. It's very important."

"That's impossible. The commandant is busy. Tell *me* what you want. I am his deputy. I decide if you need to see him or not."

"Please, Sir. My fiancée and I have been separated. She leaves Monday on the first ship and I can't go until Tuesday. We must go together."

The German's face took on a supercilious air. "That's not possible. It's too late. The manifests can't be changed."

"Please, Sir, I really must see the commandant. My fiancée and I—"

"I told you, I have full authority. What is your name?" The German glared at him from under his furrowed brows.

"Neuman. Jan Neuman."

Scowling, the German reached into a drawer, pulled out a thick folder, and rifled through some papers. "It says here, you're single. You're not family?"

"She is my fiancée. We are going to be married. In America. We must go together."

"*Es tut mir leid*, but I can do nothing for you." Grunting, he slid the papers back into the folder.

"Then please, let me talk to the commandant. Please."

The German lit a Lucky Strike and blew a column of smoke toward the ceiling as he studied Jan's face. "*Haben Sie Geld? Amerikanishes Geld?*" he muttered.

Stunned, Jan glared at him and he stared back, unblinking, eyes full of contemptuous indifference. "If you have dollars, then perhaps..." He bared his teeth in a smile.

"But I already gave—" Dejectedly, Jan shook his head. "All I have is Marks. I'll give you all I have."

The German's smile vanished into an icy stare as he slid back into his chair. "As I said, the manifests can't be changed."

He slipped the folder back into the drawer and looked away, leaving Jan standing there, crushed.

Majda cried and clung to him even more desperately when he told her. The little park became their refuge. Here they sought solace, trying to live in the moment and not think about the future that weighed on them like a blanket of lead.

Time had turned into an enemy as their world shrank with each tick of the clock, each fleeting hour. It had suddenly become physical—palpable to the point of suffocation. Each drop of water falling from the weeping trees, each rustle of leaves under their feet, each crash of the waves on the rocks, each squawk of the seagulls, each murmur of the wind, each breath and touch was a reminder of its passing. Its end was imminent. Beyond it, only a void.

*   *   *

"Sorry, but I never learned to boogie-woogie or jitterbug," Jan apologized to Majda, embarrassed, as they sat gloomily with her parents in the cantina, sipping Coca-Colas, listening to a German combo, and eyeing the dance floor alive with twisting bodies swaying to the rhythms of Glenn Miller.

She smiled sadly, politely turning down yet another request to dance from one of the young men hovering around the dance floor. "I don't really feel like celebrating."

Finally, when the band struck the Moonlight Serenade, she took Jan's hand and they danced, clinging to each other. He felt her tremble now and then, and when their cheeks touched, her tears.

"It's stuffy here, *carino,* could we get some air?" She turned pleadingly to her parents. "It's our last night."

The father looked at the mother for agreement, gave a slight nod, and smiled.

Holding hands, they strolled into the night and she led him, wordlessly, across the grassy field toward her building. "I want us to be alone," she answered his questioning look. Their steps echoed in the empty hallway as she led him up two floors past the family rooms, to a short flight of steps terminating in a single door that creaked as she opened it. It was the attic.

Only a pair of tiny gabled windows permitted the slightest amount of reflected streetlight, mostly blocked by stacks upon stacks of blankets and mattresses heaped in irregular piles way up to the rafters. The air was dry and pleasantly warm—a stale cocktail of musk and dust, the droppings of rodents, and aggregate odor of hundreds of bodies that over the years had left traces of their presence embedded in the fabric.

She stumbled and he instinctively groped for the light switch.

"No, *carino*, please," she whispered.

Only the sweet scent of lilacs told him where she was. When his eyes finally adjusted to the darkness, she was just a faint outline against the inky void where the darkness was perfect. He heard the rustle of her clothing as she undressed, and then just stood there—an alabaster statue, a pale, ephemeral, wispy apparition.

He trembled. It was the first time a woman had offered herself to him as an affirmation of her feelings—an act of love.

"*Carino...mi amore,*" she whispered hoarsely as she reached for him, tentative and pleading.

Her smooth, lithe body felt delicate against the coarseness of his clothes as she pressed herself into him. He felt her shudder under his caresses. A searing torrent flooded his mind, obliterating all thought.

"*Amore...amore... amore mio,*" she moaned softly, clinging to him as he showered her with kisses.

She stopped his words with her lips. "*Carino,* please," she begged him, tugging at his clothes, as he frantically tore at them until he was free and they melted into each other.

"Please, *amore?*" she whispered, taking his hand. "Please..."

She pulled him toward a low stack of mattresses and drew him to her. They collapsed backward on the cool, smooth fabric. She moaned under his touch and pressed herself against him as he probed the undulating landscape of her body. He touched her breasts and she shuddered.

"Something wrong, *carina?*" He pulled back.

"Forgive me, *amore.* I've never done this before. It is my gift to you. A promise. *Que Ti amo.* Only you. *Ti amo!*" She pulled him closer in passionate desperation. "*Ti amo, ti amo, ti amo,*" she cried.

"*Ti amo, ti amo, ti amo,*" he responded, stroking her breasts with his lips, intoxicated by her woman scent.

She let out a muted cry as he entered her, and then pressed herself into him with all her strength and desperation, until he could go no further.

For a few precious minutes, they were completely, perfectly alone—the only living creatures in the universe. Their rhythms, their breathing, the pumping of their hearts, the heaving of their bodies in perfect unison, in perfect union became one.

"*Ti amo, ti amo, ti amo...*" she cried out softly between his heaves.

"*Ti amo, ti amo, ti amo...*" he cried out to her between gasps.

And then their universe exploded in a dazzling display that sucked the light out of them and they collapsed on themselves like dead stars, drained of substance as darkness rushed in, lying still, spent into oblivion.

Trembling, they lay silently next to each other until she bent over him and kissed him softly.

"Did I hurt you? I heard you cry out," he said.

"A little."

"Forgive me, I didn't mean to."

"It's all right." She kissed him again. "It's just that I didn't know."

"Will you wait for me after we get to America? I swear I will come for you. I want to marry you. I give you my word. It may take time. I don't know what's going to happen. I don't know when—"

"Doesn't matter, I'll wait for you, *amore mio*. I'll wait for you for as long as it takes. As long as it takes. I'll wait for you."

"I swear I'll come for you."

"I believe you."

He pulled a blanket over them and they lay silently, holding desperately onto each other, trying in vain to keep at bay the gnawing, disconsolate thoughts descending upon them. With each heartbeat, each breath, each word, each kiss, each caress, their world became smaller, until it shrank down to the miniscule—the last couple of square yards of cloth upon which they lay and from which soon they would be torn. A great chill enveloped them.

CHAPTER 48

Jan climbed the short flight of steps to the observation deck of the bullet-pock-marked marine terminal and joined a small crowd strung along the railing watching a long line of refugees about to board one of the two ships tied up at the pier. Dragging their meager possessions, they snaked slowly toward the steep gangplank of the *USAT General S. D. Sturgis*, a Liberty-class ship, anchored in the Bremerhaven harbor, straddling the estuary of the Weser River where it met the North Sea. Agitated, the onlookers waved wildly when they would spot a familiar face, and exchanged final good-byes with those down below, laughing and crying at the same time.

Ordinarily reluctant to show his feelings, today Jan didn't care. Oblivious to the cold and blustery weather pelting him with intermittent salvoes of icy rain, he focused intently on Majda, shuffling along with her parents, slowly and inevitably moving away from him. She would turn around every few steps, look up at him and wave, and though he couldn't see her clearly through his tears, he knew she was crying. Carried by the line, she moved steadily past a small group of uniformed men checking tags pinned to everyone's clothing, mounted the gangplank and, with a last wave, disappeared into the hold of the ship.

She had clung to him that morning as they waited to board the busses taking them to the harbor. Her red-rimmed eyes betrayed her anguish. There was so much he wanted to say to her, but there was no time, so he only held her, feeling her tremble under her thin coat, unable to say anything.

She cried and swore to wait forever. He professed his love for her and assured her he would come for her, no matter what. And then she hugged him for the last time, sobbing as they boarded. Her mother wept, and her father embraced him like a son. As the buses started to move, she leaned from the window and reached out to him, and he held her hand, running alongside until he could keep up no longer and she was torn away from him. He followed on foot, along with a procession of others whom the vagaries of the alphabet had also separated from their friends.

Staring at the ship, Jan couldn't believe she was gone—the memory of her too fresh, the parting too abrupt. He still felt her presence, the way a melody lingers in one's mind after the tune has ended. The overwhelming feeling of loss was yet to make itself felt. For now, he was numb, stunned and sickened, glaring at the cavernous hold that took her away from him.

The decks of the ship filled quickly with the passengers, lining the sides, pressing against the rails to have a last look at the Old Country. She was there somewhere among the hundreds of faces, but where? With a sinking heart, he waved wildly, hoping for a response. Finally, he saw her, leaning out of a stern porthole, waving frantically, a handkerchief fluttering in her hand. He was sure she saw him.

With a long blast of its horn, the ship began to move. There was no cheering, only a sudden quiet, an eerie, almost religious stillness, broken now and then by a sob and the dull throb of the engines. A few final tentative waves from the small crowd on shore went unanswered by those on board as they stood, transfixed like statues, gazing back at their friends, the land, their pasts they were about to leave.

Majda's fluttering handkerchief grew smaller and indistinct as the ship made its way past the jetty into the open sea. A layer of mist obliterated all detail and the ship and all its human cargo became a monolith—a shape that erased the last traces of her.

* * *

The following day, laden with refugees, the second Liberty ship, *USAT General Harry S. Taylor*, unceremoniously slipped her moorings and left Bremerhaven on the evening tide. Jan put away his things and rushed on deck, already alive with the throngs gazing at the receding shore. Gone was the raucous mood of yesterday, replaced now by introspection and reflection. Most of them would never see these shores again. Unlike the previous day, the observation deck was empty. Worn by fatigue, he went to his cot below the stairs and slept.

He was awakened from a fitful sleep by a rush of footsteps on the metal stairway just overhead. Dressing quickly, he hurried topside, in time to catch a glimpse of a white smudge off the starboard bow—the cliffs of Dover. It seemed longer than almost three years that he stood not far from here on the Normandy beach, marveling at the sea, and now he was upon it, living a surreal dream whose twists and turns he could not fathom. That time seemed so remote now—reduced, like his home, his parents, his friends, his past, to a faded, static snapshot fixed in his memory. And somewhere out there was Majda. Oh, how he missed her!

The Atlantic greeted them harshly. To Jan's surprise, the motion of the ship didn't make him sick once he became accustomed to it, though from the very start seasickness began to take its toll on the others. The mess, where they took their meals at standing-height tables, was mostly deserted during mealtimes. The confined space, confused, disorienting motion, and stale air, smelling faintly but persistently of diesel, drove everyone topside where they sat, sallow-faced, lining the decks, huddling under blankets, clutching or retching into the once-white canvas bags given them upon boarding— then a source of jokes but now indispensable, turning a sickly green from their contents.

Responding to an appeal for help, he volunteered for work in the laundry. Brightly lit but small and confined, it was located deep in the stern bowels of the ship, with the massive shaft that turned the screw rotating overhead. The entire room shook from its vibrations when the screw came out of the water as she rode the mountainous seas. The work provided a welcome distraction. The monotony of the repetitious tasks lent itself to daydreaming, mostly about Majda. He missed her terribly. At night, he wrote in his diary, committing to its pages what he otherwise might have said to her. It had become her surrogate. Someday, he hoped, she would read it.

The excitement grew as the ship neared the American coast. Updated each noon, a large map indicating the day's progress became a favorite gathering place. The weather had gradually moderated until the sun became their constant companion. He saw it as an omen. The albatrosses, flying fish, and dolphins reappeared. Now and then, a ship heading in the same direction would come into view.

Finally, on the tenth day of the voyage, an indistinct darkening appeared on the horizon, becoming more prominent, gradually acquiring clear, distinguishable features—a jagged skyline of skyscrapers reaching heavenward like giant beckoning fingers. Excitement mounted and reached a crescendo as they glided by an enormous, patina-covered statue of a woman holding a torch. A fireboat trailing them sent up plumes of water. The ship let out a blast of its horn. Teary-eyed, Jan thought of Majda, wishing that they could have shared the experience together.

The sun shone brilliantly as the *USAT General Harry S. Taylor* slowed to a crawl and a pair of tugs snuggled themselves to her sides like a couple of children holding onto their mother's skirt. Slowly, majestically, they led her into the vast harbor and nudged her into a dock.

The harbor was alive with activity. From beyond its confines came the sounds of a vibrant, pulsing city. The decks teemed with immigrants gazing shoreward, faces full of awe and anticipation. Tears flowed freely. There were no bands, no friends to greet them, but they didn't care—the joy was in their hearts. America! America!

Part 2.

AMERICA

CHAPTER 49

The world continued to undulate under Jan's feet as he made his way to a drafty, cavernous waiting room smelling faintly of urine and a smorgasbord of other nondescript odors. Through a row of high, unshuttered windows, the sun sent in streaming shafts of golden late-afternoon light, made almost tangible by fine particles of dust and cigarette smoke suspended in the air. People milled about in happy confusion. Gray-haired women in starched pale blue-striped uniforms, with smiles permanently affixed to their pink powdered faces, mingled with the new arrivals, serving weak coffee and cookies. Loudspeakers blared out names over the low murmur of subdued voices, directing the recipients to several large numbered windows festooned with boldly lettered signs, "Traveler's Aid Society."

Jan heard his name called and hesitantly stepped to one of the windows.

A harried, ruddy-faced balding man finished shuffling a sheaf of papers and leaned out over the counter. "Let me see your tags, please. Says here you're going to Minnesota, eh? Had a couple of other fellas going to Minnesota yesterday, too." He thrust a ticket and a meal pass into Jan's hand and pointed toward a plump woman hovering nearby, who acknowledged him with a nod and a polite smile. "That lady over there will take you to the station. Don't worry, you'll be okay. We've already wired your sponsor. He'll be waiting for you in Minneapolis when you arrive."

"Welcome to America!" The plump woman greeted him with a tentative wave. "My station wagon's just outside, so if you'll follow me..."

They exchanged awkward small talk as she drove swiftly through the canyons of Manhattan aglow in the late afternoon sun, their jagged panorama of skyscrapers blocking out the sky, towering over traffic-clogged streets and a cacophony of sounds—the deep, almost visceral throbbing pulse of a great city. Jan choked on emotion. It was as if his old boyhood treasure – a yellowing New York postcard Father had once given him – had come to life, and he chuckled at the thought of seeing Father putting on his old Stetson and looking longingly into a mirror. Was he also reliving a dream?

"Well, here we are!" the woman sighed with relief as she swung into a reserved parking space in front of Grand Central Station. She led him inside to another 'Traveler's Aid' kiosk where an elderly man greeted her, frowning as she spoke and nodding gravely as he measured Jan with his gaze.

Jan surveyed the cavernous hall. The milling crowd reminded him of the turmoil of the past few days and especially of Majda. Only yesterday, she passed through here. Perhaps even the same woman who brought him here had also brought her and her family—he was sorry he hadn't thought to ask. He pictured her emerging from the crowd and coming toward him with a smile, but the fragile daydream vanished like a burst of a bubble.

* * *

An icy blast took Jan's breath away as he disembarked the Limited in Minneapolis late the following day. Snow covered the ground with more in the offing, judging from an occasional snowflake drifting down from a leaden sky. Bundled in heavy overcoats and hats that all but covered their faces, people scurried for the exits.

"You must be our Czech friend!" a giant of a man, made even larger by a heavy coat and a tall, furry hat, boomed, smiling. "Jan...right?"

Shivering, all Jan could do was nod.

"I'm Dr. Průcha. Welcome to America and to Minneapolis." He shook his hands heartily. "Seems our winter decided to come early this year. C'mon, I have a cab waiting. Don't like much driving in this weather." He glanced at his bag and sighed. "Is this all you have?"

Jan looked around warily. "I expected someone named Mrs. Kostka."

"I'll explain later." Dr. Průcha demurred and picked up his bag. "The missus didn't want to come on account of the weather. She gets nervous in the car. Besides, I thought we'd need the room for the bags. She'll have a hot meal waiting." He knit his brow. "We'll have to get you a coat. You must be freezing in those summer clothes."

The cab slid to a stop before a spacious home set into a hillside dense with shrubbery, bent under a covering of snow.

The doctor paid the cab driver and stomped out his cigar. "We'll go in through the garage. Do you smoke? The missus doesn't allow smoking in the house."

Smiling broadly, a silver-haired matronly woman stood waiting at the bottom of the stairs. "You must be Jan! Welcome to America! Come in, come on in. Leave your bag down here and take off your shoes."

Jan followed her up the short flight of stairs into a hallway and a brightly lit, plushly carpeted living room. "Oh, dear, you must be cold and starving. The food'll be ready in a few minutes. Just look at you, you're shivering. I'm so glad you finally made it. Come, come in and sit down. You poor dear."

Jan hesitated, ashamed of his soiled socks, his tattered clothing, his odor, and his unkempt appearance. He'd never seen a carpeted room before and thought perhaps he ought not to walk on it.

"It's all right, just come on in." Mrs. Průcha gave him a motherly smile. "This is Míra," she introduced a young man about his age holding the door open, "and this is Mr. Bernard." An older portly man wedged in an overstuffed chair gave him a nod and smiled. "Mr. Bernard was a chef at the Metropol in Prague and Míra attended a military academy before he left. They arrived yesterday, also from Germany. Perhaps you know them... No? Never mind, you'll get to know each other soon enough. By the way, do you smoke?"

"I already told him, Dear." Dr. Průcha said.

She listened intently and became animated as he described his experiences. Now and then she would cry out, "JesusMary!" and dab at an occasional tear with a lacy handkerchief. The doctor grunted in sympathy.

The meal was sumptuous. They toasted America, the Průchas, and the Old Country. Jan ate voraciously, until Mrs. Průcha admonished him gently that "in America, you eat slowly. And always leave a bit of the food on the plate, even if you are still hungry, so you don't embarrass the hostess. If she sees an empty plate, she may feel obliged to offer you more, but may not have enough to do so. And don't hold the fork and knife the way they do in Europe." She proceeded to show him. "You're in America now. May as well learn the American way. Put your left hand in your lap and the fork in the right hand...yes, that way, Jan. Sit straight, and never, never lean on the table. Good, very good." She smiled.

*   *   *

Jan cast a worried look out the large picture window at a blizzard raging outside. "My sponsor, Mrs. Kostka, was supposed to meet me at the railroad station. At least, that's what they said in New York. Is she coming for me tonight?"

Mrs. Průcha cast an uneasy look at her husband, who cleared his throat. "You'll all stay here for now," she said. "There's plenty of room. If you write, you can use our address until you get settled." She sighed. "I may as well tell you, boys. There's something you must understand. This is a great country. Don't think I'm complaining. But these aren't good times for immigrants, especially refugees like you. You have to understand, with all the soldiers home from the war, there aren't many jobs to go around. It's hard to find work. And as far as the law says, you can't take anybody's job. So what's out there for you may not be what you expect. The main thing, the *important* thing, is that you're here." Her eyes darkened under her powdered furrow. "Do you understand? I don't want to disappoint you, but you may as well know."

They all remained silent and she took their silence for the affirmative.

"On top of it all, there is this man, personally I think he's mad, a senator from Wisconsin. McCarthy's his name. You'll know about him soon enough, I'm sure. This senator has everybody running scared. Scared of communists and

387

foreigners. There's always been opposition to immigration, and now that the war's over and there are no jobs... Well, it's a miracle the immigration law even passed. Guess they had to do something since other countries took in so many—refugees, I mean. All things considered, the quota was very small, only around two thousand for the Czechs. Not much.

"I guess what I'm trying to tell you is, there's very little interest in the refugee problem in this country, I regret to say. In fact, there's even some resentment. You're very lucky to be here. You're *so* very lucky. People are confused. Afraid. Don't know what to do, whom to believe. Mrs. Kostka and a few others – your sponsors – they're all my husband's friends or clients. They agreed to help. They gave us permission to use their names in return for a small, shall I say, professional favor. They're all very good people. Good Czechs. Patriots. Hard working. Wanted to help but couldn't. Didn't have the money, so we paid. And because they only permit one single refugee or one family per sponsor, we had no choice but to ask them. However, they can't do anything for you. They're just kind people willing to help. Czechs helping Czechs. Do you understand what I'm saying? I hope you do. You're so lucky to be here."

"You put up the money?" Bernard stirred.

"That's right, boys." She smiled. For all of you. Two hundred dollars for each of you, boys."

"Two hundred *dollars*!" Jan's jaw dropped. "How can we ever—"

"When you can, if you can," Dr. Průcha broke in, smiling. "No need to be concerned about it now. There's time to—"

Mrs. Průcha continued. "Right now, we're trying to bring in a young pianist. A Czech virtuoso. An artist of some renown.

388

Firkušný is his name. He's still in Germany, and we're having a terrible time bypassing the quota. It's so frustrating. Times are so difficult."

An awkward silence settled on the room. Finally, Bernard stirred and yawned.

"Dear?" Dr. Průcha nudged his wife.

"Oh my!" she cried out. "You boys must be so tired, and here we are keeping you up. Forgive me, but all this is close to my heart, and when I get started... Forgive me. We'll have plenty of time to talk some other time."

She led them down into the basement and a room with three cots, one freshly made up, stacked with blankets and towels. "Be sure you turn off the water after you shower and always flush the toilet after you use it," she said as she bid them good night.

CHAPTER 50

Perched on top of a bluff overlooking Lake Calhoun, the Twin Lakes Country Club cut an imposing view. Surrounded by an expansive park-like setting that hid a swimming pool, tennis courts, and a golf course, connected to the city sprawled beneath its flanks by a single unobtrusive road, it was a world unto itself. "Anybody who's anybody in Minneapolis comes here," Dr. Průcha informed the boys, as he navigated his Cadillac into a vast parking area early Monday morning.

The lot was empty, except for a few older cars half-hidden by a snowbank at the far end, abutting a long barn-like structure, with a pair of gaping doors beneath a second-story loft serviced by a narrow open-air staircase. Through the open doors, two men could be seen loading tables on a gurney.

A short genial well-dressed man greeted them with a smile, rubbing his hands together. "Hullo, Doctor! Cold enough for you, huh? Come in, gentlemen, come in."

"Boys, this is Mr. Delacroix, the club manager," Dr. Průcha said. "Míra, Jan, and Bernard."

"So these are the folks we discussed, huh Doctor? Excellent. They'll do just fine." Mr. Delacroix measured them from head to toe as they shook hands. "Welcome to America and to Minnesota, gentlemen. Please, sit down. Coffee? Here, please, serve yourselves. Have some cookies, too. So tell me, how did you come to be in America?"

"Oh, my!" He rolled his eyes in mock dismay when they told him with Dr. Průcha's help. "Just don't worry about your English, you'll do fine. It won't take you long before you will— Ah, excuse me," he apologized with a pained smile, as a shrill sound of the telephone interrupted their conversation. "It's for you, Doctor."

"The clinic." Dr. Průcha sighed, putting down the receiver. "Always know where to find me. Forgive me, Bob. Sorry boys, but I must go. You understand. But you're in good hands here. Mr. Delacroix's a good friend of mine. You know how to get a-hold of us, right?"

From the boardwalk outside came stomping of the feet and a knock on the door, and two men, dressed in quilted overalls, walked in. Jan recognized them as the ones he saw outside moving the tables: an older, brawny, ruddy-faced man with a pockmarked face, curly light hair and pale blue eyes, and a younger boy, perhaps Jan's age or a bit older, hair close-cropped, stubble on his face.

"This is Ollie." Mr. Delacroix gave a friendly pat to the older one. "And this is Jerry." "They'll show you what to do. You'll be working with them most of the time. Ollie's in charge, so do exactly what he tells you—he knows everything. He's been with us since before the war, right Ollie?"

Ollie smiled uneasily, not taking his gaze off them.

"Lucky for us, he came back when he mustered out of the army. You'll be working with him. Help him setup the rooms. We have parties almost every day. He'll tell you what to do. He knows it all." Mr. Delacroix' gaze searched their faces for comprehension. "Evenings, you'll bus the tables—" He stopped short, then continued, "It's like being a waiter. You'll have uniforms. Jimmy's our head busboy, you'll meet him later. He'll show you what to do. Monday's our day off, but sometimes you'll have to work to get ready for Tuesday. Ollie'll let you know. Do you understand?" Mr. Delacroix smiled broadly, pleased with their enthusiasm.

Ollie continued to stare at them.

"Mr. Bernard, Dr. Průcha tells me, you're a cook."

"Yes, sir, I was a chef at the Metropol in Prague. That's the best—"

"A chef, huh?" An amused smile crossed Mr. Delacroix's face. "In that case, you'll work in the kitchen. Help our cooks. They can always use a hand."

Bernard bowed his head and smiled.

"Any questions anybody?" Mr. Delacroix stood up and scrutinized their faces, and when they didn't, turned to Jerry. "Would you mind showing the boys to their room? Make sure they're comfortable."

"Pick your own bunks...'cept these two. That one's Jimmy's and this one's mine." Jerry pointed to two unmade-ones in a row of six, lining the wall. "The john's over there," he nodded toward a door at the far end, "and the shower. We start around 6. Breakfast's at 7, lunch at noon, and dinner at 4. We eat early because of the guests, but you can always grab a bite during slack time." He turned to Bernard. "You're lucky. The cooks don't start till noon. That's 'bout it for now. Got any more questions?"

They met Jimmy, a gangly and sullen seventeen-year-old with an acne-covered face, during dinner. He glared at them with contempt. His face screwed up in a sneer and his eyes filled with anger when Jerry told him to show them how to bus tables. "Fuck," he swore under his breath.

With Christmas in the offing, the Twin Lakes Country Club took on a joyful air with blazing strings of colored lights turning it into a fairy-tale castle. Aglow with displays and alive with festive sounds, the city at its feet became a surreal fairyland during the night, reluctantly reverting to its earthly self at dawn.

Sprawled on his bunk and staring at the ceiling, Jan felt almost unbearably lonely. He thought of Christmas at home and of Majda. Oh, how he missed her! He had spilled his heart to her in a letter included with his Christmas card, explaining his predicament of not being able to come soon. Surely, by now she must have received it. So, why hadn't she written? Each day he called the Průchas and each day, the answer was the same— nothing. Beset by doubts one moment, he was angry with himself the next for doubting her. After all, she too had to find a niche in this maddeningly strange world. Yet, he couldn't dispel the feeling of gloom whenever he considered the distance between them and his impotence to do anything about it.

He couldn't shake a sense of foreboding. He knew it would be a long time before he could make good on his promise to go to her. His meager wages of forty dollars, half of which went to the Průchas to pay off his debt, left pitifully little to save. Besides moving furniture and busing tables, he found himself working extra long hours washing dishes late into the night, when the skid-row bums – the only ones who would take the job – disappeared into the bars and hovels of lower Nicolet after they'd been paid, returning only after their money ran out, begging to be given another chance.

* * *

"I really don't know how to jitterbug." Jan blushed, flustered by having to turn down Grace's offer to dance, acutely aware that the years spent in the camps had taken their toll. The world had moved on while he stood still. Watching the others swing and gyrate on the dance floor, he felt foolish and out of place.

The club had closed at noon that day – Christmas Eve – to make room for the annual employee Christmas party. Ollie and the boys had barely finished setting up the ballroom before the guests began arriving. Anna Swanson, the gentle, portly salad lady who spoke with a heavy Swedish accent and who took a liking to them; Grace and Alice, two full-time waitresses with their boyfriends, and three others, Hazel, Judith, and Nancy, students working their way through the university; the cooks, John and Lenny, and Helen, a dour woman in charge of the pantry, who didn't speak, but followed them with her frigid stare whenever they came within sight. Mr. Delacroix, in an ebullient mood, greeted everyone and made a speech. Jan and his friends became the instant center of attention and curiosity. People they had never seen before – families of the workers and staff – filled the ballroom.

The boys were showered with gifts and Bernard even won the raffle—a television. The only discordant note was Jimmy, who had been sharing a flask of whiskey with Jerry in the kitchen and tried to pick a fight with Míra, but Ollie quickly whisked him out of the room. They found him later passed out in the bunkhouse.

The boys spent Christmas Day at the Průchas. No sooner did they take off their coats and shoes, Dr. Průcha took Jan aside. "These came for you last week." He handed him a pack of letters. "Thought I'd hold onto them since you were coming here, instead dropping them off. Hope you don't mind."

Jan's stomach knotted as he flipped through the pack: letters from Aunt Stáska and Daniel; another one from Dick; an official-looking envelope from Immigration. Aunt Stáska's was the thickest, surely, there would be news from home. Finally, unbelieving, he stared at the last two—they were not Majda's, but his own. This couldn't be! Something was wrong! He wanted to retch.

"Bad news?" Mrs. Průcha gave him a worried look.

Jan handed her the two letters, with *Undeliverable. Return to sender* stamped on them in bold purple letters, and an arrow pointing to the Průchas' address. Someone had crossed out the street name and written above it, in longhand, "No known address."

"I don't understand." He failed to hide his distress.

"You put down the correct address, right?"

Jan pulled the precious slip of paper out of his billfold and handed it to her. "I copied it off her sponsor's papers myself the day she left."

She studied it briefly and shook her head. "Seems all right. Don't know what to tell you." She put her arm around him. "Is it a girl?"

He nodded.

"Oh, you poor dear." She embraced him. "And you gave her your address?"

"Yes, my sponsor's—"

"Mrs. Kostka's?" Her eyes widened. "Then perhaps..." She reached for the phone. "I must confess, we don't see much of each other nowadays. Fact is, I haven't talked with Sophie in weeks. Months actually. But let me see." She dialed a number, listened attentively for a few moments, and shrugged. "No answer. Sorry. I'll try again tomorrow and call you, okay?" She gave him an encouraging smile.

She called back two days later. Hearing the familiar voice, Jan's chest tightened in anticipation.

"Sorry, my dear," she said. "I finally got hold of Sophie...err, Mrs. Kostka. She'd spent Christmas at her parents. I asked her but she couldn't talk, so what do you say we go see her? It's about time you two met anyway. You can thank her in person. I'll have the doctor drive us over the next time you're off."

* * *

Dr. Prŭcha's Cadillac threaded its way carefully through the snowbound streets of East Minneapolis.

"We've been living here all our lives, and I still don't like to be out in this weather." Mrs. Prŭcha sighed. "You doing all right, Dear?"

Dr. Prŭcha grunted.

She turned to Jan. "I may as well tell you a few things about Sophie, so you won't be surprised. She's a good person and a dear, dear friend, but she changed since Karel, that's her husband, died just over a year ago. She's become something of a recluse. She never had an easy marriage. Her family opposed him from the start, and she herself broke up with him a number of times before she finally agreed to marry him. I think we were her only friends after then. She suffered a lot because of him. He was a hard worker. Worked at General Mills...you heard of General Mills?"

Jan shook his head.

"Doesn't matter, you'll find out soon enough. Anyway, he was a good worker and a union man, but he got involved in some strikes and protests back in '37 or '38. They were engaged then. Some people called him 'pinko' and 'red' and 'commie,' and he just shook it off. But it affected *her* greatly. Isolated her. One day he quit his job and, I don't think he even told her, slipped into Canada and from there to Spain to join the Internationals. Those were the people who fought in the Spanish Civil War."

"Yes, I remember the movies."

"She, Sophie, swore that she'd never forgive him, but when he returned in 1940, she took him back and married him. They had a good year, but then the war started and he volunteered to fight the Nazis. She cried when he left and again when he came back four years later, bitter to the core, in poor health, half the man he used to be. Worked for a bit, but never recovered. Spent his last days in the hospital, and that's how we got involved. Didn't leave much; a small VA pension... Ah, here we are."

The path to the small frame house half-hidden by snow drifts had been freshly cleared. The pallid gray-haired woman that opened the front door greeted them with a smile, but her gaze remained detached. Mrs. Průcha embraced her and introduced Jan. Her handshake was limp and tentative when they shook hands.

"So you're the boy the Průchas told me about. Welcome to America," she said. She led them into a room dominated by a massive fireplace and a ring of chairs surrounding the crackling flames. "Make yourselves comfortable. The coffee will be ready in a few minutes."

They made small talk and Jan told his story, to which she listened with polite interest.

"The reason we came was to see if there was any mail for Jan here at your address," Mrs. Průcha said. "He'd lost contact with his friend and was hoping that she had written here. Said he gave her this address before they became separated. His letters to her came back, so we were hoping…"

Sophie stiffened. Her liquid gaze shifted from Mrs. Průcha to Jan and back again as her hands twisted the corner of her sweater into a knot. "Oh, my God!" Her hand flew to her mouth.

"What is it, Sophie? Did something happen, Dear?" Mrs. Průcha cast a sidelong glance at Jan.

"Oh, my God." She began to shake.

"What is it, my dear? What happened?"

She burst out crying and Jan felt a sudden chill. His chest tightened like a drum.

"You know the trouble I had with Karel's politics before he died. I thought I was rid of all that, but then, last month, somebody came and asked about me. My neighbor told me. The FBI, I thought. Been here before, asking questions, while *he* was still alive. But now? Why now? Then, about that time, a letter came from someplace out of state. Virginia, I think. The address was right, but the names didn't make sense to me. Or the return address. Just didn't make the connection. All I knew was I didn't want to be involved. So, I didn't accept it. Gave it back to the mailman." Sophie met Jan's gaze and lowered her eyes. "I am so sorry."

Jan felt Mrs. Průcha's hand on his shoulder.

"So, just before Christmas, another letter, might have been a card, came from the same place. With the same addresses. I was afraid, what with all that red scare, newspapers full of stories about McCarthy and the Un-American Activities Committee and all that. I didn't want to go through that again."

"So what did you do?

"I took the letter and burned it."

CHAPTER 51

The moment Jan saw his soft fabric case sticking from under his bunk, he knew something was wrong. He snatched the bag, unzipped it, pulled out the box where he had been salting away the extra cash, and stared in disbelief. The lock had been jimmied—the money gone.

"How much was in it?" Míra said, examining the cheap lockbox, scratched and bent around the latch.

"Twenty dollars...what was left after I paid the Průchas."

"And your bag—why didn't you lock it?"

"It doesn't lock. Only has a zipper. That's why I got the box."

"Damn! You know we wouldn't—"

"I know. The door's never locked. Anybody can walk in."

"So, who else?" Míra nodded toward Jimmy slouched in the corner, drinking Coke and watching Bernard's television, pretending not to notice. "You going to say something?"

Jan shrugged. "I'd hate to start trouble. We just got here." He tossed the box disgustedly back into the suitcase.

Jimmy turned off the television and, face twisted in a challenging smirk, strolled past them toward his bunk. His eyes locked for a second with Jan's, and Jan knew—they all did.

"I'm truly sorry." Mr. Delacroix nodded gravely when Jan told him. "Without proof, there isn't much I can do. We have never had anything like this happen here before you came. Please, don't take me wrong, but could one of your friends...I don't think Jimmy or Jerry would—"

Jan bristled. "Sir, all three of us were at the Průchas. There was no way they could—"

"I understand, I understand." Mr. Delacroix flushed. "Please. I promise you, I will look into it. Let me do some checking first. If you don't mind, I'd rather not involve the police. You understand, don't you? This is a reputable...very important club. We've never had anything like this happen here before."

*　*　*

Jan stacked the last batch of dishes and pans he had been washing, slipped the heavy rubber apron on a peg next to the dishwasher, and walked out into the night. Only a pair of brightly lit windows – the bar was still open – cast a harsh rectangle of light into the darkness. The bitter cold made his breath congeal into steamy spurts.

The snow crunched under his feet as he slogged carefully toward the bunkhouse. Around the bend, where the path breached a wall of snow left there by the snowplows, a ghoulish figure stumbled out of the shadows. Jimmy!

Jan stepped instinctively off the path into the deep snow to let him pass.

Weaving and unsteady on his feet, Jimmy blocked his way. "You fuckin' sombitch," he spat at Jan, slurring his words that ended in a hiccup.

Jan tried to get by him, but he staggered so close, Jan could smell his sour breath. "You fuckin' sombitch. What yer trying to do, get me fired? You sombitch commie fucker! You tol' Delacroix 'bout me, you fucker. You tol' 'im I stole your fuckin' money, you sombitch."

"You're drunk. Leave me alone!" Jan stepped further into the deep snow.

Weaving from side to side, Jimmy put up his fists. "C'mon, you fuckin' commie fucker! What yer trying to do! Take my fuckin' job? I didn't take yer fuckin' money, you motherfucker. Who the fuck you think you are? We don't need you 'round here, you fur'n fuckers. Get the fuckin' back where yo come from." He gave Jan a hard shove that sent him sprawling.

Jan's first visceral reaction was to sink his fist into the distorted face hovering over him, but froze, recalling the admonition, given prior to his departure from Germany, that any misbehavior or infraction of the law could mean deportation. At the very least, a fight might cost him his job—and then what? Jimmy wasn't worth it. So, shaking with anger, he shoved Jimmy off and stepped back.

A window in the bunkhouse swung open and Jerry's head popped out. "Hey, what's going on out there? Jimmy? That you? Shut up and go to bed!"

"Fuck you!" Jimmy spat out and swung wildly at Jan.

"Jimmy! Goddammit—"

Jimmy swung again, slipped, and came down hard. Figures spilled out of the bunkhouse. Before he could get off another hit, Jerry grabbed him and pinned his arms. "Let it go, Jimmy! You're drunk. Shut up and go to bed. You'll only get yourself in trouble."

"That motherfucker's trying to get me fired!" Jimmy screamed, kicking up chunks of snow as he struggled. "I'll kill him! I'll kill that fucker. You're all fur'ner commie fuckers," he glowered at Míra and Bernard. He wriggled out of Jerry's grip, made another lunge in Jan's direction, slipped again, and fell. Spouting obscenities, he thrashed around for a few moments, went limp, and vomited all over himself.

"C'mon, Jimmy, c'mon." Jerry helped him to his feet.

Spitting and coughing, he shook off the snow, wiped his mouth on the sleeve of his coat, and growling, "I'm gonna get you for this, you motherfuckers," let Jerry steer him toward the bunkhouse.

* * *

One frigid February morning, a frantic expression clouding her face, Anna Swanson cornered the boys. "I don't know what's going on, but the boss wants to see you. Now."

Grim and unsmiling, Mr. Delacroix met them at the door. "Come in. Come in, fellas," he greeted them curtly, holding the door open.

Inside, four neatly dressed strangers slouched on the overstuffed sofa and chairs next to Mr. Delacroix's desk. Their eyeballs followed the boys with a cold, inscrutable look.

Mr. Delacroix's voice shook nervously. "These gentlemen are from the FBI and want to ask you a few questions."

Not moving a muscle nor acknowledging them in any way, the men measured them with deadpan stares.

Jan's throat tightened. "If it's about Jimmy..." he stammered.

"Jimmy? No, of course not, at least, I don't think." Mr. Delacroix wrung his hands. All they want to do is ask you a few questions."

One of the men stood up and snuffed out his cigarette. The others quickly followed.

Taking the cue, Mr. Delacroix sighed. "Follow me, boys, please." He led them to an empty room behind the bar, with the agents trailing close behind.

They took turns shuffling in and out of the room, and the 'few questions' turned out to be a grilling that took up most of the morning. Jan's anxiety mounted as the agents fired random questions in rapid succession: about himself, about his parents and friends, about Míra and Bernard—where he met them and how long he knew them, what he thought of them, if he thought they might not make loyal Americans, and whether he would report on them if he thought they were communists—about Sophie Kostka, the Průchas, and many others he didn't even know.

In the end, one of the agents pushed a document toward him and growled, "Read this, answer all the questions truthfully, and sign it."

Jan scanned the list of questions. Each began with the words, 'Are you now or have you ever been a member of_' followed by a name of some organization he'd never heard of, except the last one, the communist party. With clammy hands, he checked the 'No' answers and signed his name.

The interrogation left him shaken. He could understand the grilling he had received at the hands of the CIC in Passau after fleeing his home and again when he applied for immigration to America, but why this? He recalled Mrs. Průcha's admonishment about the communist scare, but surely, that couldn't include him and his friends. After all, hadn't he – hadn't they – sacrificed everything, their lives, their homes, their country, for a cause? The *right* cause? America's cause? Shouldn't *that* be proof enough?

The question weighed on him heavily. One day, when he found himself alone with Anna Swanson, he brought up the subject. "What's going on, Anna? Do you know? Something's not right."

She blanched and gave a quick look-around, and when she met Jan's gaze, her doe eyes darkened with apprehension. "I don't know, but I think somebody complained. Somebody called them," she whispered.

"Complained about us? To the FBI?"

"Ja."

"But who would do this to us? Why? Jimmy?"

Anna glanced again over her shoulder and shrugged. "I don't know. But rumor has it, it came from…" She nodded in the direction of the pantry. "Maybe others, too. I don't know. Something about you taking their jobs."

*　*　*

Mrs. Průcha turned crimson under her make-up. "You must talk to Delacroix about this." She pounced on her husband, after listening to the boys' account of the interrogation and Jan's retelling of Anna's conversation. "If you won't, I will. I'm sorry to hear it, boys," she turned to them, "and sorry to say, I'm not surprised. Wish there was some way to move you, but you are obligated. You must stay a year, that's the law. We know Delacroix. He's a good man and he's the man you have to please, but we can't vouch for the others. So, just do your work. Mind your own business. Be careful what you say. And be patient. Everything will turn out all right in the end."

From that day, the relationship between Jan, his friends, and many of the people at the club noticeably cooled. Even Mr. Delacroix seemed more distant. Where once he would stop and chat when they met, though still polite as always, now he barely acknowledged him. Only Anna would reward him with an occasional compassionate, understanding look.

Even among themselves, the boys became quieter, introspective. Was it just his imagination or did they also feel the way he did—wary and unwelcome? Or was he the only one letting the stress get the best of him? He had survived the camps. Surely, he could survive this.

He realized his world had again shrunk, his horizon again narrowed to include just his friends and the Průchas. More than ever, he felt himself an outsider. For the first time in a long time, pangs of loneliness awakened in him a longing for home, an almost amusing absurdity given the circumstances, for he hadn't thought of home in months. And he missed Majda. How he needed someone he could trust. How he needed her!

CHAPTER 52

The Greyhound came to a stop under a bare bulb-illuminated sign reading "Cincinnati." The driver swung the door open with a whoosh, and a blast of cold air rushed in from the outside, awaking Jan from a drowsy slumber. "Twenty minutes, folks, twenty minutes," he called out, stretching, before bounding out the door to unload the bags from the belly compartment of the bus.

Jan had left Minneapolis at dawn and spent the day staring out the open window, gazing at but not seeing the road unwind before him like a ribbon, preoccupied with the prospect of seeing Majda again. It filled him with a mixture of anticipation and dread—mostly dread. Would she believe that he didn't have the money or Mr. Delacroix's permission to take a few days off until this Labor Day weekend? He fingered the bulge in his breast pocket that was his undelivered letters and tried to conjure up her image and their meeting, but the thought only evoked a clutching tightness in his chest.

He changed buses in Lexington and felt a chill as he boarded the one marked 'Richmond.' The reality of it smacked him in the face. Richmond! The word had become synonymous with *her*. It gleamed from the lighted marquee above the windshield like a beacon. His mind, stoked by anxiety, raced ahead past the unfamiliar sights, the lush greenery passing by in a blur, the mileposts sliding by like a procession of pickets. Dusk fell as the bus reached the city outskirts and threaded its way to the station.

"That'll be five dollars a night, in advance." The small balding man behind the motel counter measured Jan suspiciously. "Where you're from?"

"Minneapolis."

The man gave him a pinched look. "I mean, where you're from? You speak…I mean, you ain't 'merican, ain't you?"

Jan shook his head. "No, I'm a Czech."

"Oh, I see." The man's face screwed up in a puzzled grimace. "Had a for'ner here once before. A couple o'years ago." He scowled. "Planning to stay long?"

"Two nights, I think."

"That'll be ten dollars, then. Here, put your name here." He pushed a stained ledger toward Jan.

The room was dusty, reeking of stale smoke and disinfectant, but Jan didn't care. After a quick shower he threw himself on the bed, and slept.

He awoke at 8:00 and cursing himself for oversleeping, cleaned up hastily, rushed out, and hailed the first taxi he saw. After an eternity, the taxi deposited him in front of a large two-story frame house set back from the road behind a profusion of greenery. A wide porch spanned the ornate front. A crudely painted number on the mailbox read 138 River Street, the address Majda had given him.

Heart pounding, he took a deep breath, walked up the few creaky steps, stopped at the door, and hesitated. Almost in a stupor, he felt at once immersed in the moment and yet strangely detached. Would she be there? Would she be the one to open the door? Oh, God! What would he say? What would she say? With a clammy hand he reached for the doorbell.

The loud ring inside startled him. Perhaps it would have been better not to come. What if she rejects him? Perhaps it would have been better to keep her as he remembered her— secure in his memories, sure to grow more tender with the passage of time. Perhaps—

Shuffling steps approached the door and the key turned in the lock. "Yes?" a woman's voice, *not her voice,* spoke as the door opened a crack. An eye peered at him through the slit.

Jan swallowed hard. "I'm looking for Majda...Majda Maruk. Does she live here?" His voice quivered with anxiety.

A chain rattled and the door swung open, revealing a middle-aged woman, disheveled, dressed in a hastily tied gown, streaky blond hair rolled up in curlers, traces of yesterday's lipstick still on her lips, a cigarette in hand. "Who wants to know?" Her dark eyes peered at him from behind a narrow scrim of mascara-laden eyelashes.

"Jan Neuman. Majda Maruk...does she live here?"

The woman blanched. Her hand flew up to her open mouth. "Oh my God! You must be the boy... Oh, my God!" She swung the door open and held it for him. "Come in, come in. Please. Please..."

A sinking feeling spread through Jan's insides.

She followed him in. "Excuse the house, but my husband goes to work early and I'm a late sleeper. Haven't had the chance yet to straighten up a bit. Please." She hastily smoothed a knit coverlet on a sofa and pushed aside a pillow. "Please, sit down. Can I get you somethin'? Coffee? Ice tea? It's already made."

Jan begged off. His stomach knotted.

She lit another cigarette. "I'm Lilian, and my husband's Noel. Noel Johnson. He's at work now, as I said. Works for the city. You can call me Lila. What did you say your name was?"

"Jan. Jan Neuman."

"So, you're the boy." Her eyes took on a sheen and she shook her head. "Well, the Maruks lived here for a spell, but not very long. Couple o' months, maybe. We didn't really know 'em well. Never got to know 'em. We were just trying to help. Through our church, you understand. We're Christians. It was the Christian thing to do. Anyway, as I said, they did stay with us. But just 'fore Christmas, seems there was somebody. Some distant cousin. Somebody. Spoke their language. Showed up one day 'n' took 'em with 'im. So they left. Thanked us and left. Just 'fore Christmas, as I said."

"And Majda? What about Majda? I wrote to her here."

"Oh yeah, the girl." She sighed. "Pretty girl. Kept askin' me 'bout mail. Kept askin' 'bout letters for her, but I swear, nothin' came here. Nothin.' Not one. I swear, else I'd have given 'em to her."

"I believe you." Jan patted his pocket. "All the letters I sent her came back. Got them right here. Said it was the wrong address."

"Wrong address? But how could that be," she protested.

"Here. Here's the address she gave me. Isn't it your address?"

Lila inspected the piece of paper and frowned. "Yeah, seems to be. Yeah, that's right. That's it. Oh my God, that's awful!"

"So why didn't she get them?"

"Don't know, sir, I swear." She pursed her lips and looked at him darkly. "Don't know, but I'd have shorely given 'em to her if they came. I get all the mail, and Noel, he's a good man, he wouldn't do nothing like turning 'em back. I swear they didn't come. I'd have known. I'd have seen 'em." Her eyes filled with tears.

"So, do you know where they moved? Did they leave an address?"

"No. They didn't say and I forgot to ask 'em. Everything was so confused that day. They were in a hurry. Got their stuff together. Didn't have much. Thanked us an' all that, but ne'er said where they were going. I'm sorry."

"What about Immigration? Didn't they have to pay? I mean, pay you? Give you money for their passage? Maybe if they'd send the money, or come, there'd be a way—"

Lila shook her head. "No, that feller paid us. Cash, right down to the penny. I ne'er saw them again, 'cept the girl. She came by a few times, looking for mail. Used to come every few days. So pretty, but sad—oh, those sad eyes. But then she stopped comin', that poor dear." A rivulet of mascara trickled down Lila's cheek and she wiped it with the back of her hand.

"And when did you see her last? When was she here the last time?"

"I think March." She scratched her head and took a deep drag on her cigarette. "Yeah, March or April. No, it was March. It was sometime in March when she came last. By then, she was beginning to show."

"Show? Sorry, I don't understand. Show what?"

"You could see she was in the family way."

"I'm sorry, but I still don't—"

"She was pregnant! You could see she was pregnant. She was going to have a baby. And that was the last time she came, I swear. The last time Noel and I saw her."

A baby! A fleeting memory of their last night flashed through his mind. But what if someone else... No. She wouldn't. Couldn't. It had to be his. *Theirs*. And he'd let her down! How desperate she must have been, waiting day after day for a word from him. How betrayed she must feel now. How could he ever face her? Would she believe he had written? But then, she hadn't written, either, or had she?" He recalled the visit with Sophie Kostka. "No matter what, something went terribly, horribly wrong! "Oh, God," escaped from his lips. He felt like dying.

"You sure I can't get you something?"

Jan fought a choking grip on his throat. "Is there anything I can do?"

"Dunno." Lila sighed. "Leave your address in case she comes again. But, as I said, it's been months since the last time.'Cept maybe..." Her face brightened. "Didn't you people have to register someplace? The post office? Somewhere? I know *they* registered. Noel took'em. You might check. They may know something."

"Yes. Of course! I had to register there myself. But where is it? How do I get there?"

"The main one's where I'd go, and that one's downtown. You need to take the bus, and—"

"But I don't have much time. And I don't know the city. Do you suppose... Could you please call me a taxi?"

"Be glad to. Of course." Lila pulled a telephone book from under the phone and made a call. "Be here in 'bout five minutes." She stood up. "You may want to leave your address." She offered him a notepad and a pencil, and then carefully tore out the sheet, folded it, and laid it on the credenza. She opened the door for him when the taxi pulled up, and attempted a

412

reassuring smile as he left, but her eyes flooded with tears. "God bless," she whispered."

The post office was a last straw and, like a drowning man, he grasped it.

CHAPTER 53

The post office clerk listened absently to Jan's inquiry about the Maruks and Majda, and shrugged. "Sorry, sir, but we only *collect* that information. We don't keep any files. And even if we did, we couldn't show it to you. It's against the law. Sorry."

Though steeling himself for rejection, Jan was crushed.

A patron in the line behind him shuffled impatiently and coughed.

"Sorry, sir, but I really can't help you." The pitch of the clerk's voice rose a notch. "You might try Immigration. That's where we send all the information."

"Immigration? Sorry, but I'm not from here. Could you—"

"See that tall building over there? Across the square? That's the Federal Building. It's in there."

The matronly, gray-haired woman behind the desk looked up over her half-rim glasses, smiled, and offered him a seat. An ornately carved sign identified her as Nora Smith, Immigration Officer. Behind her, the dark-paneled wall held a panoply of neatly framed diplomas and certificates, President Truman's picture, and an American flag. The room smelled of must and time. A small fan, whirring on the sill of an open window, stirred the air.

"I'm Mrs. Smith. What can I do for you, young man?" Her voice exuded warmth behind its official tone.

Jan swallowed hard and introduced himself, trying to control the quiver in his voice. "I'm looking for someone. The man at the post office said you keep records on all immigrants."

She looked at him gently, the way his mother used to look at him when he was little. "It's true we keep records, but these people, I mean, the refugees, the DPs, they don't all report once a year like they're supposed to. So unfortunately our files aren't hundred percent. Do you understand?" Her questioning gaze rested on his face. "What is the name?"

"Majda Maruk; the family name's Maruk."

"Oh, you're not related?" she cried out, knitting her brow. "That's too bad." Her voice took on a darker shade. "Wish I could help you, but if you're not family... You understand. I'm not allowed. It's the law. I'm sorry."

"But I *have* to find her! She's my fiancée. We were going to be married but we were separated when—" Jan's words came out a wounded cry as his eyes filled with tears.

"Where do you live?"

"Minnesota."

"You've come a long way." She folded her arms and looked at him kindly.

"Please, Ma'am. We were going to be married. I wrote, but all my letters came back. Got them right here. She didn't get them." He patted his pocket.

"Did she have your address?"

"Yes."

"And didn't she write to you?"

She wrote twice, but my sponsor didn't recognize the name and returned the letters. Fact is, returned one and burned the other. That was all. She never wrote again. So, this morning, I went to the address she gave me, and her sponsor said, she used to come all the time looking for mail from me. Said she spoke about me.

Mrs. Smith nodded. "And you said you wrote? How often? How many times?"

"At least four or five, but then I stopped when they all came back."

"That doesn't sound right." Mrs. Smith's frown returned.

"And her sponsor said, the last time she saw her she was pregnant. She was going to have a baby. Our baby."

"A baby?" Her jaw dropped, and for a moment, it seemed as though the air was sucked out of the room. Only the whirring of the fan broke the silence. Finally her gaze softened. "Let me see the address she gave you. You still have it?"

Jan handed her Majda's sponsor's address.

"Seems okay," she muttered, examining the precious slip of paper. "And you say they moved." Her forehead furrowed as she gave him a long, unblinking look. "Well, I really shouldn't, but I'll make an exception in your case. Just in your case, you understand? Since there's a child involved and you came all the way from Minnesota."

With a sigh, she walked over to a large file cabinet and opened one of the drawers. "Marek...Marshak." Her lips moved as she spoke softly to herself flipping through the files. "Ah, Maruk. Here we are!" She pulled out a folder, opened it, and the smile slowly faded from her face. "Let me see the address again. The one she gave you."

Jan handed it to her.

She glanced at it briefly and shook her head. "I'm sorry, but it's the same address you have. I was hoping they'd re-registered, but they never reported their move. I'm sorry."

A nauseating clamminess washed over him as his palms began to sweat. He fought the anesthetizing dullness that sometimes replaces pain. She was here, somewhere in this sun-drenched, sprawling city, walking the same streets and breathing the same air, so close, and yet, so completely beyond reach, despondent perhaps, embittered for sure, even disdainful, with their child a constant reminder of what she must have seen as his betrayal.

"Those letters you sent her, may I see them?" Mrs. Smith snapped him out of his stupor.

He handed them to her.

She studied them for several moments and sighed. "Come and look. I think I see what *might* have been the problem."

She thrust the letters in front of his eyes. "She lived at 138 River Street, right? But, you wrote, 738 River Street—seven-thirty-eight!"

"Seven-thirty-eight? That's impossible."

"Look! That's seven-thirty-eight. You wrote the 'one' the way it's written in Europe…the European way, with an extra long upstroke before the downstroke, and not the American way, which is just a single stroke. See here! To me, it's a seven. If I didn't know better, if you hadn't told me, I myself would've taken it for a seven. I'm sure the postman mistook it for a 'seven.' To an American, it's a seven. There was nobody named Maruk living at seven-thirty-eight River Street, if in fact the number even exists. It may not. The postman did the only thing he could do, send the letters back."

Jan stared in disbelief at the letters.

"I'm sorry for you, Mr. Neuman, but there's nothing I can do now." Mrs. Smith dabbed at her eyes with a handkerchief. "If you can, come back after January. That's when everybody has to re-register, as you know. Come and see me. If they register, I'll try to help you. But for now, there's nothing, absolutely nothing to be done. Nothing." She walked out, gave him a sad smile, and opened the door. "Here's my card. Take it and come see me after January. I'm truly sorry."

CHAPTER 54

"Say, young man." Someone behind Jan spoke, as he stepped off the bus back in Minneapolis. "Young man? Sir?"

Turning around, he found himself facing a tall, smartly dressed and neatly groomed soldier in khaki uniform, rows of zebra-like stripes on his sleeves, silver wings and a splash of ribbons on his chest, leaning against a colorfully decorated kiosk bearing a single sign, *Recruiting*.

"Sir?" The soldier smiled.

"Me?" He felt a chill, unable to imagine why a soldier would be addressing him.

"Yes, you, sir. You look like an intelligent young man." He sized Jan up. "How would you like to become a member of the greatest air force in the world? How would *you* like to enlist in the United States Air Force?"

"Enlist?" Jan didn't know the word. "I don't understand."

"Yes, enlist. Join. Become an airman."

"You mean—the *American* air force?"

"Yes sir, the United States Air Force. The finest air force in the world."

Jan swallowed hard. "But, I can't. I'm not an American."

The soldier smiled again. "What are you? A foreigner? A tourist?"

"An immigrant. A refugee."

"Hmm." The soldier's smile vanished. "But you're *legal*, aren't you? You do have papers? And you *do* plan to become a citizen. Right?"

"Yes."

"Then I'm sure you'll be accepted. That is, if you first pass the physical, but you look okay to me." His eyes measured Jan from head to toe. "So, how about it?"

"Well, I've always wanted to fly—"

"See, you already have the right attitude. Where you from?"

"Czechoslovakia. That's—"

"I know where it's at." The soldier made a vague motion with his hand. "Flew over it once. My last mission of the war. Unfortunately, with bombs in the belly. Bombed Pilsen. Heard it was a pretty country. Looked pretty from up there. Never saw it up close. So, what do you say? You said you always wanted to fly? I guarantee you'll fly if you join…the finest air force in the world."

"But I can't."

"Whaddya mean, you can't? I just said—"

"I have to work. The law says I must work for a year before I can leave. I still have two months."

"Hmm, I see." The soldier scratched his closely-cropped head. "Wait. Gimme a sec. Don't go 'way." He disappeared in the kiosk and came out waving a massive black binder. "Regulations," he answered Jan's curious look. He leafed through the thick stack of pages and let out a satisfying chuckle. "Yeah! Just as I thought. It can be waived!"

Jan looked at him blankly.

"It means you don't have to do what the immigration law says. You can ignore it if it's for the good of the country, and by damn, serving in the United States Air Force *is* for the good of the country, wouldn't you say?"

Jan was stunned. The proposition was so unexpected, so uplifting, after his ego had been shattered by the debacle at

420

Richmond. Flying had been his childhood dream. How many times had he lain on his back during the war, watching the bombers overhead, imagining himself 'up there'? And later, when the Americans liberated his town, how many hours had he spent hanging around a makeshift airstrip at the edge of town, watching Piper Cubs come and go, savoring the pungent smell of oil and gasoline?

After all, hadn't he left home to help liberate his country? Becoming a flyer would be an antidote to the guilt he'd carried ever since he found out he had been duped about the existence of a Czech legion in the American Occupation Zone in Germany. Becoming a flyer would get him back into the fight. It would be atonement for the pain he had caused his parents, for the loss of his friends, his home, his country. And should the liberation of Czechoslovakia ever come – and he believed it would – he would be ready.

A blue sky and fleecy clouds supplanted the tortured image of Majda in his mind. The rush of blood in his temples became the roar of engines in his soul.

"Well, how 'bout it? What do you say?" The soldier's voice snapped him back to reality.

"Yes. Yes, I think I'd like that. Yes. Yes! I'd like that very much."

"So, step up to my table. There's some papers to fill out. Will it be four or six?"

Jan looked at him blankly.

"Years. Four or six years?" The soldier was all business now.

"Six." Jan was surprised at his audacity. "Six." He would have agreed to a hundred, if that was what the soldier offered.

Míra was taken aback when Jan told him about his enlistment. "So long as they don't send you to Korea," he grumbled. Jan thought he detected a touch of envy. "I decided, soon as my time's up, to get out of here. Go to Chicago. Bernard wants to stay and that's fine, but I don't like what's been happening. I was going to ask you, too, but now that you did what you did…" He shrugged. "Hope you know what you're doing."

The ever-ebullient Mr. Delacroix handed Jan his last pay, sympathetically patted him on the back, and said he would be missed. They even held a little farewell party for him the day of his departure, and surprised him with a cake for his upcoming twenty-first birthday. Anna Swanson cried and Ernie gave him a bear hug. Even the dour woman from the pantry smiled—or was it a smirk? *Glad to see me go,* he decided. The Průchas wished him luck and permitted him to leave behind a few of his personal things he couldn't take. "We'll store them in our cabin up on the Minnetonka. There's plenty of room and they'll be safe there." Mrs. Průcha embraced him warmly. "You must write and let us know how you're doing. And come back for a visit any time," she said, dabbing at her eyes.

* * *

Jan lay on his bunk staring at the September sky through the rolled-up flap of his tent. It had been almost a week since he and a small contingent of Minnesota recruits boarded a shiny Braniff Stratocruiser for a flight to this vast training base at San Antonio in the south of Texas. It was his first flight. Gazing out the window at the setting sun and the darkening abyss below, he saw the earth for the first time from the vantage point of eagles, and the rare group of humans he hoped soon to join—flyers.

The thought of flying staggered him. It made it all worth it—the sweltering tents they had to sleep in; the dust that covered everything; the mustard-colored layer of powdery clay that was the floor of the tent that turned into mud when it rained; the smelly unwashed tatters of his civilian clothes – they said there was a shortage of uniforms because of the Korean war – with only a khaki-colored pith helmet to ward off the sun and a canteen of noxious-chlorine-tasting water providing occasional relief; even the unending stream of the drill sergeant's verbal excrement.

"You a foreigner?" The drill sergeant took him aside during a break.

"Yes, Sir. From Czechoslovakia, Sir."

"So what are you doing here, Airman? Why did you enlist?"

"To fly and fight the communists, Sir."

"Fight the communists?" A wide grin spread across the drill sergeant's face as he shook his head. "You're in the wrong outfit, Airman." He nodded sharply toward the other recruits. "See those pussies? They're not here to fight anybody. They're here 'cause they didn't want to be drafted. The infantry's the one fighting the commies. In Korea. You should've picked the Army."

"But I want to fly, Sir."

The drill sergeant gave him an amused smile, puckered his lips, shook his head, and turned away.

It left him flustered. Why would becoming a soldier be anything but a calling, a moral obligation, a patriotic duty? When Jára Soukup joined the French Foreign Legion to fight the communists in Indochina, how guilty had he felt for not joining him! Now he felt his kin. And he remembered his father's homily about fighting the good war. This was a good war if there was one, and he was in it.

*   *   *

Finally, toward the end of the eight-week stint, it was all over. Sweating under the board-stiff fabric of his starched khakis, Jan and the others enjoyed their first pass in the city, getting giddy and then boisterous on cheap beer in the bars along the Paseo del Rio. All that remained now was getting an assignment—realizing his dream. He had tried hard and done well, earning merit badges and even praise from the drill sergeant. Chest bulging with pride, he could barely contain himself, eager to hear the magic words.

The door to the commandant's office opened and the drill sergeant's head poked out. "Neuman. Inside!"

Jan's heart beat a staccato in anticipation. Saluting smartly, he braced himself. "Airman Neuman reporting as ordered, Sir."

The drill sergeant closed the door behind him and gave him a quick critical look.

The captain behind the desk looked up, returned his salute, and measured him severely. "Airman Neuman?"

"Yes, Sir."

"It says here you're from Czechoslovakia. And you speak Czech, and also some Russian. Is that right?"

"Yes, Sir. Some..." Jan looked at him dumbly.

The captain's steely gaze bore into him. "Then, you're being assigned to a special duty with the United States Army special demonstration team at Fort Belvoir, Virginia. You'll find out the details when you get there. All I can tell you now is it's a very important assignment. *Very* important. You should consider yourself lucky. Here are your orders. Good luck to you." He handed Jan a thin sheaf of documents and nodded to the drill sergeant. "Next?"

"But Sir—"

The captain recoiled. "You're *dismissed*, Airman!" The words rolled from his mouth like gravel.

The drill sergeant glared at him, ready to pounce.

"Sir, I was promised to be a pilot." An invisible hand clutched at Jan's chest.

"You were what?" The captain's eyes narrowed.

"Promised to be a pilot, Sir."

"You? A pilot? " He sneered. "Who told you? Nobody can make promises like that. You must be mistaken."

"The recruiting sergeant, back in Minneapolis, Sir. He promised I'd be able to fly. That's why I signed up...Sir."

"I don't believe that!" the captain snapped. That's not possible. You're a for'ner. You misunderstood—"

"No, Sir. I'm sure I didn't, Sir."

The captain's corpulent face turned crimson. "And I say, you misunderstood, Airman. You don't even speak correct English. You have an accent. I can hardly understand you. And in any case, I see here you don't even have a high school diploma. You have to be a college graduate to become a pilot."

"But I attended the Gymnásium, Sir. In Czechoslovakia, Sir."

"You attended what?"

"A Gymnásium, Sir." Jan's voice cracked.

"I don't know what it is. But whatever it is, it doesn't count in this country. You're in America now. You must have

American education. High school. College. You must have a *degree* to become a pilot, understand?"

"Yes, Sir."

"But even if you did, and you don't, the Air Force needs you to be with the special unit of the Army, and that is where you are going, Airman. Understood? That's an order!"

"Yes, Sir."

With a nod to the drill sergeant who hissed, "Ten-shun!" and "Dismissed," the captain turned to his papers, ignoring Jan's parting salute.

CHAPTER 55

Hidden by dense woods in the rolling Virginia countryside, Fort Belvoir was a sprawling military reservation, one of several just a stone's throw from the nation's capital. An aggregation of old whitewashed wooden barracks dating back to the antebellum dotted a landscape of scrub pine and lush greenery, crisscrossed by trails. An imposing headquarters building, high on a hill, seemingly afloat like a great white ship atop the crest of a green wave, its flags fluttering in the breeze, commanded the view of an immense parade ground. Beyond it, a manicured grove of ancient oaks, magnolias, dogwoods, and azaleas hid the imposing Colonial-style quarters of generals and other high ranks on streets bearing the names of their famous predecessors, immaculately groomed by an army of fatigue-clad privates.

"So you're the Czech guy, huh?" A young dour-faced Army captain fixed Jan with a perfunctory look from behind a green metal desk as he reported to the Special Demonstration Unit, an enclave set apart from other company areas in a stand of pines. Devoid of ribbons or decorations, the captain's uniform betrayed the fact that he'd never had to face combat.

"Have other for'ners here," he said, leaning back in his chair and measuring Jan with a steady gaze. "You're the first Czech I've seen. Here, try this on!" He tossed him a bundle that upon unraveling turned out to be a crumpled Czech army uniform. "Go ahead, put it on. See if it fits. If not, all I got is Russian."

The uniform hung limply from Jan's slender build and the captain scowled. "Hmm. I expected somebody, well, somebody more robust and less—" He stopped short and glared at Jan. "No offense, but we're trying to create a certain impression, if you know what I mean." His voice dripped with disappointment. "Oh well, guess you'll have to do. Any questions, soldier?"

"Airman, Sir—"

Glowering at Jan, the captain stood up. "Soldier! You're a soldier. Here, everybody's a soldier. Clear?"

Jan's new 'colleagues' met him with sour looks. They were a rough bunch—a ragtag collection of Eastern Europeans, mostly Ukrainians and Poles. Many, he later discovered, were first-generation Americans from ethnic neighborhoods of Philadelphia, New York, or Detroit, who had never seen the old country. Older than he and clannish, they excluded him from their loud discussions and drinking bouts, often more heavy than those performed on stage during their demonstrations. Generally, they regarded him with suspicion. He was an outsider—didn't fit.

They would travel by special bus from base to base and post to post, performing their skits in theaters before gawking audiences of a new generation of soldiers being primed for the Cold War, for most of whom they represented their first encounter with a 'foreigner.'

Dressed in ill-fitting Russian, Polish, and in Jan's case, Czech military uniforms, brandishing captured communist Kalashnikovs and conversing in simple inconsequential Russian, they were to boost the morale of the new recruits by impressing upon them the dull-witted nature of their new enemy. It really didn't matter what they said, and they made a game of making insulting comments about the captain whose pomposity they uniformly disliked. They would feign drunkenness, brandish bottles of 'vodka,' and stagger on the stage to the sounds of a harmonica. It was a first-rate theater of the absurd and the young troops loved it, preferring that to the boredom of everyday military life.

Though he tried to come to terms with what he was doing – filling the vacuum of ignorance among the young, callow minds that gazed at them from the seats of countless theaters as though they were freaks, clowns, a good laugh—Jan knew the truth to be different. Didn't the Russians turn around the war in Europe by stopping the Germans at Stalingrad, and in the ensuing six-month-long battle, which alone took more lives than all American wars combined, annihilated the Paulus's Sixth Army? He still remembered the panic of the retreating Germans as they rushed to surrender to the Americans in the last days of the war. And the Poles? Wasn't it General Anders and his Polish troops he saw languishing in the Wasseralfingen camp who had captured Monte Casino in Italy at an incredible loss of life? And hadn't the Czechs fought the Germans in France before escaping to England and fielding four Czechoslovak squadrons with more than one hundred pilots and almost the same number of 'kills' in the Battle of Britain long before America joined? He found the way he had to portray his countrymen personally offensive and demeaning. By tarnishing his countrymen, he tarnished the memory of his heroes, of his father—he tarnished himself. That he had made a mistake enlisting, that he had been deceived, crossed his mind, but he quickly dismissed it. It was too upsetting to contemplate. He rediscovered loneliness and the persistent pangs of yearning. With Richmond only hours away, he thought about Majda more intently than ever. Parched emotionally, he craved her like water.

The mail finally caught up with him and he lovingly fingered the thin stack of letters: a card from the Průchas, from Mrs. Průcha, really, wishing him luck and admonishing him to vote for Eisenhower and not for that awful man Truman who made such a mess of things in Korea, which amused him since as a foreigner, he was unable to vote; letters from Míra and one from Aunt Stáska that included a long, densely spaced and neatly written loving message from his father, and a letter from Dick, inviting him to spend Christmas with his family in Albion, Michigan.

The prospect of Christmas alone at the camp was not something he relished. He would accept Dick's invitation.

* * *

Blurry, vague shapes darted through the swirling snow, becoming human only when caught in the shafts of light cast by the shops and the piercing headlights of the bus as it came to a stop on the Main Street of Albion. A robust form, bundled up in a heavy overcoat, a furry cap pulled down over its ears, emerged from the shadows. It was Dick.

"Hullo, John. Merry Christmas! My gosh, lemme look at you! What a surprise. What-a-surprise! In my wildest dreams... Who'd have thought we'd ever meet again. And like this!"

They embraced awkwardly, patting each other on the back. Finally, Dick gave a short laugh. "Look at you. In uniform! And me, ha ha, just a fella. The last time I saw you, you were what, fifteen?"

"Sixteen." Jan smiled, handing him a large stuffed bear. "For Caroline."

Dick swung open the door of an old black Dodge sedan. "Used to be my dad's. Passed away shortly after I got home from the service. And your folks? How are they?" he inquired, and shook his head in disbelief when Jan told him.

Wanda, his wife, met them at the door. "So you're the fellow Dick's been talking about all this time." She smiled politely and limply shook his hand.

"Caroline?" Dick scanned the room.

Wanda put a finger to her lips. "Already asleep. Didn't want to wake her," she said, as she made room for the bear among a small array of gifts already neatly arranged under the Christmas tree. She gave Jan a thin smile. "It was so nice of you. She'll be thrilled."

Tall, dark haired and pale skinned, heavily made up and perfumed, with a nervous undercurrent to her cheerfulness, Wanda made Jan feel ill-at-ease, as she nestled herself in a padded chair, tucked her shapely legs under her, crossed her arms, and stared at him unblinking as he retold his story.

From somewhere came the whimpers of a child and she quickly excused herself.

Dick's concerned look followed her out of the room. "I'm sorry if she seems a bit out of sorts." For the first time, Jan noticed the hard lines around his mouth and puffiness around his eyes.

"I thought you'd still be in the army. I looked for you in Germany."

"To tell you the truth, I liked the Army, but it would've meant leaving Albion, and I didn't want to. Couldn't, on account of her folks. She and they're very close. She'd be crushed without them being around. Luckily, Dad left me the house and the car, so we're okay that way. But it's hard finding work in a small town." He sighed and wiped his glistening forehead. "Her dad's been helping us, but it's been a problem. She's a proud woman. They never wanted us to get married so quickly. Wanted us to wait. Get settled first. Get a job. But I wanted my dad to see us together before he died. He liked Wanda a lot. So…" His face returned to a cheerful beam while sending Jan a pleading look as she walked into the room.

"I made a bed for you in the basement," she said and smiled. "The house is small and with the baby… Hope you don't mind."

Snuggled under a pile of blankets in a room crisscrossed by clotheslines, Jan heard the low, muffled sound of their voices drifting in through a slit in the door. He couldn't make out the words. Only once did he hear Dick cry out, "Oh Wanda, for chrissakes," and then, minutes later, he thought he heard her sobbing.

It was still dark when he awoke to the excited cries of Caroline. Hastening upstairs, he was greeted by a gleeful Dick and Wanda watching an ecstatic Caroline hugging the toy bear. The Christmas tree was ablaze with lights.

Seeing Jan, Caroline dropped the bear, ran to her mother, and hid behind her skirt, eyeing him suspiciously, until Wanda nudged her in Jan's direction, and she bashfully planted a quick kiss on his cheek with a whispered, "Thank you."

"I think Christmas is the happiest time of the year," Wanda said, as she stroked Caroline's curly blond hair. "I miss being a child, but that's being childish, isn't it? Makes you appreciate your parents. Oh, I'm so sorry!" she cried out, realizing Jan's circumstance.

Dick cleared his throat, took her hand, and squeezed it gently. Her look softened. "We didn't know what to get you,

John," he said, "so I'd like you to have this." He reached under the tree and handed Jan a small, hastily wrapped package. "It's not much, but I hope you'll like it. It's from all of us." Jan untied the ribbon and opened the box. Inside, nested in a wad of cotton, lay Dick's gold ring—the one he'd so admired when they first met. A tiny diamond sparkled in the center of its onyx face. Seeing it again triggered a flood of memories that he fought vainly to hold back tears.

They had dinner at Wanda's parents who treated him politely and showered Caroline with affection. When he finally left two days later, Dick and Wanda embraced him warmly, and even Caroline hugged him and gave him a wet kiss. Buoyed by the renewed friendship, he basked in the inner warmth long after the last of Albion vanished from view.

*　　*　　*

Three months later, after a lengthy trip, the Special Demonstration Unit suddenly disbanded, having fallen victim to some undefinable bureaucratic 'priority from Higher Headquarters,' as the captain solemnly announced when Jan reported to his office. "I don't see how they could do this to us!" he fumed. "It's unconscionable! We're at war! People gotta be educated!"

The prickly Air Force lieutenant in the Liaison Office gave Jan a disdainful look. "I told you, flying's out of the question. There's no way, Airman. You're a for'ner. With your language skills, you'd easily qualify for Operations or Intelligence. So what'll it be?"

"But, Sir—"

"Dammit, Airman, I'm trying to do you a favor. I could just *assign* you, ya know? You can still apply for flight duty if you ever get your citizenship and schooling, but right now, you can't. So what'll it be? I don't have all day." He glowered at Jan.

Filling out the lengthy form, Jan cursed the day he had met the smooth-talking recruiting sergeant at the Minneapolis bus station.

CHAPTER 56

Jan paid the cab driver and walked up to the Richmond Federal Building. Weak kneed with anticipation, he wiped his sweaty palms on his trousers and reassured himself by fingering in his pocket the calling card Mrs. Smith, the Immigration Officer, had given him last September. With the demonstration unit disbanded, he found himself in limbo between assignments and with an opportunity finally to return to Richmond.

He hesitated at the entrance, at once drawn to and daunted by the prospect of a possibly successful outcome. The thought that he might finally meet Majda confounded him. How would she react after all this time? Would she be happy to see him? By now, she would have had the baby. But would she still love him? Would she be angry at him for having let her down? Or, God forbid – he tried to suppress the thought but it came back hauntingly time and again – would she have, in desperation, reached out to someone else? After all, it had been more than a year and a half since he last saw her. But she couldn't; wouldn't. Wouldn't? She had promised to wait, no matter what. But under the circumstances? His head felt like bursting. The 'what ifs' filled his mind with dread, and the only redemption lay in the knowing. He had to find out! Had to know. He knocked.

"Come in," a muffled voice answered.

He walked in and stopped dead in his tracks. The woman who lifted her head from a sheaf of papers and met him with a cool, questioning look wasn't Mrs. Smith.

"Yes?" she said in a curt monotone, gazing at him as he stood there, mouth agape. Much younger than Mrs. Smith, her long black hair only seemed to accentuate her pale complexion and a pair of large opaque brown eyes that peered at him over the rim of equally dark-rimmed half-moon glasses. She wore no makeup. Her dress was austere to the point of severity. The name on the desk sign was different, too. The wall behind her, except for the flag, bare. Only the fan, the same fan, he noted, stirring the same stale air. The window was closed.

He stood confused as she continued to gaze at him in a detached way. "Excuse me. I was looking for Mrs. Smith," he blurted out.

"You have the right office, but Mrs. Smith is no longer with us."

"She's not here?"

"No."

His knees buckled. "Is there some way I could—"

"I told you, she no longer works for the government. Retired last month. Health reasons." Her expression didn't change. "I am Mary Bates. What can I do for you?"

"I spoke with Mrs. Smith six months ago. Here in the office. She promised to help me find someone. A friend. Gave me her card. Said to come back."

"She did *what*?" Mary Bates' brow furrowed.

"She promised to help me find my fiancée. Her family moved and didn't register. Left no address. We had lost touch. Mrs. Smith said to come back after January to see if they'd registered. Said she'd give me their new address."

"She said she'd give you their address?"

"Yes, Ma'am."

"What Mrs. Smith did was against the regulations. She was wrong. She wasn't supposed to do that. It's against the law to give out any names or addresses. She could've gotten in serious trouble if anybody'd found out." Her icy look pricked him to the quick. "It's against the law."

"But she is my fiancée. She was pregnant. We were going to be married. Please—"

She shook her head and her thin lips became even thinner. "Sorry. I really can't."

"Then, at least, please, could you see if they'd registered? If they're still in Richmond? Please?"

She continued to stare at him.

"Please?" The word came out in a moan.

She averted her eyes and sighed. "What was their name?"

"Maruk. M-a-r-u-k."

With a jerky motion, she opened a filing cabinet and rifled through some files. She retrieved one, perused it briefly, put it back, and slid the drawer shut with a loud clang. "Yes, they've registered."

"And are they still living here? In Richmond?"

"Yes, but that's all I can tell you. They're still here." She returned to her desk, slid into her chair and looked at him sourly.

He didn't budge.

She got up, walked briskly past him, and opened the door. "Wish there were some way, but you understand. Regulations. Sorry, but there are other people waiting," she said annoyed.

Dispirited, Jan hailed a taxi and checked in at the same motel where he had stayed the first time he came.

"I remember you," the man said, grinning. "You're the one from Yugoslavia. And you're in uniform. What are you? A bus driver?"

"Air Force."

"Air Force, huh?" He chuckled. "We've got special rates for the men in uniform."

Jan spent the next two days walking aimlessly the streets of Richmond, crisscrossing the city, looking at faces, hoping for a miracle. More than once he thought he'd spotted a familiar shock of hair that made his heart skip a beat, but each time it turned out to be someone else. He scoured the telephone book but found nothing.

He took a cab to River Street. A chagrined Lila Johnson greeted him with sad eyes and a shrug. "Sorry, but, like I said, she never came back after the last time I told you 'bout, else I'd have wrote you," she said.

Finally, his time ran out. Exhausted, dejected, feeling hollow and racked by guilt, he boarded the bus and, still futilely scanning the crowds on the sidewalks as it sped through the bustling city, returned to Fort Belvoir.

Weeks later, he received a letter from Albion. It had been months since he had written to thank Dick and Wanda for their hospitality and the wonderful time he'd had at Christmas, but he had received no reply, until now. Eagerly he tore open the envelope. The letter was brief – only a note – written not in Dick's even, familiar script, but rather a disorganized, hurried scribble:

John,

The other day, two men came and asked us about you. It upset me greatly. I don't know who they were but they asked many very personal questions about you and didn't

438

say why. I don't know what's going on with you, but Dick, after many months, has just now finally gotten on with JC Penney. It is the first good job he has had since he came back from the war, and we can't afford to put it in jeopardy for any reason. So, I must ask you not to write, or call, or contact us in any way. We can't afford any problems. I'm sure you will understand.

Wanda

Jan stared at the letter, stunned in disbelief. He reread it several times, feeling the crushing weight of the words. His immediate impulse was to reply and explain about the background check for his security clearance, but in the end decided otherwise. For a time, he kept the note among his few mementos, but its very presence weighed wearily on him. Finally, one day, he tore it up and tossed the bits of paper into a trash can. With a heavy heart, he slid the ring Dick gave him off his finger. It left a whitish imprint where it had covered the skin. In time, the sun tanned the spot, obliterating all traces of it.

CHAPTER 57

Gazing with mixed feelings at the churning wake that relentlessly measured the watery void between him, the New World he'd barely gotten to know, and Majda, Jan couldn't escape a painful gnawing of guilt. And now, fate had dealt him a coup de grâce, stacking both time and distance against him— delivering the final blow. He surely would never see her again. The sense of it grew with every turn of the screw, stretching his emotions to their utmost. His feelings were raw, his remorse palpable.

Having received his new assignment, he had left New York two weeks after a short stay at Camp Kilmer, New Jersey, an overseas staging area where he and a sizable contingent of others were checked over by doctors, briefed, and finally carted by trucks to a ferry that took them to the military pier in New York harbor, and their ship, the USNS General Langfitt. Crowding the decks, even the most boisterous among them fell quiet as the ship glided past the Statue of Liberty, watching it recede and finally blend with the blurry outline of the city. Two weeks later they arrived in Bremerhaven, the same harbor from which he had departed two years ago. The circle of fate was closed.

Howls rose from the disembarking soldiers when an Army band struck "I Wonder Who's Kissing Her Now." A long overnight train ride took him and a contingent of Air National Guardsmen from Chicago to a small town of Laon in north-central France and a remote muddy airfield on which rows upon rows of hastily pitched tents clustered next to a single runway lined with black World War II-vintage B-26 bombers. Frenzied activity was underway, with engineers bulldozing makeshift streets and digging ditches in anticipation of their arrival. It had rained earlier and the air was pungent with the peculiar smell of raw earth and diesel. A complement of French pilots, who would transition into the American airplanes and then fly them to Indochina, where France was at war, greeted them when they arrived. He thought of Jára. A sergeant directed him to one of the tents.

As he was making up his bed in the corner of a tent already filled with other bunks and an assortment of cabinets and footlockers, Jan caught a whiff of a heavy sweet aftershave before he took note of the slim, dark-haired olive-skinned airman who'd come in quietly through the open door. "Hi, I'm Sal," he said. "What's yours?"

"Jan or John, take your pick. Jan Neuman."

"I'm Sal Piccolo. Salvatore—hate that name. Just call me Sal. From Providence. My tent's next door. Welcome to the mud hole." He outstretched his hand. "You're not American, are you?"

Jan looked at him warily.

"Been watching you for a while now. Saw you on the train. You seemed kinda quiet. Didn't speak to anybody. Kept to yourself. Got me to wonder."

"I don't like being ridiculed."

"You mean your accent?"

Jan shrugged.

"It's okay. So, why did you enlist?"

"To fly," Jan said softly, almost inaudibly, flushing.

"To fly?" Sal made a face and shook his head just enough to show his dismay.

"And you?"

"So I wouldn't get drafted. Hell, most of the guys here did the same thing. If you join the Air Force, you stay out of Korea. But if you get drafted into the Army, you go in the Infantry and to Korea straight from basic, and that's bad. Korea's an ass hole. Chances of being killed. *Capisce?* And besides, I want to see the world." He chortled. "Back home, with a skin and name like mine, you're a *wop* or *dago* the moment you set your foot out of Providence or Boston. So I was hoping that things would be different elsewhere."

"I had no idea. They told us all about the melting pot, and—"

"Yeah. But the Italians didn't melt. You gotta understand them. Kinda old-fashioned. Clannish. I told you, Providence is mostly Italian. They come in from the old country and never leave the tenements. Some are born there and die there. Many don't even speak English. My grandmother was like that. All she knew in English was money."

Jan shook his head.

"And they keep their customs. Like for instance, for the girls to get married early. Seventeen or eighteen. If you're not married by then, you're considered a burden to the family. An embarrassment. I got a cousin..." He sighed deeply. "Gotta understand the Italians. Am I talking too much? And you?"

Jan told him sketchily about his past, and the problems at the club and Wanda's letter.

Sal listened thoughtfully. "I think I understand what you're saying." He sighed. "I can only *imagine* what it's like being a foreigner, but I think I know what it *feels* like. I thought things would be different, but they don't like us much here, either. I mean the French. Especially the commies. Didn't you notice the signs? '*U.S. Go Home,*' and '*Eisenhower, la Peste a la Porte,*' and stuff like that? They're all over town. We're all strangers here. So I can understand how you feel."

* * *

"*Ah, Monsieur Jean! Bienvenue,*" Madame Petit, the *concierge,* cooed when Jan rung the bell at the old house on *Petit Caré* in Versailles. She unlocked the heavy gate and hugged and kissed him on both cheeks as he walked in.

His anxiety mounted with each step. He had to come. It wasn't Aunt Stáska who was the source of his trepidation – she begged him to come the moment she found out he was in France – but his uncle. They had parted on bad terms and she had never mentioned him in her letters. Jan saw it as an omen.

He knocked, and immediately wished he hadn't come.

"Oh, *merde,* it's you!" Uncle Joe glared at him from behind thick-rimmed glasses perched precariously on the tip of his nose. The *mego* in the corner of his mouth flared brightly as he took a deep drag. His sallow, stubble-covered face twisted into a hostile sneer. "She said you might show up."

A sudden rush of steps on the stairs broke the tension. Weighed down by a shopping bag full of vegetables, breathless and smiling, Aunt Stáska rushed to him, the twins in tow. "Oh Jan! Oh my God, you're here! JesusMary! You're finally here. So handsome in your uniform." She took a step back, cocked her head, and smiled. "The *concierge* told me. Tried to catch up, but I'm not as spry as I used to be." She threw open her arms and planted wet kisses on his cheeks. Tears welled in her eyes.

The twins held his hands and Aunt Stáska hung onto his every word as he told them his story over a hearty serving of *bourguignon.* Uncle Joe remained aloof, busying himself with a newspaper and sending only occasional hard looks in his direction. Around 10, he got up and walked out. "He still sees *her* almost every day." Aunt Stáska sighed deeply noticing Jan's stare.

"Lili?"

She nodded. "He's an old fool. All she wants is his money, especially now that she's not working. He keeps her on the side. Takes money from the children's mouth and gives it to her, that *putaine.* But, at least, he hasn't touched me again. Just ignores me most of the time. In a way, that's a blessing. I hear she's become a whore, that's what Madame Petit says. But I don't know. Don't care any more." Her words vanished in a resigned whisper.

They both fell silent.

Finally, she rose. "Before I forget, I do have something here for you." She unlocked an armoire and pulled out a small packet tied with a tricolor and covered with official-looking stamps. "A man from the Ministry brought it a few weeks ago—had your name and our address on it. Go ahead, open it. I already saw it. Had to open it when I signed for it."

With a chill, he carefully untied the ribbon and undid the folds to reveal a stained, unfamiliar billfold, shiny and misshapen from lengthy use, a small packet of something loose that rustled the paper, and a medal. He looked at her in disbelief.

Her pale eyes, red around the edges, filled with tears.

He opened a small *carnet* and stared at the face he'd long forgotten—Jára Soukup's. Memories, long forgotten, flooded his mind. He recalled the day Jára brought him the news of his father, their tribulations at the camp at Wasseralfingen, their

444

trek to Freiburg, and the day they parted ways in Reims as Jára went on to Perpignan and the Foreign Legion. How guilty he felt then that he didn't follow. What would have been his fate if he had?

"Your friend's dead. Killed in Indochina some time ago. Don't really know when. That's all that's left—didn't have much. They found your name with our address on him."

Obviously rifled, the billfold held only a pair of pictures hidden in one of the pockets: a young Vietnamese girl and an old, faded snapshot of a man and a woman, with two small children standing awkwardly between them—Jára's parents. The packet produced a pair of identification disks, the kind worn by the French army.

"That's all there is." Aunt Stáska wiped a tear.

"Did they say what happened? How he died? Where he's buried?"

She shook her head.

Jan turned the medal over. Its patina was dulled by time.

"Legion d'Honneur." Aunt Stáska crossed herself. "May God rest his soul."

The next day, Jan took a train to Paris and then a *Metro* to Porte de la Chapelle. Something inside – a perverse desire to retrace his steps – compelled him to go. The tunnel was still there the way he remembered, a giant gash in the earth, gaping and dark, walls stained with smoke and covered with graffiti. Once teeming with life, it was now silent, swept of all remains of human habitation, the people gone. A tall wire barricade barred its entry. A pair of gendarmes lurking nearby gave him a curious look. Only the sound of distant traffic remained, pulsing to its own heartbeat.

Three days later, he left.

"Bring your friend with you the next time you come," Aunt Stáska cried, hugging him warmly as he bid her good-bye at the door. Uncle Joe grunted as they shook hands. Good omen. The twins carried his bag and accompanied him to the train station.

He wouldn't be back anytime soon. Hunched alone in the corner of the empty compartment, mesmerized by the rhythmic clatter of the train, his mind drifted. Bremerhaven, Italy, Normandy, Freiburg, Wasseralfingen…home—his life seemed to be stitched together with the staccato of the rails. His world was passing under him and he felt detached from it, adrift—alone.

When he returned to his tent, he saw that someone had crudely scratched 'FAGOT' into the top of his footlocker.

CHAPTER 58

Gazing out the window, Jan momentarily lost sight of the ground when a swirling mass blotted out his view and as it receded far below took on the shape of a vast, infinite field of cotton. The sleek Super Constellation stopped straining. The high pitch of its engines dissolved into a harmonic drone as it settled on its course high above a solid cloudcover that obliterated all earth and ocean below. Above, the sun glimmered weakly through a hazy layer of cirrus. He and Sal, sitting next to him, had just lifted from Reykjavik where they took on fuel for the final hop across the Atlantic. Unable to rest since yesterday, having tried in vain to get some shut-eye in the crowded compartment of the Amsterdam express, they were now too excited to sleep. Early this morning, they had boarded the plane at Shiphool.

It had been more than a year since they had met. As Jan's best – and only – friend, Sal had finally persuaded him to spend his leave with his family in Providence. The real but unspoken reason was to meet Maria, Sal's cousin, with whom, at his urging, Jan had been corresponding.

At the outset, whenever he wrote, he felt like a traitor. The memory of Majda inundated his mind and every word was a stab to his conscience. But eventually he came to terms with the reality that he would never again see her. Those were the cards he was dealt. He had to go on. Maria's letters ablated much of the guilt. He knew her only from the few snapshots she had sent and from her prose that, though benign and timid, even shallow at first, often took on a more serious tone, revealing her deeper self, an inner turmoil and loneliness. His initial curiosity turned to compassion and then to attraction. Perhaps because he, too, carried a similar burden, her distress struck a chord. They connected.

Sal's mother met them at the Providence station. Eyes deep-set and glistening under a graying shock of jet-black hair artfully gathered in the back by a colorful scarf, her olive complexion and sharply drawn features reminded Jan of the classic faces of Roman goddesses that graced the terracotta vases glutting tourist stands in Pompeii. She swept Sal in her arms and looked him over with motherly concern. "Oh God! Sonny! You're so thin! Lemme look at ya. Don't they feed you over there? You must've lost twenty pounds!"

She gave Jan a big smile. "And you must be John." She extended her arms. "Welcome to Providence. Sonny wrote so much about you. I'm so glad you could come." She embraced him politely.

"Well, did the Army make a man out of you yet?" She gazed at Sal admiringly.

"The Air Force, Mother. The Air Force." Sal blushed.

Weaving through traffic, she skillfully piloted the big green Buick to the outskirts of town and a large white clapboard two-story house half-hidden by a stand of poplars at the end of a narrow dead-end street.

"Dad around?"

"No, he's at Hialeah. May be back this weekend." She sighed. "You never know with his job."

The house was warm and cozy, and smelled of garlic and herbs. Sal led Jan to an empty room next to his bedroom. "It's not much, but it beats a tent and I can vouch for the bed. It's always been comfortable." He laughed.

448

"You never told me they call you Sonny." Jan nudged him.

"Yeah. I hate it." He fidgeted uncomfortably. "All Italians call their sons, Sonny."

The next day, after showing Jan around Providence and crisscrossing the small state, Sal turned the Buick onto a quiet street lined with boxy clapboard houses, nearly identical in style. "Maria's place," he said as he pulled up in front of one all but hidden from view by tall overgrown hedges, surrounded by a low chain-link fence. A '51 Chevy was parked in the driveway. One of the curtains moved as they drove up.

Sal knocked. The door opened a crack and then swung open.

"Oh, it's you, Sonny!" A portly man rushed out, hand outstretched. "Good to see ya again. Youse look good. It's Sonny," he announced over his shoulder.

"Hi, Uncle Ben." Sal shook his hand.

The man's dull grey eyes, half-covered by drooping eyelids, measured them from under furrowing brows. Short and squat, with small eyes set deep in a long fleshy face covered with afternoon stubble, head topped with short graying hair, his ruddy complexion betrayed an affinity for the spirits. He eyed Jan with wariness. "And this must be the fella who's been writing Maria. How ya doin'?" He extended his hand.

"Yeah, Uncle Ben. This is John," Sal said.

"I'm Benito. Maria's father. *Venga, venga,* come in, meet the rest of the family. Luigi's not here, gone to Chicago to look for a job. But the girls are at home. Come on in."

A short, stout, tired-looking woman wiped her hands on an apron and turned away from a stove. A young woman busied herself setting a table.

"This is Mary, and that there's Maria." Benito nodded in her direction. "Youse'll stay for dinner and have some pasta, eh? There's plenty for everybody. Maria, two more plates."

Mary gave Jan a weak handshake. "Forgive me, just got home from work. Didn't have time to change." She half-smiled but avoided his eyes.

The water in a large pot boiled over, spilling onto the hot stove where it exploded in a staccato of steamy hisses. Benito's disapproving look erased the smile from Mary's face. "Excuse me," she said, turning quickly to tend it.

Seemingly absorbed in setting the table, Maria ignored them. Taller than her mother, complexion softened by a thin cover of makeup, full, even lips accented by a ruby shade of lipstick, her black hair fell to her shoulders in long heavy strands, providing a perfect frame for her round face. But it was her eyes that gave it charm. Large, brown, and doe-like, ringed by pronounced shadows that made them appear deep-sunk and melancholy, they seemed to exude tenderness and, above all, sadness. She blushed, sensing Jan's gaze. Finally, fleetingly, she met his eyes. He nodded and she gave him a weak, polite smile.

"Lucia? Lucia!" Benito's face turned purple. "Where's that daughter of youse?" He glared at Mary. "Lucia?"

A young, pretty, pixyish girl emerged from upstairs. "Sorry, Dad, I didn't hear them drive up." She glanced shyly at Jan. "Hello, Sonny." She rushed to Sal and kissed him lightly on the cheek before politely offering Jan her hand.

"*Mangiamo.*" Benito made a sweeping motion with his arm and sank in a chair. Mary served the pasta and they ate silently until the tension eased, then listened politely as Jan told his story.

450

"So you've been to Italy, huh? You like *Italia*? *Un bel paese...bellissimo.*" Benito smacked his lips." And you say you spea-ka da language? *Parla italiano? Capisce?*"

"*Si, capisco.*"

Benito gave him an approving smile. "See?" He turned to Maria. "I told you to learn to spea-ka *italiano*, but no."

Maria blushed.

"Children don't listen no more nowadays. Have no respect for their parents...*senza respetto per gli genitori...mi dispiace. Che peccato.*" His gaze rested heavily on her. "All they do is hang 'round the house. Now Luigi—"

"Ah, leave her alone Benito," Mary broke in pleadingly. "It's not her fault."

Maria stared into her plate.

Benito's scornful glance shifted to Mary who ignored him and continued eating. They finished the meal in silence.

Maria gave Jan a timid smile as they were leaving.

"Can I see you again?" he said, as they shook hands.

"Saturday, if you'd like." She blushed. "I'll pick you up if I can borrow Dad's car. I'll give Sonny a call."

"Pay no attention to my uncle." Sal rolled his eyes as they drove away. "*Uomo forte, testa dura...*strong and thick-headed. He's like that every time he's had a few with the boys on the way home from work."

* * *

Maria pulled up at a small park overlooking Narragansett Bay, hemmed in on the horizon by a string of low-lying flats and islets exposed by the ebbing tide. The air reeked of decaying seaweed. People digging for clams dotted the shallow estuary. Squawks of cavorting seagulls filled the air.

Jan fought the queasiness in his gut. The small talk they made and the awkwardness of the moment was nothing like he imagined. Stilted. The emotional closeness that had infused their letters had vanished. It was one thing to spill his heart to a piece of paper, another to a living being—to her, sitting silently next to him, staring straight ahead, tense. The unnerving nearness of this soft, strange girl made him feel happy one moment, remorseful the next. He had to break away from the past and forget Majda, he told himself over and over again. Reality was sitting next to him. Flesh and blood. Surely, it was more than coincidence he'd met Sal and, through him, Maria. Perhaps Fate was making amends—gifting him at once with a friend and a soulmate. He found the argument unconvincing.

He felt lightheaded whenever a whiff of Maria's perfume overpowered the stale aroma of tobacco of which the car smelled. Her sad liquid eyes met his. She attempted a reassuring smile. He reached for her hand across the narrow space and she responded with a gentle squeeze. Gazing straight ahead at the world outside their mechanical cocoon, they both sat silently. The touch sent gentle waves of pulsating warmth between them.

"You have to excuse my father." She broke the spell. "He's getting old and has a lot on his mind these days."

"That's okay." Jan shrugged.

"He's worked for years at this job. Works downtown. In a parking lot. Not much of a job, really. Hardly pays enough to buy the groceries. They've just sold it to build an office building on it. So he'll be out of work, and at his age…" Her voice cracked. "That's why Mom's working."

"What does she do?"

"Jewelry. At a sweatshop in Pawtucket. She doesn't drive so he has to take her and pick her up, and when he picks her up, he stops at a bar and stays a couple of hours with his friends while she sits out in the car and waits for him. Breaks my heart." She looked away, as her voice broke with a sob.

Jan reached to comfort her and she leaned against him limply, trembling as he held her. Stroking her hair, he searched vainly for the right words to say. Her face felt warm and moist against his cheek. Somehow their lips met and softly, tentatively, they kissed.

*   *   *

A week later, Benito invited Jan to the dog races at a track at Taunton across the Massachusetts' state line. Afterward, they made a stop at Benito's favorite bar where he bought a round for his friends who greeted him with glee and slaps on the back and Jan with curious looks. It was after midnight when Benito brought the Chevy to a jerky stop in his driveway. The house was dark and everyone was asleep, except Sal, waiting for them in his mother's Buick to take Jan back.

"I think Father really likes you," Maria commented the next time they met. "Otherwise he wouldn't have asked you to the races. He doesn't take easily to strangers."

She was able to borrow the car a few more times and they drove to out-of-the-way places, finding comfort in awkward embraces. Her tenderness was a balm to his loneliness, soothing his yearning for meaningful human contact, for a sense of sharing, a sense of belonging. He craved what she seemed to offer. When he finally summoned his courage and responded to what he took to be an invitation or, at least, encouragement, she seemed at first to welcome his groping and his awkward attempts at lovemaking in the back seat of the Chevy, but then, apologizing, pushed him away.

Perhaps it could have been anyone at this stage of his life, but it was Maria who happened along just as they both found themselves at a nadir of their lives. She seemed to understand him. He thought he understood her. In a selfish way, he couldn't deny finding her company pleasurable and welcome—an antidote.

The day before he left, she invited him to a farewell dinner at her house—recognition of sorts that her family accepted him. She accompanied him and Sal to the railroad station on the day of departure and clung to him desperately until he had to board. "Please come back. I'll write," she said in parting as she kissed him timidly one last time.

CHAPTER 59

"It's you! *Mon dieu.*" Aunt Stáska's hand flew to her open mouth, seeing Jan and Sal standing in the hallway. "And you brought your friend! What a surprise! Almost a year! I didn't know—I didn't expect you. Why didn't you tell me you were coming?"

Jan embraced her and kissed her on her cheeks. "Didn't you get my letter? I wrote you two weeks ago."

It flustered her. "The mail carriers were on strike all last week. It seems somebody's always on strike these days." She sighed. "But of course, I'm glad to see you. It's just that I don't have anything—"

Josephine and Jean-Paul eyed Sal shyly, and the girl blushed when he shook her hand and kissed her on the cheek. "Here, take this." The aunt thrust a pair of bills in her hand and hustled her out the door. "Run down to the *boulangerie* and get a couple of *baguettes.* Hurry."

"The uncle?" Jan looked around with trepidation.

She shrugged. "Still in bed. Still sleeps 'til noon, and then stays up 'til the wee hours. Goes out—"

"And Lili?"

Her answer died on her lips just as Uncle Joe, tugging at his trousers, disheveled, trailing a plume of smoke from a glowing *mego,* appeared in the doorway. "*Merde!* What's going on?" he spat out, but then, seeing them, to Jan's surprise, greeted them civilly and after the introduction, with Jan translating, peppered Sal with questions. "You picked a good time to come," he said civilly after a dinner of stuffed tomatoes, as they sat around the table sipping the last of their Beaujolais. "Tonight's the *Fête de Nuit* and the *Grands Eaux*. In the *Palace de Versailles* gardens. Maybe we can all go. It's really something to see."

They returned to the house late in the night, still buoyed by the spectacle of the immense gardens, the starry night exploding in fiery showers of fireworks, the blazing geysers of water shooting skyward from the illuminated cascading fountains to the strains of Saint-Saënz and Handel, the night resonating with thousands of voices when the orchestra struck the Marseillaise. "You two will have to share the back bedroom, if you don't mind. That's all there is since the children have their own rooms now," Aunt Stáska said as she led them through a narrow corridor to the small, windowless bedroom Jan remembered so well, barely large enough to hold a single bed. Tired and drowsy, they dismissed her concern as she gave them a grateful look and she bid them good night.

Sometime during the night Jan found himself in a dream— a vivid, incredible dream. The faceless ghost that materialized from his subconscious was—he didn't know. Majda? It overwhelmed him and aroused him. He strained to see her face but it kept eluding him. Still, the *feeling* was real. He knew what she *felt* like. Their last night was seared in his memory. His recall was total: the heady smell of lilacs; the softness of her skin, the firmness of her embrace. Her love-making... It wasn't clear, he couldn't tell. But the sensation was there: intense, burning, but disembodied.

Paralyzed by the sleepy stupor, he gave himself to the searing sensation, until the throbbing became so overwhelming he awoke with a start, painfully regretting that the dream had

456

ended. He was drenched in sweat. His penis, stiff and hard, throbbed to bursting. And then he became aware of a heavily breathing shape hunched over him, of someone squeezing and massaging his distended organ, stroking it jerkily in rhythm with his involuntary thrusts. He screamed.

Sal stopped in mid-stroke, and all Jan could hear was his heavy breathing and feel the sweaty clamminess of his grasp.

"Dammit, Sal! What the hell are you doing? Get away from me!" he struck out wildly against his friend.

Sal dodged Jan's fist and let go off his penis. His breathing was heavy, sporadic. He froze for a moment, a shape a shade darker than the darkness of the room, but then made a vague move.

Jan recoiled. "Dammit, Sal! What's this?! Are you nuts?! How could you? Don't touch me!" His body still throbbed, bathed in sweat that suddenly grew uncomfortably cold in the chill of the night. He pulled the covers up to his shoulders and drew back against the headboard.

"Boys? Is everything all right? What's going on? Are you all right, boys?" Aunt Stáska called out drowsily from somewhere in the hallway.

They both froze as her shuffling steps approached the room, heard her heavy breathing as she listened at the door for a few eternal seconds, and then retreated until the thump of a closing door told them she was gone.

Wide-awake now, Jan and Sal just sat there, two dark hulks at opposite corners of the bed, in a room that had suddenly turned oppressive.

"Don't *ever* touch me like that again!" Jan hissed.

"I'm sorry." Sal's words came out more like gasps than intelligible sounds. "I thought you knew. I thought you might—"

"How could you! I'm your friend. My God, Sal, how could you?"

Choking, Sal tried to suppress his sobs. "I couldn't help it. Can't help myself. Please, forgive me. I'm so sorry."

Jan wanted to retch. In the two years he knew Sal, there had never been a hint—ever. Or was there? Had he been stupid? He recalled an incident in Cannes, where the Air Force had provided a "rest camp," in a villa near the brilliantly white beaches, where it was easy to meet local girls at the profusion of bars lining the avenues, most famous of which was *Jimmy's*, but Sal never mixed. In fact, much to Jan's surprise, he drove away one of the girls in tears. And then, one day, he'd overheard a remark that Sal was seen in one of the 'queer' bars and cabarets that lined the back streets of this then-reputed 'queer capital of the world.' He thought nothing of it at the time, but now it made sense. Fully awake now, he recalled the word *fagot* scratched into the lid of his footlocker after he and Sal had become friends. It had meant nothing to him then, but now he saw that Sal's propensity had been a tacitly accepted open secret, and that becoming Sal's friend carried a price—being smeared by the same reputation. He had originally attributed being set apart by the other fellows in the squadron to being a foreigner with a 'funny' accent. Now he understood that they thought of him as a fagot. A foreign fagot.

Calmer now, he tried to reconcile himself to the blow his friendship with Sal had been irrevocably dealt. Forgiveness could not undo it—the memory of the deed would not be erased. The bond between them was shattered. "I'm sorry, too," he said.

Jan was glad when the visit ended. Ill at ease, he and Sal settled in an empty train compartment as far from each other as they could and fell silent.

Pretending to sleep, Jan closed his eyes but his mind was in turmoil. Through the slits of his eyelids, he watched Sal slumped motionless in his seat, withdrawn, staring out the window.

"I wish I were dead," Sal finally said, as they approached Laon. "If I had the courage, I'd kill myself."

"That's foolish talk," Jan said.

"If you tell on me, they'll kick me out of the Air Force."

"I'm not going to tell."

"I know I don't have the right to ask, but can you…can you forgive me?"

"Sure." The response sounded hollow as the distance was already there.

They seldom saw each other after that. Subconsciously, often consciously, they avoided each other. Finally, two months later, returning from work one day, Jan noticed Sal packing his duffle bag. "Hey, what's going on? You going somewhere?" It was the first time they had spoken since their debacle in Versailles.

"Been transferred. Going to Wheelus. Libya."

"Wish there was something I could say."

"What's there to say?" Sal's eyes were dark and drawn.

"I'm sorry." Jan offered his hand.

"Yeah, me, too." Sal shook it feebly, swung the duffle bag over his shoulder, and walked out to a waiting Jeep.

Jan watched him go with mixed feelings and a sense of loss. How ironic that Sal was the one responsible for introducing him to Maria. Did she know about him? Her sustaining letters continued to arrive on a regular basis and he looked forward to them. They represented his only link to a different life, a kind of life he'd created in his mind. As an only child, he had never known the pleasure of siblings, so he accepted his aloneness as a given, but not loneliness. Maria's letters changed all that. Their longing and despair engaged his imagination, making him feel worthy and fulfilled when his words seemed to mollify her fears. He clung to her letters the way a drowning man clings to a piece of flotsam.

As his loneliness increased, the ink and paper no longer sufficed. He wanted more—something tangible. He craved her presence. Besides filling the void in his life, it would show everybody he was not like Sal, he was not what they had labeled him, even by association—a 'fagot.' And so, one day, feeling particularly down and melancholy, he wrote and proposed marriage. To his surprise, she accepted.

CHAPTER 60

"How old are you, Airman?"

"Twenty-four, Sir."

"And you're an Operations clerk?"

"Yes, Sir."

"I hope you know what you're doing. She's not a French whore, is she?" Jan withered under the annoying glare of Major Glavey, the squadron commander, when he officially requested permission to marry. "Been having too many of our guys marrying French whores."

"No, Sir."

"All they're after is the dollar."

"Yes, Sir."

"She a local?"

"No, Sir."

"You have an accent. Is she from—where you're from, Airman?"

"Czechoslovakia, Sir."

"So is she—"

"No, Sir."

The Major's face twisted into a grimace; his eyes bore into Jan from behind half-closed lids. "So what the hell is she?" he snapped.

"American, Sir."

"American?"

"Yes, Sir."

The Major let out a sigh. "All right, then. Why didn't you say so!"

Jan had asked Maria to come to France to marry him and to his surprise, she readily accepted. Her parents didn't object. Later she would tell him they were relieved. Being of limited means, marrying Jan in France would preclude a drain on their thin resources, particularly now that her father was out of work and another marriage, that of her sister Lucia, was in the offing. Maria's marriage in France offered a way to save face and, more importantly, money. They set a late September date for the ceremony.

Jan had never told Aunt Stáska and Uncle Joe about Maria. When he finally broke the news, his aunt gave him an anxious look and cried, and the uncle showered him with obscenities in two languages, calling him a damned fool. Since then, they had both toned down their protestations, although the tension remained, hanging over them like a cloud about to burst as they stood on the tarmac at Orly, waiting for Maria's plane to land.

The Constellation taxied up to the terminal, and Maria's worried look disappeared when she spotted Jan. She gave him a hesitant wave.

Seeing her again was a sobering experience. His knees weakened as he stood there considering the enormity of his deed. He had been at an emotional low when he proposed. Wanting to believe it himself, he'd even told her that he loved her—something his conscience rebelled against. By the time he realized that he had acted in desperation, it was too late. Things had gone too far for them to change. Suddenly, he felt trapped.

Thoughts of Majda gnawed at his mind. His feelings for Maria paled in contrast when he permitted himself to reflect— something he had been doing more and more as the fateful day of her arrival approached. Love – true love – could not be willed nor could it be denied. It happened. There was a clarity to it that surpassed all reason, all doubt. It simply *was*. What he truly felt toward Maria was gratitude, an overwhelming gratefulness, but gratitude nonetheless, and now even that was tinged with regret.

But perhaps he was being naïve, he told himself. Perhaps true love proves itself only when it makes demands, when it is tested, and Maria saved him from his aloneness when he most needed it. Wasn't *that* an act of love? Yet, she never reciprocated—never told him she loved him, other than the perfunctory "Love" at the end of each letter. They only knew each other from their letters and had met only once. His feelings were in disarray whey they parted, and the episode with her cousin Sal sent him into a tailspin.

But all that didn't matter now. She was here. Majda was gone forever, though she would never leave his heart. It was unthinkable to back out at this point. His pride and sense of fair play wouldn't permit it. 'That's Life,' his mother would have admonished him. The only thing – the only *honorable* thing – was to accept what destiny had wrought and resign himself to Fate.

The momentary awkwardness quickly dissipated as they greeted each other, first politely, then warmly. Introductions and embraces followed. After a tension-filled evening and sleepless night in his uncle's apartment on the Petit Carré, they returned to Laon, where Jan installed her in a small hotel until the appointed day. They said their marriage vows in a small chapel on the airbase, with one of his co-workers and his wife as a best man and maid of honor in attendance, and since the Air Force did not provide on-base quarters for its married members, settled into a tiny two-room apartment in the nearby village of

Montigny. Nine months later, their daughter was born. They named her Jana.

* * *

Jan found himself in a quandary. It hadn't taken long before he discovered that the early euphoria of married life could not stand the test of reality. The Maria he knew, or thought he knew – the distraught, shy, sad girl he'd met only once and invented in his mind mostly from her letters – was a different, complex creature with a past full of longings, broken hopes, and unfulfilled promises. Increasingly morose, she turned on him. Their love-making – the only truly intimate part of their relationship – sweet and tender at the onset, had gradually drained of all passion. At times, when the rustling next to him would wake him in the middle of the night, he would find her slumped on the edge of the bed, crying.

To his dismay, he realized that the reasons that drove them together were not enough to sustain the binding commitment they had undertaken. Love, the keystone of any lasting union, just wasn't there. Sympathy, yes. Loneliness, yes. Despair, yes. Carnal desire, yes. Everything but love. At least the kind of love he remembered and still felt for Majda. Oh, Majda! If anything, the memory of her seemed to intensify his yearning with time, enshrining it in purity, elevating it to the divine. Memories that flooded his mind and filled him with mellow warmth reminded him of her loss. At first he tried to banish them, alarmed at their strength, but soon found them necessary and ultimately indispensable to his very existence.

He hated to admit his uncle might have been right. It was too late to change the course of his life, particularly now, that a child was involved. Circumstances had forced him to abandon one child. He simply couldn't abandon another. The very thought horrified him. He considered divorce, but dismissed it out of hand. Maria, a devout and practicing Catholic, would not agree to it, so he never brought it up—pride and conscience wouldn't permit it. Though not particularly religious, his inner voice still resounded with the principles drummed into him by his mother. "As you make your bed, so will you lie," she had sermonized. Marrying Maria was his "bed" and so he would lay in it. And so they both accepted their fate, even though the life they had begun together with such high hopes gradually slid into despair, blame, resentment, melancholy, remorse, and, in time, apathy. Maria couldn't wait for the tour of duty to end. Jana was the only cement that sustained their relationship, preventing it from coming totally unglued.

Two years later when they finally returned to America, Jan found himself assigned to an airbase a scant two hours away from Maria's home. Able to visit her parents whenever she chose to, Maria's disposition improved. Trips home buoyed her.

As the term of his enlistment wound down, Jan realized that with a wife and child to support and without savings of any kind (like most lower ranks, they had barely subsisted from one payday to the next) his options were few, his prospects nil. He found Maria's suggestion to move in with her parents until he could find a job unpalatable. With her father out of work, his in-laws barely managed to stay afloat on her mother's sweatshop pittance, and Jan and Maria's presence would have been an unwelcome burden. He thought about Dick, his wartime friend from Albion, and his plight trying to support a wife and a child after returning from war, Dick, who had a family and friends to smooth the way and yet was unable to find a decent job until months, years, later. Jan didn't have the luxury of time. Besides, he had to admit to himself that he liked the Air Force life, despite its parsimony. A kind of lethargy had set in, a comfortable feeling of the status quo. He found his work a challenge and school an escape. Six years invested in a career, three silver stripes on his sleeves, steady pay, and most of all, security—all that had to be considered. Who could tell? Perhaps, if he continued with his schooling, one day he'd still realize his dream to fly.

Maria didn't object. In fact, she seemed relieved when he reenlisted. Resigned to the predictability of military life, she made no demands on him. Their life had become reasonably routine, comfortable if dull. Keeping up the façade became first an art, then a habit. The question of love, which they both artfully avoided, came up only once, in an argument, when she asked if he'd ever loved her. When he didn't answer, she drew back and never raised the issue again. Jana, as she matured, began to ask uncomfortable questions, which they both deftly deflected.

CHAPTER 61

Straining to hear the Voice of America over the static, Jan tried to fully grasp the meaning of what was coming in undulating snatches over the airwaves. Having been denied flight training because he was 'too old' at thirty-six, he was slated to return to France when, in 1966, French President DeGaulle closed all American airbases and withdrew from NATO, and his assignment was changed to Germany. Had he become a flyer, things might have been different. He could have been sent to Viet-Nam instead, and not been a part of the electrifying excitement that sent an icy tremor crawling up his spine. Something unthinkable was happening in the Republic. Dubček, the 'renegade' communist Prime Minister, had decided to loosen the ties that bound Czechoslovakia to the East, and for the first time in twenty years, the Iron Curtain would part just enough to permit people to venture beyond its confines. It was like the opening of a window and letting in the fresh air. The ether was abuzz with the aptly named 'Prague Spring.'

For the past twenty years, the Cold War had enveloped much of the world. NATO and the Warsaw Pact were born. The Berlin Wall breached the city like an ugly scar. Hundreds of miles of electrified wire in a wide swath of no-man's land, laced with mines and guard towers, spanned the continent from the North Sea to the Adriatic. Each side had 'The Bomb' in sufficient numbers to annihilate not only one another, but also the rest of the world many times over. Terms such as 'détente,' 'parity,' and 'mutually assured destruction' entered the American vernacular. Things came to a head during the Cuban missile crisis, but the leaders of both sides managed to defuse the situation. All this had led Jan to believe that there never would be a direct confrontation between the two sides—only proxy skirmishes and undeclared wars, like Viet-Nam, along the periphery of their spheres of influence. It also meant that America would never risk a conflict over the fate of his homeland—after all, the Hungarians rose in '56, and the U.S. did nothing. It was hard to let go of his dreams, but he'd finally had to accept the fact that his fate and that of his country were irrevocably sealed, that he had been naïve to believe that things could ever change. Until now!

The stale and beastly hot air smelled of cinders. Dodging the streaming waves of passengers, he and Jana found themselves pacing the crowded platform of the Frankfurt main railroad station on this late June day of 1968, barely able to contain their excitement. Their anxiety mounted as the time of arrival of the International Express train drew near. The incredible was about to happen—his father was coming for a visit.

The milling crowd fell silent as the train emerged from the background clutter of freight cars, buildings, and shimmering haze, approached at a deliberate pace, let out a short whistle, and with wheels squealing and steam hissing, came to a slow, measured stop. From somewhere high in the rafters, a disembodied voice boomed, *"Frankfurt...Frankfurt Hauptbahnhof. Frankfurt."*

The clanking of opening doors, shouts of greetings, and people spilling out and streaming for the exits became a kaleidoscopic blur as Jan's look was drawn to a frail, lonely-looking figure, stooped over a cane, clutching a small beat-up valise, turning anxiously, unsure of what to do, or which way to go.

"Is that him, Dad? Is that my grandfather?" Jana squealed.

Jan nodded, choking.

They approached and the old man gave them a blank look, but then his tired eyes, puffy behind thick, round, smudged lenses, flooded with tears. His lips moved in a wordless salutation as he carefully set down his valise and extended his arms.

But he was a different father from the one Jan had expected, or rather, imagined—the frozen portrait he had carried in his memory for more than twenty years, the father of his youth. Never a big man, he seemed to have shrunk. The suit he once filled now hung on him loosely, accentuating his frailty. Even erect, he seemed crushed by the weight of time. His furrowed face was covered with stubble. A ring of silvery hair crowned his head like a monk's. Bulging veins laced his knobby and trembling hands under their papery skin. The only thing that hadn't changed was the peculiar smell of tobacco and sweat Jan remembered from his youth.

The cane dropped from the old man's hand as they hugged. Convulsing quietly under Jan's embrace, his thin, bony body shuddered as he kept moaning, "My boy...my boy...my son..."

Not understanding the language, Jana stooped to pick up the cane and the old man took note of her presence. His hand flew to his forehead in dismay. "Oh my God, how could I— You must be my little girl, my sweet Jana, my sweet granddaughter! I never thought I'd see you. Never thought I'd ever see any of you. Come, let me hug you. Come."

She approached him awkwardly and burst out crying as he drew her in, and they all stood there, locked in an embrace, overwhelmed by the incredulity of it all.

The old man finally pulled a crumpled handkerchief from his pocket, wiped the smudges from his glasses, and then the tears from his face. "If only Mother could have been here. She'd have been so proud of you."

* * *

"And Maria? She couldn't come?" The old man turned to Jan as they joined the stream of traffic of the Saarbrücken Autobahn.

"The car's too small. She'll be waiting for us with a nice meal, though," Jan said.

The old man fell silent, took off his glasses, and wiped them absently with his handkerchief. Their eyes met briefly, and Jan saw sadness in them, perhaps even a hint of accusation. He braced himself for the inevitable.

"Son," the old man cleared his throat, "I'm so glad you've made such a good life for yourself. I'm so glad you've made something of yourself."

"You're not angry at me? I thought you might—"His words, tender and loving, laden with emotion, were not what Jan had expected. "I know I hurt you, hurt you both. And Mother. I'm so sorry…"

The old man nodded sadly. "It's true that at first, when you left, it hurt me…hurt us…very much. You can't imagine how much. Hurt here." He struck his left breast as his voice broke and lips began to quiver. "It hurt, because you didn't say

470

anything. You told your friends, but you didn't tell us. That hurt, even though in my heart I understood why you couldn't."

"Mother...she wouldn't have understood."

The old man sighed. "Perhaps, perhaps. Anyway, she never got over it. I tried to reason with her afterwards, but..." He shook his head and stared out the window.

Jan reached for his hand. It was callused and rough, down to the tips of his fingers hardened by years of pinpricks from countless needles. "I'm so sorry, Dad." His chest felt like a drum. "Can you ever forgive me?"

The old man squeezed his hand. His lips quivered as he continued to gaze into space. Finally he nodded, ever so slightly, squeezed Jan's hand again, and held it. The rough pricks of his calluses became conduits that telegraphed his answer into Jan's troubled soul.

The old man relaxed under Maria's attention and showered her with compliments as they reminisced over dinner, while Jan translated in both directions. Later, he unpacked and passed out a few gifts—picture books of the Old Country for Jana, garnet earrings for Maria. "They're only gold-plated, but the stones are fine," he apologized. "It's not much, but it's hard to find anything good any more. The Communists steal everything."

He pulled something out of his vest pocket and took Jana's hand. "And here's your grandmother's wedding ring. It's the only thing I have left of her, besides a locket of her hair. I know she'd like you to have it." He slipped the narrow shiny band on her finger. It hung there loosely and he closed her fist on it to prevent it from falling off. "Someday, it'll fit." He smiled and his eyes flooded as she hugged him.

Finally, he carefully unwrapped a packet and pulled out a suit. Black, with pinstripes perfectly matched at their junctions, it was fashioned in the style popular when Jan was young. "And this is yours, my boy. I made it just for you. It's good quality. Pure wool. Been saving the material since before the war. Hope it'll fit. Had only your picture to go by and had to guess at the measurements," he said. His eyes glistened as he pressed it against Jan to confirm the fit. It was perfect.

"You know, Son?" His voice quivered with emotion. "I'd be sitting out there all alone at night, stitching it, looking at it, looking at your picture, wondering where you were. The house is so lonely without you and your mother. It's a big house. It's *your* house. *Your* home. It's all there. Your books. Your things. Everything." He paused and wiped his eyes with the back of his hand. "It's too much for me. I need you. Now that things are changing, you could come back. You could return home."

CHAPTER 62

Home! Return home! Father's words resonated in Jan's mind. Ever since that first day, the question of his return had loomed large between them like an interloper. It staggered him. He had now spent more than half of his life in exile and those years had taken their toll. 'Home' had become an abstraction, an occasional indulgence in nostalgia, but sobering reality had always prevailed. The world had changed. He had changed. His life had changed. He no longer *felt* exiled. More importantly, he had given up the hope of ever returning home again. He had a life, a family, a career—he was an American.

He wilted under the old man's steady gaze when he again brought up the subject. "You know I can't," he said.

"You could now. Things are changing. You'd be welcome. You'd be a hero." The old man's voice quavered. "You could help me. I'm old. I try, but it's hard. Look at me." He wiped his eyes.

"I can't do it, Father. I am a soldier. I have an obligation. I signed papers. And besides, *'they'* won't let me, so long as the communists are in charge."

"But that's all changing. Dubček's a good man."

"Someday, perhaps. But right now—"

"It's your home. I built it with my own hands. These hands." He lifted his trembling hands and held them up like a testament. "You were too young to remember what it took. Each time they devalued the *koruna*, we lost everything—twice, three times we lost everything. So we put everything into that house. Every single cent. Everything we had. Everything. It took years. Slaved days and nights. It's there. It's yours. Bring

Maria. Bring Jana. You'll be happy there. It's there, waiting for you." He finished in a plaintive whisper.

Jan was flustered. For now, he knew he had to say something without hurting his father's feelings. "I'll see what I can do, I promise," he said, hoping to delay the decision, giving himself time to come up with a plausible answer. "I promise."

The old man's look shifted somewhere past him into space. His jaws worked as though trying to digest the words. "You don't *want* to come, do you," he said softly, eyes glistening.

"You know I do, but I can't. Not right now, anyway. You don't know how it pains me to say this, but I have thought it over and I just can't."

* * *

Maria gave Jan a hard, disapproving look. "You're upsetting him. What's going on?"

Jan hadn't confided in her when his father first brought up the issue and now felt sheepish for not having done so. "Dad wants me to go back," he blurted out.

"Go back? Back where?"

"Czechoslovakia. Says he's getting old. There's the house. Says now that things are changing…"

She blanched. "When?"

Jan shrugged.

"And what about us?" She continued to stare at him.

"He wants us all to come, too. Says he needs me. But you know I can't go."

"I would never go, but, for chrissakes, now that he's here, why don't you ask him to stay? You know he could. He's your father."

The old man watched them with puzzled anguish and was about to say something when Jan turned to him. "Dad, now that you're here, why don't you stay? Stay with us. Come with us to America." He took the old man's hand. It trembled. "Please. We'll take good care of you. You'll have everything. You know we love you. Jana loves you…I love you."

Jana rushed to the old man and hugged him. "Oh, Grandfather, please, will you stay? Please, Grandfather, please…"

The old man kissed her gently and cradled her in his arms. His look softened. "My sweet girl…my boy, I wish I could, but I can't." His eyes flooded. "I can't."

"Please, Grandfather," she insisted. "Puleeez."

The old man, shrunken and vulnerable, face drawn, eyes glazed, wiped his glistening brow. "I don't know how to say this. You're so good to me. So kind to ask, but I can't. I can't. There was a time when I'd have wanted nothing else." He looked away and swallowed hard a couple of times. "I really can't. I'm very ill, Son. I'm dying."

Choking pressure shot up Jan's windpipe until he gasped.

"They found something on my lungs. Been there for some time. Too late to do anything. Didn't give me much time. Few months." He tried an uneasy smile. "I really don't want to die here and be your burden. I couldn't. I want to die at home. So, that's why I would like you to return. Bring Jana, Maria. Come home."

"What did you say to him? What's the matter?" Maria came down on Jan, seeing the old man slump. "He's old. Why do you torment him?"

"He says he's dying."

"I'm sorry, Son. I don't mean to cause any problems. I shouldn't have said anything." The old man wiped his eyes.

"Surely, something can be done," Jan said. "I'll have a doctor look at you. Tomorrow we'll go, first thing—"

"No, Son." The father shook his head. "I *know* it's too late. I'm tired. It's no use. I know it's time."

Jan had failed once as the 'good son,' and now Providence was offering him a second chance at redemption. His conscience screamed. He could not fail again. There was no question what he had to do. With or without Maria and Jana, he had to go. He must return.

*　*　*

"I think I know what you two were talking about." Maria's glistening dark eyes bore into him like a pair of burning charcoals. "If you tell him you'll go back, it's finished between us."

"I already told him.

"Told him what!" She glowered at Jan.

"I *have* to go back. We can all go. Can't you see, I can't just leave him like this. He's dying. There's nobody else."

Her face darkened. "Are you crazy?! He's blackmailing you! He survived without you until now. He can manage. But we can't! I know you and I've had differences, but you have a daughter. Don't we count for anything? And what about your career? After all this time, all these years, all the hardships, when we're finally a little ahead, you're going to throw it all away? Throw it all away and leave us?" She glared at him. "Always thinking about yourself. What *you* want. What *you* like. Well, not this time. I'm not going and neither is Jana. You can do what you want. You always do what you want. You always get your way. But if you do, we're finished! Understand? We're finished! *We*'re not going. *We*'re going home!"

Maria would not be reasoned with and perhaps just as well. Perhaps he really didn't want her to come. Her not coming would be a way out of the impasse, out of their tedious life. An escape. Liberation from a stagnant marriage. It would free them both from an increasingly untenable situation. It would be a chance for them both to start over. And Jana? What about Jana? Leaving her would continue to haunt him. But for now, he had an obligation, a filial duty to fulfill, and this time he wouldn't fail. He would return and take care of his father.

Jan's father's revelation cast a pall on what remained of his visit. The last days turned into a charade of pretenses: the old man's easy banter masking his pain, Jan's joy hiding his anguish, Maria superficial kindness concealing her loathing. Only Jana's feelings remained constant. She and her grandfather became inseparable.

Maria didn't accompany them on the day Jan's father left. He, Jan, and Jana remained mostly silent during the two hour drive to Frankfurt. The last thing Jan and Jana saw of him was his face drawn into a forced smile, and a handkerchief fluttering from an open window and vanishing suddenly as the train passed a curve.

* * *

"I reviewed your hardship separation papers, Sergeant," the Commander, a portly, graying Major, said. "Got'em right here." His stubby fingers tapped on a sheaf of documents he'd been perusing. "Why on earth would you want to get out, Sergeant? Throw away seventeen years of your career? Don't you like America?"

"It's not that, Sir, it's my father. He's dying. It's all in the application."

"I've read it. Your father, eh?" A short laugh escaped from behind the major's clenched teeth. "Seems you're a little late, Sergeant." He thrust a fresh copy of the *Herald Tribune* at him. "You sure you still want to go through with it?" He gave him a smirk.

Unbelieving, Jan stared at the headline. It read, in bold black letters: WARSAW PACT TROOPS INVADE CZECHOSLOVAKIA.

"Those fuckers'll jail you in a heartbeat if you go. Is that what you want?"

The world around him spun crazily. "Sir, could I, please, see the paper? I'd like to see—"

"Keep it," the Major spat out as he gathered up the documents, gave them a cursory look, and threw them in the trash can.

When Jan told Maria he wasn't going, she only looked at him coldly and went about her chores. The damage had been done. The chasm between them had deepened.

A few weeks later, a telegram from Aunt Stáska informed him of his father's death. With her dual citizenship, she had been permitted to travel to the Republic to bury him.

Losing his father and his home had never entered Jan's mind. Both had always been there—his steadfast refuge, a safe harbor. A constant. They always would be, he thought. Now he saw he was trying to hold on to the wind. A chimera. He recalled an old poem by John Donne: "No man is an island, entire of itself. Every man is a piece of a continent." The poet was wrong. At some point in life, everyone becomes an island. An island no longer connected to any continent. An island of sand, crumbling and washing away under one's feet. Now he was that island. Alone.

CHAPTER 63

Four months after his father's death, Jan had 'rotated,' in military jargon, to a sprawling Texas airbase and his new post at a Strategic Air Command flight-training school—a choice assignment. The house he and his family moved to was tucked on the far end of a Wherry housing area just off the end of the runway, and today, as almost every day, it shook to its foundation. Walls vibrated like the inside of a drum, dislodging fine speckles of dust that became visible in the shaft of light coming in through the window. He rushed out and squinted into the pale sun hanging low in the milky Texas sky just as another lumbering bomber, its eight engines trailing streams of sooty black exhaust, roared overhead. And another. And another.

He never tired of watching the planes soar. Their roar always evoked a modicum of regret that he'd not had the chance to fly, until one of the instructor pilots introduced him to sailing, which he took up with passion. "It's a lot like flying," his friend had said, "only a bit more complicated, since you deal with two elements, air and water, passing over two dissimilar airfoils, keel and sails."

He took up the challenge and in harnessing the wind, found a long lost sense of adventure and enjoyed, however briefly and euphemistically, a certain control over his fate. Fully aware it was a form of escape, he craved it nonetheless and spent as much of his free time as he could on the water, free of the drudgery of the day, the pressures of work, the tedium of home life—and Maria. Their relationship had settled into a dull and predictable groove from which it seldom veered. Ever since his father's death, a kind of emotional paralysis had set in—a numbing of emotions resulting from the acceptance of fate. They had reached a polite but safe way of conducting their lives, tolerable in the short term if neither considered the future. It affected Jana greatly, for she had begun to understand the decay that lay beneath the duplicitous veneer of her parents' lives. In turn, she divided her love equally between them, soothing them – Maria in particular – when any bitterness welled to the surface.

*   *   *

A shrill ring of the doorbell startled Jan, working on his pick-up in the garage just off the kitchen.

"Who could it be at this hour? Go see who it is, will you?" he heard Maria call out to Jana through the half-open door.

"It's a man," Jana answered. "A lieutenant."

"A lieutenant? This late? And on a Sunday?" Maria's voice showed a shade of annoyance.

"He says he needs to talk to Dad," Jana replied.

"Then, go get your father. He's in the garage. Ask the young man to wait." And then, apparently addressing the stranger, "He'll be right there."

"What can I do for you, Lieutenant?" Jan sized up the stranger with a quick glance. Young, in his early twenties, he guessed, slender under his flight uniform, fair-skinned, blue-eyed, with a shock of reddish-brown closely cropped hair protruding from under his flight cap. He recalled seeing him around the squadron.

"I need to talk to you, sir, but not here. Could you step outside?" The lieutenant's gaze shifted from Maria to Jana, and then back to Jan. "It's important."

"What is so important that you can't tell me right here? If it's anything about work—"

"Please, sir. Just for a few minutes."

"Ask the young man to come in, don't just stand there," Maria shouted. "You're letting in the mosquitoes."

"Please, sir," the lieutenant pleaded. "Not here, please."

"Don't fret. I'm going out for a while," Jan called out to her as he closed the door behind him. He turned to the lieutenant. "Want to walk?"

"That's fine." The lieutenant fell in beside him.

"So what's this all about?"

The lieutenant stopped and faced him squarely. "I'm Jurai Drugovich." His voice cracked just a bit.

"So? I'm pleased to meet you, Lieutenant. But I don't understand—"

"Your name's Neuman. Jan Neuman. Sergeant Neuman. Right, sir?"

"Yes. So?" A stab of foreboding sent his spine crawling.

"My mother is Majda Drugovich. I think I may be your son."

Thunderstruck, Jan felt his knees weaken. "What?! I don't understand," he stammered. "What did you say?" He felt the blood drain from his face and shock invade his senses. He continued to walk, like a robot, struggling to gain composure, grateful for the darkness that hid his distress. His heart pounded so hard he was sure his visitor could hear it. For a few moments, his mind refused to accept what he had just heard.

"I'm Jurai Drugovich. Forgive me, but I think I'm your son." The Lieutenant choked on the words. "You *are* a refugee. Er, I beg your pardon, sir, a former refugee? A Czech?"

"Yes." Jan strained to sound nonchalant as nausea filled his gut.

"And you were in the IRO camps in Italy and Germany, around 1950? Twenty-five years ago?"

"Yes."

"Then, you knew my mother over there, didn't you? At least, that's what she told me." The lieutenant's voice was tinged with scorn. "Her family name was Maruk. Majda Maruk. Do you remember her?"

Jan's mind was in disarray. Was he awake or was this a dream? A nightmare? Could this be really happening? After all these years? Majda! A ghost come to life. Incredible! Oh, God! She had been on his mind every now and then throughout the years, whenever he fantasized meeting his lost child. He had always imagined the child to be a girl with a face that somehow transmogrified into the likeness of Jana, and painted their meeting as a rapturous, emotional affair, and not a gut-wrenching ordeal that would turn his life upside down.

"Her name was Majda Maruk." The lieutenant's voice shocked him back into reality.

"Yes, I knew her. Forgive me." Jan fought for composure. "Of course, I knew her." A whirring kaleidoscope flooded his mind with shards of long-ago memories. "We were in love. I loved her."

"Then, if you say you loved her, why did you leave her?" The lieutenant's voice quivered. "Why didn't you come as you promised?"

Jan cringed. He sensed that under his polite but tense demeanor, the young man was seething with anger.

"I *didn't* leave her." He checked his breaking voice. "I don't know what she told you, but I loved her. Truly loved her. We met in a camp in Germany. Camp Grohn. Near Bremerhaven. Fell in love there. But the time was short. Only had a few days. Every minute, every second was precious. A gift. A treasure. We swore to each other. Made promises to marry once we got to America. But she left on a different ship. Left a day early, before I did. And that was the last time I saw her. It was a tragedy."

"She said you never wrote! Never answered her letters."

"That's not true! I *swear* that's not true. I wrote, but never got anything back from her. Never!"

The lieutenant's skeptical look didn't change.

"All my letters came back. Undelivered. Later, I found out, too late, that I had made an error in her address."

"Did she have *your* address?"

"Of course." He cringed under the lieutenant's almost tactile gaze. "But I found out that my sponsor burned all her letters. She wrote at least twice. So, the first chance I got, I went looking for her. I knew they were going to Richmond. I looked for her there at the address she gave me, but she was…they were gone. Tried everywhere. The house on River Street. Post office. Even Immigration. I did find out that they still lived in Richmond but Immigration wouldn't let me have their address. So, that's as far as I got." The words evoked a painful memory, long dulled by time.

"You didn't know she was pregnant?"

"Not until later. Months later. Her landlady told me. You have no idea how I felt." Jan paused with a sigh, feeling awkward for having to defend his sentiments, steeling himself for some reaction – condescension, sympathy, anger, anything – but, the lieutenant continued to stare straight ahead, unmoving.

"So in the end I gave up," he went on. "I thought that she'd changed her mind and didn't really want to have anything to do with me. It hurt. I knew her parents were strict. Fact is, I didn't know what to think. It haunted me knowing she was there somewhere, with our child, and I could do nothing." His voice broke and he swallowed hard. "You have no idea. I would've done anything. I *loved* her. Do you understand?"

Still unmoved, the lieutenant nodded absently.

"I looked for her again, one more time, but by then I was already in the military and got sent overseas, and that was the end of it. There was nothing else I could've done. Nothing. I'm sorry."

They both fell quiet, palpably aware of the tension between them. Wishing it all were a dream from which he would suddenly awaken, Jan stole a glance at the young man next to him, but he was real, here in the flesh. A single streetlight not far off cast a thin, tawny light, outlining his profile—a profile Jan had seen before in an old photograph of himself as a young man. It was uncanny. His heart skipped a beat.

The lieutenant, too, seemed ill at ease.

Above them, the inky sky, made even more opaque by the towering silhouettes of live oaks and cottonwoods, hinted of a storm. A shrill chorus of cicadas competed with the hum of distant traffic. A faint breeze wafted in from the west. The air smelled of rain, that strange earthy smell peculiar to the desert. Somewhere, over the horizon, a faint flash of lightning briefly outlined the swirling clouds.

"Looks like rain..." Jan broke the silence. "So where do we go from here?"

The lieutenant didn't respond.

"Why have you come?"

"Why do you think?"

"I think I know how you feel," Jan said. "I hope you haven't come here to cause trouble—"

"Why would I do that?"

"I understand."

"Do you?" The lieutenant's eyes were two shiny slits boring into Jan. "To tell the truth, I came to see the bastard who got my mother pregnant and then left her. Before I came here, I was angry. Curious, too, but angry—mostly angry. Now, I don't know what to think."

CHAPTER 64

Jan shuddered as he studied the stranger's face, his manner, and his coolness, hoping for some sign of understanding, but saw none. All he saw was a chasm that would have to be bridged before he could accept the idea of this young stranger as his son.

His mind reeled. He thought of Maria and felt a chill. What now? Obviously, he couldn't tell her. Surely she would ask about what was going on. He would have to find a way to keep it from her, at least for now. Had to make up something. But for how long? What if she found out? And what about Jana? He needed time to think. He needed time!

"I can understand how you feel, but it hurts to hear you say it," he said.

"I think what happened was a tragedy. A terrible tragedy," the lieutenant said, and for the first time, his voice betrayed a note of compassion.

"And you knew all this time?"

"No, Mother told me. About six months ago." He shifted his gaze absently into the night. "Before then, I had no idea. She never said anything. Never mentioned you. Never spoke your name, until we got the news that Dad...sorry...Stepan, her husband, was missing in action in Viet-Nam. I didn't know he wasn't my real father, until then."

"Jesus!"

"I never understood why he'd always seemed so cold toward me. Indifferent. I was afraid of him when I was young, but he never touched me. Mother was the disciplinarian." He sighed. "I knew he and Mom had problems. Argued a lot. I don't think she ever really felt anything for him, or he for her, for that matter. I couldn't tell back then. You don't pay attention to those things when you're a kid. But later, when I was older, I could see it. So, it came as no surprise when she finally told me."

"Did he abuse her?"

"I never saw him lay a hand on her, but he had a quick temper. He just wasn't nice to be around, especially after he'd had a few."

"And her folks?"

"Didn't say much. Don't think she ever told them. She was too proud. Now and then, I'd see her eyes red and knew she'd been crying. She was the one who raised me."

"So, why did she marry him if she didn't feel anything for him?"

His hard look returned. "Her folks made her, when they found out she was pregnant. Old customs die hard."

"And Stepan—is that *his* name?"

"Yes, a distant cousin. Anyway, they got married in a hurry. Quietly. That's what she said.

"That's awful!"

"He was much older than she was. *Much* older. Later, when I began to understand these things, when I looked at them, I couldn't figure out what she saw in him. They were so different. Anyway, he'd pulled a stint in the Marines sometime before they got married, and got called up when his Reserve outfit went to 'Nam. We got word he was MIA six months ago. That same day, she took me aside and told me about you. Told me everything. It explained a lot. Said she'd have waited, but she had no choice. Her baby had to have a father."

"And she named you—" Jan choked on the words.

"Jurai, after you. It's Slovene for Jan. She would've preferred Jan, but her parents objected. People call me Jerry."

"So, how did you find me? How did you know where to look?"

The lieutenant shook his head as a faint smile crossed his lips. "After Mother told me about you, I got into the habit of going through the phone books wherever we went to look for your name. It was just a game. I never really thought..." He chuckled. "Well, one evening, as I was doing it, killing time, my AC saw me and asked what I was doing. We got talking and he said he remembered a Sergeant Neuman. A foreigner – those were his words – who spoke with an accent, from Carswell, when he was here for his Tactical Refresher."

"That's incredible."

"So, soon as I got here, I looked in the phone book and sure enough, there you were. I knew I had to come. Now I'm almost sorry I came. It would've been easier to hate you." He scowled.

"I'm glad you came," Jan said. "It was a shock at first, but I'm glad you came."

"Are you?" The lieutenant looked at him warily from under a furrowed brow.

"Of course. You can't imagine what it's like to know you have a child somewhere...your blood...a part of you...the person you loved—" Jan's voice cracked. "All these years, I've been wondering. You can't imagine what it does to your conscience. I hope you never have to go through it."

They both fell uneasily quiet.

Jan's gaze traced the outline of the lieutenant's face edged in the pale glow of the streetlight. Even in the dark, he could see his eyes glisten. "Okay to call you Jurai?"

"Of course." The lieutenant cleared his throat. "Wish Mom were here." He wiped his eyes.

"Yes. Oh God, yes. Will you tell her? I hope she won't be upset."

"Of course."

"I must talk to her. You must give me her number. Her address. I must see her."

It took him aback. "I don't think that's a good idea. You're married. You have a wife and a daughter."

"They'll have to know. I'll have to tell them. But not now. I can't. I'll have to find the way, you understand?"

"It's been years. I really don't know how she'd react. It'll be a shock."

"I *must* talk to her. Explain—"

"I'll give it to you, but let me call her first. Let me break it to her. Give me a couple of days before you call. Okay?" Jurai pulled a thin notebook out of his breast pocket, scribbled Majda's address on it, and tore out a page. "It's hard to see. Hope you can make it out." He handed it to Jan.

They reached the house, now dark and silent.

"There's so much I want to say," Jan said. "So much we have to talk about. How long are you here for?"

"We're flying out tomorrow, around oh-eight hundred."

"So soon? Where are you stationed?"

"Castle."

"You can call me at work at the squadron. Will you call? I'd like to see you off, but—"

"I understand. I'll try to call Mom early, before we leave, and let you know. Shall I call you at home?"

"No, no. At the *office*. Here's my number. Call me after 7."

"Right. Good bye then."

"Good bye." Jan wanted to add 'Son' to his greeting, but the word couldn't make it past a lump in his throat.

Maria and Jana were already asleep when he walked in. Thankful he didn't have to face them, he undressed quietly and eased himself carefully into bed.

Maria rolled over with a deep sigh, stirred, and awoke. "My God, where've you been all this time? I waited up for you, but you didn't come. What's going on?" she said drowsily.

"Nothing," Jan dismissed her. "Go back to sleep."

She turned over on her side, and soon he heard her measured breathing as he lay wide awake, staring at the ceiling, listening to the pounding of his heart, washed over by a flood of shame. He didn't dare to look at her – the dark, familiar shape next to him, occupying a conjugal space that had long since become devoid of meaning. He'd often wondered why he had gone along with the charade, but tonight, more than ever, he wanted not to be there. The wall of separation between them – breached on occasions but always there – transparent until now, suddenly grew opaque. He would have to tell her. Soon. He would have to find the right moment, summon his courage, and tell her. He didn't relish the prospect.

CHAPTER 65

The shrill sound of the telephone shattered the morning quiet, and Jan instinctively tossed off the covers and dove for the receiver—they had been timed on the quickness of an alert response. The room was still dark. The glowing dial of the alarm clock showed 5:30. But then he remembered last night's visitor and froze.

Maria let out a drowsy groan and gave him a hard shove. "Wake up! Aren't you going to answer it?"

Jan fumbled for the receiver. "Sergeant Neuman," he called out, trying to sound as ordinary as he could muster.

"It's me, Jurai." The lieutenant sounded breathless. "I know you told me not to call you at home, and I'm sorry if I woke you, but we're flying out early. Just got through talking to Mom. You said you wanted to know. Hope it's not a problem."

"Of course not. It's okay." Jan winced under Maria's continuing gaze.

"She was really surprised. She cried. Said she wouldn't mind if you called...if you still want to. You have the number I gave you?"

"Yes, of course." Jan swallowed hard. "That's great news. Thanks! Where you flying to now?" He tried to sound casual.

"Back to Castle. Gimme a second, will ya?" Sound of hushed voices, a long pause, and then he came back on. "Sorry, gotta run now. Forgot to give you my address last night, but I'll give it to you the next time we talk, okay? "Hope I haven't caused you any problems calling so early, but you said you wanted to know."

"That's all right," Jan murmured. "I appreciate it. Good bye then. I'm *really* glad we've finally got to meet."

Maria glared at him. "Who was on the phone? Was it that lieutenant? What's going on?"

"It's okay. Go back to sleep. " Jan turned away from her and buried his head in the pillow.

"I don't believe you! What's going on? Who'd call at this hour? Was it that lieutenant?"

Jan remained silent as she sat up, now fully awake.

"Why would he show up and talk to you on a weekend and at night? You said last night you would tell me. So *tell* me."

"Can't we talk about this later?" Jan avoided her stare. "Please! This isn't the time. I gotta get ready for work."

"No! I want you to tell me now! Something's going on and I want to know what! What's going on?" Shaking, she glared at him through bulging eyes that shone like a pair of liquid marbles. "Just who *was* that guy you talked to last night?"

"Please, Maria."

"I have a right to know! I am your wife!"

He knew he had to tell her, but not now. Not like this. Cornered, he felt clammy all over, naked under her accusing glare.

"What's the big secret? Why won't you say? I thought he looked like you. Maybe you have a bastard son somewhere? From some whore? Is that it?"

Jan remained silent.

"So, you don't deny it?" She measured him severely. "Is that fellow your son? Your bastard son?"

"It's a long story. I never got a chance to tell you," he said, choking on the words as he forced them past the lump in his throat.

The bedroom became still. Stiflingly, oppressively still. Then, eyes flashing with pain and anger, Maria let out a shriek like a wounded animal. "Oh my God! Oh my God!" She lunged at him, shaking her clenched fists in his face. Her lips, compressed into a thin line, held back words until her eyes bulged, until she could hold them no longer and they burst out in a venomous stream. "Damn you! Damn you, you bastard! You two-timing bastard! Oh, my God. Oh, my God! I hate you! I hate you! I hate you! You bastard!" She pummeled him with blows.

He didn't try to stop her.

"How *could* you? How could you do this to me! To us! You bastard. You damned whore-loving bastard." Her last words became a stream of sobs that shook her chest in uncontrollable spasms.

"Goddammit! Shut up and calm down, will ya!" he snapped and immediately regretted losing his cool.

Jana poked her head through the door. "Mom, Dad, what's going on? What's the matter? Mom? Why're you crying?" Her voice trembled.

"Ask him! Ask him!" Maria shrieked. "Just ask him! Ask your no-good-louse of a father!"

"Dad?" Her eyes filled with tears.

"This isn't the time, honey. Please, go get yourself ready for school. We'll talk when you get back. Please."

She hesitated for a moment and then reluctantly vanished, tears rolling down her cheeks. Jan knew she was there in the hallway, listening.

"All these years. All these years, you lied to me." Maria pounced on him, face crimson with rage. "All these years

494

you've been lying to me, from the very start. How could you. How could you—"

"I never lied to you," Jan said quietly. "We never talked about our pasts. It's been years. Long before I ever met you. I never thought it would come to this—ever. It was past. Closed book. I tried to forget. Can't you see? What was I supposed to tell you? You know we can never talk. We always end up arguing. Even if I'd known, it was best not to say anything to keep the peace."

"I've been such a fool. I've been such a damned fool!"

"Please, try to understand—"

"You have never loved me. You never really loved me. Did you? Answer me! Did you ever love me?"

Jan remained silent.

"Answer me!"

"Did *you*?"

"You bastard." Her face twisted into a dark grimace. Tears rolled down her cheeks. "I curse the day we met. I curse it! I wish we'd never—" She recoiled and pulled the top of her nightshirt tightly about her. "Get *away* from me. Don't touch me. Don't you ever again touch me. Never! You understand?" She burst out crying.

"Please, Maria. Whatever happened, happened long before we met. We may not have a good marriage, but I have never cheated on you. There's never been anyone else. Ever. I swear."

She stared blankly straight ahead, sobbing quietly and dabbing now and then at her eyes with the corner of the sheet, as he told her about Majda.

"So what?" she shot back when he finished. "What about us? What about now?"

Jan shrugged.

"Do you plan to go back to her? Will you go see her?"

He didn't answer.

She burst out crying again, but then stopped abruptly. "It's up to you. If you go, that'll be the end of us. I've had it up to here!" She made a quick motion with her hand up to her chin. "I'm not gonna waste any more of my life on you."

"It doesn't have to be that way."

"Hah! You hypocrite! And what do you think—that I'll sit around and watch while you go chasing after her like the damned fool that you are? Do you really think I would? After I've given you the best years of my life? After I've stood by you? Kept your house? Given you a child? You—you—you *foreigner*! But I'm telling you, if you go to her, I'll take you for everything you got. Everything! Every single penny! Every stick of furniture! Every scrap! Everything! You understand!?" She glared at him through liquid eyes. "Oh God, why are you punishing me?" she wailed. "What have I done to deserve this? I should've listened to Daddy when he warned me about you, but I was so stupid. Oh God..." Her howling filled the room. "I hate you! I hate you. I hate you...I hate you..."

They sat in silence for a long time as she cried herself out, unmovable, untouchable, pitiful in her grief, and he drained of all emotion, feeling empty and relieved of the burden that had weighed on him so heavily all these years—the truth.

He heard the school bus pull up in front of the house and the door slam as Jana, without bidding them good bye as she always did, left for school. Maria got up and disappeared into the bathroom. The door lock clicked.

She was still there, sobbing, as he dressed. Instead of going to work, he called in sick and drove up to the lake. The boat club was empty except for the harbormaster and a couple of hands busy with maintenance. The harbormaster greeted him with a handshake. "There ain't much wind," he nodded toward the lake, "but it's a pretty morning to be out there on the water 'fore it heats up."

"Could I take out one of the Rhodes 19's?"

"Of course. Lemme get you the sails." The old man ambled off to the loft and a few minutes later returned with a bag slung over his shoulder. Jan thanked him, rigged the small boat, and ghosted out into the lake. The pale, fuzzy disk of the rising sun bathed everything in softly muted pastels. A faint breeze came up and the little boat responded eagerly. Only the rushing water broke up the silence. He closed his eyes. Drained yet relieved, for the first time in a long while, he felt at peace with himself. Slouched at the stern, feeling the vibration of the tiller under his fingers and the breeze soothing his face, he saw himself floating above all the cares, all the hurts of the world, wishing that the journey would never end.

CHAPTER 66

Jan's hand trembled as he dialed the number, closed his eyes, swallowed hard, and held his breath. His heart raced.

The phone rang several times before the familiar click. "Hello," a woman's soft voice answered.

"Hello, is this the Drugovich residence?"

"Who wants to know?"

It gave him a pause. "It's Jan. Jan Neuman. Is it you, Majda?"

"Yes..." She wavered for a moment and then gasped audibly. "Oh my God! Is it really you? Jan?" Her voice quivered. "Jurai called a few days ago and said he'd found you. Said you talked. That you might call. But I never imagined...never expected..."

"I looked for you. I wrote. I didn't want to lose you. But things happened. I swear—"

"I know. Jurai told me."

"I didn't know we had a son."

"Yes, he's a good boy." She gave a small laugh. "I keep calling him a boy, but he's been a man a long time. Do anything for me. The only real man in my life. I miss him around."

Her remark stung. He tried to fit the sounds to the image he had carried in his memory, but drew a blank. The voice he heard wasn't the lilting Italian he remembered. Instead, addressing him in English, her tone was cool and measured, soft, friendly, yet distant—the voice of a polite stranger. It filled him with trepidation. "I would like to see you."

"I know, the boy said you wanted to. But aren't you married? Don't you have a family? A daughter, Jurai said. I couldn't...it wouldn't be right."

"Yes, but my marriage's been over for years."

"Because of me?"

"No, of course not. I swear."

She fell silent for a few long moments. "It's been so long...our lives have changed. We have changed. Thing have happened. We were young then. We're not the same people any more. Maybe it'd be better to just let go, remember us as we were, remember what we once had, than to spoil the illusion...spoil it all."

"I've never stopped loving you. My feelings haven't changed."

"We're married," she replied.

"That's not what Jurai said. Didn't your husband die in Viet Nam?"

"We're not sure. They never returned his body. He's still classified as missing in action."

She began to sob, softly, almost inaudibly. His hopes tumbled.

"I can't go on living like this. Please, Majda—"

"I know, I know, but I'm so afraid..."

"If you don't feel anything for me, I'll have to accept it and go on, but I need to know. I need to see it. Hear it from you. You have to tell me. Please..."

Her sobs dissolved into silence. A sick feeling spread through him as he waited for the blow that was sure to come.

"I'm afraid I'll hurt you. We'll hurt each other again. I'm afraid. Terrified."

"But now that I've found you, I can't just walk away. Can't you see? Please, don't ask me to do that.

"I've lived this way more than twenty years…"

"And so have I. But now that we found each other, maybe there's still a chance. It may be the only chance we'll ever have."

The phone went silent again, and Jan felt himself drowning.

Finally she came on, sobbing softly. "I know. I know." Her voice trembled. "I'll be here when you come, if you come," she said almost in a whisper. "I'll be here, waiting for you."

CHAPTER 67

Jan drew open the heavy drape covering the single window and threw open the door leading to a small balcony of the second-floor room at the Airport Inn, a stone's throw from Byrd Field, the Richmond airport. The air-conditioning unit under the window hummed and rattled, and the frigid air inside reeked with the fruity smell of air freshener that did little to mask the smell of stale tobacco smoke. He turned it off.

The hot but fresh blast of the outside air felt good on his face. Down below in the manicured courtyard lush with azaleas and dogwoods, cars and people came and went. In the distance, enveloped in haze, the vague skyline of the city pierced the horizon. Somewhere out there was Majda, but at that moment, the thought of it wasn't uppermost in his mind. He was still smarting from his last row with Maria when he told her he was going and from Jana's accusing look following him as he left, with the door slamming behind him. Maria's last scream still rang in his ears. It left him strangely detached and emotionally exhausted.

He vacillated for a few moments and his hand trembled as he dialed Majda's number. Each ring increased his anxiety. Craving and yet fearing their meeting, he was at once disappointed and relieved when she didn't answer. Anxious, he unpacked the few things he had brought along and showered. The water soothed his skin and his mind.

Majda sounded breathless when he tried again. "Sorry. I'd have been there waiting for you if I'd known you'd be early, but you didn't say. Where are you?"

"At the Airport Inn. I made an early connection in Atlanta."

"Oh…"

"Shall I come there? I can take a cab."

"I think for now it'd be better if we met there. Do you mind?"

He gave her the room number and walked out on the balcony. His anxiety returned and with it a nagging onset of guilt. He felt in limbo, suspended between two worlds—the one he had just left and the other he couldn't yet predict.

Almost an hour later, a maroon Chevy entered the grounds and swung into the first empty space. A slender woman slid out. He couldn't see her face, but a shock of reddish-brown hair made his heart skip a beat. It had to be Majda! She scanned the rows of balconies, saw him, and gave a short wave. He waved back.

Silhouetted by the weak, intrusive lights of the hallway, she stood there like an apparition when he opened the door. His heart pounded. For a split second, he was transported to their last fateful night in Germany a lifetime ago. The years had been kind to her: a few crow's feet around her eyes and a sprinkling of gray hair on her temples complimented, rather than detracted from the same strawberry lips, now accented with a trace of lipstick, and the same forget-me-not eyes he remembered. He was overwhelmed, mute, frozen to the spot. Her lips parted as though wanting to say something, but broke into a smile instead as her eyes flooded. She buried herself in his embrace and he tasted the salty wetness of her tears as she showered him with kisses. A faint scent of lilacs titillated his nostrils. *Majda…Majda…Majda…* He repeated her name like a mantra, but she put her finger to his lips, begging him to remain silent, and so they just stood there, incredulous, locked in an embrace, savoring each other as the world around them, at least for the moment, became irrelevant.

She pushed him away gently and held him at arm's length. "You've changed." Her gaze explored him lovingly.

"You haven't. I was going to say so many things, and now I can't even think."

"The last time I saw you was from the ship's porthole as we were leaving. Did you see me wave?"

"Of course. I can still see that fluttering handkerchief. I stood there 'til you were gone. It was one of the most miserable days of my life. And you were pregnant."

"I didn't know it then."

"I never thought it'd be so many years. Now I'm almost afraid to believe this is really happening."

"Yes..."

The words sounded too hollow, too polite, too conventional to fit the moment. The room turned gloomy, confining. He looked at her pleadingly and she understood.

"Why don't we go somewhere else and talk? Have you eaten?" she said. "There's a place not far from here, I think you'll like it." She straightened her dress. "Shall we?"

Jan followed her out into the waning day. Somewhere to the west beyond the rolling hills, now tinted with somber hues, the sun had set, leaving the sky the color of faded denim streaked with purple cirrus turning gold around its edges. A faint breeze wafted in from the sea.

She maneuvered the Chevy into the traffic heading toward the city. "Remember Lila Johnson? The landlady?"

"Yes. She tried to help."

"She's gone. Cancer. Saw her just before she died. Told me all about you. Said you were so brokenhearted she wanted to hug you. That's how I knew you cared. That something must've happened. That's why I could never hate you." She gave him a warm smile. "I even thought of going to Minnesota to look for you, but by then I was already married and—" Her smile vanished and her eyes took on a sheen. Her gaze shifted into infinity.

"By then, I was already in the military. Jurai said your parents were very angry," Jan said.

She smiled sadly. "You have to understand. They were old school. That's why they insisted on my marrying Stepan. To save the family honor, true, but mostly to give the child a father. They did their best. Ah, here we are."

She swung off the highway onto a narrow lane that ended at a small restaurant perched on the riverbank. Etched by weather, its unremarkable facade had long shed its last shreds of paint, but the inside was friendly and intimate, with large windows overlooking the greenish water of the James River flowing sluggishly toward the Chesapeake. The far bank, a solid mass of indigo by now, punctured here and there by scattered pinpoints of light, hinted at life.

"Haven't been here since Mom and Dad died. Hope you like it," she said.

They retold their life stories over a tasty meal and then, holding hands across the table, gazed into each other's eyes like young lovers. The little candle between them flickered under their breaths, casting dancing shadows on their four-cornered world.

"You wore lilacs then, too, the last time we were together. Remember?" He closed his eyes as he drew in the air.

She blushed. "You noticed? I put it on just for you. For old times' sake. It's a young girl's scent. Now I wear something more fitting." She cradled his trembling hands and squeezed them until her fingernails dug into his skin. Her lips parted. Her probing eyes, two brilliant glistening spheres, made him flush.

"I still love you, Majda. Love you more than ever. There's no doubt in my mind," he said softly, forcing the words past the lump in his throat.

She looked at him through tears. "And I love you too, *carino*. I've always loved you. *Always*."

He probed her face. "We still have time. I'd like us to be married. Will you marry me?"

"But sweet love, you *are* still married, aren't you? And I…all these years…I don't know," she whispered, tears rolling down her cheeks. "I don't know, *carino*."

"I already told you, I'll divorce."

Her look shifted somewhere past him. "I don't want to have *that* on my conscience."

"I can't go on living like this. We've already lost so much time."

"What will your daughter say when she finds out? She might hate me. She might hate you. What then? What if she thinks that I—"

"She'll understand; I know she'll understand."

Her look softened. "Do you have a picture of her?"

He fished Jana's snapshot out of his billfold and she caressed it lovingly. "She looks like a precious young girl. I wouldn't want to hurt her. I wouldn't want her to hate me. I'm afraid. I'm afraid to think, to hope. But if everything turns out the way we want, oh God, help us, of course I'll marry you. I'd want nothing more than to marry you. I love you. *Ti amo…Ti amo…Ti amo…*" she whispered.

Outside, the river became one with the night. Only the points of light from across the water, inquisitive and unblinking, stared at them like silent witnesses. Mirror-like, the large windowpane projected their ephemeral images onto the darkness outside—two solitary souls on a ship of Fate embarking on a voyage of uncertainty.

The walls of the motel room and reality dropped out when she turned off the light. They undressed each other in the dark, fumbling like a pair of amateurs. Everything sank into oblivion as he surrendered to the intoxicating scent of lilacs and the silky warmth of her body. She drew him to her, pressing herself into him until he gasped. Exploring with their hands and lips, they melted into each other with a desperation and hunger borne of years of denial. Quenching the thirst of passion that had parched their lives for half their lifetimes became their only imperative.

In all his years of marriage to Maria, despite their virtually sterile relationship – except for an occasional relief from carnal urges followed by an onslaught of shame – Jan had never cheated on her. Until now. But was this, this pure, beautiful act of love – was this really cheating? Then why did icy pangs of guilt intrude on his mind like water seeping through cracks? Why now? Why here? Was it his Catholic upbringing, the things pounded into his young impressionable mind by his mother, playing tricks on him? Coming to haunt him after all these years?

He wavered.

Majda stiffened. "Is something wrong, my love?"

He sought to banish the intrusive thoughts from his mind. During his abortive encounters with Maria, he would rid himself of the ensuing guilt by castigating himself, driving himself to his physical limits in some punishing endeavor so that the pain would numb his senses and displace his shame. And so now, again, he wanted to hurt—wanted pain to blot out the pangs of his conscience. The act of love would become the instrument of his redemption. Almost subconsciously, he could feel Majda's fingers clawing his back and hear her rhythmic cries in concert with his crazed, painful, desperate thrusts, until, finally, they collapsed in exhaustion.

Her breath came in deep, halting spurts as they lay side by side, drenched in sweat, gently stroking each other. "You hurt me, my love," she said.

"I'm so sorry." He kissed her hand.

"Forgive me. It's been so long..." She turned to him and traced the outline of his body with the tips of her fingers. "Whenever I missed you, I thought of our last night," she whispered. "But I never thought we'd ever be like this, together again. I used to dream about us like this. Pretend, whenever *he* touched me. I thought of you until I couldn't remember your face any more." She started sobbing.

He kissed her gently. *"Ti amo. Majda...Ti amo...Ti amo."*

She put her arms around him. "I'm afraid," she whispered.

They remained entwined in an embrace, contemplating their predicament, until passion once again overtook their senses and they made love, gently and tenderly, this time immersed in its splendor, drowning in its fire, giving themselves eagerly to each other, and together, holding hands, disappearing in a momentary paradise.

* * *

They spent the next day wandering secluded spots along the river, delighting in each other, contemplating the future, making plans, filling in the void left by years of separation. She took him to her house and he couldn't help but notice the things *he* had left behind. *Their* wedding picture on *his* dresser, Marine mementos on the wall, *his* clothes in the closet. He felt like an intruder and flushed. She noticed and apologized with her eyes. At night, they made love in her bed. The next day, she made him breakfast, drove him to the motel to check out and then to the airport. She cried when he kissed her goodbye, promising he'd be back as often as he could. She promised to call. He watched her fluttering handkerchief as she stood on the tarmac, waving, and the earth dropped from under him.

CHAPTER 68

When Jan returned home, he found the house dark and musty from lack of fresh air. The garage was empty. Maria and Jana were gone. On the kitchen table lay a sealed envelope with his name on it. He tore it open and read the terse note.

I am leaving and won't be back. I am going home.
Jana is going with me. I was a fool all these years thinking
that things might work out. You have ruined my life and I
will never forgive you for it. I will not fight you. You may
have your divorce, if you want, I will not contest it. I took
some money and the car so I could take a few things. I want
you to send the rest and the furniture as soon as I have a
place to live. I will let you know.

M.

He rushed into their bedroom. Most of her clothes were gone, the dresser drawers empty. The suitcases, kept in Jana's room, were gone, too, as were her things. On the small table she had used to do her homework lay a piece of paper with something scribbled on it. "*I love you, Daddy,*" it said, with a row of Xs for kisses under it. His eyes filled with tears. He reached for the phone to call, but realizing they might not yet have reached Providence, put it down. Then he collapsed in a chair and wept.

He knew he should call Majda to let her know he had arrived, but couldn't bring himself to do it. When he finally did, hours later, Majda's anxious voice came on. "Oh, thank God, my love. I was worried about you. Are you all right? What happened? I miss you."

He told her about Maria and Jana, and assured her he was okay, but she detected the anguish in his voice and tried to soothe his frayed nerves. Afterward, eyes closed, he sought to banish from his mind the depressing desolation around him, imagining himself with Majda again, but guilt – his old nemesis – wouldn't permit it.

Two days later, he finally summoned the courage to call Maria. Benito's gravelly voice came on. "Hello! Somebody *there*?" he snapped.

"Please, I need to speak to Maria," Jan answered, feeling clammy all over.

"You sombich!" Benito let out a shriek. "You got some nerve calling here! You got some nerve! *Vai fan cullo*, you sombich!" he screamed. "*Vai fan cul'!* Get outa her life 'n' leave 'er alone. And don't call here again no more, you hear? Don't call 'er again. *Vai fan cul'!*" After a click, the phone went dead.

Maria called a few minutes later. "I'm sorry about Dad," she said tersely.

"I understand. Are you okay?"

"Yeah. Got here late last night. Took longer than I thought. Thank God Jana's old enough to drive. Drove most of the way. Please, don't make it any harder than it is. And don't call here again. I'll call you when I have a place of my own."

"Okay, but can I at least speak to Jana?"

She didn't reply, but after some scraping noises, Jana came on the line.

"Dad? Daddy? I love you. I miss you," she whimpered, sobbing.

"I love you too, sweetheart. Don't ever forget it. I know you can't talk now, but call as often as you can. Reverse the charges. Will you? Promise?"

Benito's whiny but unintelligible rant blotted out her voice. "I have to go now, Dad," she said tersely. "Sorry—" A sob, interrupted by silence, and the line went dead.

*　*　*

Time, the great healer, was kind to Jan. Work brought a sense of normalcy, Majda's and Jana's calls emotional sustenance. Maria called and let him know she had found a place of her own. He sent the furniture and the rest of her belongings, and moved out of the house into a small flat. A few weeks later, he filed for divorce. She didn't contest it. They divided what money there was and he arranged to send a monthly stipend. Oddly, stripped down to the barest essentials, he felt freer, unfettered.

He saw Majda as often as he was able to, flying to Richmond when he could or driving nonstop when money was low, arriving exhausted, just to see her for a few hours.

She'd greet him euphorically, smiling through tears, chiding him for taking the chance. "You do this just for me?" she would say gleefully, showering him with kisses each time he'd show up on her doorstep in the middle of the night.

"I'd drive to the ends of the earth for you," he'd reply. The first time he returned, he noticed Stepan's things were gone.

They spent Thanksgiving together in Richmond, almost as a family. Jurai was there, as was Jana, who had flown in after he had sent her the tickets and Maria gave her reluctant permission. He, Majda, and Jurai met her at the airport and, after heartfelt embraces and a few awkward moments, all his anxiety and apprehension concerning the meeting had rapidly evaporated.

"We must have Christmas together," Majda declared, face aglow, a few days later as he and Jana were leaving. "It would be so nice if you could come," she said to Jana. "Would you?"

"Yes, I'd like to. I'd like to very much. If I can." Jana gave her a reassuring smile.

"I understand," Majda said.

CHAPTER 69

The blustery December norther whipped the sea of dry prairie grass along the interstate into a confused, undulating mass, buffeting Jan's pickup as he tried to steer a straight course on his now customary trek to Richmond. Inexplicably out of sorts, no matter how hard he tried, he couldn't shake off a feeling of anxiety.

Instead of greeting him with her usual smile and eager embrace, Majda's pained and red-rimmed eyes told him that something was wrong! Her face was ashen, and the dark shadows under her eyes spoke of lack of sleep. She felt limp in his embrace. Her lips felt cold, without passion. He had never seen her like this. His heart sank.

Bursting into sobs, she handed him a telegram, and looked away as he opened it and read the brief message, stained and moist from her tears:

> *Dear Madam:*
> *This is to inform you that your husband, Lance Corporal Stepan Drugovich, listed as Missing in Action (MIA) in the Republic of Viet Nam (RVN), has been found alive. We are happy to report that he is currently in the Veterans Administration Hospital in San Francisco, CA, undergoing intensive care, pending release to his family. You are urged to contact the above-mentioned facility for details concerning his condition, treatment and release at one of the following numbers...*

Unbelieving, he read and re-read the message. Numb to his core, it took him a moment to comprehend the words. This couldn't be. This couldn't be. This couldn't be!

She threw her arms around him and clung to him desperately, moaning like a wounded animal, "I'm so sorry...I'm so sorry...so sorry...so sorry...so sorry..." Her body shook in great spasms, until she became incoherent and all that gave forth were dry, wheezing heaves.

He led her inside. Through the open bedroom door, he could see the unmade bed. She collapsed on the sofa and he cradled and rocked her back and forth like a child, searching for words to comfort her, but finding none. An empty, crippling sensation twisted his stomach into a knot.

"Did you call?" he finally asked.

She nodded and burst out crying. "They only told me that he had been seriously wounded, but wouldn't say much else. So Jurai called and they told him that they found him. Somewhere in Laos."

"In Laos? I didn't know we were fighting in Laos."

She dabbed at her eyes, pausing between sobs. "Said, he was on some kind of a special mission. Seems that he was the only one who survived. He was wounded. All torn up. A head wound, they said. Thought he was dead. Couldn't make out who he was. Had nothing on him except a dog tag. In his pocket. Assumed it was his. Now they say it was someone else's. Someone else got killed and he took it. Probably to report it. So, they thought he was *that* someone else. It was a mix-up. A horrible mix-up. Oh, God..."

"Couldn't he tell them who he was?"

"Jurai said, his wound, his head wound…" She shook her head and let it sink to her chest. She covered her mouth with her fist.

"I'm so sorry," Jan whispered.

"They did what they could for him. Physically, I mean. It took months. Until the family…" She burst out crying. "Forgive me, this is so hard." Her eyes seemed to have sunk even deeper into their shadowy cradles. "The other family, the family of the one with the name on the dog tag, they came to claim him and discovered he wasn't theirs. So they…the Army did some more checking, and—" Sobbing quietly, she stared at the telegram quivering in her hand.

He ached to comfort her, but instead found himself paralyzed, reeling under the impact of the crushing blow they'd been dealt. He felt betrayed and let down. "So what about us?" He looked at her pleadingly.

She lowered her head and continued to sob.

"What about us?" He insisted.

"I don't know! I don't know!" she screamed at him and burst out crying. "I'm sorry, love, I'm so sorry. Please, forgive me. Didn't mean to snap. Please, don't ask. Don't ask me now. I can't think…I can't think…" She took his hand and held it to her face. "Please, love. Please. I beg you," she moaned, as she kissed it.

"Couldn't you divorce him?"

She stiffened. "I can't. I can't, my love. I can't."

"My God, what are you saying? What do you mean, you can't?" He looked at her in disbelief "You've given him twenty years; you owe him nothing. You have the right—"

"I know, I know…but he's still my husband," she whimpered, burying her head in his chest.

"But we paid the price. Twenty-five years it cost us. Twenty-five years! Can't you see? And you don't love him! Divorce isn't the stigma it used to be. It's not the way it was in the old country. Your parents are dead. This is America."

"Please, don't make me hurt worse. Don't torture me. I can't...I can't... You don't understand. If it were that simple, I'd divorce him in a heartbeat."

"Then, for the love of God, why not? Why not! What is it?"

A torrent of tears gushed out of her eyes and she let them run freely, until her face was stained by glistening rivulets. "He's...in...a...wheel chair," she moaned through sobs. "He'll need somebody to take care of him. There's no one else. I am his wife."

Her words stopped him cold. It was one thing to argue their future, but another to fight a ghost. "What about the VA? They've kept him all this time. Can't they do anything? Keep him?" he burst out.

She pulled away and the glint in her eyes turned to ice. "I couldn't do that to him. I have a conscience. They've done all they could. Now he needs me. I can't refuse. I'm still his wife. We're still married. He's my husband. I couldn't live with myself if I did. I can't. I can't!"

He stroked her gently. "I need you, too..." he pleaded.

"Oh God, I wish I were dead. I wish I were dead." Sobbing, she held him desperately.

"I don't want to lose you again." His voice broke as he brushed her moist cheeks with his kisses.

"I'll *always* belong to you. Only you. That'll never change. Never. At least we have what we had. And we have our son." Her words dissolved into soft sobs as she snuggled closer to him, clutching him silently, weakly, like a drowning person sinking toward an abyss.

"When will you pick him up?" he finally said.

"On the twenty-second. They suggested picking him up for Christmas, and continuing his rehab locally. There's a VA Medical Center right here in Richmond."

"Oh."

"I'll be changing planes in Dallas. Perhaps, if you want…I could come a day early. We could meet." She smiled weakly and cradled his hand, but her words sounded distant and hollow, as though coming from a great distance, a widening gulf of anguish.

He shuddered. "Yes, of course, my love. I'd like that very much."

Later, when she led him to her bed and they made love, he could feel Stepan's shadow already there, the gap between them growing. He could tell. They both knew it. It made him angry, desperately angry, at Stepan, at her, at himself, at Fate, at the world. Their lovemaking was a wordless, despairing affair, each thrust a punishing blow. He hurt. She cried and dug her fingernails into him until he bled. He knew he would – could – never be back.

She embraced him weakly when he left. Her touch already telegraphed her distance and resignation. She gave him a weak wave, but looked through him, as though her mind was already elsewhere, perhaps somewhere in a future neither of them dared to contemplate.

CHAPTER 70

The road was icy and slick, making for slow progress as Jan steered his pickup toward the Dallas Love Field terminal. Christmases in Texas could be like that. The temperatures might reach near-summer levels one day, then dip into the teens overnight, bringing sleet and ice on blustery northers that would buffet street signs and send people scurrying for cover.

Love Field was a beehive of activity. By the time he parked and ran inside, the flight from Atlanta had landed and people were spilling from the exits. He spotted Majda right away, standing off to the side, looking around uneasily, a forlorn figure surrounded by a swirl of humanity.

She came alive when he waved, but approached him slowly, almost hesitantly. "Thought you might change your mind," she said as they embraced. Her cheeks, flushed from the blast of cold air, felt cool against his face. She attempted a smile, but failed to hide the sadness in her eyes and the shadows clouding her face.

"The road was icy and then the parking…everybody seems to be traveling at Christmas. How could I not come?" He kissed her.

She kissed him hard in return.

"This is all I have," she pointed to a carry-on. "It's just for a couple o' days. I'll have my hands full." She shuddered. "It's chilly here."

He winced. "Shall we go, then?" He took her bag. "There's a new Howard Johnson's not far from here. I reserved a room, if it's all right with you. It'll give us a little more time together."

They checked in and had dinner, consciously avoiding the issue of their separation. Instead, they reminisced about the past, laughing uneasily, pretending to ignore what really lay in the back of their minds—inevitability. They tried alcohol to dull their senses, but no amount of liquor could relieve the compelling feeling of doom. Borne of desperation, their lovemaking passion plumbed the depths both of delirium and anguish as they clung to each other until stupor, fatigue, and sleep relieved them of their pain.

She was again distant the next morning when he drove her back to Love. "When will you be back?" he inquired.

"Tomorrow." Her pleading eyes were two embers searing his soul. "But please, I beg you, don't come. I beg of you. I couldn't stand it. This has to be our good-bye. Please, my love. Please…"

He protested and she kept on insisting until he promised not to, though they both knew he would.

* * *

Weighed down by anxiety, Jan leaned over the balcony overlooking the grand concourse at Love and the tunnel-like passageways spilling sporadic streams of travelers into the vast open vestibule, with its vast inlay of a colorful compass rose cut into the shiny marble floor a metaphor for those scurrying over it. The incessant roar of airplanes all but drowned out the tin voices of loudspeakers paging flights and blaring out Christmas carols. The air was full of purposeful commotion.

Her flight was late. Disappointed and hurt when she didn't come out with the other passengers and thinking she'd probably chosen another flight so as not to have to face him, he was, in some strange way, relieved. Not seeing each other again would spare them a further dose of pain.

The last of her flights' passengers scattered and he was ready to give up when she emerged from the exit, pushing a wheel chair carrying a lump of a man. Eyes staring vacantly into space, motionless, hunched and expressionless, he seemed oblivious to the world around him. Stepan.

Her gaze swept the great hall and, as if drawn by a magnet, found his. Pale and withdrawn, she stopped short in the midst of her progress and just stood there, gazing up at him as the crowds streamed around her. She made no move to greet him. Even from that distance, he could see her eyes glistening. She pushed the wheelchair off to the side, bent down and, casting anxious looks in his direction, whispered something to the man. He didn't seem to acknowledge her. As Jan approached, she moved a few steps away, still within sight of the hunched figure, but behind him where she couldn't be seen.

"You shouldn't have come." She stiffened as he embraced and kissed her.

"I had to come. You knew I would come. I'll always come. I love you."

"This is reckless. Please. I can't...please, go now. Please. I can't leave him."

"I love you."

"And I love you, but can't you see? Won't you understand what this is doing to me?" She glanced uncomfortably toward the wheelchair. "I really must go. We can't do this anymore. You shouldn't have come." Her eyes flooded. "Please," she said softly, tears rolling down her cheeks.

He stood there, unable, unwilling to move. "Majda—"

"Please, don't cause a scene." Her voice broke. "Please."

"Good bye, then," he sighed, choking on the words as he kissed her lightly on the cheek.

"Good bye, Jan. Merry Christmas," she replied in a rasping voice. Squeezing his hand tightly, she pulled him to her until he staggered, and just as quickly pushed him off and let him go. "I'm so sorry…" were the last whispered words he heard.

She returned to the wheelchair and he to the balcony, and there they stood like two statues, forever rooted to their separate pedestals, unmoving, drinking in the sight of each other, eyes speaking what their lips couldn't. Time became physical, thick, oppressive, until a disembodied voice announced her flight and she moved on reluctantly, still looking up at him, straining as she pushed the wheelchair and the slumping, pitiful lump of a man, the crowd enveloping her and she becoming part of the stream, flowing with it, carried by it into a tunnel and out of sight—out of his life.

The loudspeakers blared "Joy to the World," as he retreated to one of the giant glass panes overlooking the tarmac and gazed out at the bleak landscape. The steel-gray skies hung low, casting a funereal pall over everything. Below him, her plane was loading. He strained to see her one more time, to catch a glimpse of her at one of the brightly lit windows, but without success. His heart bled as he recalled another bleak day years ago, when he stood atop the Bremerhaven terminal watching her leave. How ironic. Out of nowhere, a snippet of a melody intruded on his subconscious and refused to go away, repeating itself endlessly, obliterating all thought. It was the final strains of *Carmen. The poet was wrong! There's nothing sweet about parting sorrow—there's only pain,* his mind cried.

The engines came to life, the ramp swung away, and like a bird suddenly free of its earthly constraints, her plane slowly taxied away and took off in a swoosh. Staring at the empty spot in the sky where she had been only moments ago, Jan saw only darkness.

*   *   *

The oppressive silence of his flat was a palpable reminder of how alone again he was. Yet, wherever he looked, he saw her. His mind conjured her up even to her scent of lilacs. She was still there. She would be always. Oh God, was this really happening?

The ringing of the phone jarred him from his slumber. The clock told him she'd be getting home about now. He'd hoped for a call, but now that it came, he panicked. He lifted the receiver and stared at it, paralyzed.

"Hello! Hello! Are you there? Dad?" he heard faintly from the earpiece.

A wave of relief washed over him. "Jurai? Son? I didn't expect—" His voice shook.

"That's okay, I understand. I just spoke with Mom. She said she saw you. I just want you to know that as far as we're concerned, nothing has changed. Nothing will ever change. You're my father. I care about you. Very much. I am sorry it turned out this way. I'd do anything—"

"I understand, but this is not a good time to talk about it. Perhaps another day…"

"She still loves you."

"I know, Son. I know. That's what hurts. Look after her for me and stay in touch. I can't."

His voice broke as he put down the receiver and stared at the walls. He felt boxed in—imprisoned. His world had shrunk without her. Overwhelmed, his emotions screamed for release.

Not since his youth had he written anything of consequence. Years ago, during one of his visits, his favorite uncle had given him a small book of poetry by Baudelaire, translated from French, and introduced him to the power of words. From that time, whenever his soul cried out for catharsis, he would resort to the written word—a groping way to vent his feelings, to scream without being heard. He felt the same need now.

Reaching for his notebook, he began writing:

Between Planes at Love

Myriads of lights
Abstracted,
Reflected
In glassy windowpanes
Of a huge cage.

Inside
People waiting,
Their encased emotions
Awaiting release.

Outside,
At Love,
Silver chariots,
Birds of Christmas
Spilling out

Emotion and happiness.

You came…

Your first glance,
Seeing me standing there
Waiting,
Wanting,
Piercing in recognition,
Shattered the barriers.

The mechanical voices,
The din of cries:
Hellos,
Good-byes,
Merry Christmases
Disappeared
As you came,
And touched,
And kissed
In passing between lifetimes.

The glassy cage
At Love
Was solid,
Unpenetrable
And cold to the touch
As you left me
Alone
Inside.

The harsh lights
Screamed
Into the night
As your silver bird,
Shattering
The stillness of a witching hour,
Filled with
Christmas
And
Emotion
And
Happiness
And
Love,
Took you away,
Elsewhere,
Perhaps
Yet to another
Cage.

The next few days' mail brought a sheaf of Christmas cards. One was from her. It spoke of love and bore an imprint of her lips over her signature. It smelled of lilacs.

CHAPTER 71

Slumped against the window, heavy-eyed from fatigue and the drone of the engines, Jan gazed out at a thin smudge of gold on the horizon hinting at sunrise, as the plane broke through the low-hanging cloud layer and settled on a northeasterly course. He recalled fleetingly the happier times he'd made this trip to see Majda. It had been three years since they last met at Love, and she remained a presence, a constant, a warm glow. If anything, the memory of her was sweeter now, having acquired a patina of tenderness burnished by time. The snapshots of their encounters reeled before his mind's eye like a movie.

She still wrote to him – sporadically – each lilac-scented letter or card reigniting the fire within that never ceased to smolder, rekindling in him the urge to see her, making him relent only when the specter of a hunched figure in a wheelchair materialized before him. He craved the sound of her voice, but she never called. He didn't dare. Instead, he would spill his heart out to Jurai, whose encouraging words were a balm for his soul.

With his retirement from the Air Force only weeks away, he was surprised his commander had asked him to assist with a briefing for the Chief of Staff in the Pentagon. He'd done it a number of times, when they flew to Strategic Air Command Headquarters in Omaha to brief the Chief, but this was bigger and the commander was nervous. "I know they have some fine people there, John, but I need somebody who's familiar with the way I do things," he said with a wink. Now he slouched next to Jan, snoring lightly, an open briefcase by his feet, a sheaf of papers on the pullout table in front of him. Two other colleagues, a lieutenant and a captain, dozed directly in front.

It was mid-morning when they landed at the Washington National and took a rental to Bolling Air Force Base where they had reserved quarters. A group of Viet-Nam War protesters greeted them at the heavily manned gate as the guards waved them through. The quarters were spartan but clean.

"We don't go on 'til tomorrow and I've got some calls to make. Got to look over some of this stuff," the colonel tapped the briefcase. "You fellas got something' to do?"

"Do you need us to go over the briefing with you, Sir?" the captain inquired. "If not, we'll be at the Club."

"That's fine. I'll call you if I need you." The colonel waved him off. "And you, John? Your first time here?"

Jan shrugged. "No, Sir, but it's been a few years. I brought a book—"

"A book?" The colonel's eyebrows shot up. "Naw," he growled. "Take the rental. Go look around. See something. The Smithsonian. The Capitol. The Mall. You can read your book at night. I won't need you 'till tomorrow. The car's just going to be sitting. Just make sure you're ready to go tomorrow at oh-seven-hundred. *Go.*"

Jan swung the car out the gate past the chanting group of demonstrators into the busy street, and drove aimlessly, trying to make sense of the sketchy roadmap the rental agent had given them. Scanning a cluster of road signs, his gaze fell on one that sent a shiver down his spine: *US 1, Richmond Highway*, and under it, in smaller letters, *Richmond – 108*. He found the prospect of seeing Majda again irresistible.

The closer he got to Richmond, the more his stomach knotted and doubts seeped in, until he considered turning around, but something stronger drove him on. His pulse quickened in anticipation as he reached the familiar street and slowed to a crawl when her house came into view. It looked somber and lifeless, except for a makeshift ramp connecting the driveway with the porch. He scanned the windows for any sign of movement, but they stared back, impenetrable, opaque. Heart pounding and adrenalin flowing, he circled the block, stopped a short distance away on the far side of the street, and turned off the engine.

The longer he waited, the more foolish he felt. What if he knocked and she wouldn't see him? She'd probably put *their* wedding picture back on the dresser and *his* mementoes on the wall. She'd probably be angry at him for showing up unannounced, rekindling her pain. After all, she never even hinted about seeing him. Not once. This was absurd! He was a fool! He reached for the ignition key when a curtain moved, and a door swung open. She walked out, wrestling a wheelchair with Stepan's limp body strapped into it. Strangely detached, as though in a dream, he watched transfixed from the discreet cocoon of the car as she moved cautiously down the ramp, with Stepan's hands on the rims helping to break, steering the wheelchair around the back and into the garden where she parked it in the shade of a large oak and just stood there, impassively, until Stepan stirred and she bent down over him, spoke something as she wiped his face, laid the cloth on his lap, and slowly, hesitantly returned to the house. Overwhelmed by remorse, he felt like a voyeur.

Even from a distance she looked tired. Pausing when she reached the porch, she scanned the street, and for a split second, her gaze rested on his car. He gulped for air as blood rushed to his temples. His hands turned clammy. *Oh, God!* Had she seen him? But her look didn't connect. If it had, she didn't recognize him. He was the last person she'd expect to see. He wanted to wave, cry out, run to her, but his body went limp and his mind blank. Before he could recover, she was gone.

He stared at the door, cursing himself for being a coward. He wished he had not come. Whatever hopes he may have harbored, whatever reversals of fortune his mind may have conjured, they were now unescapably quashed. Finally, he had seen the futility of it all. Fighting tears, he started the engine and drove off without looking back.

CHAPTER 72

A red light flashed above the briefing room door. A sharply dressed Air Police guard bared Jan's way. "See your ID?" He quickly scanned Jan's visitor's badge and, scowling, tapped a clipboard holding a printout of names. "Your name's not on the list. Sorry. You're not with the retirement party?"

"No, we're here for the Chief of Staff briefing at thirteen hundred. My commander wants me to check out the setup. I really need to make sure everything's okay. Isn't there some way?"

He sighed, a bit more at ease now. Frowning, he looked at Jan and then his watch. "Can you be out in fifteen minutes?"

"That'll be fine. I'll be outta there in plenty of time."

"I'm doing you a favor."

"I know. I appreciate it. Thanks, Sarge."

Paneled in dark wood, the room was windowless and relatively small. A huge horseshoe-shaped table faced a wall of glass, in reality a huge rear-projection screen, now glowing with the words, "Fair Winds and Following Seas, Dave Fox." An American flag and service pennants hung limply on each side of the raised podium behind an ornate lectern. A small door off to the side led to the projection room. A lively, eclectic crowd swarmed around a large table brimming with hors d'oeuvres and food trays arranged around a pair of punch bowls and a patriotic display. He slid past them into the projection room.

The sergeant let out an audible sigh of relief when he walked out fifteen minutes later, just as an entourage of generals and colonels, surrounding a man in civilian clothes, arrived at a brisk pace. "Ten-shun!" the sergeant hissed under his breath, snapping into a brace, and stiffening as the party strode past them.

The wizened old man escorted by the officers seemed strangely out of place in this spit-and-polish milieu. His wrinkled face was puffy, his complexion pasty. The gray suit he wore hung loosely over his gaunt frame, rumpled and plain, except for a shiny U.S. flag pin clipped to his lapel. His bulging watery blue eyes stared straight ahead from behind thick, horn-rimmed lenses. Though stooped and walking with a noticeable limp, he nevertheless exuded an air of arrogance. He gave Jan a cold, hostile glance, and Jan felt an icy stab of recognition: He'd seen those eyes, that reptilian look—he'd seen this man before. His face was indelibly etched in his memory. Even though time had taken its toll, there was no mistake. It was Fuchs! Klaus Fuchs!

Completely stunned, he didn't hear the sergeant close the door and breathe a sigh of relief as the party disappeared inside to a burst of applause and shouts of "Huzzah!" He'd been transported in time, back to the day he'd seen his friend Jakub bloodied, lying in the dust; Jakub's uncle Isaac bleeding to death, and *Obersturmbannführer* Fuchs, face twisted in rage, holstering his pistol. He could still recall the sickening smell of gunpowder blending with the exhaust of the trucks that took his friend away.

He stood there dumbfounded, once more awash in guilt that he had let Jakub down by forgetting. He seldom, if ever, thought of him now. The exigencies of life and time had blotted the event from his mind. It had all happened so long ago, his mind seldom conjured up more than a passing uncomfortable thought which he'd been able to dismiss. Until now. But why Fuchs! And why here?

"Do you know who that was?" he queried the sergeant, trying not to sound too curious.

"You mean that civilian guy?"

"Yeah."

The sergeant shrugged. "Some big cheese retiring, I guess. Do these all the time. Gets old after while. Should say so in here." He pointed toward a small table by the door strewn with booklets. "Help yourself." He motioned vaguely toward the table. "There's plenty. They'll be trashed anyway."

Jan poured himself a cup of coffee, slid behind a desk and stared at the program. It was slim, just a few pages, standard Air Force fare—he'd seen many like it before. The cover, emblazoned with a patriotic design, framed an inscription:

Retirement Ceremony
of
Dr. DAVID K. FOX
Senior Analyst, Eastern European Affairs,
CIA Liaison Office

The inside page showed a picture of a somewhat younger man over a biographical sketch. There was no doubt, no doubt whatsoever—Fuchs. He skimmed over the customarily glowing but vague bio: "*...native of Dresden...offered his services to the American Forces after Germany's surrender...contributed crucial assistance to the CID in tracking down communist agents...immigrated to the United States in the early fifties. Offered position with the CIA...highly decorated...provided immeasurable assistance to the government of the United*

States...pillar of the community...involved in many charitable causes...member of Ahavat Shalom congregation—" Ahavat Shalom? What—Klaus Fuchs a Jew? A *Jew?* Impossible! That couldn't be...that couldn't be! Bewildered, he read on: more accolades, awards, medals, and finally the closing paragraph: *"Mr. Fox and his wife, Helga, intend to retire in the San Juan Islands in Western Washington where they plan to pursue lifelong passion for boating, hunting, and mycology."*

Someone laid a hand on his shoulder and he jerked up, startled.

"You okay, John? You seem down this morning. What you got there?" The colonel nodded toward the booklet. "Everything okay in the briefing room?"

"Yes, Sir, everything's set." He hastily closed the booklet. "It's something I picked up over there. There was a function."

"Oh? Not somebody you know?"

"As a matter of fact, yes, Sir."

"Not a friend, I'd guess, huh, judging from your expression?" The colonel laughed.

"A Nazi. I knew him during the war. His real name is Klaus Fuchs. Now he calls himself David Fox. I watched him kill a man. He sent the Jews in my town...my best friend to a concentration camp."

The colonel's jaw dropped and his eyes narrowed under his furrowed brow. *"What* did you just say?"

"I know him, Sir. He's an ex-Nazi."

The colonel gazed at him silently. "You sure?" he finally said. "It's been years. A mind can play tricks. We forget. People change."

Jan looked at him disappointed, wishing he hadn't told him. He couldn't expect him to understand. Nice man that he was, well liked by all and always friendly toward him, he hadn't lived through the war, seen it through his eyes. "There are things one doesn't forget, Sir," he said. "Perhaps if you let me explain."

The colonel listened intently. "I don't know what to say, John. I believe you, but..." He shook his head. "What an incredible coincidence." A faint smile brushed his face. "But in a way, I am not surprised. Was he an officer?"

"Yes, Sir. A *Sturmbannführer.*"

"A *Sturmbannführer?* How do you know that?"

"My father was a tailor. He commandeered my father to work on his uniforms, and my father had to sew on his new rank. Shortly after that, he was sent to the Russian front."

The colonel nodded faintly. "I know the Pentagon fairly well. Been here many times. Pulled a tour here back in the 50s as a young shave-tail lieutenant. Got my start in Intelligence, not long after Truman created the CIA. Until then, the Army was in charge of the spooky business. OSS. The Office of Strategic Services. But then the CIA took over and established liaisons with the Services. And some of the liaison folks *were* Germans, come to think of it. Experts on the Russkies and communism. We didn't have any, but they had plenty. Mostly former officers from the Russian front. BND people. That's the name of the German Intelligence outfit. Stands for *Bundesnachrichtendienst.*" He stumbled and laughed sharply.

"Yes, Sir." Jan diffidently echoed his laugh.

"So it's possible that this fellow, this Fuchs, or whatever he calls himself, is one of these folks."

"Somebody needs to know, Sir. I think I should report him."

"Report him?" The colonel's frown returned. "Now, wait a minute, John. It's not that simple. Where? To whom? Why?" He pursed his lips. "Mind you, I believe you, John, but what about the others? Do you think they'd believe you? You must have proof."

"But Sir, *I* am the proof. I was there. I saw him do it."

The colonel smiled. "Don't take me wrong, John, but think: You're just a sergeant and he's a very powerful man. Surely, you must know by now how this works. I'm not saying it's fair, but that's the way it is. It's your word against his. They'll laugh at you."

"Then I'll go to the papers."

The colonel shook his head. "What makes you think you can just walk up to somebody and make an accusation? Nobody'll talk to you. Nobody'll listen unless you have proof. Without proof—surely you've heard of slander. It'd still be your word against his, but the onus, the burden of proof, would be on you." He gave Jan a soft look, the way his father used to look at him when he instructed him as a young boy. "You'll be retiring in a few weeks, John. Do you really want to risk your career? For what?"

"I need to do something."

"Yes, perhaps, but this is not the time. Or the place. Believe me, John, you must have proof. Incontrovertible proof."

A different guard greeted them at the door. The briefing went well. The room was totally transformed, bearing not the slightest hint of the party that had taken place there just hours before, so much so that Jan had to question himself whether or not what he had witnessed actually happened. But the booklet in his hand was real. Staring at the picture of the man responsible for Jakub's death and the suffering of hundreds of others, he knew he *had* to see him again.

CHAPTER 73

The retirement ceremony was anticlimactic. Scratchy sounds from a loudspeaker of the National Anthem; the line of retirees snapping to attention; a pompous young adjutant reading the retirement orders; a solemn-faced General making a little speech, pinning medals on the soon-to-be veterans, and handing them their retirement certificates. A handshake, a salute, and that was *all*. Amazing, with what ease the bonds to almost a quarter century of military life could be severed, Jan reflected.

Watching Jurai and Jana together among the handful of attendees, he considered the whims of fate and the passage of time. Jana had blossomed, despite the vagaries of her life and the pressures of the 'Aquarian-Age.' Jurai, too, returned from Viet Nam a changed man. Gone was his carefree demeanor, the brashness, the youthful swagger. Instead, his face was lined with furrows beyond his age, his manner solemn and somber. His letters did not talk about the war, and when Jan queried him about his experiences, he demurred, "I'd rather not talk about it, Dad," making Jan reflect how that distant country had touched his life, killing his childhood friend, Jára Soukup, a Foreign Legionnaire fighting France's colonial war, and maiming and returning Stepan to deny him Majda's love. Jan was sure she still loved him. Jurai said as much. Her occasional carefully worded letters spoke volumes between the lines, and he would bury his face in them and drink in the faint hint of lilacs.

With the ceremony weeks behind him and Jurai and Jana returning to their busy lives, he found himself adrift, at loose ends. He wasn't prepared for the inactivity, and the walls closing in on him. The separation from his former life had been all too abrupt, too quick. He missed the imposed structure of the military life, however contrived and banal it may have been. Gripped by lethargy, he pondered his future.

Rousing himself, he resumed shuffling through a stack of mementoes and documents representing his twenty-four years of service, when his gaze rested on the program he'd picked up at the Fuchs, alias David Fox, Pentagon ceremony. Fuchs! The glowing write-up made his blood boil. How could it be that the same man, the 'bogey man' of his youth and the murderer of his childhood friend and many others, was here, in the States, alive and enjoying a life they never would? He had to find out. He owed it to the memory of Jakub and the others who had perished. The very thought of his presence was an affront to all he'd sacrificed when he'd left his homeland and put on an Air Force uniform. He had to find Fuchs and confront him. And then? He knew his colonel was right. He could do nothing without evidence. Nothing at all. He must find a way to expose him. His conscience wouldn't let him rest until he had proof and laid this one last specter of his past to rest.

* * *

"That's Mount Rainier out there, folks, on our left, in case you're interested," the matter-of-fact voice of the captain came on over the intercom. "We're on our final approach and will be landing soon."

A majestic peak piercing the puffy sea of clouds seemed to float by, appearing disembodied from the ground below. The pitch of the engines changed. The plane dipped into the cloud cover and shuddered, for a moment obliterating all view, before re-emerging over a vast estuary punctuated by islands, inlets, lakes, and a sprawling metropolis dominated by tall buildings and a thin needle-like spire: Seattle.

Jan checked out a compact from the car rental agency and drove out into the thin drizzle. Two hours later, under a bright sunny sky, wearing crowns of puffy clouds, the heaped bluish-green mounds of the San Juan Islands came into view.

An old wizened clerk at the Islander Inn looked up from the guest register and frowned. "Canadian?" he said, peering at Jan over his half-moon spectacles.

Jan shook his head, smiling.

"Hmm." He scratched his head. "You here on business? The season's almost over."

"I came to find somebody. Somebody I knew, long ago."

"Hmm," he grumbled. "Gonna be with us long then?"

"I don't know. Lives somewhere in the Islands. Gotta find him first. Could be a week, maybe two."

"Then I'll need a deposit," the old man said, pushing the register toward Jan. "And your car make 'n license, too. Take only cash or American Express."

Jan paid him and he grunted. "There's places to eat just down the block on Commercial, if you want. You can walk. Good fish 'n' chips at The Hatchcover."

The room was clean but musty. Jan opened the window and looked out over the harbor, letting in the fresh breeze, oblivious to the cries of kingfishers and seagulls, feeling nervous at the prospect of what might lie ahead. He unpacked and pulled out a stiff-looking pouch, the kind thinly lined with lead and sold by photo stores for protection of films from X-rays, and shook out a miniature tape recorder, a tiny microphone, and a pair of tapes. He rifled through the tourist brochures and ferry schedules neatly arranged on the night table, and then fished the Island County phone book from under the telephone and turned the pages to governmental offices. The County Courthouse was on San Juan Island, a couple of hours of ferry-ride away. He would start there.

When he walked out, the sun was just dipping behind the islands. Wispy mare's tails high in the deepening blue sky promised a fair tomorrow. The fish and chips at The Hatchcover were as good as the old man had said. Looking up and down the busy avenue, he caught sight of a forest of masts only a block or so away in a bay under a massive wooded promontory.

"She's a sweet little boat, ain't she," someone behind him uttered softly. "Yeah, real sweet."

Absorbed in looking at a derelict of a boat, he turned around, startled.

A smiling, rotund, middle-age man, a fisherman's cap cocked jauntily on his head, extended his hand. "Skip Nordlund. I'm with the Cove Marine. She's one of ours."

"Looks like she's been sitting a while." Jan nodded toward the faded sail cover stained by gull droppings, weathered wood work, and thick green strands of algae fouling her waterline. "Sailboats ought to be sailed."

"Yessiree, that's true. She don't look all that pretty right now." Skip shook his head. "But she's a fine boat. A Kendall, if you're familiar with boats. You a sailor?"

Jan nodded.

"I see, I see." Skip nodded knowingly. "Been here a few months. Be hauling her this week 'n doin' her bottom'n some maintenance. She'll look a lot different then." He swung into the cockpit and gave Jan a big smile. "Care to see 'er below? C'mon aboard."

Fetid stale air met them as they slid below.

Skip threw open a switch, reached into the cockpit, and pushed the starter. "Gotta run the diesel every few days," he said. It turned over a few times and sputtered to life. "Yeah, she'll make somebody a fine boat. Yessiree, she will."

"How come she hasn't sold?" Jan fingered the fine woodwork.

Skip pursed his lips, took off his hat, and scratched his head. "Well, she don't sell 'cause she's got a hex on her."

"A hex? What do you mean, a hex?"

"Yeah. Her skipper died on board. Right here at the dock. Drives the customers away."

"How come? What happened?"

"You notice she carries Alaskan registry?"

Jan shrugged.

"Don't matter. Well, there was this couple. Older couple. Lived in Anchorage. The husband went up into the oil fields to work so he could buy a boat 'n' sail 'round the world. He and I used to talk. Told me all this. Anyway, she, his missus, I mean, she hated the idea, but wouldn't say anything, hoping it'd pass. But it didn't. So finally, he had the money. Got the boat and quit his job. Was ready to go, but she balked. Called him a crazy old fool 'n other things I won't mention. Of course, he wouldn't go without 'er, so in the end she finally gave in, provided if she didn't like it, she'd git off at the first stop, 'n he'd go on alone."

"Yeah?"

"Anyway, the passage wasn't all that bad. It's mostly inside. No open water. But I guess she still didn't like it. Argued a lot, even 'bout her name. He wanted something like *Alaskan Dreamer* 'n she taunted him with *Charlie's Folly*—his name was Charlie. So they ended up not naming 'er at all. Anyway, they got 's far as here, 'n stopped to provision. Probably would've cost them their marriage at this point, 'cept one day, she came back from somewhere 'n found him down below. Right here." He made a vague motion. "Sprawled out on the sole. Dead. His heart gave out on 'im, that poor old sombich. So she buried him at sea. Scattered the ashes, I mean. Left the boat here, 'n returned to Alaska. Said, 'Sell that damn thing for whatever it brings. I don't want to see it again. Ever!' So, that's why she's here, like this. As I said, been here a few months. She's worth at least thirty, mebbe even thirty-five, but I might let her go for twenty-five, or even twenty-four, just to get rid of 'er. She's costing me slip space 'n maintenance, 'n just sitting ain't good for 'er, either. You know what I mean. Interested?"

"Naw." Jan shook his head, smiling. "Can't."

"Here, take my card anyway. Our office is just 'round the corner on Commercial. Just in case." He closed the hatch, slipped the bronze padlock through the hasp, slid the keys under the coils of line in the coaming compartment, and shrugged sheepishly, noting Jan's puzzled look. "It's easier this way if I have to show 'er. Saves time running back to the office."

Jan lingered after Skip left. Gazing at the derelict gently tugging at its mooring, he felt a strange kinship to her master, the stranger he'd never met but understood. He saw the universal parallels of Life as a voyage, where the ebb comes without warning and we are carried away regardless of plans, ambitions, or desires.

CHAPTER 74

The ferry made a wide, sweeping turn as it entered a narrow inlet that gradually widened into a broad sheltered bay surrounded by stands of pine and cedar, and came deftly to a halt at the San Juan ferry landing. Cormorants and seagulls, competing for roosting space atop the tall pilings, took off in a start. Disturbed by the prop wash, a scattering of sailboats anchored in the placid water came alive, tugging at their moorings. From atop the upper deck, Jan surveyed a quaint assortment of picturesque houses clustered around the waterfront—Friday Harbor.

A short walk up the hill from the landing took him to the rustic weather-beaten building housing the county offices. A graying woman, glasses drooping from a chain around her neck, looked up from a sheaf of papers and smiled politely when he told her why he had come. "Well, sir, we do have records of all the transactions and they are, indeed, public records. But you can see for yourself," she made a sweeping move toward a stack of large registry books and boxes of documents, "it may take you quite some time to go through all this." Her forehead wrinkled in a solicitous smile. "But, if you say, all you want to do is find where your friend lives, then perhaps you might try the *Gazetteer*. That's the local paper. Just down the street. Publishes a real estate supplement every week. Lists all the county transactions. Be much easier for you to find what you're looking for. But," she shrugged, "if you want to start here, that's fine with me, too. Up to you."

"I need to look up at least the past two years. Maybe more."

"I don't think they'd mind. Just tell them Ellen from the county offices sent you."

A small bell attached to a coiled spring atop a massive wooden door sprang into action as Jan entered the *Gazetteer* office, a large room with a counter and low partition up front, separating a small vestibule from the pressroom. Almost hidden by stacks of newsprint, a printing press crowded a pair of desks and a row of bulky shelves holding an assortment of supplies. Along the back, more shelves overflowed with back issues of the *Gazetteer,* some bound in well-worn hardcovers, others – more recent – stacked loosely in cardboard boxes labeled with the years of publication. A heady smell of ink, paper, and musk hung heavily in the air.

Two men, seemingly mesmerized by the rhythmic clanging of the gears, gazed intently as the press swallowed sheet after sheet of newsprint and spat it out on the other side, stacking it gently onto a large pallet. In the corner, stooped over a light table, a young woman in a white smock busied herself pasting loose pieces of copy onto a large mat. A cat lay comfortably coiled in a cardboard box at her feet.

"So Ellen sent you, huh?" The older of the men snorted, taking off his green-billed visor and wiping the brow with the back of his hand. "My cousin." He sighed. "So what can I do for you?"

Jan told him, and he smiled. "No problem looking, so long's you put everything back'n the same order it's filed," he said, unlatching the gate. "Come on in. I'll make some room for you on one of the tables. Want some coffee?"

Jan poured a cup and settled himself in a creaky old chair. The stacks were daunting, as the highly compacted small print in the real estate supplement, a narrow column among the plethora of ads, was hard to read, until the girl, smiling shyly, passed him a loupe. He went back two years, three, and then four. Nothing! He didn't know when Fuchs may have obtained the property. Could have been years ago. He may have come all this way for nothing. It left him empty and yet, strangely, relieved. He was about to give up when he saw a small two-line blurb almost lost in a sea of similar blurbs: *Plot 719F, Perm. Reg. SJ068719, Fox D., Dolphin Bay Road, Orcas Is.* A chill pulsed up his spine. He stared at the words, not believing his luck.

*   *   *

Dawn of the next day was just breaking as he drove up to the ferry terminal, bought a ticket to Orcas Island, and swung into the assigned waiting lane. A thick opaque fog obliterated everything but a few lights glaring from the mist, exposing the liquid clouds of droplets rolling past in giant swirls. A line of cars were already there, waiting, their occupants invisible in the dim light, save for the occasional glow of a cigarette. From somewhere out over the water, a horn sounded three long blasts and an array of moving lights materialized as if from nowhere. The ferry came to a halt, and after disgorging a string of cars and a gaggle of walk-ons, began loading again.

Wishing to remain anonymous, he didn't join the stream of passengers rushing topside to a warm cabin and a cup of coffee, but instead sank deeper into his seat, pulled his collar up around his face, and studied the map of the island, committing to memory the layout of the thin web of roads, and one in particular, hugging the tortured shore of a deep bay in a series of precipitous turns—Dolphin Bay Road.

The fog lifted and a pale disc of the sun rose timidly from the mist by the time they reached Orcas. The few disembarking cars quickly dispersed and he found himself alone on a narrow undulating road bisecting the island. Suddenly, there it was—a narrow lane veering off at the fork, the letters 'lphin' barely visible on a weather-beaten sign. The emptiness in the pit of his stomach turned to nausea.

After a short drive, the pavement played out and the washboard road turned muddy, dipping into pools of standing water gouged out by traffic. A towering canopy of moss-covered pines and old growth cedar admitted only weak sunlight in chimerical streaks. Foggy wisps of vapor spiraled slowly skyward. The air was pungent with the smell of wet earth and decomposing wood. He thought he'd heard something and stopped the car, turned off the engine, and listened, but other than an occasional splat of giant crystalline water drops on a thick covering of debris, the silence was complete.

Relieved, he drove on as the road twisted and turned along the steeply sloping shore. Here and there, a mailbox would appear at the head of a path or rutted tracks leading to a house or cabin hidden by the dense undergrowth. Some mailboxes had names, others only numbers. Some carried neither.

Trying to decipher the faded, weathered letters, he felt a mix of frustration and relief each time he drew a blank. He really didn't relish confronting Fuchs. But then, there it was! An ordinary mailbox with a single name painted over a number: Fox! A lane peeled off toward the bay. The house itself was invisible, but the faint acrid smell of burning wood wafting through the air told him it was there. Nailed to the trunk of a large cedar were two newer signs: one read, *Private Road*; the other, *No Trespassing! Violators Will Be Prosecuted.*

He was both elated and stunned by his unexpected success. The knots in his stomach sent a creeping dullness to his head. He needed time to regroup, steady his nerves, and steel himself for what might lay ahead. He needed to think. Clammy all over, he turned the car around and drove back as though chased by a ghost, jarred to the bones by the bumpy road, until again reaching the level pavement and a while later, the town. He pulled up at a fast-food kiosk, ordered a sandwich, and then drove on at random into the countryside until he reached a secluded lake. He parked out of sight of the road, ate, and found himself alone with his conscience—a conscience once fed by hatred now mitigated by time. The hatred was gone. Only his resolve, his sense of obligation to his friend remained. He'd come this far, he had to see it through.

He drove back to Dolphin Bay Road and almost missed the turnoff at the Fox mailbox in the weakening light. Mashing on the brake, he slid into the rutted lane, backed the car into the bushes, slipped the recorder into his pocket, pinned the microphone under his lapel, and set out on foot.

CHAPTER 75

The road played out at a house built over a rocky precipice. Facing the bay, its front extended to form a deck. The rear hid a small barn that doubled as a garage, holding a shiny black Mercedes, partially covered by a tarp. A beat-up Chevy pickup loaded with trash and dead branches sat outside on a crumbling slab. A footpath connected the house to a set of steps ending at a dock and a large cabin cruiser tethered to a mooring. Peering through the branches, Jan saw no signs of life, though a thin ribbon of white smoke rose slowly from a rock chimney.

The boat's cabin door swung open and a man, lugging a bulging satchel and a cooler, backed out into the cockpit. Fumbling with the keys, he locked the cabin door, eased himself onto the dock, and started cautiously up the steep steps. Jan recognized him immediately. Fuchs!

A door creaked open and a ghost-like, wispy woman walked out on the deck. Everything about her was gray—from her pasty, wizened skin and her mousy hair gathered in a small tight bun at the back of her head, to her sweater and slacks under a faded green apron. Shuffling about stiffly, she sat a large tureen on a table, leaned on the railing, and gazed impatiently at the dock. *"Kannst du nicht schneller machen?"* she called out as Fuchs came into view. *"Die Suppe wird kalt."* Fuchs grunted something unintelligible and she frowned. *"Komm, komm. Beeile Dich!"*

Just another old guy, if he didn't know better, Jan considered, watching Fuchs with his gangly legs and baggy shorts, loose-fitting shirt, hat askew on his balding head, and face ruddy from exertion under thick stubble that resembled a hedgehog's coat. Heart pounding, he checked again the tiny microphone under his lapel, switched on the recorder, took a deep breath, and stepped out from behind the pickup.

The woman gasped. Her hand flew to her open mouth. Her faded blue eyes, set deep in purplish eye sockets, bulged.

"Klaus Fuchs? *Obersturmbannführer* Fuchs?" Jan called out in a quivering voice.

Fuchs froze in his tracks, and then, turning around slowly and warily, glared at Jan for a few long, silent moments. "What is this? Who are you? What do you want?" he snarled, measuring him with disdain.

Jan met his gaze—the same cold bulging eyes, made even larger by the thick lenses of his glasses, eyes that gave him chills whenever he dared to dredge up the past. "You probably don't remember me, but I remember you. We met in the Pentagon. During your retirement. You walked past me and looked at me. I was sure you recognized me."

Fuchs sneered. "Recognized you? I don't even know who you are. Get the hell off my property!"

Jan made no move.

"Who are you? What do you want?" His pale bulging eyes flashed with anger.

"We met during the war. In Czechoslovakia. And then again in Italy. In Rome. In '48."

It threw him off balance. A heretofore invisible scar on his left cheek turned pink. His bushy eyebrows arched in mock surprise. "Aah, of course. Your accent. That explains it. I should've known." He swallowed hard, sending his Adam's apple up and down under the flaccid skin of his throat. "Still, I don't know who you are. I don't know you. You're mistaken.

You have me confused with somebody else. My name's Fox, David Fox, not…what was it you called me?"

"Fuchs! Klaus Fuchs! You *are* Klaus Fuchs!"

He glared at Jan and shook his head. "Perhaps you have the wrong address. I don't know how you came to the conclusion—"

"No, I'd know you anywhere. Anywhere! You *are* Fuchs. You haven't changed. I'd know that scar anywhere."

Fuchs' eyes narrowed into two slits. The scar on his left cheek darkened, as he reached subconsciously and touched it. "*Scheisse!* I've had enough! How dare you! How *dare* you come here like this! Who do you think you are? You're trespassing! This is my property. I have rights! Helga! Please! Go and call the sheriff!"

The woman didn't move.

"Helga! *Bitte!* Do as I say."

Staring at Jan in terror, she remained frozen in place.

"Go ahead. Call him!" Jan snapped. "Go ahead! I'll be glad to tell him what a sonofabitch you are. Tell the world all about you."

The woman stared at them through liquid eyes, whimpering softly.

"Look, fellow." Fuchs's voice turned nervous, somewhat conciliatory. "I don't know who you are. Don't even know your name. Don't know why you're here, but if it's money you want, I'll give you some. Take it and go, and we'll forget the whole thing." The words rolled out of his throat like gravel.

"What makes you think I want money?" Jan shot back. "My name is Neuman and I don't want your money. But why would you offer me money if you had nothing to hide? It's because you *are* Fuchs!"

Fuchs glowered at him, unblinking. "So what if I am? So what? The war's over. What's it to you?" he sneered.

"You killed my friend." Jan's voice trembled. "You killed my best friend! You sent him and his family, and God know how many others to the concentration camp. And you shot his uncle when he tried to help him. I saw you do it. The whole town saw it. You *made* everybody watch. Remember? I saw you. I saw it all."

"Kill? Your friend?" Fuchs smirked. "I don't remember killing anybody."

"In my town. In Čekaná. You Germans called it Kieseldorf. And you...you were the chief of the SS garrison there. Back in '39 and '40. I was ten years old then."

Fuchs laughed. "Ten years old?"

"Yeah, ten years old, but old enough to understand. You knew my father. You even came to our house a few times and—"

"What! I knew your father? I came to *your* house?"

"Yes. To *our* house. He was a tailor. You made him work for you."

"Huh?" Fuchs's brow furrowed, and then he smirked. "Ah, the little tailor. *Ja*, I remember now. I remember him. A fool, but did good work." He smiled faintly. "So, that was your father? Caught him once listening to London. Could've had him shot."

Jan's jaw dropped open.

"*Surprised?*" Fuchs bared his teeth in a 'gotcha' grimace of a smile.

Dumbstruck, Jan continued to stare at him.

"You don't believe me? Do you think I was stupid? Who do you take me for? You think I didn't know what was going on? You think I didn't know he was listening to London? He and the others? He wasn't very smart. Not a good liar, either, as I recall. I could've had him shot, and his cronies, too. But I didn't." His eyes narrowed. "I could have, but I didn't. I let it go."

Jan remembered that day well: Fuchs walking in late at night; Father scrambling to hide the telltale shortwave antenna; the glowing tubes; the heady smell of ozone; the panic; the waiting for the knock on the door in the middle of the night; the days of unbearable fear; the nights of terror. Was Fuchs sincere or a rat backed into a corner? A self-serving coward? Should he believe him? Did he *want* to believe him? Having always seen him as cruel, despicable, and hateful Nazi, the way he'd always viewed all Nazis, he found the idea of his having a humane, compassionate edge bizarre. "You're a liar! I don't believe you."

"Am I?" Fuchs bared his teeth again, but this time he didn't smile. "Think!"

"Still, that doesn't change anything. You killed my friend. You sent others to their deaths. I haven't forgotten. I could *never* forget. Never!"

Fuchs shook his head. "What can I tell you? It was the war. Wars are ugly, no matter on which side you fight. It's been years. You expect me to remember one little town and one little Jew?"

"His name was Jakub! He had a family!"

"So? I'd been to hundreds little towns. Saw thousands of Jews. It was the war. I had my orders!"

"Orders, huh?" Jan was seething. "It's not enough you killed him. You insult him. You insult him with your lies. And even more by passing yourself off as a Jew." Jan snatched the program from his pocket and thrust it in front of Fuchs's face. "Here! You can't deny *that*! It says so right here!"

Fuchs recoiled, but then a faint smile crossed his scarred face. "Ah, but, you see, I *am* a Jew."

"You? A Jew? That can't be." An invisible hand squeezed Jan's throat. "Jesus! "

"I *am* a Jew. I have always been a Jew." Fuchs looked off and shook his head faintly before returning his gaze to Jan. "I don't expect you to understand. I was a German first and a Jew second. Never a Zionist. Never really practiced. I believed in Germany. It was my country. My home. I loved my country. I was born there. Expected to die there. Was willing to die for her. For my Fatherland. I was a patriot. A believer. I come from a military family. My grandfather was a soldier. My father was a soldier, a *Hauptman*. Killed at Verdun. After he died, I decided to do what I was expected to do. Follow in his footsteps. I was angry then. Young and angry. I suppose like *you* were, back then. Like you are right now, from what you say. And why? Why was I angry?" He glared at Jan, unblinking. "You have no idea.

"Imagine Germany in the '20s. Devastated. Didn't lose the war, but paid the price. Horrible price. Reparations. Social unrest. Hunger. Disease. Inflation. Can you imagine four million marks to a dollar? Can you? Everybody was a millionaire. We carried money in baskets and it still didn't buy anything." He sighed and swallowed hard. "So when Hitler came along, we saw him as a savior. He was our Kennedy. Forgive the reference, but he was. He was our hero. He restored our pride. He gave us self-respect. He had a plan."

"But Jews were persecuted!

554

"*Ja*, but not all Jews. There was a system. You've never heard of *Generalfeldmarschall* Milch? Of course, not. The *real* father of the Luftwaffe. A Jew. And Generals Wilberg and Zuckertort? Jews! And Admiral Rogge, Commander Ascher, Colonel Hollaender—do you want me to go on?"

"But how could they—"

"Because they were patriots. Like me. Answered the call when they were needed. So Hitler himself, and Goering, too, against all odds, decreed them to be Aryans."

"And you? How did *you* manage to stay in the military and out of—" Jan was unable to get the words 'concentration camp' past the lump in his throat.

Fuchs smiled. "*Glücksfall.* Let's just say, I was in a position to make certain papers disappear. We lived in Leipzig then. Helga, my wife, she is from Leipzig. Had a lovely home there. The only problem was her sister. In a mental institution. We never got to *her* papers. Caused us a great deal of grief. They could have gotten us through her. Spent months, many months, living in fear. She was deported to Dachau soon after they began rounding up everybody. Was one of the first. Luckily, for *us* anyway, one day the British bombed the city and wiped out everything. Destroyed all the records. That saved us. We never told our son. So, you see, in the end, especially after the Kristallnacht, it became a question of survival."

"But that doesn't excuse—"

"You *still* don't understand. At first, I didn't object. Fact is, I wanted to go along. Later, I *had* to go, whether I liked it or not. I had a family to protect. We had to survive."

Jan stared at him in disbelief. "Still, Jew or not, how could you do that? Didn't you have any conscience?"

Fuchs continued to glare at him from under his furrowed eyebrows. "I'm sorry about your friend, but I don't apologize. I'm trying to explain. I never stopped being a German. I bled for my country, here," he struck his chest with his fist, "but I could never leave her. I had to follow orders. Do my duty, or risk the lives of my family. Had no choice. If I hadn't done it, someone else would. Do I have regrets? *Ja*. Do I have conscience? You don't believe me, but *ja*. Oh, *ja*. But I can't change the past. The past is past. Gone. Irreversible. I assume you have a family somewhere. Wife, children perhaps. What would *you* have done?"

Jan didn't answer.

"In a way, you and I, we both have paid a price," Fuchs went on. "You lost your country, I lost mine. You lost your friend, I lost my son. On the Russian Front. Only eighteen. Broke our hearts."

The glasses slid to the tip of his beak-like nose and he peered at Jan over their rims. Was there a glimmer in his eye? A tear perhaps? Gazing at him, stooped and disheveled, his spindly legs pale and knobby, face sallow, lined with wrinkles and contorted by age under the stubble, a caricature of his former self, Jan almost felt sorry for him. Almost—until he thought of Jakub.

"You say all these things and I wish I could believe you, but why should I?" He scanned Fuchs's face for some sign of contrition, but found none. "I don't believe you. Just as I don't believe this country would let in criminals like you. Jew or not, you were an SS officer. A Nazi. Fact is, people like you are still being hunted down. Arrested. Tried. Expelled...even worse. They got Eichmann—"

Fuchs shook his head in disbelief. "So that is, perhaps, why you came? Turn me in? Do us harm?" His tone turned icy, cutting. "Let me tell you something. You can believe it or not, don't matter, but let me tell you anyway. You say you saw me in Rome. I don't remember it, but if you did, as you say, I was on my way to Argentina. I was in the Odessa pipeline on my way to Argentina when they got me."

"Odessa." Jan swallowed the word, recalling Gregor's explanation back in the camp after his return from Rome of the SS organization that helped SS soldiers escape to foreign countries, mostly in South America. "When *who* got you?"

"The Americans, of course." He chuckled. "Who do you think? The A-me-ri-cans!" He paused, waiting for the words to sink in. "How do you think I *got* here? Offered me a job. I didn't have to ask—*they* asked me. Begged me. Practically kidnapped me, just like the others: Von Braun, Oberth, Debust, Rudolph, Blome, Schreiber—hundreds of others. Hundreds! They all were, as you say, Nazis. I could go on. Have you never heard of Operation Paperclip?"

Jan looked at him blankly.

"Of course you didn't. Well, look it up, sometimes. You may learn something."

"But why?"

"Why?" He chuckled again. "Who do you think got America the rocket science? Who put America in space? On the moon? Who did America's dirty work in Eastern Europe? Who had the intelligence? The expertise? Who benefited from our medical experiments? Huh? And not only the Americans. Someday, you may find out about the Brits and Operation Unthinkable."

"Did you tell the Americans you were a Jew?"

"Of course not. Not then, anyway. Later, it didn't matter. Eventually, it proved useful. Now they know all about me, probably even more than Helga does. I held the highest security clearances. Did more for America than most Americans. Got medals and awards to prove it." He sighed. "And you? When you saw me at the Pentagon, were you a soldier?"

"Yes, Air Force. Twenty-four years."

Fuchs pursed his lips and nodded faintly a couple of times. "So, you left Czechoslovakia after the war?"

"No, after the communist coup d'état in '48."

Nodding again ever so slightly, Fuchs looked off into the distance. "So now what?"

Jan had not anticipated this turn of events.

Fuchs' voice softened, turning solicitous, almost fatherly. "You're not young any more. I'm an old man. Seems, whether we like it or not, we both spent our lives on the same team. Fighting for the same cause. And what have we accomplished? Nothing. What has changed? Nothing. If anything, it's become harder. Each side has dug in its heels. Your home's still under the communists. Mine, if there is one, is behind the Wall. You can't go back. I can't go back. Not that I'd want to at this stage of my life. Yet, in another way, everything's changed. Just look. Who are America's best friends today, huh? Germany! *Ja*, Germany. And Italy. And Japan. The old Axis. And now even China...*com-mu-nist* China! You and I, we both have spent the better parts of our lives fighting against communism, and now this. Nixon and Kissinger kowtowing to China. It defies all reason. And yet here we are. We've become obsolete. Misfits." His look turned long as his voice trailed off, but then, in a flash, his face drained of color, except for the scar on his cheek. His stare rested on Jan's chest. "That thing under your lapel, what is it? That little clip…and that, is that a wire? Is it a microphone?" Glaring at Jan over his smudged glasses, his veneer of civility vanished. "*Scheiße!* Are you *recording* me?"

Jan stared at him. The caricature of the man before him had in a flash transmogrified into the old Fuchs, the contemptuous, arrogant steely-eyed Nazi barking out orders, brimming people's hearts with terror.

"So that's why you came. To *entrap* me!" His gaze bore into Jan. "What else? To turn me in? To blackmail me?" Beads of sweat glistened on his forehead in the afternoon sun, and he wiped them with the back of his hand and pushed the glasses up to the top if his nose. "You're making a mistake. *Big* mistake. I have connections. Important connections. In the highest places. You can't touch me. Nobody'll believe you. So if you're smart, you'll go, or I *will* call the sheriff. But first, give me the tape. *Now!* Stop the recorder and give me the tape!" He made a couple of nervous beckoning movements with his fingers. *"The tape,* I said!"

Jan didn't budge.

Fuchs made a quick move and whipped a gun out of his satchel. *"The Tape!"*

"I am not armed." Jan's arms instinctively went up a few inches, his sweaty palms turned toward Fuchs. His mind reeled. The Parabellum in Fuchs's hand was just like the one he had used when he shot Jakub's uncle back in Čekaná.

"It's just you and me here," Fuchs hissed. Nobody else around. So, just give me the tape and go, and we both will forget about this. The *tape!*"

Jan shook his head. "I can't."

"You will. I'm not playing games. Helga! Helga! *Bitte.*"

The gray woman stared at them from the deck, eyes wide, mouth open.

"Helga, *bitte*, call the sheriff."

The woman didn't respond.

"Helga!" Fuchs broke the eye contact and shot an angry look at the woman.

Jan's body uncoiled like a spring, and with a heave he went for the gun, smothering Fuchs in a lock, grasping his flailing hand. Wheezing and groaning, they fell to the ground, rolling in the shrubbery, struggling for the gun. A shot rang out, muffled somewhat by their entwined bodies, and Fuchs went limp.

The woman screamed.

Jan stared at Fuchs crumbled at his feet. A small trickle of blood pooled in the dirt. The gun lay next to him, still smoking faintly. The smell of cordite wafted through the air.

The woman came to life. Shrieking at the top of her lungs, she virtually threw herself off the deck and scurried to where Fuchs was laying. *"Oh mein Gott!...oh mein Gott!...oh mein Gott!"* She knelt over Fuchs and raised her knotted hands skyward, crying uncontrollably. *"Oh mein Gott...mein lieber Klaus...oh mein Gott!* What have you done to my Klaus? *Was hast Du gemacht?"* Her tearing eyes flooded with hate. "You killed my man! *Du bist ein Mörder! Mörder! Mörder!"*

The scar on Fuchs's cheek had drained of color, and his face turned pasty, the color of parchment. Jan bent over him and reached out to check his pulse, but the woman screeched and shoved him away. *Mörder! Mörder! Mörder..."* she wailed. *"Oh, mein Gott!"* His mind was reeling. They both grasped the gun. For all he knew, it might have been Fuchs himself who pulled the trigger. But the woman called him murderer, and that is how he would be seen. His word against hers. An unwinnable situation. He felt sick. And then panic set in. In one swoop, he kicked the gun into the bushes and ran, stopping just long enough at the house to yank the wires out of the telephone junction box.

Behind him, the woman continued to scream, *Mörder, Mörder, Mörder…*"

Driving like a madman, bouncing over ruts and potholes, physically exhausted and emotionally drained, he reached the ferry landing, boarded without incident, and remained in the car, sliding down low in the seat as other passengers filed by. Finally, he became aware of the hard bulge in his pocket. The recorder, still running. Fuchs's confession. He turned it off.

CHAPTER 76

The grey woman's *Mörder, Mörder, Mörder* echoed in Jan's mind as he merged into the line of ferry traffic moving briskly along a narrow winding road leading to town. His mind continued to replay the terrible scene. One thing was certain; he had to get off the island as quickly as possible. From around the bend, a flashing red light came into view and the tail lights of the cars ahead began to glow as they frantically yielded way. Nerves on edge, he pulled off to the side and held his breath, as moments later a police car whizzed by at high speed, light flashing but siren silenced, heading in the direction of the ferry landing. Someone behind him honked and he realized that he had sat there in a stupor, paralyzed, not noticing that traffic had resumed. He was drenched in sweat.

The old man looked up from a newspaper when he walked into the motel office. "Ah, Mister Neuman!" He smiled. "Something I can do for you?"

"Yes. Something came up, and I need to leave very early in the morning. My flight leaves SeaTac at 6," he lied, "so I have to be outa here no later than 3. Would like to check out tonight, if it's possible."

"I take it you didn't find your friend?"

Jan shrugged and smiled.

The man nodded knowingly, scratched his head, and sighed. "That'll be thirty dollars then. Have to charge you for tonight. Just leave the key on the table."

Jan felt the man's gaze following him as he walked to his room, locked it, slipped the recorder and the tape into the lead-lined bag, and repacked the suitcase. Making sure the old man was gone, he slipped the bag into the trunk and drove out into the falling night. His churning stomach reminded him that he hadn't eaten all day. He pulled up at the Hatch Cover, found a dark booth at the back across the bar, and ordered fish and chips. The blaring of the television, mixed with the lively chatter of the patrons, suddenly faded as the set went silent, and a news bulletin sign flashed across the screen. The camera switched to a harried announcer shuffling some papers, and then, seeing that he was on, smiling apologetically:

*Forgive me, folks, but this just in. Authorities have been called to a site of what appears to be a robbery-murder on Orcas Island. The facts are sketchy at this time. All we know is that a retired high government official has been shot during an apparent robbery attempt. The assailant disabled the telephone line as he left, but the victim's wife was able to contact the Coast Guard over the VHF radio on their boat, and the Coast Guard in turn notified the authorities. The victim was airlifted to a hospital and is in critical condition because of a massive loss of blood from the gunshot wound. The assailant is described as a white male in his mid to late forties, possibly speaking with a foreign accent. Authorities caution that he may be armed. Our reporters are on the way to the scene and as soon as we have more details, will report them to you. Again, a retired high-level government official is in a hospital fighting for his life...*The announcer repeated the story.

There was a momentary hush as he finished, but gradually the patrons returned to their food and interrupted chatter. Jan was stunned. So Fuchs wasn't dead! He might even survive! He felt a mixture of relief and chagrin, wishing he could stay and watch the news for further developments, but reason spiked with fear won out. Gulping down his food, he paid the waitress, and feigning nonchalance strolled out into the street, feeling exposed and vulnerable. With a sigh of relief, he slid behind the wheel and, resisting a temptation to speed, cautiously headed toward the highway out of town. Passing the familiar street, he caught a glimpse of his motel and gasped. A police car was idling next to the office and a policeman was talking to the old man.

The traffic picked up, as it had each time a ferry landed, and he joined the procession, finding safety and anonymity in the numbers. Cresting a small rise above the bridge separating the island from the mainland, he gulped and instinctively slammed on the brakes. Lights flashing, a pair of State Police cruisers blocked the way, with two troopers checking papers. Heart pounding, he swung onto a side road and checked the map. It showed two other roads leading off the island: one crossing a small bridge spanning the channel at its southernmost end of an Indian reservation, and the other connecting adjacent Whidbey Island at a place called Deception Pass.

Somber and deserted, the reservation road ran straight among tall stands of old-growth cedars, hemlock, and a curtain of thick undergrowth, virtually impenetrable in places, widening only to form an occasional shallow clearing with a dilapidated hut tucked away in its niche, or a faint lane leading deeper into its bowels. He stepped on the gas and focused on dodging the chuckholes that kicked up small torrents of sand and gravel where the asphalt had worn off as he hurtled over them. When he next looked up into the rear view mirror, he saw a flashing red light almost on top of him, coming fast.

His heart raced. It was over! He had been found! The blood drained from his face. His body went limp. Instinct told him to run, but where? How? He couldn't outrun the trooper, and on this narrow stretch there was no turnoff, not even a place to pull off—the shoulder dropped off sharply into a muddy ditch and beyond it, an intertwined maze of bramble. Shaking all over, he resigned himself to his fate. Pulling as close as he could to the side, he expected the flashing light to pull up behind him, but the cruiser streaked past without even slowing down, spraying his car with a shower of stones. A few seconds later, it disappeared behind a bend.

Shaking, he stared into the void, realizing how lucky he was. They still didn't know his car! It left him weak, but relieved. But the reservation bridge was out. That left only the Deception Pass, his last hope. True, Whidbey too was an island, but a huge one, and he could easily get lost on it, hide, wait things out, or with any luck, even make his way into Seattle and the mainland from its southern tip by way of a ferry. He swung the car around at the next clearing and headed back toward town.

Deception Pass traffic was sparse and moving smartly. It buoyed him somewhat. The way seemed clear as the soaring span came into view, but then a red flash from behind the scrub on the other side of the bridge caused him to slam on the brakes and swing into one of the pullouts, heart racing. A trooper, flashlight in hand, was directing cars into a parking enclave. He was trapped.

Fighting panic and trying not to speed, he turned around and followed a winding coastal road until it narrowed at a headland overlooking the strait, found a brush-covered turn-off camouflaged by shrubbery, and parked. Ahead of him, the sea was a stream of indigo, with the craggy silhouettes of islands resembling a flotilla of battleships. Somewhere beyond them, the Pacific. He thought of the day on a windblown Normandy shore when he saw the ocean for the first time, and how it had awed him then, as it did now. Now as then, he felt he stood at the edge of the world, and again, the horizon beckoned. Again, the sky and the water became one. A line of murrelets skimmed the waves, flying by silently to destination unknown. He envied them. A chill breeze made him shudder. Unseen and unheard, he was relatively safe here, finally able to collect his thoughts, all of which had a single focus: Fuchs. Alive. At least for now. But what if he dies? It's ironic, but in a way, Fuchs held his future in his hands. If Fuchs were to die, he would be forever seen as a murderer. A wanted man. On the run. The confession would have little value. If anything, it would hurt. His word against the grey woman's. She only saw Fuchs go down. She would be credible. They'd believe her before they'd believe him. But if Fuchs were to live, he would have to face Jan in court. Answer questions. Defend his confession. Would he want to risk it? What if he was bluffing about being untouchable? About friends in high places? If he wasn't, why would he pull the gun? That was no bluff. Was he afraid? Of what? Was there something he had kept from the Americans? From his patrons? Things that might come out in a trial? The confession could be credible. It could cost him. Expose him. Maybe more. But if he were to die, Jan's fate would be sealed. He wouldn't stand a chance against the word of the grey woman. He could still hear her in his head: *Mörder! Mörder! Mörder!* He needed Fuchs to live! And above all, he needed to stay free. Run! Hide! But where?

CHAPTER 77

More comfortable under the cover of the night, he once again joined the traffic and drove out to the main bridge. The flashing lights were still there. There was no point trying the other crossings. Turning around, he drove back to the marina, parked in an inconspicuous place, and cautiously walked out on the dock. It was deserted. Only the creaking of the docks and the splashing of the water broke the silence. The old boat was still there, tugging gently at its mooring. He swung aboard and felt the coaming pocket for the keys. They were where the salesman had left them. He unlocked the hatch and slipped inside.

The air inside the boat was stale. He flipped the big red master switch and turned on a small red map light to get his bearing. The heavy curtains shielding the portholes were drawn shut and he breathed a sigh of relief. A pile of Skip Nordlund's business cards still littered the galley counter. A chart with a pencil and a ruler where someone had left them lay unrolled on the navigation table. A pair of foul-weather suits lay crumpled on one of the berths. The ship's log and a stack of neatly arranged books, held in place by a bungee, filled the shelf above the navigation table. A felt-lined lacquered box revealed a sextant. Bags of sails filled the forepeak. The lockers overflowed with gear and provisions. It appeared as though the former skipper had just walked out and would return at any moment. He could hide here for the night. He turned off the light and collapsed on a bunk. The boat under him swayed gently, and the rocking calmed his nerves. He lay there, staring into the darkness, contemplating his options, when suddenly he saw the way out of the impasse. It was so simple and yet so audacious it gave him a chill. His body went limp with the thought.

For years, he had been salting away a little money whenever he could spare it, and now, with his mustering-out pay, could easily match Skip Nordlund's quote. His hand trembled as he wrote a check to Cove Marine and a note to Skip asking him to forward the sale and registration documents to Jurai's address in California, slipped both into an envelope, and climbed out into the crisp air. The coast was clear. Dazed, almost breathless, he walked to the Cove Marine office. It was deserted and locked at this hour, but there was a mail slit in the door. He hesitated, but then, overcoming the bursting pressure in his chest and numbing buzz in his head, lifted the brass cover and dropped the envelope through the slit. Coming back, he pulled the suitcase from the trunk of the rental and, with a sigh, locked the keys inside. Now, there *was* no way back. He was committed.

Off to the side of the harbor was the harbormaster's office, now dark and locked, but the adjoining kiosk with a public telephone was lit. When he was sure the coast was clear, he placed a collect call to Jurai.

"What's going on? How come the collect call? So late? Where are you? Are you all right?" Jurai's voice quivered with concern.

He proceeded to recount sketchily the day's happenings, his inability to leave the island, his purchasing the sailboat. "So I will try to contact you when I get to San Francisco or some place along the coast," he said, "and when you bring the papers, I'll tell you the whole story. For now, would you call

Jana and your mother? Tell them? Explain? If all goes well, I'll see you in a couple of weeks. Wish me luck."

   *   *   *

The darkness provided a perfect cover as Jan untied the mooring lines and nudged the boat out of the slip. For all its heft, it responded easily, almost eagerly. He tethered her briefly to a piling, carefully hoisted the sails, sheeted them in, let go of the tether and, pushed by a building breeze, headed silently out of the marina.

Caught by the outgoing tide, he sensed the surge in speed. In the wind shadow of the looming cape, far enough not to he heard, he flipped the switch and pushed the starter. To his great relief, the diesel turned over after a few sputters and quickly settled into a muffled rhythm. The boat surged ahead, meeting the light chop of the channel with ease. He rounded the forested headland where he had stood only hours earlier, bore off to port and into the strait, and turned off the engine. The sails filled with a dull thump. Responding to the nudge of the tiller, the boat healed gently and settled into the steady rhythm of a long starboard reach. Only a sprinkling of sharp unblinking pinpoints of light hinted at the dark mass of the island to his port. A pair of smaller islands slid into the darkness behind him. The wind shifted, and the dark craggy hint of a coastline fell astern, blending with the night.

At the crack of dawn, after a bit of tinkering, he succeeded in setting the self-steering vane. From the stores under the settee, he pulled out a can of Spam and devoured it. Nothing had ever tasted better. He made coffee and turned on the radio. To his surprise, the familiar strains of Dvořák's *New World*

Symphony from a Canadian station filled the cockpit—the perfect send-off. He took it as an omen.

Continuing to sail westward, he hugged the Canadian shore, fighting the tide, and eagerly spinning the dial every hour to pick up the news. Finally the announcer's sonorous voice told him what he had hoped to hear: *"...In other news, the high-government official, whose name remains classified and who was the victim of attempted robbery-murder on Orcas Island, has been airlifted to the Seattle Olympic Medical Center, where he will undergo additional surgeries to repair severe internal damage. He remains in serious condition but is expected to live. Search for his assailant continues. He is reported to be a white middle-aged male speaking with a foreign accent, with dark hair and..."* Jan turned off the radio and realized he was shaking with relief.

The sun dove into the sea, sprinkling the waves with a shower of liquid gold in a long, undulating path, beckoning him to follow. With the wind caressing his face and the boat alive under his feet, he felt reborn. Until now, he had been adrift in the world, without any permanent harbor. The military life was all he knew. But while the Air Force gave him a sense of belonging, it also left him without a sense of place. The only roots he had ever known and really yearned for, the only two things he still felt attached to, were unattainable—his home behind the Iron Curtain, and Majda. With her, he could have lived anywhere. But that wasn't to be. She still wrote now and then, and the scent of lilacs sent his heart racing. But reading between the lines, he detected a mounting tone of desperation, and ultimately resignation. Now, at long last, he had found his place. His world. His life reduced to essentials. Surrounded by a roiling expanse of the ocean, it was the only concrete thing that mattered, that made sense. It gave him a measure of belonging, but most of all, it restored his self-respect. He was the mover now, in control of his fate, in concert with the ocean, in concert with the world—in concert with the universe. The world was his destiny.

Perusing the books on the shelf – navigation tables, manuals, routes and passages, a few novels – he spotted one he had read before, Huxley's *Brave New World*. He had treasured a copy for years, re-reading it now and then, feeling a kinship with the hapless hero, Savage, a curiosity and a foreigner in his own land, a misfit like himself. A true kindred spirit.

He slid below and came up with a bottle of faux champagne covered by netting, the kind sold by marine stores for the christening of boats—one the former skipper never got to use. Tethered to a jackline, he made his way carefully to the bow where a massive anchor lay snubbed in its chocks. Hard pressed to keep his balance on the undulating deck, he flung the bottle at the metal, and as it shattered into a shower of luminescent fragments, proclaimed solemnly and jubilantly, "I hereby christen thee *Savage*."

CHAPTER 78

The shiny Mercedes bus looked incongruous as it emerged from the green curtain of the Guatemalan jungle and came to a stop on the outskirts of Rio Dulce, a small hamlet whose dominant feature was a soaring concrete bridge spanning a short but swift-flowing river of the same name. Spilling out of Lago Izabal on its short course to the Caribbean, the river and the town had acquired a reputation as an ideal 'hurricane hole,' and it was why its three marinas overflowed with an eclectic collection of wanderers thrown together by a common desire to wait out the hurricane season.

Jan had arrived at Marina el Paraiso only a week ago, during the waning days of September, having spent weeks crossing the Pacific and transiting the Panama Canal on his way to Houston to renew his expiring passport. He arrived too late to safely cross the Gulf and had decided to wait for a spring weather window before continuing. He didn't want to take the chance since the 1989 hurricane season was already well under way and the storms were particularly heavy because of the *La Niña*. The time at Rio Dulce would be well spent performing the perpetually needed maintenance on *Savage* and visiting Tikal, the Mayan ruins he'd always wanted to see. In the spring, he hoped to meet Jana and Jurai in Corpus Christi, and make up for lost time somewhere on the Padre Island and its pristine expanses of beaches. He needed to reconnect with them, see them in person. All he could do during his years of wandering was to rely on the mail and an occasional phone call—an unsatisfactory arrangement owing to the uncertainty of his itinerary, contingent on the weather, and the vagaries of the postal systems in the out-of-the-way places he visited. Today, he boarded the bus to take him to Morales, the district capital some twenty miles inland, to visit the post office and check for mail.

A heavily armed guard met him at the entrance and followed him inside, measuring him with a curious frown. The clerk behind the counter diligently studied his passport for several moments, and then retreated to a large box marked *Poste Restante* at the back of the counter. After some rummaging, he returned with two envelopes: one from Jurai, and the other from Majda. Both bore time stamps more than three months old. "You're lucky. Normally, we send them back after three months," the clerk said, handing them to him. "In case you didn't know."

Jan thanked him and walked out into the square, filled with hawkers and tortilla vendors. He had a two-hour wait for the return bus, so he found a small café, ordered a drink, and with shaking hands opened Majda's envelope. The expected whiff of lilac was not there, nor was there a letter. Instead, the single sheet of paper carefully folded revealed a bold black-bordered imprint, and he realized he was looking at a *parte*, a death notice still used by some of the 'old country' immigrant communities. A stabbing chill ran up his spine as he stared at the simple announcement. Stepan, Majda's husband, was dead.

Jurai's letter provided details. Stepan's health had improved somewhat as he remained in Majda's care, with regular visits to the Veterans Administration Medical Center there in Richmond. One day she found him sitting in the garden, unconscious, the result of an aneurism. He died on the operating table in the VA hospital and was buried at the Richmond

573

National Cemetery with full military honors. "May God bless his soul," Jurai concluded. "He never knew I knew."

* * *

Jan first got an inkling that something momentous was underfoot on a steamy November morning after a pelting rain made sleeping late that much sweeter. A pounding on the *Savage's* hull got him up in a hurry.

"Hey, Yank, you up? Are you awake?" a familiar voice bellowed as the pounding resumed. "Hey, Yank, get up!"

"I'm up. What's up?" Jan half-rose sleepily and then sat up, recognizing the voice of his neighbor, a Brit by the name of Harold.

"Hey, Yank, if you don't hurry, you'll miss it! C'mon! It's important!" Harold sounded almost frantic.

Jan didn't mind being called Yank, since he was the only American in the tiny marina and *Savage* carried American registry. He and a handful of other itinerant mariners had shared stories of their pasts during the lazy days of waiting out the season, usually in the large *palapa* that doubled as a bar, restaurant, meeting place, and marina office, where the center of attention was a large television set, usually tuned to the weather channel.

"What's going on?" Jan slid back the hatch and came face to face with the heavy-breathing Harold.

"Sorry, old chap. It's on the telly. You'll see when we get there. Hurry. C'mon!"

Heavy drops from last night's rain dripped onto the rickety wooden floor from the thickly layered palm fronds forming the *palapa's* roof as Jan and Harold rushed in. Stretched on loungers and sipping coffee, two other sailors already there nodded to them without taking their gazes off the screen. It showed a huge crowd raucously jingling their keys, chanting slogans, waving tricolor flags. Jan felt his throat tighten as the camera zoomed out, revealing a large equestrian statue of St. Wenceslaus seeming to float above the sea of humanity. He knew the place—Wenceslaus Square in Prague—now filled to overflowing with Czechs chanting, *Svobodu! Svobodu!* Freedom! Freedom—laughing and crying under a sea of fluttering Czechoslovak flags.

"I was afraid you'd miss it. That anyplace near where you're from?" Harold nudged him, grinning broadly. "I knew you'd want to know."

Jan gaped at the spectacle until the screen flickered and the announcer came back on with the rest of the news. The latent image of what he had just seen stayed fixed vividly before his mind's eye. Could he believe what he just saw? Could he believe his eyes? Or was he still asleep and it just a dream? Was the impossible really happening? For all these years, the communist regime in his homeland seemed as solid and impenetrable as the Iron Curtain that shrouded it. Home, when he thought of it at all, had become but a wisp of nostalgia, a static set of images bleached sepia by time. He had resigned himself to Fate, that great unpredictable mover that had toyed with him and shaped his life in ways he could have never imagined. He had long ago stopped expecting he would return.

Harold's voice jarred him back to reality. "Well, what do you say, old chap? Wasn't that smashing? I'm so glad we didn't miss it. What do you make of it?"

Grinning, eyes glistening, a stray tear rolling down his cheek, he was enthralled by the image of roaring crowd and fluttering flags.

"I say, does it mean you can go back now? Can you go home?"

"I don't know. I don't know." His voice broke. "Depends how it all plays out. It's so hard to believe. I never thought...It's been so long." His mind already leapt ahead to getting the boat ready, dodging the storms up the Belize coast, pausing at the tip of the Yucatán, and then finally making the jaunt across the Gulf when a weather window opened. Sometimes after Christmas, probably early spring. Putting *Savage* on the hard somewhere, most likely at Corpus where he'd berthed before, and then...oh my God, then— He shuddered at the very prospect of it all.

CHAPTER 79

The Gulf greeted Jan first with mountainous swells – the aftermath of a storm – that robbed *Savage* of wind in their troughs, making progress under sail almost impossible, and then with steep and confused seas, when the north-flowing Gulf Stream collided with a procession of lows barreling in from the Texas plains.

On the fifth day, the inky night sky ahead turned flickering yellow, and then, one by one, glimmering dots of light emerged from beyond the horizon. The air turned foul. When he got closer, they transmogrified into massive platforms ablaze in lights, with spidery derricks burning off gasses.

At the crack of dawn of the seventh day, he reached the buoy marking the entrance to the Intracoastal Waterway and followed a procession of red and green buoys into the Corpus Christi municipal marina. It was deserted at this hour and he regretted the noise of his diesel shattering the idyllic peace. He guided *Savage* carefully through the forest of masts to the harbormaster's office when a ghostly silhouette materialized from the patchy fog drifting above the harbor. It couldn't be Jurai, he surmised as he headed for a guest slip. He had called him from Isla Mujeres on the Yucatan, but did not expect him to be here, since he had missed his estimated time of arrival by more than four days because of the storm. The figure became more distinct and he drew a deep breath, realizing it was a woman. A tingling stab of recognition shot through his spine. Quickening her pace, she turned toward *Savage* and waved. His belly filled with flutter. There was no way. It couldn't be. It *couldn't* be! But it was. Even from a distance he knew it was Majda!

She reached the slip, hesitated, and stopped. "Don't you recognize me? I am—"

"Oh, God! Of course I do!" His heart raced. How many times he had imagined such a moment when he permitted himself to daydream, and now that it was really happening, he could only stammer. "It's just I didn't expect—"

"Jurai told me you were coming. They weren't sure when at the office. Said you were overdue. So, I've been coming every day. I didn't think you'd mind." Her forehead wrinkled.

"I just don't know what to say. It's been so long. Years!" He smiled and the furrows disappeared from her brow.

He helped her into the cockpit, and as the boat swayed under their feet and she lost her balance, caught her in an awkward embrace. She stiffened and he relaxed his hold.

Her pallid face felt soft against his tanned skin as her hair, still curly but sprinkled with grey, brushed against his cheek. "It's been a long time. Forgive me," she said, apologizing with her eyes, still pale blue but filled with sadness from behind a frame of deep shadows.

They gazed at each other awkwardly, the way strangers might, unsure of what to say. He offered her coffee, and she accepted with a smile. He rolled up a chart spread on the table, and they sipped the brew, avoiding each other's gaze. Tension mounted with the silence.

"Reminds me of the place on the river when we first met," she finally said, gazing out the porthole over the water. "Not there anymore. Burned down."

"I am sorry about Stepan," he said. "Sincerely. I mean it."

She looked up at him and burst into tears.

"I missed you," he sighed, offering her a handkerchief. "You can't imagine how much."

She wiped her eyes and took his hand. "I missed you, too. Terribly. I saved all your letters. They gave me strength. I wouldn't have survived without them. Whenever I'd receive one or a post card from some exotic place, I'd imagine myself with you. I know I'd sent you away and it pains me. I have no right to expect..." Her voice broke and she suppressed a sob. "Still..."

He cupped her hand. "I would read your letters and sense the despair in them, and see the futility of it all. Lost all hope of meeting you again. I still have every single one. I used to fantasize, imagine meeting you again...seeing you, but now that we have, I feel like a stranger."

"Oh, *carino*. But I haven't changed."

"Neither have I. I mean my feelings. But it's been years. Twelve years. Things happened. Our lives have changed. Things could have been different if—" He caught himself and looked at her sadly. "Sorry."

She looked away. "Have you come to stay?"

"Just long enough to renew my passport and store the boat. Jurai didn't tell you? You must've heard what happened in my old country, in Russia, in Europe. The Cold War. It's over."

"Yes..." Her voice fluttered.

"My parents are dead, have been for years. But there's the house. My home. They struggled incredibly to keep it. Would have wanted me to have it. Hoped that I'd return. So I must go and see if it's still there. It's the only place that still touches me. Emotionally, I mean. I have to live with my conscience, so I have to do this. I *have* to go."

She looked at him forlornly through glistening eyes. Her lip quivered slightly. "After all these years..."

"There's something you have to understand. This is a wonderful country. It's given me a good life. But being in the Service did strange things to me. With all the moving around, here, there...overseas, I never felt like I belonged. Like I belonged anywhere. No roots. No friends. Except Richmond, once. And now, this boat." He smiled faintly, but her eyes clouded. "Maybe I am deluding myself, but the only place I still think of is the place I grew up in. My home."

Wiping a tear from her cheek, she nodded absently. "I understand. I didn't have much time to think while Stepan was alive...took up all my time. But now, without my parents, I feel lost."

"What about Trieste? You could go back now."

She replied with a long anguished look. "Back to what? It's not home any more. There's nothing there for me. No family, no friends. Nothing." She looked away and fell silent, and then, turning to him, said hoarsely, "Do you plan to stay?"

He shrugged. "That'll depend on what I'll find or what I'll decide to do."

Her eyes became two dark pools. "And what about the children?"

"They're grown. They have their own lives."

She reached out to him. "Take me with you." Her voice quivered.

An icy pulse shot through his body. He brushed her hand with his lips. "I love you. I never stopped loving you. But I couldn't ask you to waste your life, to give up all this. You deserve better. I have nothing to offer. Don't know what I'm going to find. What the future will be. It wouldn't be fair. And even if I'd come back, I couldn't live in Richmond, or anywhere. I told you how I feel. I don't have anything except this little boat. I couldn't ask you—"

"Would you go back to sea then?"

"I might. It may sound selfish, but I've grown to like it. Like it a lot. There's a big world out there. Amazing places that welcome you. Embrace you. Make you feel alive. People are poor but kind, the way I remember my home. Simpler, but fuller lives. No stresses. No wars. No problems, at least not the kind that can't be handled."

"I'd like to share it with you. I'll go anywhere you go. I'll live anywhere you live. I'll come, if you'll have me."

He wilted under her look. "God knows I want to. You know I love you, but I have nothing else to offer you. No security, no place to live, except this little boat. I don't know what I'll find in the republic, if I'll find anything. And the sea doesn't forgive. It can be incredibly beautiful, but it can also be incredibly dangerous. Terrifying. So much so, you can't imagine. We could die."

"I don't care. I've been dead for years. Now, I feel alive again. We can't keep saying good-byes to each other. Time flies. We could be left with nothing but regrets. This could be our last chance. I want us to be together, no matter what. Until the end."

Her gaze rested on him, boring into his very soul as he considered her words. "I have to do this alone, but I'll be back, no matter what. And when I get back, will you marry me?" he said softly.

She froze and blanched for an instant, and then burst out crying and collapsed in his embrace, and he felt the salt of her tears as she smothered him with kisses.

"I'll never let you go," he whispered.

The reunion with Jurai and Jana was exhilarating. Seeing them brought tears to his eyes. Both were elated when he and Majda told them about their plans. "I don't think you have to worry about Fuchs," Jurai said, when the conversation turned to the old Nazi. "No one ever came and asked about you. Seems to me I'd be the first one they'd question about your whereabouts, that sort of a thing. But nothing. I checked around, called, and they told me that he fully recovered and is back to the islands. So I wouldn't be concerned, if I were you."

"Still, I think I'd better take a copy of his confession with me. Will you keep the original for me? Just in case."

That night, Majda offered herself to him, first with her eyes and then with her body. As they lay together in gentle embrace, he again breathed in a scent of lilacs. Their lovemaking was gentle, almost tentative, the way he remember it during their first encounter there in the camp in Germany, some forty years ago. It seemed an eternity.

She accompanied him to Houston to get his passport and later to the airport when he was leaving, and hugged him desperately as he boarded. "I'll be here waiting for you when you come back," were the last words he heard.

EPILOGUE

The lights of Houston fell away and the whine of the Lufthansa Boeing 747 powerful engines dropped a notch as the plane settled into its cruising speed and turned eastward toward the Atlantic. Jan slouched in his seat, eyes closed, but sleep was out of the question. If anything, he was feeling a touch of nausea. After forty years, he was going home. Going home! Just the thought gave him the shakes.

The young woman in the seat next to him stirred and yawned. She reminded him of Jana. Their eyes met and he gave her an encouraging smile. "Long night," he said.

She blushed. "It's my first trip overseas. Are you German?"

He shook his head. "No, American, but born in Czechoslovakia. And you?"

"I'm from Austin. Got a job teaching at the American High School in Wiesbaden. Don't speak German. Don't know anything about Germany." She smiled timidly. "Is it—"

"You'll like it. It's all modern now. Not what it used to be...what it was like when I first saw it. Back in '48."

"Forty eight? That's—"

"Forty years. Forty years ago. Before you were born, I'm sure."

She puckered her brow. "You said you were born in Yugoslavia—"

"Czechoslovakia," he corrected her, soothing her embarrassment with a smile. "I was a student back then, probably younger than you are now, and an activist. You might say, a political activist. There was a coup, an overthrow of our government by the communists, and I would have been jailed if

583

I'd stayed. So I escaped to Germany. Spent a couple of years in refugee camps. Was fortunate to immigrate to America."

Her gaze clouded and she nodded. "So why are you flying to Germany?"

"You know, the Cold War's over. The regime at home has changed. So, I thought I'd go back and see. Retrace my steps. Close the circle, so to speak."

The young woman fell asleep and he himself finally drifted off, not knowing how long he slept, but he woke up with a start as the plane dipped in altitude. It was an automatic reflex, developed over years as a single-hander. Sailing alone, he was used to sleeping lightly and in spurts, with the alarm clock always at the ready. It had sharpened his senses and attuned him to his environment, to anything out of the ordinary, whether it was the sudden flagging of the sail, the change in the hissing sound of the boat going through the waves or of the wind in the rigging, or the dreaded sound of the surf on a lee shore. Anything out of the ordinary made him react, because any change might portend danger. He let out a sigh of relief, realizing he was not aboard his boat but in an airplane about to land.

He pressed his face against the window and watched as the countryside below rose up as if to greet him. His coming was an impulsive act. Now that he had had a little time to reflect, sober thoughts intruded. What would he find? His father was dead, as was his favorite uncle Alois, so there would be no one to greet him. He was the last one. Still, the desire was overpowering, almost primeval, like that of migrating birds that travel thousands of miles to the places of their birth, or like the salmon that brave countless dangers to reach the headwaters of their origin, only to die.

The plane landed with a thump and taxied to the Frankfurt terminal. The young woman wished him luck and disappeared with the Army escort who met her at the gate. By the time he cleared Customs and picked up a rental, the lights in the great bustling city were coming on. There was no point going any further tonight. He found a Novotel near the autobahn and letting go of all his emotions, tired to the bone, fell into a dreamless death-like sleep.

*   *   *

The rolling countryside around Regensburg was just as he remembered—a checkerboard of raw-earth fields emerging from their wintry slumber. Yet, the city itself had changed, a vibrant metropolis in place of the piles of rubble and bleak streets he had once wandered after his harrowing escape. No traces of the Goethestrasse camp where he had spent the first days of his exile, only a modern school alive with children's voices. The ghosts of the past were gone. The two villages, Bishofsreuth and Heidmühle, he had once viewed with distress through the periscope with his father from atop the tall mountain were now peaceful pastoral picture postcards. He thought fleetingly about the wizened farmer and his family in the mountains who took him in as he ran for his life under a hail of bullets. No doubt they, too, were gone. All the relics of those times had vanished. Now he was the relic.

The sun was high in the sky when he finally reached the border. A single German customs man waved him off when he tried to hand him his passport, but a passel of guards spilled from a lichen-covered bunker when he reached the Czech side.

His heart fluttered as he passed under his country's flag – his flag – swaying in the breeze over the roadway.

"Halt! Documents!" One of the guards stepped into the road with his arm raised, while the others just stood there, glaring at him with mistrust.

Jan handed him his passport. Dressed in Russian-style uniforms, looking surly under their saucer-like hats, the guards eyed him with a frosty stare. *Only a few weeks ago, they'd probably have gladly put a bullet through me,* he reflected, a chill crawling up his spine.

"American, eh?" The guard gave a sneer.

"A Czech. I'm a Czech. I was born here—"

"American. It says American here." The guard cut him off. "Where are you going?"

"Čekaná."

"Čekaná? Why Čekaná?" The guard raised his eyebrows.

"It's my home. I was born there," Jan retorted.

"Number? Address?"

He shrugged.

"When you get there, you must register at the District office, understand? Within two days."

"Yes, of course," Jan replied in Czech.

The guard grinned widely. "So you still speak the language, eh? You speak with a foreign accent." He chortled. "What's in the bag?"

"Just personal stuff."

"Open it."

Jan opened his suitcase and the guard poked in it before letting the lid down with a grunt. "Forty dollars. Every foreigner must pay forty dollars."

Smirking, the guard pocketed the money and lazily touched the bill of his hat with two fingers in a salute as Jan drove away from the guardhouse, followed by the glare of a half a dozen condescending eyes.

The highway ahead was rutted. Passing a huge scar bulldozed into the undulating landscape, dotted with vast piles of wire fence and concertina wire, and remnants of what he guessed had been guard towers, Jan realized that these were what was left of the electrified barrier that was the Iron Curtain, designed to keep the 'enemy' out and people like him in. Until a few weeks ago, he was the enemy.

The road snaked past deserted homesteads and lifeless villages, all the while skirting the mountain where as a young boy he had visited his father at the gun emplacements before the start of the war. The serpentine access road leading up to the bunkers was still there, as were the tank traps, now lichen-covered and crumbling. The mountain, broodingly enmeshed in mist, foreboding and mysterious, still overwhelmed him.

The sun was dipping when he finally reached the turn where the road dove into the valley and stretched, arrow-like, under a swaying canopy of poplars, toward his town. The closer he got, the more difficult it was for him to suppress his expectations. He felt like a child at Christmas. Shivering, chest tightening, he drove down the familiar street. And then there it was—his house, his home, incredibly just like the day he left: the same pink stucco with white trim and red-tiled roof, and geranium boxes in the windows, and the gate and the cobblestone passageway. Everything. It was all there. Untouched. Nothing had changed. Nothing!

Was he *dreaming*? Had his memory been playing a trick on him? Light-headed and flushed all over, he looked around in disbelief. And then panicked. Feeling suddenly like an interloper, he gunned the motor and, spinning the wheels on the little Ford in the loose gravel, took off, driving randomly through town, past Jakub's house, still there but the store front cemented over, past the Clauder manor, still pristine behind its high stone wall, past the river, no longer a frolicking stream but a muddy rivulet full of slimy algae, past the silo near the railroad station, still riddled with bullet holes from the strafing by the American P-38s he'd survived back in '45, past the old synagogue, now a hollow decaying hulk with its windows knocked out and roof caving in, past the town square, now shabby under the perpetually resplendent canopy of lindens. It was all there, precisely as he remembered. Everything. Except one thing: The bleak, deserted streets had a decaying feel about them. The life had gone out of his town.

Finally, he pulled up at his house again and stepped out. He thought he saw a curtain move. The door in the house next to his creaked open and a wizened old man ambled out. "Are you looking for someone?" he said, measuring Jan suspiciously.

Relieved to see a face, Jan smiled. "I used to live here."

"Here? You used to live here?" The man's gaunt face screwed in astonishment and he rubbed his eyes a couple of times before returning his glare to Jan. "Then you wouldn't be—"

"Jan Neuman. I used to live here. This was my home."

The man swallowed hard a couple of times. "Then you remember me. I am Zdeněk. Or maybe you don't remember? We went to grade school together when we were kids, remember?" He gave a short, wheezing laugh and shook his head in mock disbelief. "Jan Neuman. Jan Neu-man. Who would have thought?" He scowled. "But you're a little late."

"Zdeněk?" Jan was taken aback, unable to accept the wreck of a man before him as his peer. Time had not been kind to him—he was aged beyond his years. But his disdainful look and acrid words stung. "What can I say? I know, but I couldn't—"

"You know your old man was jailed after you left? Came back broken. Sure could've used you here. Lived there all alone. I watched him every day. In the end, couldn't even walk, take care of himself. Couldn't do anything for himself."

"I told you I couldn't—"

"Yeah!" Zdeněk spat deliberately into the dust.

"Couldn't you—wasn't there someone who would, could have helped? I couldn't—"

"Helped?" He laughed again and spat in the dust. "You don't understand. Nobody would even speak to him. Much less help him. Because of you. He was watched. Was treated like a leper. People were afraid. Suffered while you were out there in America living it up like a *king*."

Jan averted his gaze and drew a deep breath, fighting the thickness in his throat. He wanted to shout, *What right do you have,* but instead managed only a terse laugh. "Living like a king you say? You have no idea—"

"He sure could've used you. If more of you had stayed behind, things could have been different. Could've ended sooner."

Though seething inside, Jan didn't want to be drawn into an argument. "I really don't know what I could have done. You *know* what they would've done to me. I don't want to argue with you, but—"

A young blue-eyed, flaxen-haired, pink-cheeked girl ran out of Jan's house into the street, stopped short, and gawked at them with childish curiosity.

The curtain moved again and a young disheveled swarthy man rushed out into the street. "Alenka! Get back in! What did I tell you—" He stopped short when he noticed Jan. "Forgive her, but she is a precocious child. She shouldn't have. Alenka. Alenka! Inside, I said, or—"

"Excuse me," Jan said, "my name is Jan Neuman. I used to live in that house."

The man's jaw dropped. "You…you used to live *here*?"

"Yeah, Frank, years ago," Zdeněk cut in. "He's been gone forty years. That's Jan Neuman, old man Neuman's son. From America."

The man continued to stare.

Jan felt cotton-mouthed. He wished he were somewhere else. Finally, he summoned his courage. "I wonder if you would mind…if I might step inside just for a few minutes. You understand, just to see. If you don't mind. I don't want to impose."

Without changing expression, the man shrugged, uttered a single word, "Please," nodded silently to Zdeněk, and turned to the house.

The familiar echo of the slate-tiled hallway brought back a new flood of memories as Jan followed the man into what used to be the workroom of his parents' tailor shop, their domain, around which his life had revolved, now transformed into a great room with a green ceramic-tiled stove in one corner and a large table in the center. It was nothing like he remembered, nothing like the image burnt into his mind all these years. Only the clock was still there – his father's clock – ticking away loudly, measuring time with a deliberate pace. A young flaxen-haired blue-eyed woman sat on a faded sofa under the window, breastfeeding a baby. Inexplicably, he felt a rising flood of resentment toward these strangers (*squatters* flashed through his mind) for robbing him of his dream, for usurping one of his long cherished memories.

"This is Mr. Neuman from America," the man said. "This is Věra, my wife, and little Sláva. You already met Alenka. I am Frank, Frank Vondra."

Blushing, the woman gently pushed away the baby, covered her bosom, stood, and extended her hand. "JesusMary, is it possible? An American? From America?"

Overcoming his chagrin, Jan managed a smile. "I saw the Prague demonstrations on television. The crowds on Wenceslaus Square. The flags. I never thought it would happen. Came back as soon as I could."

She offered him a seat and gazed at him through narrowed eyes.

"He says he used to live here. He wants to see the house," the husband said.

The blood drained from her face.

Trailed by the little girl, offering only cursory comments but watching him hawkishly, the woman led him through the familiar rooms, the courtyard, and the garden. There were changes, to be sure: The washroom had become an indoor toilet. The pump in the garden was gone, replaced by a spigot inside. The goat shed had become a storage shed. The orchard, his father's pride, had grown into a twisted unkempt jungle of broken trees.

"That's not ours. The State owns it. They used to graze goats in there until last year," she said, seeing his sour look.

591

"How long have you been living here now?" Jan asked.

"Six years, come next month. The State took over the house after old man—" She caught herself and blushed. "Sorry, after your father died. We were lucky to get it. They wouldn't let anyone have it unless they belonged to the Party." She flushed and stopped abruptly.

Jan remained silent.

"We had to belong...everybody had to belong. You couldn't live if you didn't belong. We weren't really political or anything. We had to survive."

"I understand." Jan shrugged. "Doesn't matter." He looked at his watch. It was 5:30 and he was getting hungry. "I guess I better go and see if I can find a hotel for the night. It's getting late." A chill in his spine made him cringe. He wished he hadn't come.

She smiled sadly. "There isn't anything in town. There used to be one, but..." She fell silent. "If you're not too fussy, you're welcome to have supper with us and stay the night. There's a small room upstairs...a spare. Nothing fancy. Just a bed. I know Frank wouldn't mind."

She finally broached the subject after supper. Jan sensed the stiffness in her demeanor and apprehension in her voice. "If this is your house, are you going to take it back? Ask us to leave?" she asked.

The room suddenly became airless, oppressive. Only the soft whimpers of the baby in her arms and the ticking of the clock on the wall disrupted the silence. Frank looked into his plate but her gaze was on him, clinging to him, full of fear and despair, eyes beginning to tear.

The question pierced a wall, releasing a flood of realities he never thought he'd have to face. He felt like an intruder. In his own home! Choking, he returned the woman's look, shook his head, and averted his gaze.

They didn't talk much after that. A void, a remoteness, had sprung up between them. She led him to the room upstairs. His old room. Even his bed was still there, with its straw mattress and creaky boards. He didn't sleep well.

In the morning, after a breakfast of black bread, strong coffee, and awkward conversation, he thanked them and walked out into the crisp air. The streets were still devoid of life. He drove to the cemetery. The lichen-covered wall had crumbled in places; the headstones tilted this way and that. He found the family grave. Not particularly religious, more a seeker than believer, he nevertheless stood by the cold weathered slab of marble and prayed.

Walking down from the cemetery to where he had left his car, he stopped on the weathered granite steps under a crucifix that had been there since long before he was born, and looked down on his town. It was there just as it had always been—a stage upon which a drama had finally played out.

He felt the cool moisture of an unwanted tear trace a path on his cheek and fought to suppress the tightness in his chest. His heart ached. He felt painfully alone, the way one might feel in the absolute loneliness of space or the vastness of the desert or the middle of the ocean—a solitary actor clinging to his imaginary spot long after the play had ended, the audience gone, the applause an echo in the recesses of his mind. Only the props remained, resplendent but spiritless, and the mustiness so characteristic of stages—a strange mixture of antiquity and nostalgia. Somewhere along the way, he had missed his cue. The play was over. He no longer belonged. Thoughts of Majda and *Savage* came alive in his mind and he felt a stab of longing.

He got into his car, drove down to the highway and, without looking back, turned westward toward Germany.

THE END

AUTHOR'S NOTES

FULL CIRCLE is a work of fiction. Any resemblance to real persons, living or dead, is purely incidental. The settings are accurate as best as I can remember them. Many no longer exist and others have been transformed, eradicating all traces of the past. This novel attempts to acquaint the reader with some of the locales and events that made this period so memorable, and leave a record for those who may one day wish to revisit the past. It is but one story of thousands such untold stories of people displaced by the two wars, the Second World War and the ensuing Cold War; stories of people overwhelmed by the onrush of greater events—the flotsam left behind by the tide of history. It begins at the onset of the Second World War with the betrayal of the Czechs at Munich, and follows the protagonist through the Cold War. It covers both wars because they are indelibly linked—the second being the consequence of the first.

WWII drove 12 million people from their homes, leaving Europe awash with refugees. The newly emerging Cold War cut short the euphoria of victory over the Nazis as the Iron Curtain slammed shut. Three years after the war, there were still more than 800,000 refugees in 370 camps in the three Occupation

Zones of Germany, and 25 in Italy. More than half were in the U.S. Zone. Regardless of their former status, the refugees became known as DP's, or Displaced Persons. This was an acronym that hid a multitude of affiliations: People from all over Europe who at various times were sworn enemies; ethnic, religious, or economic emigrants and their entire families, seeking a better life elsewhere and able to carry as many personal possessions as they were able to haul; enemy collaborators or sympathizers trying to elude justice, or political refugees, mostly single persons, uprooted by a brutal political system and having to flee their country with only the clothes on their backs to evade persecution.

The Czechs and Slovaks escaping the communist regime following a coup d'état in 1948 were an unexpected mix in this volatile cauldron. Many fled their country hoping to join a patriotic legion they believed was being formed in the American Occupational Zone of Germany by an exiled Czech general, but instead were stripped of their political refugee status, and first absorbed by and then submerged in the stagnant Displaced Persons pool. Their hopes of returning home as liberators were dashed. Ultimately, they were scattered to the four corners of the world, principally to Australia, Canada, Argentina, and a host of other countries. U.S. Public Law 778, the Displaced Persons Act of 1948, passed by Congress on the last day of its session, initially excluded the Czechs, but ultimately permitted 2,000 to be admitted to the United States, if they had a sponsor.

The initial surge of Czech escapees tapered off as the border, the Iron Curtain, became a maze of electrified barbed wire and clear fire zones. But still they came. The numbers are difficult to come by, but over the years, the estimates run from the low of 65,000 to a high of 200,000—a substantial number for a small country. Over the course of the Cold War, more than 8,000 were shot at the border trying to escape or died during the subsequent interrogations by the StB, the Czech Secret Police, whose methods reportedly rivaled that of the Gestapo; 240 were executed for political reasons, and as many as 7,000 died in prison because of inhumane treatment. About 250,000 were imprisoned, many in the infamous uranium mines of Jáchymov, and their untimely deaths continued beyond their statistical relevance.[1] None of the Czechs escaped with the idea of emigrating. They all hoped to return and continue their lives under a democratic system—a dream not easily extinguished.

Emigration is the answer to hope and desperation, but an emigrant's scars never really heal. Torn from his home, family, and country, from life and the predictability of future as he knew it, from the comfort of common language, friends, relatives, and parents, from the intimacy of customs and the familiarity of the national fabric, the immigrant refugee faces an uncertain future laced with apprehension. Invariably, he finds himself at odds with the new culture, foreign in all respects, from language and its nuances to history, customs, politics, and attitudes. He may manage to disappear in it, but is brought back to reality each time he utters a foreign-accented word. In truth, he never fully assimilates, remaining imprinted with his past so long as his mind is able to remember his roots. At best, he remains a curiosity, an oddity, a presence in, but never an imbedded part of his adopted land.

---

[1] Křivka, Zdeněk: Twentieth Century Communism Through the Eyes of its Victims, (Komunismus ve dvacátém století očima jeho obětí), Confederation of Political Prisoners of the Czech Republic, 2009.

ABOUT THE AUTHOR

Joe Vitovec was born in Czechoslovakia. As a young man, he saw his country overran by the Germans during World War II, liberated by the Americans and Russians in 1945, and taken over by the Communists in a coup in 1948. Fear of arrest because of political activity in the school and desire to join a Czechoslovak Legion forming in the American Occupation Zone of Germany led him to escape the regime into Germany with the hope of returning as a liberator. However, the Legion didn't materialize and he became a refugee, a 'Displaced Person,' or 'DP'-- one of 800,000 still languishing in the camps three years after the end of the war. His having spent more than two years in German, French, and Italian DP camps enables him to accurately portray the plight of refugees who, having lost everything, were defying Fate in seeking a new life.

After immigration in the USA and working off his passage at a Country Club in Minnesota, the author made the US Air Force his career. There he spent most of his time in information technology and development of instructional programs and aircraft training simulators. Concurrently, he graduated MCL from Texas Christian University with a Degree in History, attained Master's Degree in Urban Studies from the University of Texas, and instructed in political science at the Tarrant Community College in Fort Worth, Texas. He and his wife Ruth currently reside in Anacortes, Washington.

Made in the USA
Columbia, SC
01 June 2022

61181501R00333